# OTHER BOOKS BY JENNIFER DEBRUIN

## A Walk with Mary

*A Walk with Mary* was an outstanding book. You've hit every emotion in this old man's heart! Every chapter keeps giving and giving, and I've just had the aromas of butter tarts (at the barrister's home) and banana bread (at Mrs. Wright's home) waft through the sun porch, as the sun goes down. I enjoyed it so much, and it meant so much to me, having lived in and around the community of Moulinette. So many aspects of the story touched my life. Incredible! — Jim Brownell, President, Lost Villages Historical Society

\* \* \*

I read *A Walk with Mary* and fell in love with every minute of it. Jennifer writes in such a way that the book flows from one chapter to the next with such vivid description of what life was like during this time period. It really made you feel you were living life right there with the characters. Not many books can make me cry but this one did. *fantastic* job! Can't wait for the next one. — Michelle L.

What I like most about the book is your writing style that immerses readers into the picture . . . Your mix of fiction and fact makes it very readable. Thanks. — J. Ford

*A Walk with Mary* is a charming and highly readable book. DeBruin's words paint pictures of the times and places and her characters live and breathe in that space. — L. Worrall

I just finished reading *A Walk With Mary* — What a beautiful story . . . I felt I was right there on every page. I cried when the babies were born and when there was a death. I sort of feel like the invisible aunt that watched over the lives of everyone . . . wonderful . . . I absolutely loved it! Rating: 5 out of 5 hearts! — B. Outhouse

# Shadows in the Tree

*Shadows in the Tree* is an inviting and riveting story . . . DeBruin most skillfully explores the emotional toll on women and their families as they leave behind all they knew and face a dangerous and unknown future . . . I heartily recommend this book to anyone wanting to examine the human experience of many a Loyalist refugee. — The *Loyalist Gazette*, review by Grietje R. McBride, UE, B Sc.

\* \* \*

Thank you for taking me on another incredible journey with Eliza. It is a *powerful* and *emotional* journey. What I can only being to imagine, you put into words and make images so vivid in my mind that I felt like I was on the trail with Maria Catrina. I cried and rejoiced along with her. Congratulations Jennifer, the book is wonderful . . . It truly is a heartfelt story and I know that others will feel it as deeply as I did. — S. Seymour

My sister just gave me your second book, *Shadows in the Tree*. Jennifer, I couldn't put it down. You are truly a gifted writer. You make the reader a participant in the story, a reader who is transported all those years ago to share in the joys and trials of the times. Thank you once again for a brilliant novel and I am looking forward to your next book. Keep them coming. — M. Craig

I just finished reading your second book and had to tell you how much I enjoyed it. Your descriptions of scenery and events were good, but those of the heroine's emotions, exceptional. You brought reality and drama to the pages. — Sheila H.

# Daughter
## OF Conflict

Jennifer DeBruin

Published by Jennifer DeBruin
*www.jenniferdebruin.com*

ISBN 978-0-9947461-2-2 (pbk.)
ISBN 978-0-9947470-0-6 (mobi)
ISBN 978-0-9947461-9-1 (epub)

Copyright © Jennifer DeBruin 2015

Cover art, design, typesetting:
Magdalene Carson, New Leaf Publication Design

Cover photo: Magdalene Carson
Cover model: Anneke DeBruin, descendant of Sarah Allen.

Printed in Canada

Library and Archives Canada Cataloguing in Publication
DeBruin, Jennifer, 1971-, author
Daughter of conflict / Jennifer DeBruin.
Issued in print and electronic formats.
ISBN 978-0-9947461-2-2 (paperback). –
ISBN 978-0-9947470-0-6 (mobi). – ISBN 978-0-9947461-9-1 (epub)
I. Title.
PS8607.E383D38 2015      C813'.6 C2015-904702-1
C2015-904703-X

*For those behind the veil whispering their stories, and for Sarah:*
*in journeying with you through time, if only through imagination,*
*a grateful granddaughter remembers you.*

*. . . and to my family and friends,*
*without whom Sarah would have remained in the shadows.*

# Inspired by True Events

This book was inspired by real individuals in the author's genealogical history. It should be noted that this is a fact-based historical fiction, and some details have been changed to accommodate this story. This novel has been extensively researched to ensure historical accuracy, and as a way of honouring those who experienced this incredibly wrenching history, the names of individuals remain true to those found themselves swept up in continental conflict.

Some cultural terminology within this novel is used in a historical context, and does not reflect the point of view of the author.

Use of the term "Canada" within this novel relates specifically to the St. Lawrence River Valley.

"New France (French: Nouvelle-France) was the area colonized by France in North America during a period beginning with the exploration of the Saint Lawrence River by Jacques Cartier in 1534 and ending with the cession of New France to Spain and Great Britain in 1763.

The territory was divided into colonies, each with its own administration: Canada (St. Lawrence River Valley), Acadia, Newfoundland (Plaisance), and Louisiana." (Source: *https://en.wikipedia.org/wiki/New_France#cite_note-FrancisJones2009-2*)

The locations within "Canada" in this novel are the outlying areas near modern-day, Montreal, Quebec (known as Ville Marie in novel time period), including: Kahnawà:ke, Quebec (Mohawk Territory), Sainte-Anne-de-Bellevue, Quebec (known as Beaurepaire in novel time period), Baie-D'Urfé, Quebec, and Fort Chambly, Chambly, Quebec.

Learn more about the Raid on Deerfield, Massachusetts (incl. map):
Pocumtuck Valley Memorial Association
(PVMA)/Memorial Hall Museum
*http://1704.deerfield.history.museum/*

# Daughter of Conflict

# Prologue

❧

"I have never been so far . . . alone."

"Sarah, you shall have great fun with Esther, for how long has it been since you have had occasion to speak with her? I think you shall find these six days lacking in duration and will want for more." Mercy's warm embrace and soft, gentle voice cannot comfort her fears as they once did.

"I will not, for I will miss you all in the utmost." Pulling back, Sarah looks to her dear sister, beseeching her to understand. Mercy's steady expression and lovely smile cannot hide what Sarah sees in her eyes. They are of one heart. Falling into Mercy's arms, she renews her weeping, for she cannot help but feel as a frightened child.

"Dearest, do not fret, for you have a heart for adventure. Even now, when the days are cold, I see you looking to the fields, wondering what places lie beyond. Imagine yourself on one of these journeys, and when you return, you may tell me of what you have seen. I shall not sleep a wink until such time."

She loves her sister all the more for trying to replace her dread with anticipation, but Sarah's tears speak to her heart's desire — and to its fears. "Yes. But when I imagine such adventures, we are all together."

\* \* \*

Swift, almost silent footsteps approach. Suddenly, a door is violently thrown open, followed by another; the reverberation of each echoes clearly above all else. Besieged by a surge of terror, Sarah closes her eyes, despite the darkness. The door to the bedroom they are sheltered in swings open with a deafening bang, sending Sarah and Esther further under the covers as shadowy figures approach. Seized viciously by the arm, Sarah is hoisted from the bed and instantaneously dragged towards the door, followed by a flailing Esther, screaming, "Help, Papa! Help!"

Attempting to save herself, Sarah catches the doorframe with her free hand, holding as tightly as her cold fingers allow. The effort made in vain is no match for the violence of the response, resulting in her hand being cut open with one powerful tug of the assailant.

# 1

**"S**arah, get Samuel back inside at once!"

Her mother's shriek startles her and Samuel in equal measure, though he is but a babe, having only joined the family but a year and a half ago.

"You are to tend the children, and should you not heed my command, you will be punished most severely."

Sweeping Samuel up in her arms, much to his delight, her mother brings him very near to where she and Mercy are preparing the evening meal. *If only Mother knew how dreadfully quick he has become now that he is able to run about. It was much nicer when he was yet set in the basket at Mother's feet.*

"I am sorry, Mother."

"Please, Sarah, you know your father's warnings not to go beyond the confines of our home."

Her voice is no longer angry, but rather peculiar sounding, almost as if she is trying to hold back tears threatening to burst forth.

As she takes Samuel, Sarah notices a look pass between Mercy and her mother. The glance seems to reassure, for her mother quickly resumes kneading the bread, all evidence of her strained expression gone.

"Sarah, please take Samuel to the other room and entertain him," Mercy says calmly. Her kind smile reminds Sarah of the days when they still played together. Though only three years separate them, Mercy seems much older than her now, having turned into a great beauty, like their mother, whose name she shares.

"There now, you sit and do not go outside." Sarah tries to take a stern tone to mark her warning, but as Samuel looks up at her with eyes the colour of the sky, and curly golden locks set about his rounded, rosy face, he commands the same reaction in her that he seems to command in all who know him, and she smiles. *He is seemingly so pure, having the very look of the angels, but his disposition is yet to be seen,* Sarah thinks skeptically. Having only come into her care these past few weeks, he is still not well known to her. Mercy, now deemed an adult at fifteen, no longer cares for the children, but helps their mother in her work, leaving Sarah to determine the children's true natures. Already they are much different with her. She fears that as the weather warms, she may find herself taxed in preventing Samuel from dashing for the door, as he did today. *Oh, I pray he is not precocious — for that is what they call me.* She does not know what this means, but she imagines it is not a good quality for the way in which they say it.

Samuel now occupied by three of his older sisters, Martha, Jemima, and Hannah, watches carefully as the girls attempt to instruct him on how he may make the ball come to rest in the cup of the Bilbo Catcher their brother Edward has made them. Satisfied he is controlled for the moment, Sarah looks out the window, watching the breeze make the newly sprouted leaves sway and dance. *Why should we not be permitted to go outside and enjoy such a day? It was not always so that we should be kept within the walls of our home.* Thinking it a dreadful waste of the day, Sarah laments, *Surely the Lord made it for our enjoyment as much as for Father and his work in the fields. What work are we to do, those who are too young to take on the responsibilities of adulthood? There is so little to entertain.* Thinking to the previous spring when they played in the lush, green grasses that came to life again after the long winter months, she is left wanting for days past.

"Sarah? Why did Mama yell before?" Martha's look of concern mimics her mother's so well that Sarah is taken aback by how much she begins to take on her very appearance. While lovely in her disposition, Martha is so dreadfully quiet Sarah does not think she will ever really know her.

"Samuel ran from my care into the garden."

Pulling Samuel to her, Martha wraps her arms around him tightly, as he squirms to escape her grip. Sarah wonders why she, too, embraces him as if he were very nearly lost, for he was only in the garden.

Gathered around in each other's confidence, Sarah's charges continue playing on the floor, leaving her to sit by the window imagining herself elsewhere. The days pass in such dull routine, closed off as she is from exploring the forest and river she knows lie just beyond her view. To be trapped in a house that warms dreadfully as Mercy stokes the fire in preparation for the meal is most unbearable, and Sarah wishes they were free to enjoy the cooling breezes that carry the butterflies flitting about outside.

"How I wish I were a butterfly," Sarah whispers under her breath, longing for the freedom to go where she wishes, to do as she pleases, and to spend the days being carried off by the winds to destinations she can only imagine. Her life here is small, and she cannot help but want for more — to sit by the river, to watch the eagles soaring above the wide expanse of the field, to chase her butterflies once more. *I wonder if this shall ever be so again.*

# 2

With his family at rest, Edward sits at his small desk, a memento of his father's making. Pensive for a few moments, he looks over the workmanship by the dim light of the candle set upon the corner, and remembers his early life. Finding his memories of the past stir his emotions, he cracks open the new leather bound book before him.

18 May 1703

I am afraid this new journal, which has just arrived from Boston, will serve as a document of a life no longer led. If it be so, I trust I will convey the depth of experience we, the people of Deerfield, live through and why we ardently hold true to such an isolated place. It must not be in vain that we have existed, for surely it is a noble life to settle such places of grand beauty and abundance, ensuring a future for our children and generations to come. It is this future I dream of, and our daily work is but laying the foundation for such a vision. To you, the reader, I convey my deep gratitude that you should come understand who we are . . . should we no longer exist.

Such tension grips our colony and we, set here on the western frontier, are utterly isolated. The rumblings of war grow, and we are beset once again with the strain of the unknown. We know all too well the terrible cost. Continental conflict has spilled into our small places. Only a year ago, the King of France asserted that control of the Spanish throne was rightfully his, and now our five years of civil relations with the French are shattered, and we are in a renewed state of readiness. Our arrangement with the French was never a true peace, for we were ever at the ready, knowing their ambitions for our colony. I must shield my dear wife, Mercy, from this burden. Her nerves were much affected by our previous troubles, and she will surely be unable to bear further aggravation. Do not misinterpret my words, dear reader, for she is the loveliest of creatures. Such feminine beauty does not exist in such abundance in many a woman, but she is of noble stock. Descended from the founders of our earliest days on these shores, such a lady is not suited for life in the wilds. An obedient wife and child of God, she is understanding of what we build and the importance of our efforts, but I should think her much more suited to the society of her native Newport, rather than to this isolated existence. She leaves unspoken her yearning for such a life and is ever faithful in her work. To one who does not know her as surely as I do, she would appear no different than any other of this community — except in beauty; in this, she is set apart.

Dear reader, if you will indulge me, I should like to hold you in my confidence and share more of who we are. The news of yesterday weighs heavily on my mind and heart, and I feel the outcome may be decisive. When before I had fewer in my care, I now have seven children and a wife looking to me for protection, and I falter in the belief that I should be able to safeguard all adequately. I shall pray on this, for I know the Lord holds us in His care, and that it is our righteous duty to make His land bountiful, but I confess to you, my unknown confidant, there is less surety in my heart.

Having called us to the meetinghouse, Reverend Williams shared news from our Governor Dudley that Governor Cornbury of the Province of New York has informed him that we are to expect a party comprising one hundred French and their Indian allies. We are put on high alert, and scouts have been assigned to confirm such news. At a disadvantage, Deerfield has only three fortified houses within its palisades. How should so many find refuge? The palisade walls, weathered and worn these fourteen years since their construction, were newly improved and expanded a year ago. The improvements of 1697, completed during our last hostilities, proved lacking in their ability to withstand our enemy's molestations, and our governor answered our call for aid in this regard. Of course, these provide decidedly more assurance than our cluster of homes set south of the village. Here, we are exposed with no hope of protection, except for the defence we may mount. In the event of an attack, I do not believe we can make the home of Jonathan Wells, which is the only fortified house outside the walls. The fourteen men representing our cluster at the meeting looked to one another, understanding the same. We shall meet again to discuss our defence. It will be with the spilt blood of the French and their Indian allies that we mark our victory over such a transgression of our God-given rights. My anger threatens to overtake me when thinking upon this, and though much is to be done, perhaps you must come to know who we are before you may come to understand our convictions.

As night brings the end to our daily toil, I find myself yet unable to rest, listening instead into the silence of the night, beyond the sounds of the Lord's creatures, to hear what I might of these men who stalk us. I pray for physical strength to remain a sentry, but the need for sleep overwhelms me, and I am sorry to say, dear reader, that I shall have to share more in my next entry.

Until then, I remain your humble servant,

Edward Allen

# 3

"We are called to the meetinghouse tomorrow."

Sitting in opposing chairs in the sweltering room now emptied of the children, all fast asleep, Edward and Mercy maintain an uncomfortable conversation. Despite the heat, the windows are closed tight, as though this may provide some form of protection. Not looking up from the sewing she attends to, Mercy repetitively pulls each thread through with her needle, making slow but steady progress on the filthy, threadbare shirt she is mending for Edward, testament to his arduous days in the fields.

Closing his Bible and setting it upon his lap, Edward continues, "Our son remains here to keep watch." Looking to Mercy, he can plainly see that the worry has taken a toll on his lovely wife. The deep furrows upon her brow age her, yet her natural beauty radiates. Even in the manner in which she sits, doing such a simple task, she seems much in contrast to her humble surroundings.

"I am afraid your noble stock makes it more difficult for you, my dear. I should encourage you to continue improving such skills as you have, for you are a fine wife and mother, and worry will do you no good; that is my burden to bear alone. Rest assured, I will return before night falls."

Setting down his shirt, she looks to Edward. The anguish in the depths of her intense blue eyes takes him aback.

"I shall abide by your command, my dear Edward, but with tensions renewed, I find the burden of my constant companion difficult to bear."

"Do the children cause you grief, my dear?"

"No, Edward, the thought of losing another does."

Knowing his assurances would be to no avail, he does not try. She cannot relinquish that which troubles her. He, too, feels the sting of such loss. Picking up his Bible, Edward begins to read once more, leaving Mercy, now gently weeping, to mend while thinking of those she has lost, and may lose yet.

\* \* \*

"Why should I not help you in your work? Have I not been a worthy aid?" Sarah's brother Edward pleads, following so closely that when his father stops in his tracks, Edward barely avoids colliding into him.

"My word is final, and I caution you to heed it. You will tend to the garden and go no further than a sprint to the house. Of this I will speak no more."

Equal in nature, as well as in name, Sarah's father and brother glare determinedly at one another for a brief moment. Edward only acquiesces when it is clear there will be no further negotiations, for his father's expression is as stern as Sarah has ever seen it, frightening her. Striding to the house, Edward slams the door behind him, making Sarah and the children jump as the sound echoes within the walls. Sensing it is best to stay out of his way, she ushers the children into the adjoining room to begin their daily routine.

Her father's recent insistence that her brother, now nearly a man at sixteen years, not go to the fields as he once did signals a change in the dangers that lie beyond their home. He dutifully tends to chopping the wood and helping his mother in the garden, but does so with such a sour disposition that Sarah knows it must serve to further their mother's grief. She often wants to tell him so, but with the young ones to attend to, it leaves no time for addressing such things.

Preoccupied since his visit to the meetinghouse two days ago, Sarah's father frequently leaves with a worried expression upon his face. He arrives home late at night, long after she has drifted off to sleep, and when he rises upon the morn, seems more distressed. Even without overhearing what troubles him, Sarah fears it nonetheless. Her mother, too, has become melancholy and worries where the children are at every moment. Helping where she might with the younger ones, on warm, sunny days Sarah finds it difficult to corral the children indoors. *How I wish for winter, for it would be more bearable to endure being indoors if such beauty of spring were not just out of reach.*

# 4

As the sun dips below the horizon, extinguishing another day, Sarah is glad to hear her father's heavy boots upon the floorboards at the door. Despite the fear that darkness brings, she cannot help but welcome dusk, for it is then that the pace at which the family has been labouring eases.

*I pray this night is good. I think I shall ask Mother to tell us the tale of Captain Lamberton*, she decides, hoping for the escape it provides.

After supper, the family gathers by the hearth, now lying dark with the return of the warm evenings. A lantern set on the mantle casts a soft glow in the room as the children gather upon the floor to listen to their father read the Bible.

Sarah loves to hear him read the stories of the Lord's life and teachings. His deep voice, reverent and steady, does not mask his passion for the passages he reads. She believes that if he were the storyteller in the family, a position her mother holds, they would instantaneously be swept up and carried off to the places in his stories. As it is, tonight they listen quietly to Psalm 27.

"The Lord is my light and my salvation — whom shall I fear? The Lord is the stronghold of my life — of whom shall I be afraid? When the wicked advance against me to devour me, it is my enemies and my foes who will stumble and fall. Though an army besiege me, my heart will not fear; though war break out against me . . . " Her father pauses for such a long time, Sarah wonders if he has lost his place. Looking directly at her mother, he speaks the next line slowly and deliberately, reciting it by heart, ". . . even then I will be confident."

Despite his reassuring smile, fear lingers in her mother's eyes. Wishing she were an adult to know all that her parents share, Sarah senses they seem to understand one another even with an absence of words. As if his unspoken message is understood, her mother returns his smile. *If only I could provide such comfort to her when we work side by side,* she thinks helplessly. Vowing to take her father's lead tomorrow, she prays a small gesture, such as his, will work.

Once finished, he bids goodnight to the young ones, leaving Edward, Mercy, Martha, and Sarah sitting with him as their mother escorts the three youngest children upstairs. Knowing it will be dreadfully hot up there this night, Sarah does not envy them, as the breeze which provided some relief has departed, leaving the air still and lifeless. Listening to the world outside, she hears the frogs by the river's edge calling to one another in their secret language; she imagines the fairies must understand them, but try as she might, she has yet to find a fairy to ask.

*I dare not confess to Mother that I yet believe in such magical beings.* But when she sees a small flashing light outside the window, she cannot help but think it a fairy in disguise. *By what natural method could such light be possible? I wonder if the creatures of this unknown world feel fear as we do.* Thinking they must not, she is all the more envious of them, for without fear, they are free in this world. *Man asserts he is the master of all creatures, and yet we are confined in our fortress, closed off from the world inhabited by the frogs and fairies. Such wondrous lives they must lead,* she thinks. *How I wish . . .*

"Sarah. Sarah."

Startled back from her reveries by her father's voice, Sarah turns from the window to find all eyes upon her, making her flush despite her effort to appear innocent.

"What do you see that holds your attention so?" Her father's expression shows such concern she fears his reaction should she share her true thoughts. *Surely he will understand even less the world of creatures and will think me a frivolous, ungodly child.*

"Please forgive me, Father. I was looking to the stars, for they begin to appear in the sky."

"Your time is better spent reading the Bible. The stars will still be there when you are done."

Her father seeming content with her apology, Sarah opens her Bible. Edward, however, casts a mean-spirited look at her, as though her looking to the stars has somehow offended their father, and Edward believes it his duty to scold her. *Perhaps I am beginning to understand the silent language of my parents, for Edward's message is quite clear.*

With a smug smile, Edward takes up his reading once again. Finding the correct page, Sarah stares blankly at it for some time. Reading the same line over and over, she does not understand any of its message, for though she keeps her head down to appear devoted to the task, her eyes wander about their home. The love she has for it makes her sorry she should ever have to leave it once married. Hearing the voices of the youngest children through the floorboards, repeating after their mother, "Now I lay me down to sleep, I pray the Lord my soul to keep," Sarah yearns for days gone by. *How I loved when Mother led the nightly prayers.* Her soothing voice often made Sarah fall asleep as soon as their prayers were completed, and, she is ashamed to remember, sometimes before. Now, saying them alone in her darkened room makes her miss it all the more.

Martha, like Sarah, has reluctantly left behind the carefree days of childhood. At eight, she must assume her place amongst the older children. Appearing lost without Jemima by her side, she looks forlornly at the stairs where her most trusted companion has been led away. Sarah believes her sisters share a soul, each possessing half of the whole, and has heard her mother say the same many times. Despite the pain of separation, they do not protest, abiding their Christian values, as they all must.

Sensing the walls closing in around her, Sarah is drawn to the window once more. The scene that only a moment before revealed but a few flickering lights is now filled with countless dancing stars emerging in the darkening sky. She thinks to the many creatures, and people, that may be looking at the same stars. *Not more than two hundred and sixty people live amongst us, and our visitors are rare. I wonder at all that more should exist.* Suddenly a reminder that they are not alone in their isolated existence once again appears at the window — a small flash of light brings a greeting from the outside world.

A gentle breeze rushing past lifts the corner of her mother's cross-stitching set upon the chair awaiting her return. It catches Sarah's attention, and she watches it wave about in such a fluid motion it reminds her of the butterflies she loves so much. She yearns to be light and carefree, released from the realities surrounding her. *If ever Father and Mother were to know what is truly in my heart, I should think they would be most concerned with my prospects.* She has overheard her father telling their neighbour how she is growing into a fine girl, and by the man's response of how fine his son is, Sarah believes they are plotting to marry them off. She knows she should be excited for such things, but she is not. *I want to stay here, on a night just like this, with my family as one.* Her most ardent prayer is to stay as she is now: not old enough to marry, yet old enough to help her mother in her work.

Gentle footsteps upon the stairs bring Sarah back from her troubling thoughts. Her mother descends slowly, trying to ensure the little ones stay at their rest. Upon reaching the final step, she turns the corner with lantern in hand, illuminating the faces of Sarah's loved ones. Weathered by many days spent in the fields and his recent concerns, Sarah's father still has kindness in his eyes. This is where she looks for the true nature of people, for it is easy enough to smile, but one can always tell the truth in a person's eyes. His concerned nature results from ensuring their safety, though she does not understand what they should fear.

Now drawn and tired, her mother sits upon her chair and resumes her cross-stitching. The purest soul Sarah knows, she seems incapable of truly masking what she most deeply feels. When she tells her stories, she always seems pensive, her voice often trailing off as if she is lost in some memory. Sarah believes it is because she yearns for her family, whom she has not seen since settling the western edge of the colony many years earlier when newly married. She has never met her mother's family, but their occasional letters give her reason to like them nonetheless. *I do not want to be like Mother, for she carries such a burden of separation.*

Closing his Bible, Sarah's father sits in quiet reflection for a moment longer, which strains her ability to sit quietly, for now it becomes the time of evening she enjoys most. They are finally able to simply enjoy each other's company without the burdens of their daily work or prayer. Sarah knows she should not think of prayer in this way, else she will surely burn in the afterlife. *Dear Lord,* she prays silently, *Please forgive me. You know I am truly thankful for your many blessings, but with the world made so wonderfully, as you intended, I should want to enjoy it, as intended. Forgive my wickedness and help me to be your ever-obedient servant. I wonder if Mother . . .*

"Mother, will you tell us a story tonight?" Sarah asks, unable to contain herself any further. Her mother, who has been holding Martha in her arms, looks at her with a curious smile upon her face. Confused, Sarah looks to her father, but he appears to be of the same mindset.

"And what story would you have me tell, my dear?"

"Of great-grandfather."

"Which one, might I inquire?"

"Captain Lamberton, please."

"It has been a while since I have told this story. I do hope I remember the details." Sarah is glad to see her mother's radiant smile return.

"If you do not, I can help."

"I am sure you could, daughter," her Father adds, stifling a laugh and cocking his eyebrow at her. *Why should he laugh? I am very good at remembering the details of my favourite story.*

# 5

12 July 1703

Good news finds us, dear reader. Governor Dudley held a conference at Casco Bay but a fortnight ago and finds our alliances with the Abenakis renewed. We have been assured that should the French and their allies attempt to affront us, the Abenakis will thwart such efforts. This evening, I shared this news with my dear Mercy, and she finds comfort in it as I prayed she would. She is much affected by the troublesome accounts delivered upon the pulpit. I continue to instruct her to find guidance and strength in the Lord's words, but she falters in her belief that we are truly safe under His protection. It is my duty to remind her most sternly that this is sinful and that her increasing fear is not a testament to her faith. I pray she finds comfort in the Bible verses I have suggested. What I have imparted tonight will surely prove His grace.

I believe my son Edward may be safe in joining me in my work once again, though we must remain ever vigilant, for the French are not to be trusted. It shall not be long before he embarks on working his own land, and any time now lost in his instruction will surely prove detrimental to his future success.

My family suffers under the oppression the French have inflicted through their unjust and ungodly assertions, but I now feel a return to the life we once enjoyed. Perhaps I shall instruct Mercy to allow the children some time in the garden.

Much work is yet to be done, dear reader, if we are to yield an abundant harvest, and so I must take my rest. The veil of sleep falls over me, and I feel sure that tonight I shall truly find respite and wake upon the morn renewed.

Edward

# 6

**"S**arah."

"Yes, Mama . . . Mother." Sometimes forgetting that she is older, Sarah yet calls her mother by the name she once used.

"Please clean and dress the children and bring them down once they are ready."

"Yes, Mother."

Gathering the little ones, Sarah must ensure their obedience. It is difficult to do with Samuel and Hannah, who cause much grief on the Sabbath, as they do not always heed her warnings. Try as she might to learn the ways of her mother, who can silence the children with a mere look, Sarah has had no success at this and often feels overrun. Now with Samuel walking quite steadily, she exhausts herself in trying to keep up with him. *They frustrate me so! I shall ask for the Lord's grace and lessons so that the children will not be damned for their terrible behaviour.* As laborious as her dear sister Mercy's work may be, she envies her, for Sarah is convinced she has the more difficult task.

*The Sabbath brings such relief!* The moment the family steps outside to walk to the meetinghouse, Sarah is surrounded by the trees, birds, and creatures that she loves so dearly. Though it renews her spirit, she is aware that when once again confined within her home, she will feel their loss more profoundly.

Turning back, Sarah sees Edward and her dear sister Mercy taking up the rear, for now this is how they must walk: her mother and father in front, followed by Sarah in the middle with her younger siblings, who are followed by the two eldest siblings. Jemima and Martha are so in tune with one another that they require very little of Sarah's attention. She envies their sisterly affection for one another; their friendship seems to keep them from feeling loneliness as Sarah does. *At one time, my dear Mercy was my most trusted companion, but now I am left alone. If only we could hold on to one another as we once did.* Even in the silence of their walk, there had been pleasure. Noticing Sarah's glances, Mercy beckons with a quick nod to continue to face forward, but does so with a sweet smile, and Sarah understands that she, too, remembers.

At the cusp of adulthood, Sarah is made more aware of the changes in her life, and she finds herself sorrowful. *The aggravations caused by the French and their Indian allies must be the cause, for Reverend Williams most vehemently denounces them upon the pulpit each Sabbath day.* Sarah prays her father may yet go to heaven though he curses "the damned French" quite regularly as of late. She has had to caution Hannah a few times not to repeat such words, but at five she can hardly be convinced of going to hell. Luckily, it has only been in Sarah's presence that she curses. Giving her a swift slap on the hand Sarah reminds her to watch her words. Inevitably, she cries most passionately, bringing her mother to comfort her, while casting a stern look in Sarah's direction. It seems Hannah can do no wrong. Sarah does not blame her mother, who does not know the sinful nature of the little sprite she comforts. Sarah fears Hannah may have a temperamental nature, for she is sure by the glint in her eye she knows plainly the reaction Sarah will receive in scolding her.

"Every effort must be made to defend God's will. Our duty is to thwart all efforts of these self-righteous and pompous French, with their extravagant ways and usurpation of our lands. Such greed is surely the result of darkened hearts that do not follow the will of God, but use His name in vain to do their evil work. The French and their savage allies must be made to answer for their sins, if not by the weapons of our defence, then by the righteous judgement of our Lord, who will see them burn in the eternal and damning fires of hell."

Instantly, Sarah looks to Hannah, hoping she will glance over so she can employ the glare her mother often gives to control them. There is no doubt the word will bring the need to correct her once again. But, she gives no opportunity. *She does not even pay attention!* Scanning the surroundings, Sarah is sure one of the deacons will see and chastise their mother for allowing such behaviour. *Oh, how these young ones grieve us!*

"Pray, dear folk of Deerfield, for we face an enemy of God, and this enemy must be met with the might of our bodies and the strength of our convictions. Pray! Pray! We must not let up our defence. Do not have fear in your hearts, women of our community, for you must take up the sword of faith and defend your children."

Reverend Williams continues to rail against the French, and one man in particular. *Marcus Vodroy,* Sarah repeats over and over in her mind, fascinated by the foreign-sounding name. Finding it difficult to follow his words when the sun shines so brilliantly out the small window, she silently commends the Reverend on his endurance. *His passion must prove stirring to one who understands what he speaks of, but surely we have been sitting on these benches for an eternity!* Sarah knows she must endeavour to heed his words, but she has never seen the enemy he speaks of, and on such a day, it hardly seems possible that such things could happen. *Surely he exaggerates to ensure our souls are dutiful to the Lord.* Looking to the faces of the women and children surrounding her, Sarah sees that most fear the words of Reverend Williams, save Hannah and Samuel, who are sinfully preoccupied with looking around. Catching her mother's glare, she faces forward at once. Straining her eyes to look about the room while appearing as if she is paying attention, Sarah sees the men nod in unison. Even her brother Edward, surrounded by the other boys of the community, seems to understand the Reverend's warnings. Try as she might, she cannot find much interest in them.

Seeking her friend Esther amongst the congregation, Sarah looks to where the Reverend's family take their usual seats. Sarah and Esther have not had occasion to speak with one another in many a day. Sheltered in their homes, they are not only hidden away from the world outside, but also from each other. The girls are kindred spirits. Of course, Esther is often punished for her nature by her father, and seeing the strength of his convictions on this day as he raises his voice louder — "We will prevail only with the strength of God at our side!" — Sarah imagines the punishments are most swift and memorable, for Esther does not look around at all.

Seeing a deacon motion, Sarah tenses, knowing he has spotted a wayward member. *It must be Samuel. Dear Lord, have mercy on us.* Feeling a gust of wind as the deacon brushes past her on his way toward the back of the meetinghouse, she cannot see who he has warned, but he is very soon back in his position, keeping a steady watch on all. She vows to pay closer attention so that she does not bring shame upon her parents, but something catches her eye — *is that a bird resting in the treetop? I think it must be. I wonder when the Reverend will let us out. It begins to warm terribly.*

*Thank you, dear Lord!* Finally permitted to exit into the day, Sarah does not know what time has passed, but notices the sun has begun its descent in the sky. However, with days now lingering, there is yet time to enjoy it. Their walk home will have to be enjoyed in its entirety, for it will be her only opportunity, she fears, to breathe fresh air until the next Sabbath day.

As the family makes its way down the road, the palisades seem to grow larger and more imposing as they approach. *I would not like to live within their confines, for they shut out the beauty that surrounds the village.* She is thankful to live amid the trees and animals, for even when the sun sets she may enjoy its last glimmering rays on their natural horizon, while the good folk within have night come swiftly as the sun sets on the top of their fortress. *Such a waste, for I believe it the most beautiful time of day.* The mist settling upon the fields in the distance stirs her imagination, and she thinks of the creatures that inhabit such places. It is only in these last moments when strokes of orange, pink, and lilac paint the sky that Sarah truly feels privy to the Lord's canvas. The shifting light, the deepening colours — *yes, this makes me most sad to think the people within the palisades will not enjoy His gift.*

# 7

**"S**amuel, slow down!" Sarah cannot deny her brother such abandon, for they have been set free once again. It has been a year since she and her siblings were last able to enjoy their beloved river, but she has been there every day in her mind.

"Do not allow the children to get wet, Sarah, and keep them in your care. You must not fail in your duty. You must not." She can still hear her mother's stern warning as she chases her devilish brother. Her mother's aim was to set fear in her heart, but it did not diminish her joy. *Surely Father would not have allowed our venturing to the river if we were in any danger,* she reasons. *He and Edward are only in the adjacent field. I do not believe we are under any threat.* Though Reverend Williams is as impassioned as ever in his loathing of the French, he has reverted much of his sermon to the congregation going to hell, a fate they seem unable to escape. Sarah reasons if her fate cannot be changed, it seems the only course is to enjoy this life while it is to be had.

"I shall take care of them, Mother. Do not worry," she calls back as she rushes to Samuel, who is unsteady as he runs over the furrowed ground.

Martha and Jemima giggle as they roll a hoop that their father has newly fashioned from the strapping of an old, decrepit barrel and a straight branch he found on a recent expedition to fell trees. Hannah chasing behind, pesters the girls to try. They stop to instruct her, but she clearly has no patience for it.

"This game is not fun! It will not do as it has for you and Jemima!" she cries, making Sarah's early understanding of her truer with each passing day.

"Come here, Hannah, and hold my hand. You shall not display such anger, for the Lord will smite you for it."

Unconcerned by the warning, Hannah yet does as told. Sarah holds tight, for, as expected, she tries to pull her hand away. Giving up on Samuel entirely, Sarah gathers him in her one free arm as he kicks and protests. *Why am I burdened with such wilful children? Do they not hear the Reverend's words? Do they not heed such dire warning?*

"I will set you down, Samuel, but should you continue to carry on in such a manner, I shall have to take us all home and reveal to Mother what you have done."

He instantly stops, and with a complete change of expression, he puts both hands on Sarah's cheeks and quietly pleads, "No. No home. Me see fishies. Pease Sarah?"

"Okay, but you must abide by my words."

Setting him down, she holds her breath expecting a sudden dash. Neither Samuel nor Hannah struggles to release their hands. It seems the threat of being shut away has instilled in them a deep sense of fear. In truth, even uttering the words overwhelmed her with sadness. As they walk, they listen to the abundance of birds singing in the trees and the faint sound of the river coming from within the forest beyond the fields through which they pass.

"I see it, Sarah," Martha announces, pointing to glimmers of light dancing on the flowing waters through an opening in the trees.

"Yes! Is it not wonderful to see it again?" Sarah smiles back at her, and Martha rushes off, understanding the silent message. The last time they were here, they were in the care of Mercy. Watching Martha and Jemima move to the river hand in hand, Sarah's joy is tempered by missing her own companion. *How Mercy would have loved a day such as this.*

Just as Sarah and her siblings are swallowed up by the trees, she looks to the far field, seeing her father and brother working amongst the growing crops, now nearly reaching their waists. Sarah cannot see his face, but she knows Edward is most pleased to be at their father's side once more. She doubts he envies his siblings, who may frolic by the water's edge, for he takes much interest in his work, often talking with their father about his future life working his own land. *It is wonderful to see men dotting the fields, working together with their sons. It must please them to be amid such natural beauty.* From the fields, one can see the rounded ascent of land in the distance, as their valley is surrounded by hills and mountains. Sarah has never seen the mountains, but imagines them vividly from her father's descriptions. *This place is surely made by the hand of the Lord.*

"Sarah, might Jemima and I go and pick those flowers over there? We should like to bring them to Mother." Martha asks, pointing to a cluster of delicate white daisies on the bank of the river.

"You may, but no further."

Sarah releases her grip from the two little ones, who are now marvelling at the minnows swimming in the shallows very near their feet.

"Can we try and catch them?" Hannah asks, having seemingly tamed her wilfulness of earlier. *Surely it will do no harm to allow the children to be entertained by the river.*

"Mother does not want to see you coming back sopping and in disorder; you may catch the minnows, but only in the shallows. Take off your stockings so that you may chase them, but take care not to let the hem of your skirt brush the water."

"Oh, I shan't. Thank you, Sarah."

Abruptly, Hannah sits upon the ground, desperately pulling off her stockings. The relief of the cooling breezes under the shade of the trees releases Sarah of any final apprehension and she pulls off her own itchy stockings.

Gently splashing the brisk water with her toes, Sarah watches Hannah and Samuel attempting to scoop up the little creatures tormenting them with their proximity. Just as they reach into the water, the minnows scatter with such swiftness that they seem to disappear altogether. Realizing their defeat, the children look around their ankles, finding the minnows returning once again. This game seems endless, but Hannah and Samuel are immersed in its gaiety, and Sarah in watching them.

The torrent of water at winter's end has threatened Sarah's family many a time, but when the abundant season is upon them, the water flows no deeper than a creek in most parts and welcomes them to its refreshing pools. Such a changing personality it has. It seems alive, knowing of what it does. Sarah imagines herself as the river, flowing through the land, twisting and turning at will, and when the snows melt, roaring and boiling with no boundaries to stop her wilful nature. She wonders about the journey of the river and the lands and people it sees. While she does not know from whence it comes or where it may yet go, she believes it must witness such wondrous sights.

"Sarah, look what we have picked for Mother." Holding on to one another, Sarah's sisters are radiant with the bounty of flowers they have assembled.

"Oh my, surely she will put them on the table for this evening's meal. They are beautiful."

Standing with one arm behind her back, a sheepish grin on her face, Jemima reveals a delicate bunch of purple violets. "These are for you."

This thoughtful, unexpected gift moves Sarah to tears. "Thank you," is all she can muster.

Looking very proud that their surprise has had its intended effect, the girls set their mother's flowers upon the bank and begin to help the younger ones in their game of trying to catch the elusive minnows. Sarah feels all at once grown. It did not strike her before, but she now realizes her sisters see her as their elder and afford her the respect of such a relationship. So often she feels as though she does not have a place in her family and that, with Mercy grown, she does not belong to any one person. But, smelling the sweet aroma of her delicate bouquet, her own flowers gifted to her by her dear sisters, Sarah knows she is not unseen.

Allowing Martha and Jemima to assume responsibility for Samuel and Hannah, Sarah traverses a submerged tree reaching from one bank to the other. Feeling the rush of water over her feet, she thrusts her arms to either side to maintain her balance on what is proving to be a much more slippery passage than she remembers from years past. Knowing all eyes are on her as she accomplishes this feat, Sarah shows the others how she keeps her balance so splendidly.

"Sarah, I want to try."

As she turns to see Hannah stepping onto the tree, Sarah falters.

"You wicked girl!" she cries, but before she can utter another word, she slips, and is instantly engulfed by the river.

"See what you have done with your disobedience!" Sarah sputters. Struggling against the current, made more demanding by the weight of her soaking skirt, she grasps Martha's hand, extended to bring her to safety. Martha and Jemima quickly gather the children to reassemble them with stockings and shoes, leaving Sarah to fume in peace. The girls lead the children away from the river, along with their ring and stick and their mother's flowers, with Sarah following behind. Just as they emerge into the brilliant sun of the open field, Jemima runs past Sarah back into the shade of the trees.

"Jemima, come back here!"

"You forgot your flowers." Yet dripping, Sarah smiles at her young sister as she takes the flowers. Jemima rushes off to rejoin the others. Knowing she will be punished for disobeying her mother, about this, much as about going to hell, she can do little. Sarah decides to simply smell her lovely flowers and enjoy what she may of this day — and pray she dries before they reach home.

# 8

**"S**uch news as I have, friends, is dire indeed," Reverend Williams announces as he mounts the pulpit. Hastily finding places upon the benches where they sat only three days prior on the Sabbath, Edward and the other men await the details of what has been expected for many months.

"Our scouts report enemy tracks but five miles from Deerfield, and we find ourselves in the path of imminent attack. We have called for the colony to come to our assistance, if we are to shore up the western front. As during our past troubles, our brethren living by the sea are the first to experience the assault, but we, too, must expect raiders at our doors once again." Pausing, the Reverend allows the severity of his message to fall upon the men, whose expressions harden as they await more details.

"This is as before, dear neighbours. Once again we must look to the Lord for His strength, for it will surely be needed to rid the world of this blight." The Reverend's voice, loud and simmering with rage, takes on a more fervent tone as the men join in with mumbles of agreement and discontent.

"Defend ourselves, we will!" the Reverend thunders. "Protect our good wives and children, we must! We shall not let Deerfield, nor the western front of our beloved colony, fall! The Lord will not forsake us, for we are the righteous and true people of this place!"

"Who has been attacked?"

"What casualties?"

"When are we to expect our enemy upon our doorsteps?"

The rapid, successive questions of John Stebbins, Thomas French, and Godfrey Nims echo the concern of all gathered.

"Saco, Wells, and other settlements have seen their homes burned and many a man killed or taken captive. Colonel Partridge has reported the French and their allies sweep through as a force said to be numbering five hundred men." Stunned by the strength of the enemy bearing down on them, the men cease all conversation, and the Reverend's voice alone fills the meetinghouse. "We know the fearsome nature of such battles, many of our own men having been lost in troubles past, yet Deerfield stands testament to our fortitude."

Incensed, many a man abandons any attempt to disguise his anger at Governor Dudley for having denied their previous requests to leave this place and settle in less exposed and isolated communities. Deerfield, they believe, survives not from fortitude, but because of forced settlement.

"What of the governor's agreements made only six weeks ago? Are they now broken? Do the alliances not hold?" Edward calls out above the angry voices. Noting the Reverend's demeanour suddenly change, Edward braces himself for the dreaded truth.

"They do not."

He slumps to his bench in disbelief, and the shock reverberates through the crowd.

Captain Jonathan Wells stands, and the crowd hushes. "Such details are none that we should hope to hear ring in our ears once again. The truce of these five years has afforded a fleeting reprieve to improve and make prosperous Deerfield and its lands. We are in a state that finds us woefully unable to protect ourselves against such aggression. What would the governor have us do, set here isolated and without men and supplies to mount a defence? The militia I now lead does not provide such numbers as would serve our people in such circumstances."

Having seen the result of defence in the service of the king in his youth, Jonathan Wells stood out as leader amongst men. Surmounting impossible odds as a boy of sixteen, he had pulled himself from the brink of death despite a grievous leg injury at the hands of the enemy. Lost for many days in the wilds, he languished in a terrible state, slipping in and out of consciousness. Through sheer will, he survived the arduous ordeal, spawning tales that seemed impossible if one did not know the man himself.

"Governor Dudley has sent word that we shall not be abandoned. He has called on the aid of Governor Winthrop, who forthwith deploys soldiers from Connecticut to stand with us. We are directed to make ready our people in thwarting the attack. Our militia and sentinels upon the watch are called to be ever vigilant in their duties," instructs the Reverend.

John Hawks, who resides in one of the few fortified homes, cries, "Though we may have our newly reinforced walls to protect us, we have but three fortified houses. With our numbers growing, and now an untold number of soldiers arriving, how are we to shelter so many?"

"Aye!" rise shouts of agreement.

"We shall make do, as the Lord commands us to protect one another. If our earthly comforts are sacrificed in the defence of our neighbours, then we may be assured of the Lord's favour in His kingdom." The stern voice of Reverend Williams ends all further discussion. With no alternative but to rely on the Lord, Governor Dudley, and the might of their own militia in mounting a defence, the men quietly disassemble. Opening the door of the meetinghouse, they pour out into a day that holds faint hope that they should be spared their apparent fate.

On his way home, Edward passes Captain Wells's fortified home, the only one beyond the palisades. He takes count of how many paces lie between their houses: "Forty-three . . . forty-four . . . forty-five . . ." but with many yards between them yet, he stops counting, coming to the terrible realization that there is no need for such knowledge, for with so many in his care, it will never be made necessary.

# 9

19 August 1703

Dear reader, our changing fortunes give rise to a grim reality. Attacks have been reported in the colony at Saco and Wells, putting us on the defence once more. With the arrival of fifty-three soldiers sent by Governor Winthrop in Connecticut, we receive word that reports by our own scouts of the enemy lurking upon our doorstep have been misinterpreted, and no evidence of such has been discovered within thirty miles of Deerfield. The soldiers left after but two days in our midst. While the soldiers' news brings some reprieve from the oppressiveness of the vigilant mind, it leaves one no less ready for future harassment. Damn this Marquis de Vaudreuil! How may he claim nobility when he shows himself a wretched beast? He may hold the position of Governor General of New France, but surely he does the work of Satan himself, leading legions of devilish and ungodly men in the name of the Lord — such blasphemy! My anger boils over, spilling onto these pages, and for this I am sorry, dear reader. How much you must not understand, reading the words of one you do not know.

The harvest we have toiled these many months to cultivate nears, and I pray we are not called away from this work, for if we do not bring in its bounty, we shall all surely perish. The quick blow of the tomahawk or a shot from a French musket should be preferred to the less merciful end to our pitiful lives through starvation. To see us starve in reach of such abundance is too cruel; I pray we see the harvest realized.

My son, Edward, works by my side once more with the news that no enemy lies in wait . . . yet. In truth, I missed him during the planting. He will not be long in choosing a bride, and his instruction is most necessary to set forth a prosperous future. I am left conflicted, wondering if I put his life in peril, exposed in the fields as we are. With so much work to accomplish, it seems a risk I must take. Edward has been privy to the

discussions amongst the men of our community and seems
to comprehend the risk he takes, but he does not request to
be released from it. He is truly a man in many ways and must
assume his responsibilities, as all men must.

My dear Mercy, exceedingly unsettled, continues to find
her faith weakened. Often, when she believes me at my rest,
she weeps in the night, but I do not — cannot — provide comfort, for she must learn to strengthen her fortitude. This is
the reality of our life; sympathy will not aid her in accepting
the truth of it. But to you, dear reader, I confess that on more
than one occasion I did reach out to her. Each time, as my
hand approached her back, I stopped, reminding myself that
my duty is to protect her, not allow her to give in to despair.
There is always a heaviness lying upon my heart when I turn
away from her and try to rest. Sleep has been elusive as of
late. My mind is much occupied with the many responsibilities I have, and how we might be called to defend our homes
in the face of so many. Governor Dudley once moved swiftly
in supplying men for our protection. This time, I pray our
intelligence, proven unfounded, does not dissuade him from
being so quick if truly needed. Should he withhold for further confirmation, the aid, I fear, would be too late in coming.
Even with our own militia, our exposed position gives us only
the slightest hope of thwarting the enemy. I, too, must pray
for renewed faith, for I am afraid Mercy does not find herself
alone in faltering. Such sin washes over us that I suppose it
the evil of the French and their influence bearing down on us.

I shall not burden you further with my news and the
troubles that plague us. Perhaps it is best to now share with
you who we are and from whence we come, for I should
think it important information for one to know even in making acquaintance through the pages of this journal. I confess I
am sorry not to know your name, dear reader, but thank you
for your attention to my words.

I was born in the year of our Lord 1662 at Ipswich in
the Massachusetts Bay Colony no more than thirty years
after its founding by the revered John Winthrop, the once
governor. After serving Cromwell during the Civil War,
my father, Corporal Edward Allen, left his native Scotland
to settle along the beautiful, abundant river named for our

town. He and my dear mother, Sarah Kimball of this colony, moved to Suffield some years on to yield abundance on new land. I learned to farm by my father's instruction, and I pray that my son, who carries on the name of this great man, will find such success as I am blessed with. The sage advice of my father — to set forth with no fear and bring bounty to the land — resonates still, though he has been departed these seven years. I shall ever be sorry we did not have occasion to see one another again once I settled in Deerfield.

My dear Mercy hails from Newport, in the Rhode Island Colony on Narragansett Bay, where the salty waters flow from the mighty Atlantic Ocean, which spans to the distant shores our people once called home. My Mercy is the daughter of Shubael Painter and his wife Mercy Lamberton. While her parents were not affluent, Mercy's status in society is assured by the right of heredity to her grandfather Captain Lamberton, one of New Haven's founders. My children delight in my wife's stories of the Captain. I oft think that had I the gifts of the great bards, it would make good work to record such stories as are told in our humble home of this impressive man and his grand adventures. As it is, our work and my limited skills in matters of literature leave this to one more suited.

My wife's status, the troubles caused by her father's sinful ways — which I will not disclose on these pages to save her good name — and our current troubles have made her disposition delicate, and she requires much care and guidance. We are ill afforded such luxuries. It is difficult to live in such wild places, but the womenfolk, with their weak constitutions, seem to suffer all the more. Although I assure Mercy that we are under the Lord's protection, it appears I am unable to quell her fears in their entirety. Despite this, my good wife remains resolute in her efforts and does not let the hindrance of her sensibilities impede her in her work.

We know the blessings of many children: two sons and five daughters, though there ought to be seven. I will write more of them in future entries, but find myself waning.

I must rest now, for much work is to be done with the dawning of the day, and so I bid you well until my next entry.

Edward

# 10

Having removed the ashes from the hearth, Sarah stands a dreadful mess with her skirt and hands so black that no amount of scrubbing would remove it entirely. However, she cleans with a happy heart, for her mother has allowed her and her younger siblings to go and watch their father and Edward bring in the hay — once the children's lessons are complete. Such entertainment is to be had watching the change in the fields and the men working in unison. Ensuring she instructs the children as her mother expects, she will not suffer foolishness that will delay her enjoyment of such a lovely day.

"Martha, please fetch the book for your lesson. Samuel, Hannah, Jemima, gather round. I shall not repeat myself today; you must listen and learn well. The Lord will not look kindly upon children who are disobedient, and if you do not want to be 'damned' as the good Lord warns, you must heed my instruction." Sternly looking to each, she gives a silent warning akin to her mother's.

"We shall, Sarah," Martha says, nodding to each for agreement. She is becoming an ally amongst so many young ones, and Sarah is pleased when she takes Samuel in her arms, controlling his usual custom of running off.

Carefully opening the worn book, their only copy of *The New England Primer*, Sarah fears the spine will give and the pages will tumble from it. With no doubt that she will be held accountable for its demise, she gingerly turns to one of her favourite pages, and the whimsical images welcome her as an old friend. Memories of dear Mercy instructing her, just as she now instructs the small group in front of her, bring her such happiness.

"Children, today we practice our alphabet. It is an essential skill that you will need throughout all your days; therefore, mind what I say. A: In Adam's fall, we sinned all. B: Thy life to mend, this Book attend. C: The Cat doth play, and after slay." When she gets to "S" she reads, "S: Samuel anoints who God appoints."

"Dat me Hannah, Sawa say me Samooel!"

Hannah looks to Sarah with wide eyes, quickly putting her hand over Samuel's mouth to avoid any more outbursts.

"No more speaking out of turn, Samuel!" Sarah scolds, as his interruption threatens their time outdoors. Grieved to see his familiar pout, which can only lead to tears and further delay, she mutters under her breath. "Children are such afflictions!" Coming to her aid, Hannah offers a pacifying kiss upon his cheek to sooth him. Relieved to find her efforts rewarded, Sarah continues.

"Z: Zaccheus did climb the tree, his Lord to see." Except for Samuel, Sarah is impressed by the children's attentiveness, and surprised that it is Hannah who has proven to be her finest pupil.

"Reflect on my instructions, children. I shall return in a moment." *Perhaps now Mother will allow us to escape the confines of our home.*

Entering the kitchen, Sarah is instantly struck by how stifling the room is. Intense flames lick the bottom of a simmering pot, and the open door provides no relief at all, making her all the more eager to be given the permission she seeks.

"Mother?"

Her mother and Mercy look up from their mending and the private conversation they seem to be enjoying, and Sarah's heart is struck by their similarity in appearance and mannerism. They seem as equals, and she knows her dearest sister is truly lost to her. By the time it is Sarah's turn to aid in such work and enjoy such companionship, she knows Mercy will surely be gone, raising a family of her own.

"Yes, Sarah?"

Startled from her unhappy thoughts, she swallows hard to stop her childish tears. "May we now visit Father in the fields? I have completed the children's instruction."

"It seems far too little time to have accomplished the task. Are you quite satisfied with the result?"

"I am. I was very clear in cautioning that they should work diligently."

"Very well, you may take them to see Father and Edward, but do not burden the men with your presence." Her mother smiles at her, and she is pleased, for it does not happen so often anymore. Perhaps the thought of the oncoming winter months and the dour Reverend Williams take a toll on her mother, as they do on Sarah herself. But these last warm days seem to welcome such levity back into their midst, that even the Reverend cannot affect it. As the women return to their work, Sarah makes haste to gather the children.

The sun hits Sarah's face as she bounds from the house, and she feels as the flowers swaying about them in the warm summer breezes racing through the meadow. *Such gaiety we may revel in on our walks,* she rejoices, renewed by the release from their daily toil. The Reverend often cautions the congregation not to allow such wicked behaviour in their children. Knowing her dear friend Esther enjoys few of these days, Sarah is thankful that she and her siblings may partake in it at all, but in her heart she is left wanting more.

Seeing countless orange and black monarchs flitting about upon a branch in the distance, Sarah longs for the freedom to rest upon the ground and watch them throughout the day, waiting for the moment when they fly off as one. For two summers she has excitedly raced to visit them only to find them departed, leaving her to wonder why they should not make her privy to such a sight. The joy in their gathering is tempered, for it signals the harvest. Though she delights in the season, it is much too fleeting.

Sitting amid the stems of newly shorn grasses at the edge of the field, Sarah and the children do not disturb their father and brother, as instructed. Setting Samuel upon her knee, she watches Hannah force her way between Martha and Jemima, who are sitting together, as always. They allow the intrusion, giving no evidence of being disturbed by it. It is not that Sarah dislikes Hannah, but she does not pretend to hold her in the same affection as the one now sitting upon her lap, for Samuel is not as bold. In her sensibilities, Hannah is akin to Edward; both are stubborn and cause Sarah much consternation. However, judging by his manner towards her, Edward holds Sarah in the same esteem, so she is not alone if such sentiments be wicked.

Sweeping to and fro, the scythes fell the towering golden grasses that now grow much beyond the height of Samuel, and even Hannah. Such lovely expanses are revealed with each fluid, slicing motion: haystacks dotting the fields where their neighbours work rival the beauty of the distant hills. She imagines it must be difficult for the men to remain focused on their labours, but they do not seem to notice in the least.

"Me see Papa!" Samuel attempts to release himself from Sarah's grip, but she holds him tight, certain that if he troubles their father, she will be punished. Deciding it might be best to explore their surroundings to divert his attentions, she begrudgingly leaves the scene before her.

"Come children, let us go see the calves yonder." Standing, they brush off the grass that sticks to their skirts and Samuel's britches. They hardly have a chance to make themselves presentable before Hannah grabs Samuel by the hand and the two dash off in merriment. Coming to Sarah's side, Martha and Jemima link arms to skip together, offering Sarah an arm to join. Seeing no harm in it, she dashes along with the others. *Such fun!*

Clamouring upon the rails, beckoning to the calves in the paddock, Samuel and Hannah capture the attention of their neighbours, Mr. Williams and Mr. Nims, who tend the animals. They greet the children with a wave, and they wave back as they settle themselves on the fence to enjoy watching the calves frolic. Sarah holds Samuel tightly at the waist, as he is on the verge of falling from his perch. Watching the calves bounce about playfully, Sarah notes how they have gained in size over the summer months. That they will sustain many in the community makes her no less sad to know their fate.

"How many do you see, Samuel?"

Happy to play the game Sarah has begun, Samuel looks at her excitedly before he begins. "One, two, tree, fowr . . . Sawa, dey run!"

"Yes, Samuel, they will move about. Do not be frustrated. Let us begin again." Taking his small hand in hers, Sarah extends his little finger and the two count together.

"Sevteen. Hooray! Me tell Mama."

Before she can correct that there are many more, Samuel begins his rapid descent from the rail, running home to tell his mother. Sarah sighs. *I suppose it is time, for the day draws to a close.*

"Martha, Jemima, Hannah, we must get home and finish our chores." Grabbing Samuel's hand to slow his progress, Sarah turns back and sees Martha and Jemima helping Hannah complete her own count.

"Twenty-two, Sarah. There are twenty-two!" she yells, running to her. Taking Sarah's free hand, Hannah looks up and announces again, "Twenty-two calves."

Gazing upon her radiant face, Sarah is sorry to have thought less of her, for she is surely a good and sweet child, despite her occasional wickedness. Nearing the house, Sarah looks back to catch a final glimpse of the scythes moving in unison. "An even more wonderful sight," she whispers, finding her father waving at her as they leave the fields.

# 11

25 September 1703

The autumn moon framed within my window, once considerable upon the horizon, has turned from a fiery orange to a radiant white as it rises ever higher in the sky.

We are blessed to have our abundant harvest being stored for the desolate months ahead, which are not long in coming. The days shorten, and, though the world is ablaze with colour, the cold chill of the nights signals the approach of winter. With much work yet to be done, we must not abate in our efforts, but feel more assured now with so many working in the fields.

No further evidence of the enemy has been found by our scouts or sentries. We do not let our guard down, but have had pleasure in our lives. On occasion I have granted Mercy's request to allow Sarah to take the children to explore the fields and river. I am ever watchful. Though they may be sorry to see the season end, I confess I will welcome the deep snows and deathly cold of winter, for it provides reprieve from the threat of attack.

Even now, as I write, I hear a few distant calls of geese that are gathered upon the river beyond our fields. As dusk ushers the day into night, the skies blacken with hundreds of them as they prepare for their collective departure from this place. Their understanding of the changing season is a mystery unto the Lord, for it seems their ways can ever be counted on to signal what is to come. The contemplation of such changes on the horizon brings many concerns to mind, which will only serve to impede my rest, and so, dear reader, it is best to end the day and wish you good night.

Edward

## 12

"**M**ercy, where are the children?" Edward calls, rushing to his wife. Their son slams the door shut and begins barricading it behind him, while Mercy pivots to meet her husband's alarmed expression.

"Where are they?" he repeats, grabbing her forcefully by both arms and shaking her to attention, a look of unbridled fear in his eyes.

"They . . . The children . . . " she stutters.

"Father, they are together in the back garden," his daughter Mercy answers, running to her mother's side and holding her tight to stop her trembling, which overtakes her with terrifying violence.

With no words, Edward pushes past them with such haste that a chair crashes to the floor, startling his wife to her senses.

"Save them!" she cries out.

Not wanting to alert the enemy skulking in the shadows of the trees surrounding them, Edward silently locates the children sitting upon the grass, delighting in the leaves that fall about them. Seizing Sarah by the arm, he pulls her up, whispering in an alarmed tone, "Take Samuel and run immediately to the house. As fast as you might." Roughly taking hold of Hannah, he clumsily hoists her under his arm. With his other hand, he grabs Martha, pulling her toward the house, followed closely by his son, who has taken Jemima in his arms in a similarly indelicate fashion. Tripping upon her skirts in her effort to keep pace, Martha falls to the ground, forcing Edward to lift her by the waist on the last stretch towards the house. With the last footstep upon the threshold, the men throw the children to the floor, slamming the door behind them. Pulling the table from the center of the room, Edward flips it on its side, pushing it hard against the door. Piling chairs against it and any item that may add weight to the growing makeshift barricade, he yells in a loud commanding voice, "Wife, take the children to the inner room and lay upon the floor!" Sweeping up a tearful Samuel into her arms, Mercy does as she is told, much to Edward's relief.

Realizing no more can be used as a barricade, he pushes his son away from the pile of furniture that nearly reaches the ceiling.

"Go watch over your mother, brother, and sisters. Should we fall under attack, it is your sole duty to protect them. I will stay here and obstruct any attempts at entry. If our home should be breached, exit the window and make haste to Captain Wells's home."

Attentive to his father's wishes, Edward signals his understanding with a nod and immediately leaves his company. Left alone by the hearth, Edward knows his instructions are a desperate attempt to create the illusion that such escape would be possible. He strains to hear something in the silence beyond the door, but only the noise of the rustling and falling leaves fills the void.

"Mother, what is happening?" Whispering over Samuel's incessant sobs, Sarah is not sure her mother has heard her at all, for she just keeps repeating, "Shh, shh, Samuel, you must be quiet." Bringing her skirt to his face, muffling his cries, their mother rocks him rapidly. Not looking at any of the children, she keeps her eyes fixed upon the door. *What is beyond it that sets such fear in Mother — and Father?* Sarah wonders, struck by an unknown panic.

"Mama?"

"Sarah, mind me. You must *not* speak." It is not the sternness of her voice, nor her serious glare, but her tears that frighten Sarah most. *What evil must we be facing?* She repeats silently to herself, *I must not cry, I must not cry, I must not . . .* The effort proves futile.

Huddled in the dimming inner room, dusk plunging them into darkness, Sarah's mother finally pulls her skirt from Samuel's face, for he now sleeps soundly, unaware of their torment. Sitting still as the dead, they listen into the silence that masks certain doom.

After what seems hours, Sarah's sisters Hannah, Jemima, and Martha lie sleeping upon the cold, hard floor. In the shadowy confines of the room she shelters in, Sarah sees her mother cock her head occasionally, turning her ear to untold dangers, but listen as she might, Sarah can only hear her own breathing. Tapping her mother on the shoulder, Mercy pulls Samuel's limp body from her, cradling him tightly in her arms to soothe him back to sleep as he stirs from being jostled. They remain mere silhouettes to one another. Keeping an ear pressed to the door, Edward has not let go of the handle, bringing reassurance they are protected by his vigilance. Sarah is confused to be so frightened of something unseen. The passing time does not soothe her nerves. Pulling her knees close, she pretends she is in a cocoon like one of the butterflies she loves so well.

Brushing away what she believes is a bug on her shoulder, she is glad to realize it is her sister Mercy lightly tapping her. Squeezing her hand, Sarah is relieved by her sister's presence. Mercy pulls Sarah to her, and she huddles in close, laying her head upon her sister's shoulder. As she moves, she is careful not to disturb Samuel, for he will surely put them in peril if he were to wake. Sarah cannot forget the sight of her mother nearly suffocating him — for it seemed that way. At first, when he stopped wailing, Sarah thought him dead. Sickened by the realization, it was only when he shifted slightly in his mother's arms that she realized he was not harmed. Closing her eyes tight, Sarah tries to banish the memory of it. As Mercy tenderly strokes her shoulder, Sarah finds herself suddenly tired. Not wanting to seem as a child to her brothers and sisters, she struggles to stay awake. *How I long for sleep; perhaps I will close my eyes for just a moment.*

Roused by her brother Edward's faint voice, Sarah jolts awake.

"Mother," he whispers almost imperceptibly, "we have not heard Father move in many hours, and I have not yet heard a noise that should cause alarm. Might I see if he requires my assistance with the watch?"

Worn out by the innumerable thoughts of devastation running through her mind, she wearily consents, "Yes. Go to him."

Cracking open the door, Edward pauses momentarily to assess the risk before escaping the confines, and then hastily shuts his mother and siblings in once more.

"Father?" Still staring out the window into the darkness, Edward turns to his son. The panic of hours earlier having subsided somewhat, he beckons him to his side.

"Might Mother and the children exit the room and take some supper?'

"Yes. I will remain a sentry while the others partake, but I must insist that no undue conversation take place. And we must limit ourselves to one candle to provide only the most necessary light."

Privy to what was so fearful, Edward leaves to convey his message.

Sarah does not mind her brother's warnings not to make too much noise, for that they may finally rejoin her father brings such relief.

Leaving Samuel and Hannah to sleep, they venture into the kitchen, Sarah holding tight to Mercy's hand. They are unable to see much, as the kitchen is as black as their shelter. Striking the flint the candle flame sputters to life and they are met by a shocking sight. With furniture piled high against the door, their home, in shambles, is unrecognizable, and Sarah knows it must hurt her mother to see it so.

"Come, Edward, bring a candle," Sarah's father whispers from the far reaches of the room.

Leaving his mother and siblings around the cold hearth, he moves to his father, handing him a candle. Sarah is stunned by her father's distressed expression, now visible in the candlelight. She has never seen him in such a state and prays that she never will again.

"Father," Edward says, "I will keep a careful watch."

"Very well, we will take turns throughout the night." Resting his musket by Edward, Sarah's father brings the candle and sets it in the ashes of the hearth. Afforded only a dim view of one another, what is revealed takes Sarah aback. They look as strangers.

Picking up the partially baked bread, Sarah's mother tears off small pieces, giving each a morsel. It is not enough to satisfy, but at least they are together.

Throughout their brief few moments together, Sarah tries to imagine what has happened from the peculiar glances her mother and father exchange, but she can make no sense of it.

"Tonight you will all sleep upon the floor of the room I earlier sent you to," her father says. "Off now, the candle must soon be extinguished."

Taking a few pieces of bread for Hannah and Samuel, Sarah and her siblings do as their father instructs, but she knows she will not sleep at all. Her mother stays behind to speak with their father, and Sarah prays she will not be long, for without their mother or Edward, Sarah and Mercy, as the oldest siblings in the room, are left to defend the others alone.

"Edward, might I inquire what causes such alarm?" Plainly exhausted, Mercy does not seem as terror struck as when last he saw her hours earlier. Glad for it, he senses she is able to understand the severity, but he limits the detail to spare her further grief.

"Zebidiah Williams and John Nims are taken or killed. I cannot say which, for when the first shots rang out as Edward and I were in the field, my only thoughts were to get to the house and shore up what defences we may be afforded."

"Was it the French, as we have been warned?"

"I do not know, for I maintained my sights upon our home, thinking to you, good Wife, and our children within it." Too worn out to assume his usual assured manner, Edward exposes his true feelings. Staring at the candle flame rising higher with the absence of movement, Edward has no more insight to offer.

"I looked." Breaking the tense silence, their son Edward, unsure if he should confess such when he was told to flee without delay, tentatively repeats, "I looked back, Father."

"And? Was it the French?"

"It was Indians, Father. I saw no French amongst them."

Upon the horizon faint hues of pink signal the returning light of day, bringing with them a new reality: they exist in the midst of the enemy.

# 13

The next day, sitting at the righted table to eat a small meal of dried meat, the family is jolted from their solemn state by a loud knock upon the door. Rushing to the window, Edward sees his neighbour, Eleazer Hawks, standing stern-faced, obviously as overwrought as Edward himself. Removing the few remnants of their barricade, now but two partial barrels of ale, he opens the door.

"We are summoned to the meetinghouse," Eleazer announces before leaving abruptly to meet the other men delivering messages to their neighbours.

"Edward, you will join me," he says to his son. Taking the meat he was apportioned, he turns for the door. "Replace the barrels once we are gone," he instructs his wife. "Do not, under any circumstance, allow the children to leave our home."

Mercy nods her understanding. Alarmed by his altered demeanour, seeming as if his anger threatens to manifest at any moment, she turns to find her son mimics his father's disposition. Seemingly unconcerned, even eager, to meet the enemy, he loads his musket.

Where once she might have implored her husband to spare Edward relinquishing his youth to such full measure, she can see he is already changed. Her protestations would not recover what is so evidently lost.

*This above fear, above uncertainty, is the cruelty of war*, she sighs regretfully, watching her son slip away from her.

In the meetinghouse, the men's voices rise as everyone speaks at once.

"We must bring in the remaining harvest or we will find our families starving upon the winter!"

"Neighbours, take your places."

"Our defences are poor and we cannot stay in this place with any hope of survival!"

"Sit and listen, men of Deerfield."

Precipitated by fear, fatigue, and uncertainty, the unruly atmosphere will not be easily quelled by the booming voice of the Reverend on this occasion. The men continue their angry tirades, frustrated at how poorly defended they are.

"Stop!" Resounding beyond the walls of the meetinghouse, the Reverend's cry reaches as far as the homes within the palisade walls; he stands in his usual commanding manner. Finally order is brought to the chaos, and the men sit awaiting the Reverend's guidance.

"Pray for the souls of our neighbours Zebediah Williams and John Nims, taken from us so violently, for they surely endure suffering beyond measure." Bowing his head, the Reverend leads the men in a moment of quiet prayer and reflection, which is the first pause in many hours fraught with panic and disbelief.

"The course of safety dictates that families enter the walls each night, taking shelter in the fortifications we have."

His words destroy the newly wrested calm. The men erupt in wild gestures, expressions of exasperation, and comments out of turn.

"We will make do as before," the Reverend cries above the discord. "Though it does not afford comfort or dignity, it does afford *salvation*." The last word momentarily quiets the room.

"How are we to improve our land under such threat?" Nathanial Brooks calls out.

Realizing force will not quiet the temper of fearful men, the Reverend composes himself, replying in a matter of fact tone, "We must not concern ourselves with further improvement; it is the harvest that now becomes our sole concentration. There will be time, good neighbours, to make Deerfield and its lands prosperous, but to do so we must ensure our survival, and in this effort we must remain steadfast. To see our good wives and children suffer at the hands of such treachery would not serve our purpose upon this earth. I shall write further to Governor Dudley, for he has promised not to forsake us in our valiant efforts to protect the edge of the colony. As before, he will surely send us soldiers to aid in our defence. Until then, I call upon Captain Wells to provide direction in what further measures we may take to mount adequate defence until such time comes that we welcome reinforcements."

Captain Wells rises to the pulpit, dressed in his uniform. Relinquishing his role as a farmer, he exhibits the commanding mannerisms of his rank as he addresses the men in a calm and steady voice. "I have sent word to Colonel Patrigg, whom we may expect forthwith. Until such time, we will send our scouts to gather evidence of the enemy, and we will install additional sentries to keep watch of our village. But it must be with haste that you prepare your families to be at the ready. All may be called upon; even the youngest will not be spared. Show your sons how they may defend their mothers, brothers, and sisters. Do not falter in this, for even with soldiers at our side, the enemy comes at us with silent ferocity from which no man, woman, or child may escape. We have seen such methods before and know the French will call upon their allies to do their bidding. No alliances hold. Trust only the men of our village and the soldiers sent to us — and no more. If you see a stranger, assume him foe and sound the alarm as you are able. We rely solely on one another to defend what God has righteously provided His people. It is our duty, men of Deerfield, to defend and protect this gift."

Jonathan Wells displays such discipline that every man sits straighter at attention, heeding their commander's words as though they were now soldiers in Her Majesty's forces, not farmers on the frontier.

Calling upon his faith to overcome his own fatigue and disillusionment, Reverend Williams summons what strength remains and stands before his flock. "The Lord commands your obedience. Go and instruct your families to pray for those already taken, and for our souls, for we surely see the first blow fall upon us. We will be rewarded for our faith and our courage to meet the enemy."

Startled by the creaking of the door opening, revealing the blackness beyond, Mercy sits alone by the hearth, bracing for the inevitable. The faint light of the dying fire casts deep shadows upon Edward's troubled expression. Exhaling, she is relieved fate has not found them. Wearily, their son heads directly to his bed chamber, ignoring the food she has left out for them. Pulling a chair out from the table, Edward slumps onto it and in quiet defeat shares, "This night shall be the last we see in this place, for all must now shelter in the protection of the walls when night begins to fall."

The horrifying prospect of such undignified living conditions is quickly accepted with the reality of the alternative.

"And how long should this be so?"

Pensive for a moment, Edward does not look up when he finally delivers the answer. "The length is unknown."

"Might we return upon the morn to maintain our family, our home?"

"We may, but we must endure the nights away." Consumed by the burden of their changed circumstance, Edward stares at the last few radiant coals of the fire, not sensing the chill settling upon them.

Putting her hands upon his slouched shoulders, Mercy whispers gently, "Come, take your rest, dear Husband. The day has been long, and morning arrives in but a few short hours. Surely no more may be done this night. We are in the Lord's care, and in this we must take solace."

Glad for her unwavering faith and the reassurance of her touch, he looks to her, tears welling in his eyes. Holding her hands that rest softly upon his shoulders, he feels the cold she endures.

"Go to bed, Mercy. I shall stoke the fire to warm us this night. Take comfort in your own bed, and sleep well. I will join you presently."

Edward gives her a weak smile and releases her. As he watches her move into the darkness, the light from the candle she carries fades with each step, and sorrow overwhelms him.

"Mercy . . . I love you."

Turning back to him, the flickering candlelight reveals her beauty, which remains despite such severe worry. A genuine smile crossing her lips, she displays a strength he has not witnessed before.

"I love you, dear Edward."

# 14

9 October 1703

Dear reader, I shall not delay in sharing with you that we find our neighbours Zebediah Williams and John Nims taken captive. It seems they were not killed upon the fields outright, for some say they witnessed their being led away, but we do not expect to see them in this place again. These accounts further my belief that this journal may one day be the only evidence of our existence. I entrust it to your care, and what you do with the contents are yours to determine; that my words resonate after our departure from this sinful world will be enough.

Through the growing and harvest seasons we have had our sons at our sides. Edward is of the age to accept such risks as we take in the fields, but sons not yet thirteen are sent back to their mothers. Many a man will struggle to maintain his work without their aid. Edward has a resolute nature, and I am proud to have such a son, however, I am not unaware of his mother's fears.

Such hope endured in the quiet weeks preceding this blow. Our focus had been drawn away from our troubles to the promise of the coming harvest, and we find ourselves proven naive. Ever are we under the malevolent watch of the enemy and those who do their bidding. Curse the French and their allies! We face much strife, but, as before, we will rise to meet their affront, and should we not endure in this life, we shall be comforted in knowing we endure in heaven, where the Lord will welcome us triumphant.

Such anger wells in me, though it be subdued by my need for sleep. My belief that we must do as commanded will provide strength to overcome these mortal weaknesses I now suffer. The Reverend has written to Governor Dudley to beseech aid, and with this we may be assured.

Encouraged by my good wife's manner, I may rest knowing her faith is restored, for only before I put pen to paper did she demonstrate a resolve that will surely aid in her endurance during our displacement and the uncertainty of awaiting further aggression. My children are distressed by the unknown events of these two days, but the youngest, who is spared the knowledge our eldest must endure. My daughters do not voice their concerns, but it is evident by their constant gaze set upon the fields and forest beyond our home that they understand something lurks just out of sight. I think they believe signs of the enemy may be had by such vigilance and that they do their part in this way, but this is for naught. As we saw when the unfortunates were taken from us, no sound, nary a bird signalling the intruders, will be given. Such ways these allies of the French employ that we are spared the worry of listening, for what is coming we will surely never be made aware. Though we travel to the confines of the palisades in the remaining light of day, it is not certain that we will make the gates of Deerfield.

Our moving outside the walls to our cluster of homes, now called the Bars, has allowed expansion of our lands and has given us hope that our way may be prosperous. However, I now wonder if such dangers that come from being set apart and exposed are the levy exacted for such ambitions. Now we must all huddle together within the palisades, penned as the animals in our barns. My mind wanders with fatigue and so, dear reader, I bid you goodbye, for I do not know if we shall again meet in this journal. Much is unknown. Should you find all pages henceforth vacant, I implore you to pray for our souls, and I wish you well in the life you may yet enjoy.

Edward

# 15

24 January 1704

I am sorry I have not had occasion to write upon these pages in many a week. With the threat of attack by the enemy, our efforts to bring in the harvest were redoubled, occupying much of my time. This effort, coupled with the lack of privacy in the homes inside the palisades, left me with no opportunity to maintain my journal. Since the end of the harvest, I have concentrated on instructing Edward on furthering his skill with his musket, and I am pleased to report he is now quite capable with the weapon, providing some peace of mind that I may have him by my side in defending my family.

Winter has released us from unbearable oppression and the indignities we endured in protecting ourselves. It is a blessing to be restored to our home and our usual ways. With the reprieve afforded by the deep snows, I have just this day been to the meetinghouse for our year-end session and am happy to report that our discussions were to taxation, future land uses, and appointments.

Colonel Patrigg heard our concerns and sent reinforcements for a few weeks. Now, with the onset of winter diminishing the threat of attack, only a few remain to give guidance to our Committee of Safety, of which I have been made a member. We now assume the lead in ensuring our security. I am glad to report that little came of it, as we have passed these interim months peacefully, with no sign of the enemy. There has been news delivered to us that Zebediah Williams and John Nims yet live, though they suffer in captivity. It is unknown which fate is worse, but we have hope that they may yet be redeemed.

I am sorry to end my entry so soon, after such a long pause, but my son and I have much work yet to accomplish before we may take our rest, as it is bitterly cold this night and we must provide additional bedding to the animals. I bid you well, and pray to soon find myself sharing more upon these pages.

Edward

# 16

"Edward, might I have a word?" Reverend Williams asks, catching him by the sleeve as he leads his family out of the meetinghouse.

Nodding his agreement, Edward stands to the side, awaiting the last of the congregation to spill out into the biting cold of the midwinter day. In truth, the variance in the chill from within the meetinghouse to that beyond its walls is nearly indiscernible. Taking their seats on the benches once again, the family waits.

Shutting the door behind the last of his flock, Reverend Williams joins Edward at the side wall.

"Might Sarah come to stay with us and provide some assistance in our household? I understand she is quite needed at home, but I offer additional instruction in her faith as incentive. Our Esther, ever her mother's aid, has found the task of caring for so many children difficult to manage. My wife, as you know, has been troubled since the arrival of Jerusha these six weeks, and in her weakened state has become fearful of her ability to endure. I assured her I would find aid from within our community, by which she was very encouraged. With our troubles seemingly at bay for the time being, I should think it would be safe enough for Sarah to join us."

"Of course you may have her in your service, but might I inquire when you would like to have her attend your home? We will need to make such arrangements as is necessary, you understand."

"Yes. Yes. Thank you, Edward. We would be most grateful if Sarah might attend us tomorrow until the Sabbath, when she might well return to you. I pray her aid will not be necessary beyond this — but if it is, might we revisit the terms?"

Sensing it difficult for the Reverend to admit the weakness of his wife and resulting family situation, Edward offers, "You may have use of her for as long as you need. I expect your instruction will serve her well."

Looking to Sarah attempting to keep Samuel occupied as they wait, Edward knows the burden her absence will put on his own household, but recognizes Mercy's capability to withstand such adversity. Proven in the months since the assault, her resolve now exhibits a determination well suited to their isolated life – the answer to so many of Edward's prayers. Sarah's yearning for adventure is apparent by her very nature, and he is sure she will welcome the opportunity as he equally welcomes her added instruction. While obedient enough, she still lacks the placidity sought by many a young man and will need to be brought into check if she is to make a good wife one day.

"Very well," Reverend Williams says, shaking Edward's hand heartily in thanks. He motions to his own family waiting silently near the front of the meetinghouse; his wife Eunice rises slowly from her bench. It is apparent today is not a good day for her. Esther holds her infant sister, Jerusha, as her mother is helped to her feet by her younger siblings. All have the strained look of a family struggling with a great many burdens of the mind.

Mercy and the children join Edward to begin their strenuous journey home through drifts at times reaching Edward's knees. The winds that had whipped the snows into a frenzy, causing the piercing cold to penetrate the walls of their home in the days before the Sabbath, have now given way to calm, clear skies. Despite the challenges such wintry weather poses, with the warmth of the sun on their faces and the respite from fear, the Allens rejoice in the day.

Glancing back, Edward sees Reverend Williams holding the hand of his six-year-old son, John Jr., who gazes up at his father towering over him. Watching the family slowly and somberly walk in the direction of their home near the meetinghouse at the edge of the village common, he knows the Reverend's family does not share in the blessing of the unburdened mind.

# 17

"Sarah, come here."

Surprised by her father's unusual request, she turns to see him standing at the door. Handing Samuel to Martha, she follows him into the kitchen, away from the children, with whom she has only just begun daily lessons. Worried that her daydreaming was noticed during evening prayers, she awaits her inevitable punishment.

"Reverend Williams requests we send you to their assistance for a time. We will leave henceforth. I ask that you gather your clothing."

"How long will I be gone, Father?" The thought of being under the watchful eye of the Reverend terrifies Sarah, for surely he will condemn her distracted nature, which she finds nearly impossible to control, despite her prayers to overcome it.

"As long as you may be needed, Sarah, but for the purposes of preparing your belongings, you may plan for six days. Should you be needed beyond the Sabbath, we will arrange to bring you more."

Sarah's heart beats so forcefully it pains her. So many days she has longed for adventure, to go beyond the confines of her plain and solitary life, but now faced with the prospect, she finds herself wanting for nothing more than to remain within its confines.

"Father, might I aid Sarah in her preparations?" her sister Mercy asks from the doorway. *Oh dear Mercy! I will confess my fears to her. Please, Father, allow it.*

"Yes, but do not delay. The winds are picking up again, and I do not want to be caught in a tempest."

Moving swiftly to Sarah's side, Mercy squeezes her hand, always her secret message of comfort, and leads Sarah away to prepare.

"Edward."

Startled from his thoughts, Edward looks to his wife, who is now facing him with a worried expression on her face.

"Do you think it wise to allow Sarah so far from home?"

"Mercy, it is our Christian duty to provide aid to the Williams family in such times, and as it has been so requested by the Reverend himself, we shall not decline."

Taking a place upon the chair by Edward's side, she grabs his hand, passionately begging, "Dear Husband, such risk we take in sending our dearest Sarah away from our protection. Who shall come to her aid should the enemy find them? Surely we risk too much. Please reconsider the request. There is many a woman who may be of more assistance than a girl Sarah's age can provide."

"We send her, and of this we shall speak no more. The Reverend has requested it." Edward's severe response, precipitated by his own reservations, comes across more harshly than intended. Seeing his wife's tear-filled eyes, he clasps his hands around hers, softly assuring, "The world is frozen over and the snows are deep, good Wife. It would be much too arduous to venture into our lands under such conditions. I am comforted by this, as you must be. Only having taken these conditions into consideration have I granted Sarah's aid. Martha is able enough to help with the children, and so no discord in our family will come of her departure." Praying his reasoning has placated her fears, he looks to Mercy, hoping to find her resolve renewed. Raising her eyes to meet his, her tears are replaced by a silent, stern warning that his words best prove true.

"We shall make do well enough, dear Husband, and I am glad that Sarah may provide comfort and assistance to the Reverend and his family, but I will be in constant prayer until my child returns to our care nonetheless."

Edward cannot chastise such a sentiment, for he will be doing the same. "I will be meeting with the Reverend on some business matters and will return before dark."

Silently working with Mercy gathering what may be needed, Sarah feels the weight of separation from her dear sister as never before. Though they are separated by the divide of age and responsibility, the thought of physical parting, she believed, was beyond them yet. *Will this be what it feels like when we leave one another for new homes?*

"I have never been so far . . . alone."

"Sarah, you shall have great fun with Esther, for how long has it been since you have had occasion to speak with her? I think you shall find these six days lacking in duration and will want for more." Mercy's warm embrace and soft, gentle voice cannot comfort her fears as they once did.

"I will not, for I will miss you all in the utmost." Pulling back, Sarah looks to her dear sister, beseeching her to understand. Mercy's steady expression and lovely smile cannot hide what Sarah sees in her eyes. They are of one heart. Falling into Mercy's arms, she renews her weeping, for she cannot help but feel as a frightened child.

"Dearest, do not fret, for you have a heart for adventure. Even now, when the days are cold, I see you looking to the fields, wondering what places lie beyond. Imagine yourself on one of these journeys, and when you return, you may tell me of what you have seen. I shall not sleep a wink until such time."

She loves her sister all the more for trying to replace her dread with anticipation, but Sarah's tears speak to her heart's desire — and to its fears. "Yes. But when I imagine such adventures, we are all together."

# 18

❧

"**M**on Dieu, thank you for providing signs that we are the righteous against false claims and heathen beliefs, for the snows that have so impeded our movements to this faraway place have now provided the means by which we shall make our silent entrance. Dieu, for the snows that drift and pile high along the palisades, we are most thankful. Dieu, for the protection of our men who carry out this work commanded by our king, I pray we shall see all return to us. Should this not come to pass, we commend our spirits to your care and rejoice in joining the realm of the angels and saints. We pray for the souls under the watch of this Queen Anne, and while no salvation may come in the kingdom of heaven for them, we further pray, as our priests have counselled, that some may yet have hope in conversion. To Your glory, when we return to Fort Chambly, they will be sent immediately to the parishes of Canada to receive the grace of baptism. Au nom du Père, du Fils et du Saint-Esprit . . . "

"Lieutenant deRouville, we are ready at your command."

". . . Amen."

# 19

❧

"Hello, Mr. Allen, please enter." Stepping aside to allow Sarah and her father to pass, Parthena averts her eyes. Sarah does not think she is paid for her services, for she has heard her brother speak to his friends about the slaves. But as he caught her listening, he scolded her terribly, leaving her knowledge of the details spare. With so few in the community that can afford a slave, they remain a mystery to her. Moving to close the door behind them, Parthena catches Sarah's gaze, giving her a friendly smile. Curious to know more of her life and from where she has come, Sarah hopes this visit provides such opportunity. Startled by the Reverend's bellowed greeting, she is left to ponder such things later.

"Good afternoon, Edward. Thank you kindly for bringing Sarah to us. We are ever grateful."

"It is our pleasure, Reverend."

"Parthena, will you take Miss Allen to her accommodations and have Esther instruct her on what is needed of her." Speaking as though Sarah is not in the room, the Reverend motions Edward to follow him to the study, where they are to discuss community matters.

"Yes, Sir."

Parthena's demeanour has become more serious in the Reverend's presence. It seems his effect is universal.

Picking up the bag that holds her few belongings, Sarah looks up to meet her father's gaze.

"I pray you will be a blessing to the Williams family. Do not forget to be ever thankful that you may be so."

"Yes, Father," she replies, poorly concealing her apprehension.

"We shall see you upon the Sabbath, but six days from now."

*An eternity!* Watching her father leave to join the Reverend and two soldiers seated in the study, Sarah turns to follow Parthena, who is already several paces ahead.

Parthena unpacks Sarah's bag with such efficiency that within minutes they are on their way to meet Esther, who they find caring for her younger brothers and sisters in a small room.

"I must attend Mrs. Williams now, Miss. You will find Miss Esther knowing all that must be done," she says before disappearing out of the door. Sarah is glad not to have the care of Mrs. Williams, for she looked so sickly at services the day before. She is ashamed to admit that it was difficult to look at her. With Mrs. Williams' breathing laboured after only a few slow steps, it was as if Sarah could feel the pain herself.

"Sarah! I am so happy to have you with us," Esther cries. Setting Jerusha in her basket by the large window, she rushes to Sarah, embracing her exuberantly. "Though we may have much to attend to while you are here, I know we will have a most wonderful time together. I do not tell Father, but it is often dull with such routine. A friend makes such a welcome distraction."

With Esther's words, Sarah's misgivings are replaced with excitement at having such a friend to work with.

"I, too, am happy that I may help, Esther. Will we be looking after the children together?"

"Yes. They are such dears, but with our poor Mama confined to bed, but for the Sabbath, it makes much work for me. Parthena must attend to Mama's needs, and so I prayed Father would send for assistance, and it seems the good Lord has answered my prayers, for which I am ever so thankful. When we pray together tonight I will be sure to say so. I do hope your own mother does not suffer your absence." Hardly taking a breath between thoughts, it seems Esther is as desperate for companionship as Sarah is.

"Mercy will take my place with the children, as she once did. Mother assured Father at our departing that she would find the strength to assume the duties she must to accommodate such a request." Thinking to her mother's tears and tender kiss upon her forehead makes Sarah miss her terribly already. She decides not to think more on it, for if she does, she will burst into a fit of tears, a display she is sure Esther will find childish, and the Reverend, sinful.

"Wonderful! It would not be so enjoyable if it were not so."

"Is she not beautiful, Sarah?" Esther coos, taking up Jerusha from the basket. "I have oft wondered these weeks since her arrival why Mama has been so grieved by her ailments. While my questions have not found answers yet, my prayers are answered as she gains strength daily. However, we should not see her walking about. Her strength is protected so that she may attend services upon the Sabbath, for to take this away from her, Father says, would be as death itself. You will find we pray most ardently, Sarah, for her returned health. Father provides the most wonderful instruction, and we are happy for it."

Esther's enthusiasm seems forced, and Sarah senses her friend is more pained by her mother's illness than she lets on. She has seen the strict hand and heard the severe manner of the Reverend's beliefs upon the pulpit, and she is often sorry for Esther and her siblings, for they seem to lack much joy in life.

Moving to see Jerusha, Sarah passes by the other children sitting upon the floor and cannot help but notice how docile they are. They peer at her with the most curious expressions upon their faces. Sarah gives a faint smile, but this elicits no response.

"Mama so rarely has opportunity to enjoy Jerusha. She grows well now, but in the beginning we did not know if she should join our Lord after being on this earth but a short time. It was Parthena who used her skill to ensure she lived. She has many mysterious medicines, Sarah, and though Father will not admit it, for he says she may not be saved, he is yet glad she provides such care." Suddenly quiet, Esther stares at Jerusha. Almost inaudibly, she says. "Mama would love her so, if she could."

"I am sure your mother will rally." Sarah reassures, not wholly believe it.

Esther's sadness lifts and she looks upon the now sleeping baby in her arms. Placing Jerusha into her basket once more, she covers her with a small blanket to keep her warm in the chilled room. "Come now, you must help me with the other children. We are woefully behind in our lessons today with so much excitement."

Turning to the children, Sarah smiles broadly, attempting to show her pleasure in being with them. She will seek forgiveness for her falsity in her prayers, for she would rather be at home. Despite the effort, they remain firm in their dour dispositions, so much like their father's.

"Children, you all know Miss Allen. She has come to aid in your instruction and care. You must attend her as you would me. Please stand and introduce yourselves, giving your age so that she may know what can be expected."

"Miss Allen, I am Stephen Williams and am soon to turn eleven."

"Stephen, I have asked that you give your age. Sarah does not need to know how old you may be. Begin again."

He frowns. "I am Stephen Williams, and I am ten years old," he says clearly aggravated. Esther shoots him a look of warning, one Sarah knows well.

Esther nods to the next child.

"I Wawham."

"I am Warham," she corrects.

"I am Wawham Wiwiams. Fo-war year."

"Next," Esther continues, her frustration growing at the missteps in the introductions.

"I am Eunice Williams, and I am seven years old." Intelligent and bright-eyed, she reminds Sarah of her own sister Martha. Her evident desire to make her sister proud sets her apart from the other children. Sarah feels sorry for the final child as they wait an uncomfortably long time for his introduction. He is a shy, timid boy.

"I am John ... "

"John, look at Sarah when you address her, please," Esther says in a tone that is equally encouraging and demanding.

"I am John Williams, and I am five years of age." Much more formal in his mannerisms than the others, John, despite his young age, has the makings of a man of some status. Sarah can see, even now, that he will follow the path of his father and eldest brother Eliezer, who is already away pursuing a religious education.

"Very well. Thank you children, you may be seated." Esther's firm tone and habit of correcting and chastising the children makes Sarah realize that, while jovial enough with her, she is evidently learning much from the Reverend.

"Sarah, perhaps you would like to instruct the older children today. I have much work to accomplish with the others, and I am afraid they are sorely lacking in discipline to make the advances they ought."

Glad to have a change in routine, Sarah sits to one side, positioning herself close to the hearth, as the room has quickly become cold with the fire reduced to but a few glowing coals in the ash. Noticing no wood present, she hopes her proximity will provide some relief to the chill she yet suffers from her journey here. Joined by Stephen and Eunice, Sarah is sure she will make gains with so few to instruct.

"What lessons have you been concentrating on?"

Quickly offering a hand in response, Eunice is eager to share.

"Yes, Eunice."

"We have been reading and discussing the parables."

"Very well then, where do you keep your Bible?"

"Over there," comes the cheerless response from a still-dejected Stephen, his mood making the room seem even more gloomy. Following where his finger points to the tall oak bookcase along the wall, Sarah moves to fetch it. The vast number of books upon the shelves are as none she has ever seen. Picking up a large Bible from a lower shelf, she examines the other leather-bound volumes, many with gold titling engraved on their spines: *The Reasons of the Christian Religion*; *New England Judged by the Spirit of the Lord*; *The Snake in the Grass or Satan Transform'd to an Angel of Light*. *No doubt where the Reverend acquires his inspiration,* she surmises.

Opening the Bible to the first reading, Sarah notices the tips of her fingers tinged with the blue of cold setting it. Rubbing her hands together to bring relief, she notices the others do not seem concerned with the chill and are merely awaiting her to begin.

"I will read, and then we shall discuss the passages."

A slight smile upon her lips, Eunice appears eager, while Stephen stares at Sarah, expressionless. Undaunted by his lack of enthusiasm, she begins. "Not everyone who says to me, 'Lord, Lord,' shall enter the kingdom of heaven, but he who does the will of my Father who is in heaven."

Heavy footsteps approach and the wooden floor cracks and moans with the weight underfoot. Sarah is relieved to see Samuel, and not the Reverend. The oldest of the Williams children yet at home, he enters the room with a large bundle of wood to stoke the fire. *Thank the Lord!* Sarah gives silent praise as she looks to the frost gathering upon the edges of the window. Paying no mind to them, Samuel goes about his work in rebuilding the fire, returning the room to a bearable warmth. After observing the flame is truly taken, the only evidence he is satisfied is his hasty departure from the room. Perturbed by his lack of civility, she imagines Esther must be equally affronted. But she did not seem to notice his presence, nor his departure. *Such differing ways! I shall be glad for the Sabbath and my return home.*

"Miss Esther, your father wishes your company, and that of Miss Sarah, in the study," Parthena says, standing in the shadow of the doorway. Sarah cannot help observing her, but attempts to disguise her curiosity, for she knows it is not right to stare. With only the faint glow of the candle to shed light upon Parthena's face, it is the kindness in her eyes that captivates Sarah. Her pleasant disposition, evident from the curve of her lips, makes her seem at the ready to smile at Sarah, but when in the presence of the Reverend, she changes quickly to suit the needs of this austere household. She exhibits a tenderness with the children; even in her few short hours in the home, Sarah has witnessed this. Her manner of dress seems extraordinarily plain compared to that which Esther wears, or any in the community. *Perhaps to distinguish her as a slave?* Sarah wonders. While Parthena had served the family supper, Sarah resisted the urge, with much difficulty, to study her features, for she was sure the Reverend would have reprimanded her for it.

"Oh, thank you. Tell him we shall be there forthwith," Esther says over her shoulder without looking directly at her. Immediately leaving to deliver the reply, Parthena seems unconcerned by the lack of consideration for her presence. Esther continues folding Sarah's clothing, setting them in the drawer emptied for her use. Patting the last item, Sarah's apron, she closes it.

"There, all done. Let us go and see what Father wants of us." Esther seems excited by the request to meet with her father, but being well acquainted with the Reverend's doomsday prophecies, Sarah feels a familiar sense of dread. She forces a smile in return to Esther's, and her friend stops.

"Do not look so forlorn, dear Sarah. Father is most kind, though you may not think so. He does such important work in saving us. He is often much occupied, and therefore, unable to show such kindness as we are blessed to know in our own home."

Hoping what she says is true, Sarah tries to rally, showing a brighter smile in response. Following her friend down the dimly lit hallway, feeling a little less hesitant, she holds on to a degree of doubt, just in case.

"Good evening, Esther. Miss Allen." The Reverend rises from his immense desk, where many books and papers are scattered about in piles. Sarah is shocked to find such disarray, for it contradicts the strict manner in which the Reverend presents himself.

"Much work occupies the mind — and time — of Deerfield's Reverend. It is the Lord's work that must be ever attended to, and it does not always lend itself to order upon one's desk. Please forgive the untidiness."

Embarrassed that he has noticed her observations, Sarah is relieved he does not seem angry. The Reverend motions for the girls to join him by the fire.

"I ask you both here tonight so that I might provide special instruction to you, Sarah. Esther will no doubt benefit as well from the opportunity, and as such, I have allotted our time to this endeavour until we take our rest. Your father has been most kind to send you to us, and I shall not neglect my duty in repaying this kindness." From the increasingly serious tone and reverence he is once again assuming, Sarah feels her worry return. Her fears realized, she prepares to be lectured about the sinful ways of man and half expects a berating of the "damned French" to be thrown in.

Hours later, exhausted by the long sermon, which was interrupted occasionally by an older and more sombre male slave stoking the fire, Sarah finds the new experiences of the day have left her wanting for home more ardently. *Mercy will be most disappointed, for no news of adventure will I have to tell.* Sarah vows not to wish for adventure again, for it is lonely without her own people. Shortly after she slips under the cold covers of the bed she shares with Esther, Parthena enters the room carrying a shiny copper warming pan. Gleaming with decorative details pierced into the metal, it puts Sarah's family's plain warming stones to shame. Parthena slides the pan under the covers at their feet, and Sarah eases into the warmth. Observing Parthena silently as she builds the fire and tidies their clothing, Sarah ponders her circumstance. *How old is she? She looks older than Mercy. Could she perhaps be as old as Mother? Does she like it here? Am I allowed to address her?*

"A good night, Misses." Taking up the candle set on the dresser, Parthena closes the door gently behind her.

"Good night," Sarah answers sheepishly, unsure if she should, for Esther does not.

Watching the flames dance about in the hearth, Sarah is unable to settle, despite her fatigue. "Esther, from where does Parthena come?"

"I do not know," she answers drowsily. "She has always been with us. I believe Father said he bought her when Samuel arrived, or some such thing."

Unable to suppress her next question she hesitantly asks, "Where does one *buy* a person?"

Esther's lack of answer and steady breathing leave Sarah alone in contemplating such things. To soothe her troubled mind, she closes her eyes and listens to the crackling flames consuming the logs, imagining it to be the familiar fire of home.

# 21

<br>

"**R**un! Save yourselves!"

Groggy with sleep, Sarah wakes in the dark of the early morning, believing she is dreaming the strange, chaotic sounds that abound beyond the door. "You bastards!"

Released from slumber's final grip by a sudden intense squeeze of her arm, she realizes it is her friend grabbing her in fear.

"Father," Esther gasps in terror. With eyes ill-adjusted to the murky light, neither can make sense of what is upon them.

"Stop! Stop! No! N — " The instant silencing of Parthena's voice is followed by the equally sudden commencement of Jerusha's shrieking cries. Seized by fear, Sarah's thoughts are clouded and confused.

"Stop! Dear God!"

Flinching at the brutality of the noises, Sarah holds desperately to her friend.

"Mama," Esther whimpers.

BANG!

"Stop!"

Shots ring out amidst the explosive crash of furniture and shattering windows, but only the voices of the family are heard. The fearful assault they face seems at the hands of a spirit, for it makes no sound.

"No, not my boy!" The scream emanating from Mrs. Williams is inhuman in its shrill, terrorized timbre.

"Mama, M — " Caught mid-word, the naive pleading abruptly ceases.

"John! My boy! My innocent boy!"

"Murderers!"

Dragged by some unknown force out the front door, the distraught cries of the Reverend and Mrs. Williams fade.

"Papa! Papa!" Eunice's frightened pleas, too, quickly become indistinguishable amidst the multitude of screaming, tormented voices, escalating with every passing second.

Swift, almost silent footsteps approach. Suddenly, a door is violently thrown open, followed by another; the reverberation of each echoes clearly above all else. Besieged by a surge of terror, Sarah closes her eyes, despite the darkness. The door to the bedroom they are sheltered in swings open with a deafening bang, sending Sarah and Esther further under the covers as shadowy figures approach. Seized viciously by the arm, Sarah is hoisted from the bed and instantaneously dragged towards the door, followed by a flailing Esther, screaming, "Help, Papa! Help!"

Attempting to save herself, Sarah catches the doorframe with her free hand, holding as tightly as her cold fingers allow. The effort, made in vain, is no match for the violence of the response, resulting in her hand being cut open with one powerful tug of the assailant.

Gripped by fear and stinging pain from her open, bleeding wound, Sarah's mind races. Desperate to find any method of survival, only visions of her father and mother appear, and she yearns to call out to them for rescue. Utterly trapped by terror, she is left mute. Scarcely able to keep pace with her attackers, Sarah catches a glimpse of the small, wailing figure upon the floor ahead of them. Illuminated by the earliest light of day coming from the open door of the house, Jerusha has spilled out of her basket just beyond the reach of the bloodied figure of Parthena, who yet seems to reach for the babe. Turned toward them, Parthena's once beautiful face is twisted in a frozen expression of terror, while vacant eyes look into the abyss. A gaping wound on her head, creating a pool of blackened blood growing upon the floor, threatens to engulf the flailing baby.

Seeing her sister abandoned with such cruelty, Esther screams "Jerusha!" just as the tomahawk renders its death blow. Numbed by the gruesome violence, Esther instantly goes limp in the arm of her attacker, who seems to take no notice as he drags her in the direction of the meetinghouse, where many neighbours are now being hauled.

Fighting against the blackness threatening to overtake her, Sarah stumbles and lags but remains upright, aroused to full consciousness by the agonizing cold upon her exposed feet, making each step feel as if it cuts through flesh. The image of Jerusha's brutal end is replaced by the foreign scene of Deerfield falling into ruin. The screams of neighbours and animals mix in an otherworldly desperation that speaks to unfathomable horrors. Acrid smoke coming from the homes, where the cries of frantic occupants yet emanate, fills her nose and mouth causing her to choke. Sarah is sickened by the frenzied brutality of men, women, children — babies — and animals being cut down around her, the ghastly smells, and sudden awakening into

Armageddon, and she retches. Undaunted, the Indian, who she can now clearly make out in the growing light, pulls her brutally onward through the drifts of snow piled high by the howling winds. These winds whip the flames into infernos and fill the sky with a smoky haze, making the scene more as a nightmare not to be believed.

Sarah looks back to the home she has been wrenched from and sees the hoisted figures of Warham and Stephen being delivered in the same direction. Her ears filled with the treachery about her, she is not able to hear them, but can see they thrash about, indicating their survival. Taking strange relief in this, she regains control. With the last few excruciating steps to the meetinghouse, Sarah scans the surreal scene, searching in earnest for the familiar faces of her family.

⤬

## 22

Lying on the floor in a heap, Mrs. Williams cowers amongst the women and children who have already been herded into the cold meetinghouse. The open doors allow snowdrifts to form within. Esther, left at the cusp of the doorway, lies exposed, not only to the elements but in manner of dress. Her torn shift shows her bare legs nearly to the thigh. Unable to bear her friend suffering further indignities, Sarah chances pulling her into the confines of the building by her cold, limp arm. Despite the fear of drawing attention, she sees the attackers are much occupied with their ongoing assault, so takes the opportunity. Esther, heavy in her unconscious state, leaves Sarah struggling to pull her at all. Startled by the sudden extension of hands grasping Esther's arm above her own, feeble with cold, she is relieved to find the combined efforts finally bring her friend to her side. Once inconsequential details seem vibrant: Mrs. Frary's aged, weathered hands upon Esther's smooth, porcelain skin surprise Sarah. *She must be at least sixty years, and yet finds the strength I cannot.*

"Thank you, Mrs. Frary."

Without a word, the woman instantly resumes her desperate search for her own people.

Instinctively stroking Esther's hair, Sarah holds her close in an effort to shield her from the cold, and provide comfort to them both. Lost in her observations, she revives with the jerking motions and mumbled protestations of her friend.

"Jerusha . . . no . . . not the baby . . . " Awakening from the reprieve unconsciousness afforded, Esther sobs as reality once again takes hold.

"Shh, we must remain calm."

Looking up to the familiar face of her friend, Esther stops, realizing she is not dreaming. Sarah's expression confirms it their hellish reality.

BANG! BANG! Ferocious, unremitting musket fire shatters the last vestiges of decorum.

Crouching to the floor, Sarah glimpses the figures of unknown men outside the windows at one corner of the building trading fire with the Stebbins' home, visible through the doors left slightly ajar. Held in captive disbelief, she watches as the men are enveloped in white smoke with each blast of their muskets, shrouding them. Her heart pounds so forcefully that her breath is taken from her; only terrifying voices yelling indistinguishable words give evidence of their being flesh and blood, not demons.

Suddenly plunged into an eerie silence, Sarah sees the figures sink below the windows. Their bodiest scraping down the outer walls indicate they are only removed from sight, not from proximity, leaving those in the meetinghouse in no less danger.

"Have you seen Father and Mother, Sarah?" Esther begs. Pulling herself upright, she takes care to guard her modesty with the tattered fabric of her once fine, white shift.

"Your father looks to us now."

Following the direction of Sarah's gaze, Esther sees him standing amongst the other men in the distant corner of the meetinghouse. Bloodied about the face from a seeping wound on the side of his head, Reverend Williams offers only the comfort of a knowing look to his daughter before turning back to that which draws his attention. With eyes akin to the vacant stare of Parthena yet lying on the cold floor of the house, Sarah can see Esther's mother has not fared so well. Sitting against a wall, Mrs. Williams holds her knees to her in a rigid embrace. Isolated in a state of oblivion, without care of being in such an undignified position, she is incapable of giving comfort to those who need that which only their mother can give. Burying her head in Sarah's shoulder and shielding herself from the sight, Esther hesitantly asks, "Who remains?"

The piercing screams penetrating the walls of the meetinghouse and the unavoidable smells of death and destruction induce retching at the thought of their source. Panicked, Sarah, succumbing to the blackness filling her view, grabs hard to Esther's arm. "Do you see my family?" she pleads breathlessly. "I have not seen my family, Esther; I should not have left home."

Confused by her own insurmountable distress, Esther begins to cry as passionately as Sarah, though they muffle their cries in their hands so as not to alert the enemy they know to be on the other side of the wall. It seems others understand the same, for most remain quiet. The horrified expressions of those in the meetinghouse were but hours before placid, faithful people, confident that no such attack was possible. Through her blurred, tear-filled vision, Esther takes account of who survives: *Father, Mother.* Looking to a dim corner where many children huddle together, she whispers each name, "Samuel, Stephen, Warham, Eunice" Assaulted by the ghastly vision of Jerusha's end and the memory of her mother's screams filling her ears — "No, not my boy!" — she knows there are no more. Turning from her dear ones she meets the blank stares of many, and the beseeching eyes of others. She searches amongst the bewildered crowd for familiar faces, the doors occasionally swinging open as the attackers deposit more bloodied and delirious neighbours; a crushing weight bears down on Esther. Turning to look upon her orphaned friend, she whispers regretfully, "I do not see them, Sarah."

# 23

The battle rages for what seems hours. With each opening of the doors, Sarah expects death itself to be revealed, but only more battered people arrive — none her own. The fleeting images afforded such horror that it should have been impossible to look, yet she found herself mesmerized by every clear, repulsive detail: menacing, deep-orange flames licking the grey sky; black smoke engulfing the enemy taking position against homes where people yet defend themselves; bright-red, blood-soaked trails in the pure, white snow, often leading to the doors of the meetinghouse. But it was one image that stood out above all others: a woman, unknown as she is, with black hair strewn about her face, lying face up in a heavy drift that slowly consumes her. Sarah imagines it is her, and in this, there is peace.

At first, the steady, muted beat of the approaching sound gives no warning that numerous men march in unison toward them, but as a loud command rises above the riotous, frantic screams and musket fire of the ongoing battle, a few desperate sobs in the crowd bring Sarah to her senses. "Dear Lord, forgive us for our sins. I know I am unworthy, but please spare my family and bring them to me. Please, dear Lord. How I wish to see Father, Mother, my brothers, and sisters safely here. Please do not leave me alone," she desperately prays in a hushed voice. With the sound coming ever closer, the meetinghouse goes silent, with all looking intently at the frost-covered doors.

Opening with such force, the door splinters, and startled shrieks ring out. Anticipating the answer to her prayers, Sarah is bitterly disappointed when only the forms of several soldiers appear. A few move ahead of their commander, throwing the heaps of clothing they carry to the floor. Unnerved, no one moves to attain the warmth the clothing would provide. The commander scowls at the captives. "Dress!" he yells in a heavy accent. Abruptly turning to leave, his soldiers follow, slamming the broken door behind them.

The Reverend looks over the many pitiful faces yearning to take such marginal reprieve of his guidance from the misery of the penetrating, damp cold they have endured these many hours. His slight nod is met with an immediate rush of bodies seeking what articles they can grab from equally desperate neighbours, friends, and family. Shocked by the sight, Sarah does not move as Esther scrambles to take what she can. The shameful spectacle is in such opposition to their usual reserve that she cannot reconcile herself to join. "Father, Mother, where are you?" she quietly begs, staring mournfully at the door. Numb from the hours sitting upon the frigid floor with little protection but the simple, thin shift she wears, Sarah shivers uncontrollably. Distraught to find herself alone, she tucks her head into her knees, attempting to escape the reality she finds herself in.

Sensing a growing warmth about her, Sarah lifts her head to find Esther securing a large, grey woollen cape about her shoulders. Summoned from her prayers, she joins the others in clothing herself. Pulling the additional shift and petticoat over her head that Esther had laid at her side, she examines her deplorable state. Much too large for her frame, it is better suited to a woman much taller and slightly wider in girth. With no stay, stomacher, or kerchief to cover the shifts she wears, Sarah, ashamed to be exposed to the men and boys in this way, blushes.

"Sarah, we do as we must, dearest; Father will forgive us for our transgressions of propriety. We must make haste," Esther says, now more in command of herself. Glad for her friend's guidance, Sarah quickly fastens the strings of a cap to cover her head and pulls up the stockings, affixing them with a knot tied at the top of each, for no garters are to be had. Finally, sitting upon the floor, she puts on a pair of woefully tight shoes. Examining the others around her, she can see, even in the midst of this mayhem, she is fortunate. With merely two kerchiefs wrapped around her feet, Elizabeth Corse is pitifully left with no further aid. With every article of clothing claimed, the bedraggled villagers in their ill-fitting, but warming, garments sit once again upon the benches and floor, awaiting their fate.

# 24

❧

The doors open once more and reveal not the French soldiers, but a myriad of men that affect such fright that the children and women begin to cry without reserve.

Hauling the uncooperative captives from the floor with a manner equal to the disdain shown when they were first taken, the Indian allies move quickly to empty the meetinghouse. Without hesitation, a fearsome warrior, his true likeness masked by black-and-red war paint, grabs Sarah by the upper arm, pulling so hard it instantly breaks the rigid bond of her and Esther's interlocked arms.

"Sarah!"

Struggling to look back at Esther calling out in vain, the warrior forcefully holds her arm, compelling her to move in the direction his might commands. Exiting the meetinghouse, Sarah strains to find her family amid the chaos. The cloud-filled sky, having become white as the snow blowing around them, shields her view. Moving erratically to avoid slaughtered animals littering the path they take, she takes one last glance back as they exit the north gate of Deerfield.

With musket fire ringing out behind them, Sarah and the other captives are forced to run through the deep snows of the meadow, heading for the hills she so oft looked upon, wondering what lay beyond. *Oh, Father; Mother.* Weeping with a desolation of spirit that threatens to draw all strength from her, she is kept alert only by the sharp, permeating cold and the pain of her ill-fitting shoes. Their captors' shouts, pulling and prodding signal their intent to carry them off from their beloved Deerfield to places — and intents — unknown.

Stirred by sporadic muffled sounds, Edward, reasoning them to be the howling wind causing branches to strike the boards of their home, turns over, attempting to resume his fitful rest. Troubled by the weight o promise to his dear wife, who remains unconvinced of allowing Sarah to be away from home in such times, his own resolve was shaken, particularly as night fell. Noticing the earliest signs of day upon the horizon as the darkness gives way to a dull grey of the looming, overcast day, Edward is reassured thinking, *It is but six days until Sarah returns to us. These first hours prove trying for Mercy, but she will find her irrational, motherly fear proven for naught in a few days.* Having calmed his own irrational fears, Edward closes his eyes, allowing sleep to take hold again.

# 25

"**A**ttack! Attack!"

Edward bolts from his bed with the assault on his raw nerves. Waking to frantic yelling and pounding upon the door, his dreaded suspicions are realized. Stumbling to the stairs and trying to gain his full senses, he instinctively calls to his son. "Edward, dress!"

Opening the door, he is blown back by the cold gust of wind and snow, making him truly aware of his surroundings. Just as the bloodied, blackened body falls toward him, he catches the exhausted unknown man in his arms. Dragging him into their home, Edward struggles to shut the door with his foot as it strains against the force of the powerful winds.

"Deerfield is aflame . . . There are many attackers . . . My own family burns in our home . . ." Overtaken with the severity of the words coming from his own lips, Samuel Smead, relinquishing what strength remained from his treacherous, desperate sprint to the Allen home, begins sobbing uncontrollably.

Taking the inconsolable man under each arm, Edward and his son carefully set him upon a chair. Mercy, standing at the bottom of the stairs, abandons propriety and rushes to hear the news this neighbour has brought. Wringing her hands, aching to ask the question paining her to the core, she blurts out, "Sarah! Have you seen my Sarah?"

"So much blood, so many sickening screams . . . My children called for me." Distraught, Samuel is unable to understand what is being asked.

Mercy kneels at his side, shaking him by the shoulders in an attempt to bring him to his senses. "Sarah! Where is my Sarah?"

Her hysterical cries penetrate his delirium and he looks directly into her eyes, as though he were not affected in the least, and with disturbing calm, answers, "She is most surely lost. They are all lost."

Mercy collapses to the floor. Edward watches helplessly as his wife, deathly silent, is consumed wholly by the immensity of her grief.

Turning to his son, who is stunned by his mother's altered state, Edward thrusts the musket into his hand. "We must make for the Williams' home! Do not hesitate, your sister relies on our rescue."

Edward stalls momentarily at the open door, expecting his father to offer some comfort to his destitute mother. The severity of the situation becomes alarmingly apparent when none is offered. Exiting the house in a rampage, Edward moves swiftly in the direction of his only consideration.

Driven by his limited knowledge of the grave dangers Sarah faces, Edward's unyielding urge to protect his daughter carries him at an unnatural pace; the haste with which he makes it through such impediment as knee-deep, drifting snows, defies logic. Edward runs to equal his father's speed, being winded with the effort. The silence of their march to Deerfield is soon broken by the increasing musket fire and shrieks in the distance, but even this is not as alarming as the black smoke rising in great, menacing clouds before them. With every step, the sky above blackens as angry, crimson flames emerge from several dwellings.

"Edward! Edward!"

Roused from his dreaded thoughts, he turns to see a group of men coming to meet him.

"What news?" he apprehensively inquires of John Field who is soot-covered and half dressed from his desperate escape from his house, now aflame.

"We are finding survivors at our door, with many having gone on to alert those further afield," he answers breathlessly. "Men of Hatfield and Hadley are now arriving."

"How long has this been going on?" Edward asks, gesturing towards a burning Deerfield. Unconsciously trying to shield himself from the deathly images forcing themselves into his mind, he is unable to utter the word "attack."

"It is nearing two hours, from our best estimation."

Stunned by the revelation, he can no longer avoid the reality of what he might find. With renewed vigour, he presses forward, wanting no more details. The image of his singular goal appears before him: her face, desperate and pleading, as clear as though she stands before him. Through sounds of destruction now fill his ears, he clearly hears, *Father*.

"I am coming Sarah. I am coming." Entering the south gate, Edward, his son, and the group joining them are suddenly thrust into hell.

# 26

Halted as if by some invisible force, the apocalyptic sight before Edward and his son is so foreign they cannot reconcile it to be the village they love so well. The sickening realization that Samuel Smead has escaped, leaving his own family in the blackened, smoldering shell before them, makes any attempt at rescue unnecessary. Cupping his hands about his mouth to appease his rising panic, he yells, "Sarah! Sarah! Where are you?"

Through the suffocating haze engulfing them, the Williams' home, untouched by flame but wide open to the elements, briefly comes into view before heavy smoke falls upon them, impeding this glimmer of hope. Ignoring the pandemonium around him, Edward darts for the home he knows in his heart lies empty, whether by abandonment or by void of life within. Such thinking is inescapable. Searing his nostrils and imprinting such stark reality on his heart, the smells, sights, and sounds of death abound in all directions. Abandoning all concern for his own safety, he ignores the remaining musket fire at the north gate of the village and runs headlong, looking only to the open door now becoming clearer with every step. Suddenly, Edward falls to the ground. Stunned momentarily by the intrusion into his racing thoughts, he finds the ground unusual and his footing mired as he struggles to right himself. A strong arm hoists him from the ground. "Father, do not step on her."

The abhorrent sight before him is unnatural. Black strands of hair cover much of the face, but in his fall, he displaced the snow his own daughter had seen consume this poor woman, revealing vacant green eyes looking to the desolate sky. Gingerly bringing himself to a standing position, Edward is careful not to disturb the body further. Kneeling, his son gently closes her eyes, covering her once more with snow as if to provide some dignity to this fallen soul. Moving carefully around her, unsure if the drifts about them shield more unfortunates, Edward, now more aware of his son's presence, looks to him, a terrible understanding passing between them.

Crossing the threshold of the Williams' home, the blinding snow gives way to a darkness within, momentarily obscuring their ability to see. Closing the door behind them, they set about their work, listening intently to any interior sounds as they await the return of their sight. A sliver of light reveals two figures upon the floor adjacent to the study where Edward had but a day before sat in conversation with Reverend Williams and his guests. This sight leaves no doubt his fears are well founded. Knowing his son has not yet seen what lies before them, he cautions, "There is much in this world we have not known until this day, but in the name of finding your sister, we will endure what we must. Sarah's survival depends on it."

Thinking his father's warning in reference to what they have already seen in the village, Edward watches his father move to the side, allowing the sight to come into full and shocking view. Repulsed, Edward heaves. Overwhelmed, he can scarcely make sense of how to react, looking upon the small figure consumed by the black pool just beyond the outstretched arms of a protector yet hidden in the shadows of the hallway.

"Sarah? Sarah!" Edward calls out to his daughter, hoping some voice or faint sound will echo in response. Entering the study, he cautiously moves the furniture strewn about to ensure she does not lie injured below it.

"Father, what if the attackers lie in wait?"

Knowing the house lies abandoned, Edward turns to reassure his son, who is peering suspiciously out into the hallway.

"Do you hear the musket fire in the distance? Our men give chase; there are none to fear within these walls."

Noting the sadness in his father's voice, Edward quickly moves to search the room directly across the hall. With the movement of each impediment, he dreads what sight may lie in wait. Scarcely able to quell his urge to retch, he brings Sarah's image to mind, focusing on it to carry him through. When last he saw her, she had been upon the floor with his young brother and sisters, telling them of Captain Lamberton's adventures. With children rapt in her animated telling, he liked her in that moment, and despite exasperating him from time to time, he would gladly have such annoyances now. "Sarah!"

Finding no evidence in the rooms, each quickly reappears in the hallway. The grim task of moving past the bodies upon the floor is made necessary to search the upstairs. The cold, noticeably as gripping in the Williams' home as outside in the village common, indicates to Edward it has been many hours since his Sarah last occupied this house. He knows they search in vain, but only in searching does he feel any subduing of his rising torment. *I should not have let her go.*

Evidence of violent struggle is most profound in the upstairs hallway. Deep gashes in the walls and shattered glass crunching underfoot are all that remain of windows, which now allow gusts of bitter wind to howl throughout the space, and all doors are left ajar, but one. The closed door, signalling a faint hope that some may yet shelter within, sends Edward instantly running to it. Slowly turning the handle, he stands back as the door swings open, revealing dolls strewn upon the floor along with clothing of Sarah's size. Elated by the possibility that fate has been cheated, Edward springs into the room, frantically looking behind furniture, under piles of discarded clothing, blankets, and the mattress pushed from its frame.

"Sarah! Sarah!" Once strong and boisterous, his voice dissipates into whispered defeat. Upset to see his father so broken, Edward leaves him alone in the empty room, moving on to check the few that remain. Coming to the final room at the end of the hallway, he finds young John. Lying upon his blood-soaked bed, it is obvious he had no chance to ward off the attack.

Entering the room soon after, Edward joins his son, staring at the grievously injured boy. Signalling the end of their search, he puts his hand upon his son's shoulder, saying in a quiet, calm voice, "Let us say a silent prayer for young John, and the others, for surely they are in the kingdom of heaven."

With John afforded no dignity in death, Edward reaches for a blanket at the foot of the bed and covers the young boy. Taking another from an empty room, upon reaching the bottom of the stairs, he raises it high into the air, allowing it to billow and fall gently upon the baby and her guardian.

"Will we not bury them, Father?" Unable to look away from the forms now covered in a white blanket taking on the red hue of such destruction, Edward simply replies, "No. There are many to bury, Son. We will wait to lay them to rest with the others."

Opening the front door, Edward takes his first lingering view of Deerfield. He follows the sounds of musket fire echoing in the distance, and finds men giving chase to unseen attackers in the meadow out the north gate. Before him, man and beast lay scattered about either dead or dying. Above the crackling sounds of fire erupting from rooftops and windows, soot-covered faces watch in horror as attempts are made to rescue those sheltered inside, while men from neighbouring villages pour in from the south gate.

An eternity, a lifetime, has transpired in the few short minutes since their arrival through that very gate. Once he passed through its portal, no semblance of the life he had known could be salvaged from the ruins. Thrust into a dismal abyss, Edward cannot reconcile the news he must deliver to Mercy: their daughter has been taken by unknown evil, dragged into the wilds. Edward sickens knowing their young, innocent Sarah would have been best served lying amid the drifts of Deerfield.

❧

## 27

"Lieutenant, you are wounded."

Stumbling along, trying to maintain his pace, deRouville waves off the assistance of his men, angrily protesting, "Non, non, I am quite able. Move on; we must put distance between us and our pursuers. They will soon tire, and we can attend to this minor issue then."

Assessing losses as he can in such a hurried manner, amongst his injured allies and their captives, he notices his younger brother, René, unconscious and hoisted upon the back of a sturdy Abenaki warrior, one of only a few allies to assist them until the end of the battle. Bleeding profusely, deRouville tries to ignore his own intensifying pain from his ragged arm wound. He fumbles to reach the fabric of his shirt from under his heavy woollen coat, affixed with cumbersome gold buttons. Finally grasping it, he tears a piece from the bottom. As he presses it hard to the wound, a shock of severe, stinging pain ricochets through his body, causing a momentary lapse in his footing, sending him tumbling into the deep snow. Reaching for a tree limb above, he falters, finding the exertion overwhelming. Attempting time and again to right himself, he at last allows his men, standing at his side awaiting approval, to pull him to his feet and provide aid in his retreat. He is angered not only by the unexpected burden of injury, but by the discord amongst those in his command. The impulsive departure of his allies with their prized captives, left him and his soldiers to complete the work of decimating Deerfield to ensure it could not rise up from the ashes.

Supported by his men, deRouville grudgingly concedes, "Les Anglais are formidable, but we have done as commanded by our king, and our survival proves we are protected by the hand of notre Dieu."

Met with grunts of agreement, and buoyed by his rage, he regains his balance, waving off further aid. Moving quickly through the thick forest and treading the path laid in the snow by those who retreated early, every step upon the trail fuels his anger. *If it has not been made clear to our allies who commands them, it will soon become very plain.*

# 28

❦

As deRouville advances with his men, he sees that the landscape is devoid of any perceptible human presence. Unsure if this change is due to lack of pursuit or distance, he maintains his pace, eager to confront his allies for what he deems desertion, a crime he will not see go unpunished upon their return to Fort Chambly. Incensed, his thoughts of retributions mask the pain and exhaustion his body felt but moments earlier. A faint noise in the distance catches his attention, breaking his intense focus. Signalling his men to stop their advance, he listens for any distinct sounds over the blustery winds. Assured it must only be a distant bird calling out, he orders them on. "Allez!"

Sighting movement in the forest, deRouville picks up the pace of their gruelling march, quickly closing the gap to the larger group ahead of them. The group appears to have injured amongst them, for some are being carried. Passing a young girl lying face down adjacent to the trail, the blood-red snow surrounding her confirms the noise was not of nature, but of a woman who can now be clearly heard screaming out in the direction he heads to. Averting his eyes as he passes the body, deRouville simply moves forward, paying no mind to the sight.

Reaching his allies, deRouville, enraged by their single-minded effort to bring their captives to their villages, unleashes his full fury. "How dare you abandon the cause before we have completed what we came to do — what you were commanded to do! Are you so driven by your want for these prizes that you would abandon us? You will hang for this. French justice demands it, and I shall personally see to it that each of you answers for this crime against the French cause. You will find the price of these captives high — and absolute!"

Unmoved by his outburst, only a few allies take any notice of him at all. Sensing no protest will be made to his declaration, deRouville turns to his men, allowing them to attend his wound.

Unexpectedly, a calm, deep voice penetrates the tense silence. "We help les Française, but mind your judgement of us, Lieutenant, for we are not your subjects; we merely have our ambitions aligned — for the moment."

The veiled warning of the Mohawk warrior, moving steadily toward him through the group, is not lost on deRouville. He has seen these now allies on the field of battle in an opposing manner. The ferocity for which they are now sought to provide assistance to the French is also to be feared. Aware that diplomacy alone will maintain this shaky alliance, deRouville ceases his admonition, addressing this leader amongst them in a much more conciliatory tone.

"It is true that we rely on our allies to assist in our righteous cause, and for this we are most indebted. It is our mutual gains that I look to safeguard, and as such, I merely assert that we must work in accord with such plans as have been made. Only in this way may we ensure our victory, and our survival."

The stark realization that not only are they outnumbered by their allies, but that their making Fort Chambly depends on their knowledge in surviving such harsh circumstances, deRouville knows his allies now have the advantage. Further complicating matters are the tenuous alliances of the segregated groups of Huron, Mohawk, and the many tribes making up the Wôbanki alliance, including the Pennacook, Abenaki, and Pocumtuck, the complexities of which cannot be discounted.

Negotiated, broken, and struck again, these peace accords have never proven long lasting. Avoidance of bloody wars and advantages to be attained in such campaigns are the foundation of these most recent alliances, but with each tribe having claimed this expedition's prizes, no further reasons exist for them to remain allied to one another, much less to the French.

Having claimed their spoils, deRouville's allies are clearly the deciding factor on whether he and his men will live to enjoy their own success.

Satisfied with deRouville's contrite manner, the warrior rejoins his own tribe, having made their point clear.

"Why kill one so innocent?" Reverend Williams cries, charging at the wounded Lieutenant being attended by his men. "You call yourself a gentlemen, yet you would have the men in your command slaughter a girl of three. This savage behaviour is precisely why the continent must be rid of such evils."

Drained by the long, demanding day, and the effects of his injury subduing him, deRouville looks to the defiant Reverend, cautioning,

"You would do well to serve your 'flock,' as you call them, by sitting amongst them and remaining silent. Pray to your 'God' as you wish, but do so in absolute silence, Monsieur, for your protests, and those of the others, will not fall on deaf ears." Callously glancing to the woman yet calling out "Marah!" in the direction where the child lies dead, deRouville minds his simmering anger yet raw below the surface. He continues in a low, guarded voice. "While your protests will not cause me and my soldiers to act against you, over our allies, we have little control. So, I say to you, Monsieur, sit." His eyes, full of dire warning, confirm the truth of the message.

Understanding his people are at the mercy of an enemy that even poses a threat to one another, the Reverend moves to provide comfort to Hannah Carter, sitting with a small group of bewildered neighbours, unable to give any. Holding her remaining child, a baby wrapped in her own skirt, close to her chest, she still calls out in a raspy, fading voice, "Marah!"

Bending down to her, the Reverend puts his hand on her head, and whispers, "Enough."

# 29

❧

Night quickly falling upon them, deRouville, realizing his allies have no intention of making further gains on this day, orders his men to prepare to bed down. A fire, only big enough to provide the most basic necessity of preparing what meal as may be found in the forest, is set by a few of the allies. Shifting towards it, the captives try to take comfort in its feeble heat. Having earlier disappeared into the dark woods, a number of the warriors soon return with but a rabbit or two for their respective group. Not nearly enough to sustain, each offering is met with a desperate gorging and obvious disregard for respectability. Such concerns begin to give way to survival.

The whimpering of Marah Carter is still fresh in Sarah's mind. Her need to be constantly picked up by her captors, and the futile efforts of her mother, yet weakened by the birth of the child she carries in her arms making her unable to protect her, instilled in all a knowing that if one could not keep up, death would be swift and brutal. All too well, Sarah had seen the result in Deerfield in the once-assumed safety of the Williams' home, but the abrupt silencing of the Marah's cries stunned her with its brutality, and she gave no resistance. Handed icy-cold water drawn from the river adjacent to their encampment, the refreshing coolness in Sarah's dry throat lifts the stupor she had been in for hours. As she emerges from her state of confusion, the ardent yearning for her family resurfaces.

As they camp along the north shore of the Deerfield River, Sarah's mind drifts to the summer days spent in its waters. Even as she convulses with the penetrating cold, the familiar river provides a thread linking her to Deerfield — to home. Lost in her memories, Sarah smiles absentmindedly, easing into the warmth of the arms caressing her.

"Rest now, young one. Keep your happy thoughts close." Not wanting to relinquish herself fully to this reality, she looks to Mrs. Frary, the kindly old woman from the meetinghouse now stroking her hair.

"I am glad they are not here, for it is lovely to think them yet at home safe in their beds."

Pulling her own cape around them, Mrs. Frary rubs Sarah's hands, trying to ease the trembling she knows to be the result of more than just their exposure to the bitter cold.

"I am sure my brothers and sisters sleep, and Father and Mother will soon be welcoming me home. Father said he would come for me on the Sabbath, and his words can ever be counted upon, for I have heard men say so when speaking with him. Mercy attempted to make me feel glad about leaving, saying that it would be an adventure, for they often say I have a heart for it, but I know she was sorry for it. Oh, what joy she will feel to see me home again so soon! Father will come, I know it . . . for he said so."

It is evident from her furrowed brow that doubt creeps in. Allowing Sarah her comforting delusion, Mrs. Frary looks down at the pitiful child in her care giving a faint, forced smile in return. "Yes, Sarah, he will."


Stirred from her uneasy sleep by the sounds of their captors chanting, Sarah watches them dance about a now roaring fire. Looking on with disdain, the French do nothing to quell the seemingly jovial celebrations. Mrs. Frary's concerned expression, and those of many others she can see in the brightening firelight, renews the panic Sarah's rest had provided a short reprieve from.

"Is that French they speak, Mrs. Frary?" Sarah whispers, unable to make out their strange words.

"Shh, we must remain silent, Sarah. It is their own language they speak. Please, avert your eyes, dear."

Putting her head to Mrs. Frary's shoulder, despite her fear, she squints to see the curious spectacle.

Frank, the Williams' slave, tries to remain standing as the warriors surrounding him prod him with branches torn from trees. They taunt him as though he were but a plaything, an entertainment. Praying in an increasingly determined voice, Frank does not give his captors the satisfaction of bending to their will. With each fall to the ground, he picks himself up, looking directly at them. His defiance has the effect of enraging them further, and they begin hooting and hollering loudly, causing the other captives to cower.

"I do not fear, for the Lord saves me. The Lord guides me to His favour, and I shall not fear you!" His insolent yelling into the face of his attackers signals his end. A figure coming forth from the group, which had moments before been in a state of revelry, raises his war club high into the air. Knowing his fate will be rendered, Frank cries out, "Parthena, dear wife, I come to you now."

The captives exchange horrified glances as Frank is dragged into the woods. Trying to conjure her mother's face, Sarah finds it clouded by visions of the day's horrors. Afraid of the dark, and painfully convulsing as the frigid night bears down on them, she desperately pretends Mrs. Frary is her mother. *I can hear her singing.* As Mrs. Frary's embrace tightens around her, Sarah says dreamily, "Good night, Mama."

# 30

⟨❧⟩

The captives are woken in the pre-dawn to begin their march, with the misery of only a few minutes of restless sleep. Drenched by a steady, frozen rain, they shuffle in the direction in which they are being driven, and in some cases, the young ones are carried. The treachery they suffer exacts a heavy toll on a number of women and children who weep aloud. Piercing the silence of the forest, their cries begin to affect others, and just as the voices of discontent begin to overtake many more, the group suddenly stops.

"Silence!" DeRouville's command echoes from the darkness ahead of them. Most obey instantly, but a few have little control of themselves. Soothed by those closest to them, and fearing their own fate if the command is not obeyed, the group soon goes quiet. Now understanding that resistance puts them in grave danger, they follow as commanded, in silence.

Sarah strains to see the familiar faces of Esther and her family; her separation from her friend, even the Reverend himself, leaves her feeling abandoned. Thrust into an unusual relationship, Sarah and Mrs. Frary, nearly strangers to one another a day ago, walk arm in arm, now wholly reliant on each other. While Sarah gains comfort from the older woman's presence, Mrs. Frary relies on the bodily strength of this young girl as she wanes in speed on the demanding march through heavy, wet snow. To see each restored is the hope they cling to.

Mired by her rain-soaked petticoat, heavy and cumbersome, Sarah stumbles, nearly falling with every step.

"Pick it up for now, dear."

Following Mrs. Frary's instructions, she lets go of her arm and pulls up her petticoat, feeling the true weight of it. Glad for the relief, she finds herself able to maintain the pace once more. Keeping an eye on Mrs. Frary, who at times has to be encouraged to stay by her side, Sarah finds refuge from the pangs of hunger and numbing cold that penetrates her inadequate clothing in her memories of home. Over the many hours of the demanding march, she is only occasionally stirred from her thoughts by the renewed protestations of Hannah Carter yet calling for her child.

Mrs. Frary watches suspiciously as a couple of their captors speak amongst themselves, occasionally looking to a few people in the group. She senses a growing tension as others have also noticed where their glances are directed. Moving ahead on the trail to speak to deRouville, one of the warriors from their own group motions in the direction of those who have fallen behind. DeRouville's seemingly angered response results in an animated exchange. The discussion brief, he looks in their direction. In his hardened eyes, Mrs. Frary catches a fleeting look she surmises is pity. Turning to the soldiers awaiting his command, he shouts, "We rest."

With the unexpected stop, the captives immediately drop to the ground, exhausted. The arduous trek over increasingly hilly terrain and dense forests makes the effort seem insurmountable, but threat of death spurs them on. Those who could not keep the unnatural pace of the French and their allies, set through advantage of their snowshoes, were roughly hoisted upon the backs and shoulders of their Indian captors.

Taking what brief opportunity presents itself, Mrs. Frary grabs the fray of Sarah's tattered petticoat and pulls hard, tearing away the bottom few inches to make it easier to walk through the deep snow. Not wanting to waste what little they have, she wrings the excess material and ties it around Sarah's head and neck, creating an extra barrier from the elements.

The warriors move fast in the direction that has been the focus of their discussion. Shrieks of terror follow their movement amongst the groups. Ten-year-old Jemima Richards and Hannah Carter are ruthlessly pulled to their feet. Despite being weakened, Hannah fights off those threatening to take her and her baby. Her guttural screams and violent physical protests make the others fear her primal manner. Drawing Sarah to her, Mrs. Frary nervously instructs, "Put your hands tightly about your ears and pray aloud, my dear. Do not stop until I say so."

Looking over Mrs. Frary's shoulder to the sight of Jemima being carried off and Hannah Carter ferociously resisting several men dragging her away, Sarah's world suddenly goes dark. Putting her hands to her ears as tightly as her diminishing strength will allow, she prays in a voice only loud enough to muffle the sounds. "Dear Lord, please deliver us from this evil which steals us from our homes, from Mother, Father . . ."

Wrapping her arms around to her young companion, Mrs. Frary watches in horror as the baby, whom she herself had helped deliver but seven months before, is thrown to the ground in the melee. Unceremoniously picked up by her tiny arm, she, along with her thrashing mother, now sobbing, "No! No! No!" is carried off into the forest, followed by the pitifully weakened Jemima, now too sickly to call out.

Reverend Williams, understanding no protest will change their fate — and perhaps might seal the fate of the many others in his care and protection — waits for the silence to return, signalling all hope is lost.

"Sarah."

Hearing Mrs. Frary's saddened voice calling above her prayers, Sarah pulls away from the shelter of arms wrapped tightly about her to find tears welling in her protector's eyes. "Is it done?"

"What, dear?"

"Are they gone to the Lord?"

Gazing upon the remaining Carter children orphaned on the trail, she finally looks to Sarah. "Yes, dear, they are." No ardent prayer, nor futile method of shielding her senses, could prevent Sarah's knowing.

Signalled to their feet, Sarah, Mrs. Frary, and the others continue their forced march to an unknown destination. No sooner have they picked up their usual pace than Reverend Williams requests to speak to deRouville. Unconcerned by the consternation this will cause the Lieutenant, the Reverend's captor, the Mohawk warrior who had earlier given warning to the French commander, agrees.

"Instead of slaughtering the young and helpless, might we not provide aid? Such madness must surely affront your sensibilities, Lieutenant?" The protests, which had seemingly fallen on deaf ears, are renewed with vigorous protestations. "You, Sir, are doomed to the hell fires! You are a heathen and savage; you care nothing but for war and blood, even if this must come of those most defenceless! Is this how French victory is defined?"

Halting the march, deRouville cautions his soldiers with the slightest gesture to sheath their swords, which are at the ready to slay the irate Reverend. Infuriated by the insinuation, deRouville, unaccustomed to such disrespect, minds his anger. Turning to the group, he addresses them in a steady voice, knowing it will accomplish his own goal.

"We must make where supplies for our journey await. There you will find warm clothing and footwear supplied by our allies. I trust this will motivate you to continue, for surely the thought of bodily comfort drives your thirst for it."

The Reverend feels the sting of defeat as his flock moves forward at the command of deRouville. Among them, he sees his own wife near collapse; she had been weak when in the comforts of their own home, and he cannot imagine what carries her forth now, but prays it will sustain her. Though his protestations of killing the innocent had seemed in response to those already cut down, it was in preventing future, much more personal tragedies, he had pleaded to avoid.

❦

## 31

For many gruelling hours, each helps the other navigate the perils of the unbroken trail, for the loss of more life seems unbearable to all. What strength exists amongst them is now freely shared, for it is as much to save each other as oneself.

Having veered away from the river, which served as the guiding feature, the captives' sense of connectedness to their far-off home is broken. Darkness quickly overtaking them, signals another bitterly cold, desolate night will soon be upon them. The pelting rain finally subsides, providing some relief that they may dry by the fires sure to be set as the night before. The reward of such minor relief is the only factor encouraging their endurance.

"We make camp past the creek ahead," a soldier orders harshly. Holding tight to Mrs. Frary who is weakened by a fever, Sarah prays it is merely rest she requires. A squeeze of her hand gives the reassurance she needs.

Coming to the edge of a creek running swift with the rains, each woman is aided across by the men in their own group. They are forced to step on slippery stones, most below the surface of the rushing water. Their feet numbed by cold, few are able to steady themselves as they cross. Ebenezer Nims, a friend of her brother Edward, offers a hand, and Sarah turns to help Mrs. Frary's crossing, just as so many are doing along the length of the creek. Hearing a loud splash, Sarah searches the murky scene, finding Mrs. Williams engulfed by the fast-flowing water. Instantly becoming waterlogged, her clothing drags her into the frigid water despite the desperate efforts of the men giving her aid to cross. Many more of her group try to grasp what fabric they can. The last of her strength drained, she makes no attempt to save herself.

Having walked many miles in a state of delirium, she now seems to have a momentary return of clarity as she looks to her husband with mournful eyes. Understanding her fate, she bids him a silent goodbye. Remaining on her knees in the middle of the creek, she meets with a cruel fate rendered by the tomahawk.

"Eunice!" Held at bay, Reverend Williams cries out from the depths of his soul, harkening that of Hannah Carter.

Hastily pulled to safety, Mrs. Frary looks to Sarah who is standing motionless, mesmerized by the forms the red strings of blood make in the clear, crisp water. Watching them swirl about before cascading over the rocks, she cannot look away. Transfixed by the intricate patterns before her, she does not equate them to the horror that rendered them. The sobs of Eunice Williams' children echo about her, separated from one another as they are, but Sarah's world is quiet.

Turning from the sight of what he hopes is the last of the day's killing, deRouville is not entirely sorry for Eunice Williams' demise. Its effect on the Reverend is not lost on him, for it sends a message words can ill convey.

⚓

## 32

"Father must have been able to ward off the attackers as before."

"Pardon?" Surprised by the sudden voice of her once sleeping companion, Mrs. Frary is taken aback by Sarah's cheery tone.

"My father must have kept the attackers at bay. He will surely come for me. I think I shan't be on this march in a day or two. He will save us both, you will see. He will be ever so glad to know I had your company."

Mrs. Frary moves closer to this fragile little girl. "Yes, my dear, your father is sure to come for you. Take heart."

Yet speaking as if to herself, Sarah continues, "Yes, I am sure Father is on the trail now. Mama cried, you know. She did not want me to go . . ." Mrs. Frary looks down upon the pitiful child lying with her head upon her lap, and gently strokes her hair, knowing its calming effect.

"Rest now, my dear, for tomorrow we must have our strength to endure what we must." Minding her as she would her mother, Sarah slips back into the oblivion of sleep.

# 33

Awakened by the loud, angered voices of the sentries charged with keeping watch by night, the groggy captives huddle together for protection. Observing their captors have reapplied the red-and-black paint that masked their faces as when they first attacked, Sarah is terrified by their unnatural appearance. Alarming yelps given in warning ring out as tomahawks and war clubs are now plainly shown as a threat to each other.

Believing her asleep, Mrs. Frary moves to cover Sarah's ears with her cape, praying she will remain at rest until the trouble passes. Surprised to find her eyes open, Mrs. Frary is taken aback by her unaffected look. Shielding her eyes as before to spare any further account of the violence that is robbing Sarah of her ability to comprehend what is happening, Mrs. Frary knows that if reality is lost, her endurance will wane and any hope for her future will vanish. Leaning in close to Sarah's ear she instructs in a gentle voice, "We must pray. It is our duty to hold steadfast to our faith and look to our Lord for salvation."

There is no response. Removing her hands from Sarah's eyes, Mrs. Frary caresses her face, finding a far-off gaze. "You must listen, dear. Do as I say. You are young and strong; surely you do not want to expose the others to your demise. It is your duty to thank the Lord for sparing you, and you must honour His grace by doing as you must to survive. It may be true that such things we have seen ought never to exist, but they do, Sarah. They do." Mrs. Frary watches the terrifying spectacle of the warriors, now shoving one another and raising tomahawks high into the air, only missing each other's heads and bodies by the sheer speed at which each strike is evaded.

Feeling Sarah's cold hand touch her own, Mrs. Frary looks into now aware, tear-filled eyes. "Am I the cause of all this?"

"My dear, why should you think such a thing?"

"In my heart I always wanted for more. I was never happy with my plain life and often thought so. Perhaps it is my ungrateful nature that has brought this to pass. I am being punished, and many suffer as a result. I am so very sorry." Sobbing, Sarah repeats over and over, "I am sorry."

Cradling her guilt-ridden companion who is exposed to more than she can admit is endurable, Mrs. Frary despairs thinking of the needless burden Sarah carries. *A child's reasoning is cruel. So much of their world is unknown to them, shielded as they are. Such shocking events as these few days have brought must surely seem retribution to one so young.* Putting her cape around them, Mrs. Frary attempts to soothe with action where no words seem adequate.

"I do not think Father will look for me, for surely they do not want such a girl in their midst." Pushing Sarah from her, Mrs. Frary's eyes well, overwhelmed to know Sarah's youthful spirit dims. "Listen to me. This is not the result of your wanting for more; we are swept up in a conflict we do not understand. What has befallen us these past days is the result of men, not the punishment of our Lord. These men are the evil we pray to be delivered from, but to lose hope, to lose our faith, Sarah, is a sin." Trying to control her own intense emotions, Mrs. Frary passionately consoles, "Your family will come, but you must survive not only in body, but also by keeping your spirit, your faith, intact. It will be the only sustaining force, I am afraid."

As the shouts become louder, Mrs. Frary remembers the need to remain unnoticed. Quieting her voice, she whispers, "No father, no family, would be so easily parted from a girl such as you, Sarah Allen. Already your companionship has brought much to improve my own resolve. The Lord only asks for your faith, Sarah, and in all you will endure, you will find salvation, no matter the outcome."

Set apart from the larger group to afford some distance from the misery precipitated by the ongoing protestations of the captives, deRouville watches the rising tensions carefully, knowing the intervention of his men must only be made if absolutely necessary. His own alliance with these warriors having already been tested, he does not want to enter the politics playing out in the firelight. As much as they moved as one, the motives of each tribe remain specific to their own particular purpose. If challenged, each will protect what they have already claimed, and deRouville knows slaughter of both captives and allies alike is at stake. Biding his time, he makes his men ready should the violence manifest into warfare.

Fully anticipating the need for escape, deRouville is relieved to see the warriors suddenly dissipate at the cusp of war. He is unaware of what provoked the encounter, as his understanding of their methods of violent negotiation, for this is most surely what transpired, remains elusive.

Attending the fire that was neglected during the tensions, the warriors return to making a watery corn soup to shore up the captives, though many sleep already. Ordering his men to take their rest, except two who maintain a watch of his allies, deRouville finds himself unable to do the same, for he is preoccupied with determining what strategy will see these factious groups organize, as the treacherous trek north requires. They are at a disadvantage upon the trail; his only means of ensuring their survival, to see his victory realized, is to organize the efforts of all by negotiating a peace amongst those in his command. This, he knows, will not be easy. Each tribe has met as enemies for centuries. *What effect could words have against such history?*

# 34

"**M**es amis, we rely on you to bring us the victory we seek." Closely guarded by his soldiers, deRouville addresses his allies convened in council to discuss the grievances arising amongst the divisive groups. They are increasingly torn further apart by competing motivations, stresses of the changing season, and the burden of so many captives, an unexpected occurrence. He proceeds with caution, knowing in such wild places survival must be negotiated.

"It is but to our mutual advantage that we placate the tensions amongst ourselves and reach an accord that will see us all victorious. Mes amis, bring forth such grievances here that we may end this now, with many miles yet to journey." His deferential tone requires much effort, for his opinion has not changed: as leader of the expedition, he has the authority to command each. It is only the reality of what he has seen in conflict, particularly ones of similar circumstance, that tempers his disdain for such negotiations. Rarely has winter expeditions seen the lot, soldiers and captives, return to Canada alive; he dares not tempt those who hold the fate of all in the balance.

Speaking without hesitation, a young, fiery Huron warrior, seeming at the ready for war, brings forth the concerns of their group. "There is an uneven disbursements of the captives: some having many capable of the march ahead, and we, burdened by the young, sick, and injured, will see our rewards dwindle until we arrive in our villages with none at all. It is only by our aid that such great success is realized. Trades must be made, or we will take our rightful reward and leave!"

Beside him, their grievously injured chief closes his eyes, satisfied with the message given in his stead.

"We thank you for the strength of your force," deRouville says calmly, addressing the chief directly. "We will endeavour to negotiate that which is fair and just." Bowing his head slightly to indicate his approval, the chief is removed from council by two of his warriors to take his rest. DeRouville knows from here on he will be forced to deal with the chief's volatile nephew who will soon assume his place as their leader.

"Tomorrow we continue to our villages. Our concern is not for those who we do not claim, it is of no consequence whether they live or die," says a stern-faced Mohawk warrior staring directly at deRouville in warning. "But we will not sacrifice our prize waiting for the weak and disorganized groups."

His insinuation that it is the disorganization of those around the fire that has created this situation meets with riotous declarations of retribution for such insult. Leaping to their feet, the warriors assume stances suggesting war is at hand. DeRouville, equally affronted, holds his temper, knowing they teeter on the brink of massacre. Signalling his men to stand down, he yells above the increasing noise of their allies, quickly transforming into enemies once more.

"War will not serve our purpose! Our mutual enemy, the transgressors of your land, the murderers of your people, is a common enemy. Do not lose sight, for les Anglais will use our discord to their advantage. Even some amongst them," deRouville cautions, looking to the despised Reverend, "will deliver news of our weakness, and you will find them renewed in their effort to rid you of your land. Will you see your elders, wives, and children cast out? If we do not succeed in our current mission, we will see such consequences."

Allowing the truth of his words to fall upon them as the tomahawks they wield, he sits, indicating his intention to continue the council. A hush falls upon them signalling the realization amongst all that the captives, whose faces show their distrust and fear, keep a careful watch for the dissention he speaks of. Staring directly at the men standing in place before him, he silently prays his words have subdued their desire for revenge, for nothing can be done to abate violence once it commences.

One by one, each grudgingly rejoins the circle around the dying fire. As the council reconvenes, deRouville motions for his soldiers to set more logs upon the fire. As the flames rise high into the air, the returning warmth eases the misery of the damp cold bearing down on them. Again able to ignore the discomfort of his injury made worse by shivering, deRouville continues in a relaxed manner.

"Merci, mes amis, for we now come together as allies once more. I ask that you trust my leadership, as I trust you to guide us all to our victorious return." In extending his respect and acknowledging his need of them, deRouville finds the gesture met with agreement from all but one.

"Our divisiveness comes not solely from the strains put upon us by the challenge of such a journey, nor by the numbers we guide. It is the irritation of one amongst them who stirs their hearts, making our captives rally to his cause. The resistance he encourages, whether by word or deed *will* end." Finding agreement from his own people, the Abenaki warrior continues with renewed vigour. "To rid ourselves of such an instigator would do much to subdue their spirit, making our march easier, and ensure *your* success, Lieutenant." Pausing, a smug look of satisfaction crosses his face.

Insulted by the mocking remark, deRouville seethes, realizing the art of diplomacy, even done with false intent, is not unique to the French.

"Let us assert our full control." Rallying to his call, the warriors of the other tribes join the Abenaki warrior in demanding the Reverend be sacrificed.

Regaining control of the situation is imperative before deRouville's own prize is forfeited. Despite the relief the Reverend's demise would bring, his own feelings on the matter are not to be entertained. "Just as your captives bring the advantages of trade, labour, and to some the promise of renewal in delivering children to ease the pain of the great loss suffered, I, too, have been charged with a duty — to bring victory to our king. Does the life of one man equal the lives of many? Do you not require the king's favour in protecting, no, in *defending* your land? Les Anglais are ambitious and will not stop their bloodlust for your lands. They do not seek to build an alliance as we do, but seek to take and rid these places of you for all eternity. We face a common enemy, and the will of the king must be considered if we are to defeat such evil."

Attempting to regain the advantage of command as a palpable shift in allegiance rises, the Abenaki warrior defiantly counters, "What is one man if we offer the king many? Surely those amongst us are eager to please him with the riches we may offer, for we do not have need to take all to our villages, and les Français may share in the spoils."

"I do not disagree," deRouville concedes. "The Reverend's presence is disruptive in maintaining control over your captives." Sensing his allies require the evidence of necessity of the Reverend, he continues, "His death would surely serve to subdue any resistance, but Gouverneur Vaudreuil requires such a man to negotiate the release of our own highly prized captives now in the hands of les Anglais. Were it not necessary in the absolute, we would not have set out in such circumstances. But as it is, we must ensure his arrival. We fight under the flag of New France, and to ensure the king's continued supremacy, we must pledge our loyalty to carry out our orders as commanded."

Breaking the tense silence, the Mohawk warrior who had previously challenged deRouville's leadership ends any further discussion. "We have many miles before us; it is best served with our alliances intact."

Disbanding, each man rejoins his own group to begin redistributing their numbers as negotiated. Given charge of the Reverend, the Mohawk warrior, found to have demonstrated sound leadership at the council, agrees to deliver him to Fort Chambly. DeRouville's own large group is comprised of his soldiers, their own captives, which include three traitorous French fur traders who lived amongst les Anglais. One, a former neighbour in Chambly, Jacques de Noyon, even married a woman of Deerfield. Unable to ensure the Reverend's survival under such circumstances, he offers a reward for his safe arrival. The deal struck, deRouville is glad to be rid of a man whose mere existence holds the fate of so many, giving him a power for which deRouville hates him.

# 35

⚜

Unable to subdue his increasing resentment of the Reverend and the captives for the position they put him in, deRouville sits by the fire lit many hours before, watching the undulating ripples of brightness flow over the glowing coals.

Wanting to make a record of what has already proven the most trying mission of his career, he pulls a piece of paper from his pack, and knowing the inkwell is frozen, searches for a nearby fragment of charred wood.

2 March 1704

I have not wavered in my charge, despite bodily injury, which grieves me, but my resolve to do as commanded in one regard is tested.

Some captives have perished, and it is the counsel of their own Reverend Williams that marks the fate of many to come. They would be well served to be rid of him. Though they look to him for comfort and guidance, they are ill-advised to do so, for he does more to steal their salvation from them than provide it. Our priests wait to educate them and save them from damnation. This fool can only provide an eternity of suffering. Surely he has seen enough of it these three days to suffice his gluttonous appetite for it. I do not expect to have him subdued long, for despite the loss of his wife, resistance is evident in his manner. Even now, I see he attempts to send secret messages to the men able to see him in the dim firelight. Damn him!

I do not mourn the heathen lost, nor put credence in the warnings and protestations of the impassioned Reverend who calls such actions "savage" and punishable in the fires of hell. Our allies do as they must, for mercy's sake; it is swift and without undue suffering. Should we leave these unfortunates to bear the agony of the frozen trail, as he suggests? He is misguided to think such hope exists for rescue. The weak

should not want for such a fate, and I damn him for suggesting that he wants this for his people. If retribution plays
a part in such actions, for this I pray forgiveness that I am
not sorry. No mercy is afforded by those who murder and
decimate our allies' people. Too many villages have we come
upon in our many campaigns where the very young and their
revered elders linger in their suffering, surrounded by the
many who succumbed to the brutality laid upon them. These
Anglais complain most vehemently for suffering as they do
now, but what of the suffering inflicted by the command of
their distant, unfeeling Queen Anne?

It is common for our allies to slay the weak and very
young, for they endanger all by hindering our ability to survive such harsh conditions as are on the march to Canada. We
must trust them, for they have proven to be most successful
in previous actions. Those who may yet survive must turn
away from the Reverend and embrace the hope of salvation.

Lieutenant Jean-Baptiste Hertel deRouville

# 36

❧

After three desperate days marching through soaking rains that make the penetrating chill of night excruciating, the nerves of both captive and captor are raw. Ill-prepared for such a journey, they cannot escape the stabbing pain of frozen feet and limbs, forcing each to be present in every enduring second of this tortured existence. Even the horrifying memories of Deerfield burning, or the want to take refuge in their memories of home, are trumped by such bodily agony. Shuffling leaden limbs made unresponsive by the cold, and despite crushing exhaustion, they move forward at the pace set by their captors, who take only the need to make ground into account, not their capability to do so.

The relative warmth of the day hints at the coming spring. Intermittent glimpses of sun escaping a blanket of heavy grey clouds brings about a renewal of what little yet sustains the group, including the Reverend who loudly prophesizes to his flock.

"Pray, good people of Deerfield, for the evil of these French and their heathen allies will be defeated. Our unwavering faith will call forth the Lord's retribution. Take heart, for we are the righteous. They may have taken much from us. . ." Pausing momentarily, he struggles to regain his composure. Grief-stricken by the violent end of his children and beloved wife, Eunice, he finds her final mournful glance affects him most deeply. "They slay the weak for they themselves are weak. But we find peace in knowing our family and friends await us in heaven, and we shall be welcomed. Rejoice!"

Unable to bear hearing the Reverend's voice ringing out any further, deRouville turns back on the trail, pushing captives harshly out of his way as he rushes past.

"Monsieur, do not presume that I allow you to profess your blasphemy out of weakness. You may continue to prophesize to your people, for soon they will be yours no more. You will submit to the will of the Holy Catholic and Apostolic Church, and your children will be given to our allies as they wish. I care not for your people's safe arrival, Monsieur; but for our allies, they would not be here at all. Your people are the spoils of war we have promised in exchange for our glory of victory over you. Our victory, Monsieur, the victory of our king, lies in the smoldering ruins of your Deerfield, not in your lives."

Taking one more step, deRouville, now unnervingly close, stares intently at the Reverend, his eyes full of rage. "Your words may provide solace, but to *our* end, and to *our* advantage, they provide means of control, ensuring our spoils live to have our victory evidenced by all in New France." With laboured breath, he lays one final degradation upon him, "Monsieur, you are no more than a ghost; you hold no real power or influence in the fate of your flock."

# 37

Frightened by the unexpected appearance of more Indians ahead, Sarah grabs Mrs. Frary's arm as the piercing shouts of their exuberance resounds. Sweating profusely with the exertion of marching many miles, Mrs. Frary seems relieved in seeing the group before them. Confused why more of the enemy should be welcome, Sarah braces herself for the end she believes their appearance signals. Panting heavily, Mrs. Frary looks to her to see what panic has set in. Noticing Sarah's wide eyes fill with tears as she focuses on the men awaiting them, she leans in, whispering, "They have supplies." The fear that has occupied her every moment on the day's march — that death should visit before she can see her family again — is subdued, for the moment.

Set upon the ground in their newly formed groups, the captives watch as ropes are released from the bundles held upon the sleds with a precision indicating this has been a well-planned attack. Reverend Williams realizes they have long been marked as pawns of war.

Looking to those who falter in their ability to keep pace and those carried thus far, he prays for their souls, knowing they will not be invested in. Seeing them bypassed as moccasins and clothing are distributed, his fears are confirmed. Too weak, or too young to cry, they are carried off. With the last of these unfortunates vanishing into the dense forest, the Reverend renews his praying, joined by the few who also notice. Most are spared the knowing, as they desperately affix the clothing on their frozen feet and bodies. Only moments later, the returning chatter of the warriors coming from the darkness is heard; the only evidence of the captives' demise is their absence. So silent was their end it seems as if they had not existed at all, were it not for the few family members and neighbours mourning their loss.

The captives seem much changed since deRouville's earlier warning to Reverend Williams. Most now understand that if the Reverend could not save his beloved wife, he can have no effect in safeguarding their lives, and so their boisterous protestations cease. Despondent, the Reverend observes his flock move from the want of spiritual salvation to that of their bodily salvation. While he, too, feels the pain inflicted by such cruel circumstances, he holds steadfast to his convictions. Watching his own children desperately working against frozen hands to tie the clothes and moccasins on themselves, he prays they will not lose sight of his many teachings, and will cling to the deliverance offered only through adhering to the teachings of the Bible. Filled with dread at the thought of losing their young souls, he calls out, "Pray, people of Deerfield, pray! It is not these heathens who provide relief to us now, but our Lord. It is by His hand alone that we are given such bodily comfort, but do not lose sight of His greatest gift. He spares us yet that we might profess His true word to many when we are redeemed."

Not but a few think of redemption, as most are consumed by survival, but Sarah, believing her prayers about to be answered, stops dressing. As if in a trance, she listens intently to the Reverend's words.

"Most surely, our own families are not but a few miles behind. Only through prayer will they find us."

No longer obscured by agony, Sarah's loved ones appear clearly before her. Released by renewed hope, she prays aloud, giving thanks, "Dear Lord, I knew you would bring them to me. . ."

"Sarah, No!" The harsh slap across her mouth shocks her, and she begins to cry more at the intrusion into her familiar world than the pain it causes. The warning in Mrs. Frary's eyes is dire. Obeying her guardian, she allows her family to be swallowed by the shadows once more.

Turning to the Reverend, others, too, slowly emerge from their defeat, seizing the promise he offers, and begin praying in unison.

"And what agreement hathe the Temple of God with idols? For ye are the Temple of the living God: as God hathe said, I will dwell among them, and walk there; and I will be their God, and they shall be my people."

DeRouville, noticing his allies becoming incensed, knows if the captives are to live, if his own victory is to be realized, they need to remain defeated. He moves to quash the looming disaster.

"Arrêtez!" His booming voice leaves no doubt of the seriousness of his intent. "You will be silent, or you will find yourselves silent in the utmost." Tired by this continued irritant, deRouville nods at one of his allies, who instantly subdues the defiant Reverend with a blow of a war club. Though he bleeds, he breathes.

# 38

$\infty$

Pained, empty stomachs are soon filled with an abundance of deer meat taken from parcels apportioned to each group. Some captives are so starved that only a few bites of the rich meat prove too much, and they heave what little they attempt. Seeing this, Mrs. Frary gives warning.

"Eat slowly, and only a morsel at a time, dear." Tapping Sarah's hand occasionally to remind her to restrain herself, she is glad to see her eat most of what has been given, and not suffer the effects of gluttony, as some.

Set by the great, roaring fire to regain strength from its warmth, the captives experience the agonizing pain of restored feeling to frozen extremities, making many wish for the return of numbness that masks the damage they suffer.

The intense flames, reaching high into the air, give the first opportunity to see the effects of their wretched march. Horrified by the ghastly sight before her, Sarah watches as Thomas French, of their own group, removes his stockings, wringing them of blood that flows freely from his warming feet. Around her, neighbours, seeming ashamed of their state, attempt to tidy themselves as they are able. Men and women alike mend their tattered clothing with strings hanging from the ragged edges, having been shredded and torn by hidden underbrush and trees in the thick forest. In this new reality, rituals of everyday life, once done absentmindedly, are now held to irrationally. These fragments of the familiar shore up their spirits, giving them reason enough to attempt to carry on.

Sarah pulls her stockings from her own feet, as white as the snow, and winces in pain as Mrs. Frary rubs briskly to bring sensation back to them. Seeing the many scratches marking her ankles, some red and inflamed, she realizes the lack of feeling saves her certain pain on the march. Without a word passing between them, Mrs. Frary carries on, seeing the colour returning, as Sarah's toes begin to wiggle in response.

"I remember these toes, big as they now may be, perfectly formed, and wiggling from your earliest days." Dispensing of usual propriety, for such sensibilities now seem trivial, she quietly continues, "Yes, I told your mother you were trying to walk from your very first moments. You seemed as if you had someplace you wanted to go."

Captivated by Mrs. Frary's comments, their effect binding her to her mother again, Sarah looks to her, her eyes beseeching more.

"You see, I helped to bring you into this world, as I did many here." Intrusive and cruel, the memory of Hannah Carter's baby being torn from her mother's arms takes her breath as if by some vicious blow. Pushing it from her mind, she looks instead to Sarah's drawn, but beautiful, face. "My part, of course, was small, for it was only by the will of the Lord and great effort of your mother that you arrived safely. However, I am pleased to have offered such aid, for in knowing you as I do now," she pauses, "I am thankful, for you are most certainly destined for greater things, Sarah. You, my dear, will endure."

Rapt in the story, Sarah listens attentively, forgetting what is happening around her.

"You most certainly gave us all a scare, for your mother laboured many hours — two days, come to think of it. She and you alike were most destined for the grave, but when it became unbearable, I found your father knocking at my door, begging my help. Well, it was no surprise to be awoken in the night for such things, but the face of the man who greeted me upon opening the door did strike me. I could see his desperation, and we wasted no time making our way to your mother. When I entered the dimly lit room, I could scarcely believe the ashen woman before me was yet alive. Only an occasional reaction to the terrible pain roused her from her despondent state." Noticing tears brimming in Sarah's eyes, Mrs. Frary quickly assures, "Do not worry, dear, this story will take a turn for the better." She gives a slight smile, realizing Sarah has not yet made the connection. "I arrived without a moment to spare, for it was almost too late. Your mother was exhausted and slipping away, and I checked the baby, only to realize it was facing the wrong direction. I am sorry to say, I had lost many a mother and child this way, and prayed this would not be one of those sad times, for even with my many years of experience, it is never easy to lose a life. When one has not had the opportunity at all, it seems such a pity, but we must trust it was the Lord's will, and I take comfort in it . . . even now," she says in a trembling voice. Gathering her thoughts, she continues, "We had no choice but to try and turn the baby."

"How does one do that?" Sarah inquires, utterly confused by the miracles of life.

"Well, I shan't provide too many details of such things, for it is not proper, but when a child is to be born, it must be in the right position within a mother's womb, and this one was not."

Unable to imagine what this means, Sarah senses she does not want to know, and so despite her ignorance, a vivid scene plays out before her.

"I set to work, pushing the baby into the correct position, but there was no movement with only my effort. It was evident from the lack of response from the mother that time was of the essence, and even the child within did not move as it ought. With no option, I called the husband to aid in one final desperate attempt to make right the baby and save one or both lives, Lord willing. As one might imagine, the poor man was horrified to witness such things, for it is not the place of a husband to be privy to such private matters. But watching his wife slip from him, knowing that many relied on her for their care, he abandoned such sentiments and did as I asked. A man without a wife and young children to rear is left in such a pathetic state, but the source of his fear was something more. I had seen the way he looked to her when we had occasion to meet on the Sabbath. Do not misunderstand, he treated her no differently than any good Christian would, no lack of the usual ways, but he could not entirely conceal his great love for her. She reminded me so much of the delicate flowers that bloom in early spring, susceptible to the lingering frost. The harshness of our temperamental weather, isolation, and separation from our own people, so much the defining characteristics of the life we led in Deerfield . . ." Already feeling the distance from such a life, she corrects, ". . . we *lead* in Deerfield, caused her hardship. She was a fine lady, finding such harsh realities difficult to adjust to. But with great love comes great sacrifice, and she never wavered in her efforts to make him happy, to make a home with him at the edge of the colony." Thinking upon that night, its outcome unknown as it was, she cannot help but yet be struck by the willingness of this man to forgo all propriety, and through tears, encourage his wife to remain with him. "He was strong, Sarah, and his strength was all that could be relied upon in the end." Sarah's lip quivers as a tear rolls down her cheek, and Mrs. Frary grabs her young companion's hands, confused by her reaction. "What is it, Sarah?"

"I do not want to hear more if there is no happy ending to this story."

"Why, Sarah, you *are* the happy ending," Mrs. Frary assures, with a broad smile. "It is your mother and father I speak of, and only their great love for you matches the love between them. That night, not so many years ago," she says gazing upon the still young girl before her, "I witnessed the power of such love."

Welcoming the relief of her memories, Mrs. Frary drifts back to Deerfield. "When you made your very dramatic entrance into the world, we were all overjoyed to find our fears were for naught. You were a curious creature, strong and precocious from the very beginning. I should think this will serve you well in life." Mrs. Frary's prays these once defining traits remain steadfast.

"Mercy said I have a heart for adventure," Sarah offers, encouraged by the assurance that these were not wholly sinful traits.

"Your sister is not wrong, for I could see it flickering in your eyes the day you were born to this world. Hold fast to these, dear girl, for they are gifts given by the Lord."

Too exhausted to attend to her own feet, deadened with cold, Mrs. Frary pulls her cape about them, instructing Sarah, "Say your prayers like a good girl, but in silence." Closing her eyes, the old woman, sweating profusely even as she trembles with cold, begins reciting her evening prayers. Before finishing, she falls into a restless sleep.

❧

## 39

Drawn back from her despair by Mrs. Frary's story of home and the relief afforded by the food and clothing supplied, Sarah takes her first real notice of the others set about in groups around the central fire. She hopes to find her friend, Esther, amongst them. No words can express what is so plainly etched on the faces of those she looks upon. Contorted with anguish, the stains of grief mark each profoundly, altering them into strangers. Recognizing herself in their pained expressions, she turns away, unable to bear the intensity of her own torment.

A faint howl in the distance captures her attention. Listening for the response she knows will come, she takes strange comfort in the familiar, haunting call. Many a night, tucked into her own bed, she listened to the wolves moving about as they explored the world outside her window. Safe in their home, she did not fear them as Mercy, who always pulled close when hearing them. Even now, Sarah searches into the shadows within the forest, hoping to catch a glimpse of a creature she has only on one occasion seen. Without a sound, it emerged from the forest surrounding their house, watching as she and her brothers and sisters played under a maple tree nearby. Observing it carefully, it seemed to be as curious about them as Sarah was with it. She marvelled at the detail of its large, muscular body: thick, mottled fur of grey, black, and white; long, sleek legs; an upturned, black mouth set against a white mask of fur on its face, making it appear as if it smiled shyly at her. As the creature studied the children, its ears, moving independent of each other, seemed to seek the direction the various giggles and squeals came from. Cocking its head one way, then the other, it seemed to listen to the very words the children spoke, as if attempting to understand. Sarah smiles unconsciously, remembering how peculiar, how human, the reaction was. She knew she should fear it, but did not. Instead, she wondered what places it had travelled from and why it should call out in the night. Not wanting to scare it away, she motioned for the children to hush, but upon seeing where her gaze rested, they panicked and raced, screaming, for their mother and the shelter of the house. Spooked by the intrusion into an otherwise peaceful encounter, it bolted into the forest and out of sight. Stomping into the house, chastising the children loudly for ruining her opportunity to study the graceful creature, Sarah met with a stinging blow to the buttocks from the ever-handy paddle, her mother managing the swift justice despite the children holding tightly to her skirt. Stirred by the memory of the punishment, she turns her attention from the fading howls in the hills surrounding them to the fire, and her devastating reality.

Unable to close her eyes without confirming Esther survives, Sarah forces herself to look once more upon the forlorn groups. Finding her lying motionless upon the snow-covered ground, Sarah shifts slightly to see past the brightness of the fire. Unexpectedly, their eyes meet. The void of spirit scaring her, Sarah pulls back, allowing the flames to block the stranger from view. Distraught to find the friend she knew gone, she lays her head upon the cape set down for her, and listening to the melancholy calls echoing in the distance, she cries herself to sleep.

# 40

"**M**onsieur, you may announce that we make for Canada, and that it is our intention that all should see it, but there can be no falling behind or consternation caused by your flock." Still incensed by the Reverend's hold on his people, deRouville uses it to his advantage, giving what information is necessary to secure their obedience.

"We are ill-prepared for such a march," the Reverend replies, shocked by the destination. "Do you not see how the women and children suffer? It seems quite impossible that all will endure. Negotiate our release now before we set more miles between us and Deerfield. Take what reward you will receive for our lives and go back to Canada knowing you have done much to decimate our village and people. Surely this will give you satisfaction."

Unyielding, the Reverend's fiery temper is not so easily suppressed, despite captivity and the continued threat of impending death. In any other circumstance, deRouville would appreciate such strength of will, recognizing a match to his own determination and character, but, as it is, he finds it impossible not to contemplate how he may yet achieve victory while ridding himself of such an aggravation. Seeking any who may prove a worthy pawn releasing him of the necessity of the Reverend, he scans the haggard lot, frustrated to find them all wanting.

"Allow me to take them back," the Reverend persists, "and I will negotiate that no retribution will follow you." DeRouville's demeanour becomes disturbingly calm, surprising the Reverend, as his intention was to further frustrate the Frenchman.

Finally satisfied to have information that will quash the Reverend's ambitions, deRouville replies, "Ah, Monsieur, you may follow the trails from whence we have come; keep to the rivers as your guide, and mind the bodies marking the trail." He pauses, a sinister grin crossing his lips. "Surely you will recognize *her* — excuse me — them. Oui, you may take your flock, but without the expert knowledge of our allies and our protection from any that may find you upon the lonely trail, I doubt *Reverend*," he says with contempt at the use of the word, "you will make the twenty-five miles back to your smoldering village."

Stunned by the distance now separating them from home, the Reverend realizes he cannot ensure the safety of his people. Overcome by the memory of his wife's last mournful, knowing look, he slumps, losing all conviction.

Invigorated by his feeling of supremacy, deRouville straightens himself as he has not been able since being injured. Standing tall and commanding, he savours his victory as he waits for the question he knows will come.

"And . . . how many miles are yet?" the Reverend asks in a low, despondent voice.

"Two hundred and seventy-five."

DeRouville walks past the shaken Reverend, brushing against him roughly. Stumbling back, he barely rights himself before falling to the ground. His confidence restored, deRouville leaves no further doubt amongst his allies about who is in command.

# 41

With a few of the youngest children already set atop the sleds, the snowshoes are distributed to all but a number of men forced to do without. The success of the raid being greater than planned leaves inadequate supplies. The captives stumble and fall, encumbered by their unfamiliar use. With mountains looming in the distance, they know they have to master the skill exhibited by the French and their allies, who seem to find it easy to make steady progress. Breathless with the effort, the captives are spurred on by the constant fear of being killed. Unspoken prayers echoing in their minds, they eventually find their footing.

Now, upon the frozen surface of the river, they move with more ease. None exhibit the tell-tale signs that brought such brutal ends to their neighbours in the previous four days. Sustained by the improvement in their physical comfort, even Reverend Williams welcomes the relief for which he chastises himself, believing it given by the hand of Satan. *The insidious nature of these French and their savage allies are the work of evil. Such temptation as we all face tests us, and my resolve must carry us all. Dear Lord, every step towards the treachery we face in Canada is done in your name. I pledge my faith and pray that none will be lost to you.* Despite his impassioned, silent prayer, the thought of two hundred and seventy-five miles of misery shakes his resolve.

Neither the sun attempting to escape the gloomy clouds of so many days, nor the many hours since witnessing further horrors improves Sarah's spirits. The exertion of her struggle to march in the foreign contraptions upon her feet and of lifting her heavy petticoat, dripping with the wetness absorbed from the deep, melting snow, takes its toll. Overcome with fatigue, her burdened mind drifts to Deerfield, even as her body moves ever onward.

*"Mercy, I am returned!"*

*"Oh, Sarah, do tell of your adventure."*

*I feel her hands holding mine tightly, and their warmth signals I am home. Her face is as sweet as it ever was, the details of which my nightmare would not allow me to remember. But is has lost its hold on me, and I study her features: deep-blue eyes shining as our beloved river on the clearest of summer days; curly-brown hair, perfectly placed with only a few strands escaping her cap; and her rosy cheeks, accented by the curve of her smiling, rose-coloured lips. I envy her beauty, and am glad to call her sister, for she knows me as no one does, and yet she does not fault me for it.*

*"It was no adventure whatever; it was a nightmare that I could not wake from. Such things I imagined. So real are the images that even now I should think they truly happened. Oh, Mercy! Such terrible things I dreamt."*

*"Now, now, Sarah, what of your friend Esther? Did you enjoy your time together?"*

*"Mercy, I cannot think to what we may have talked about. She seems lost to me, her eyes stare at nothing . . . and behind them, nothing. She is much changed in my memory and does not resemble my friend at all."*

*"Well, never mind, it has surely done you good to be away and experience a little of what it will be like one day when we are grown and married with families of our own."*

*I squeeze her hand tightly, but she pulls away at the strength of it. "But I shall never leave home again, Mercy. I shall tell Father I cannot bear to be away from all of you." I cry, not caring how childish I may look, for surely if anyone were to understand, it is my most beloved sister. The warmth of her embrace eases my mind. Finally, the nightmare is over and I am home.*

"Sarah, Sarah, hush. Sarah, stop. Stop now." The sternness of the whispered voice brings reality flooding back, stealing Sarah away from home. Seeing not Mercy's soft, supple hands holding her own, but ones weathered with age, she is shocked by the realization that what she is hearing is her own voice crying aloud.

"Sarah, *please*," Mrs. Frary begs as she desperately shakes her.

Suddenly lucid, she looks anxiously about to see if she is noticed. Finding a number of warriors observing her, she walks as if nothing at all has happened, though dread threatens to consume her at any moment. Praying she will not meet her end, Sarah faces forward, ignoring the continued attentions of a watchful enemy.

Even after a number of miles, she remains unsure if her time with Mercy was real, for though her mind tells her it was only imagined, her heart yet feels the ache of it.

Hoping to catch Mrs. Frary's attention, that she might apologize for endangering them, Sarah is taken aback to find her sweating profusely with the effort to take each shaky step. She, too, feels the strain on her legs and body in continually lifting the heavy snowshoes, but it does not produce the same reaction. Thinking it the distress she has caused that precipitates the effect, she is sorry for it. Cautiously peering behind her to ensure they are not being watched, she grabs Mrs. Frary's hand. Briefly closing her eyes with the relief of the welcome touch, she turns to her young companion.

"I am sorry," Sarah silently mouths, still looking ahead to shield her secret message.

Fighting against the pull of the delusion that would provide escape, Sarah allows herself to feel the agony of the excruciating cold to hold her captive in reality, thwarting any further outbursts. Her full senses restored, she notes the sound of rushing water ahead.

The cascading water now poking through the icy surface falls over a large tree wedged across this narrow point; its eerie familiarity brings back the horror of Esther Williams' final moment in the creek the evening before. To know what happened to those led away does not match the brutality of witnessing it.

Veering from the open water, Sarah watches the others begin to climb a steep embankment. To reach the top, each fights against unwieldy snowshoes mired in the heavily crusted surface of the snow, the steepness of the rise, and their own weariness. Just as she crests the top, Sarah hears a commotion behind her.

"No! Please. Mama, No! I shall provide aid. I am young — let me help her. Mama!"

Sarah sees Ebenezer Nims pulling desperately at his poor, weakened mother, lying upon the river's frozen surface, unable, or unwilling, to move. Down river, two more women are ruthlessly thrown to the ice by the warriors who had carried them for a number of miles.

"No!" The sudden cry of this pitiful boy rings out, forcing Sarah to look once more upon the gruesome scene, which she can neither avoid by proximity, nor morbid curiosity. Viciously hit upon the wrist with a club, Ebenezer loses his grip, just as the tomahawk deals its fate. Dragged up the embankment, Ebenezer speaks not a word. Though their eyes meet, he does not see her.

With Mehitable Nims slumping to the river, Sarah, bewildered by the grisly scene playing out before her, watches fate now cast its shadow on Hepzidah Belding. Seeming already dead, she lies motionless, staring directly into the sky above as if glimpsing heaven awaiting her.

"Sarah, take my hand!" Turning from the sight of the blood-soaked snow, she turns to find Samuel Williams' hand extended in an attempt to pull her to safety. Just as she reaches his fingertips, she hears a familiar voice pleading, "No, you must go. Do not sacrifice yourself for that which cannot be saved." Releasing her feeble grip, she turns to search for Mrs. Frary amongst the many frantically pulling themselves up by any means — crawling on hands and knees, or clinging to one another in some cases. Sarah finds her guardian just as those attempting to give her aid abandon the seemingly lost cause. Lying face down, Mrs. Frary is being slowly consumed by the deep snow cascading over her with every movement of those continuing their desperate climb. Making no further attempt to save herself, she closes her eyes, saying a murmured prayer as she awaits the fateful blow that will surely come. Sarah pushes through the crush of people moving in the opposite direction, but none attempt to convince her otherwise, except Samuel. Faintly heard, his desperate calls rise above the sound of her fiercely beating heart. "Do not go, Sarah. Come to me."

Falling as her snowshoe catches the edge of a hidden rock, Sarah lands in a heap, tangled up in her petticoat. Struggling to right herself, through sheer will she gains her footing and immediately begins searching the snow. Finding her friend panting heavily, she whispers, "I will pull you up, but you must try. You must." Sensing the warriors move about her, having finished their ghoulish work, she knows she has but one opportunity to save Mrs. Frary.

Looking up to her young companion, Mrs. Frary knows Sarah's innocent plea comes from a fear of being left alone in this ill-fated place.

Summoning all her strength, Sarah pulls Mrs. Frary's upright, steadying her on the uneven ground. With her full weight upon her, Sarah purses her lips tightly, trying to control grunts threatening to escape with the arduous climb up the embankment. The sight of Samuel's extended hand keeps her moving. The hope provided by this simple gesture, carries them both the impossible final step, just as the warrior who killed Mehitable Nims moves past.

Grasping Sarah's wrist, Samuel hoists both to the top. Speaking not a word, he keeps Sarah by the arm as she holds tight to Mrs. Frary, and together they lumber to the area where the others now gather.

Dropping to the ground in a heap, Sarah turns to Samuel to thank him for his help, but finds him already returning to join his own pitiful group. Her thoughts confused and her vision fading, she tries to control her rapid breathing threatening her consciousness. Amidst the disturbing chaos that brought such decisive outcomes, Sarah's only concern was to keep Mrs. Frary safe, for the thought of losing her is more than she can bear. In the moment, she did not consider her own fate, but as she takes off her snowshoes and those of her companion, Sarah keeps an eye to their captors, who in equal measure watch them. Young as she is, she understands their survival is not yet assured, and only in wanting to live, does she not cry.

As they rest, partaking of what food is offered — a few grains of dried corn and pieces of tough, smoked deer meat — Sarah gazes at the river to the water flowing freely at the narrow.

"I do not fear my end as a result of the tomahawk," she says, as though to herself.

"You must not speak of such things, Sarah; you will surely cause more grief thinking of that which will surely not happen," admonishes a somewhat revived Mrs. Frary, disturbed by her young companion's grim thoughts.

Wounded by the scolding, Sarah turns her attentions to where a child's retching and crying rise above murmured whispers within their group. Mary Alexander, not yet two, whimpers as her desperate mother tries to force food into her small mouth, even as what morsels she swallows come back up instantaneously. Tormented by the sight, Sarah can no longer contain herself.

"But I must tell you; my fear consumes me," she says emphatically, biting her quivering lip in an effort to control the emotion threatening to burst forth.

Mrs. Frary, abandoning her effort to prevent the unnerving conversation, moves closer so that none may hear. "What is it that you fear, dearest?"

"It is not meeting my end, but to be left abandoned, not buried amongst my own people. I should like Father, Mother, my sisters, and brothers to find comfort in knowing where my body lies, to know what has become of me. Mercy will surely bring flowers from our garden to set upon my grave, and even in death I will be glad for it."

The innocence of Sarah's fear strikes at the core of her own.

"If I might not go home in life — " Stopping abruptly, Sarah knows if she continues, the tears already welling will not be impeded. She looks again to the clear cascading water below them, seemingly full of life, before it disappears under the icy surface, much like those now left behind.

"On y va! We go!" The distant command of an unseen soldier rings out, ending their fateful rest. Strapping her snowshoes upon her aching feet once more, Sarah is relieved to be moving on.

# 42

***❧***

"**I** will not see Canada, my dear." Mrs. Frary announces without looking away from the growing flames of the nightly fire.

"But why should you not? We must!" Sarah cries. Setting down the meat she eats with tempered pace, she stares at Mrs. Frary. Though drawn, as many are, she seems at peace, which should ease Sarah's mind, but instead instills a sense of foreboding.

"You have witnessed the result of those who hold the group back. I have used the last of my reserves, and my strength leaves me. It will be on the morrow that I will surely meet my fate."

"No, no. It is not true; you will be fine. I will help you. I will. I promise." Her desperate pleas reveal Sarah's young heart — which still believes all may be possible if wanted ardently enough.

"Were it only for your faithfulness, I have no doubt that I should make it, but it is not. Our fate is determined by the strength of our bodies alone, and mine is old and feeble. It will deny me salvation in this world, but I take comfort that I shall find it in the next. My only regret will be to leave you."

Realizing Mrs. Frary speaks a plain, unguarded truth, Sarah feels disoriented, breathless. Overwhelmed by the enormity of what is to come, she studies the details of Mrs. Frary's wrinkled features, committing each to memory: the soft lines of her pale face, her forced smile to ease profound heartache, and her kind, hazy-blue eyes reflecting what Sarah realizes is love. She does not want to lose her to the shadows, as she did her family. None of their images can be conjured in the slightest when awake, and even fragmented dreams in the night do not bring forth their true likeness, but rather distorted images, leaving them out of reach. But to succumb to the dangers of delirium, as before, is her only way to see them. Sarah knows this would see her deepest fear realized, putting her in a desperate situation; if only to have hope of being found alive, or dead, she *has* to endure this horrific reality. Despite this, her mind drifts off.

Finding Sarah slipping away from her, Mrs. Frary takes on a much more serious tone. "Sarah, you must listen now. Heed my instruction. Sarah?" Slapping her hand to keep her attention, she is relieved to see her aware of her presence once more. "Hello again, dear one," she says giving a weak smile to her companion, whom she now thinks of as one of her own. "Sarah, you must use your youthful strength, your spirit, to survive. You must promise you will not let hope extinguish in your heart; it will sustain you through much, diminished as it may be. Hear my words echo in your mind and *endure*. Promise you will endure." Pausing momentarily, she recalls the night Sarah was born. "Remember, my dear, you survived once before, and you can do so again."

"But I cannot," Sarah protests, tears now streaming down her face. "I am afraid of the dark."

Embracing her tightly, Mrs. Frary cries with her. Sarah's thin body, swallowed by the ill-fitting garments weighing her down, makes her seem all that much smaller — all that much more fragile — and Mrs. Frary is sorry to leave such a vulnerable child. She yearns to protect Sarah, but to allow her demise to come as a shock seems too cruel.

"I am sorry to leave you, but I do not regret that we met, even under such circumstances. I must give thanks to the Lord, for our meeting upon the Sabbath was no more than a fleeting glance, but here, in such despairing times, the memories of but a few days with you brings my life to a beautiful conclusion. Your face, amongst those of my own children and grandchildren, will be my last in this world; such joy, such comfort it provides." While thinking to the next life devoid of such brutality brings a sense of relief, she is sorry for the burden it will cause her dear one.

"Will you try?" Sarah pleads through whispered sobs. "Maybe you will endure, though you may not think so now." Desperate to change Mrs. Frary's mind, as if it were but a decision made, Sarah implores, "Please say you will try."

Knowing her fate cannot be changed, she offers a heartfelt, but hollow, assurance, "I will try, my dear . . . I will try." Cradling Sarah, she holds her for one final night in the dark of the forest.

# 43

6 March 1704

If you will indulge me, I shall henceforth call you friend, for the words upon these pages will convey that which I cannot express to those who look to me for their care. My guilt consumes me, but to share such sentiment with my dear tormented wife, Mercy, would serve no purpose but to bring further grief to an already unbearable situation.

These seven days, we have been burying our dead and taking account of those violently taken from us. We have now determined that forty seven citizens of our own small community lie dead, and one hundred and twelve are taken captive. A mass grave has been determined to be the only course in such times. A few have had family claim them for burial, but most lie together in death with but a simple stone upon the mound — 29 February 1704 — chiselled into it. Our attempts to reclaim our own taken from us results only in finding those killed by our enemy in retreat. We gave each the Christian burials they were denied. I will not describe the sight of coming upon the youngest amongst us left as they were in the forest. Word has been sent to Eliezer Williams, spared only as he was away at school, that he is all that remains of his people at Deerfield. A boy of sixteen should not suffer the burden of burying his beloved mother, young brother, and sister.

Such grief bears down on us; such words I write upon these pages seemed impossible when in my dazed state of disbelief. Not wanting to make them true, I have avoided putting pen to paper, but as the shroud lifts, the severity of what has occurred is inescapable. I have no choice but to meet this offensive reality with what faint hope I have for redemption.

Where once we lost two dear children, our lovely Elizabeth, nearly twelve, and our tiny Consider, but a mere eighteen days, knowing they are safe in the care of our dear Lord makes it tolerable; the lack of surety that Sarah lives grieves us in the utmost. I am consumed by guilt. Were it not for those who rely on my care and protection, I should set out with no consideration of my own well-being and find the truth of what has happened to my daughter. Such incomprehensible circumstance! She must be frightened beyond reason. Dear friend, what am I to do with all this grief, anger, and yearning? It seems too much, and I should take dear Sarah's place in but a moment if it were possible. I am castrated in my duty as protector.

I am sorry I have not written more of my children before now. Their care has been so much my responsibility that I do not think I have conveyed my deep love for each of them. The unknown fate of our Sarah leaves me possessed by hate and desperation in such measure I cannot think clearly. When I join Mercy at day's end, I hear her cry herself to sleep. She is unable to look at me, holding me responsible for such tragedy that has befallen Sarah, though she will not say so. What measure of judgement she feels does not approach that which I bring upon myself. I, alone, am responsible.

Looking out my window into the black night, I am lost in thinking of how she might fare. She fears the dark. She was spirited by day, but I could see her yield to her childish fears once the sun set. To think of her in the frigid night as I warm myself by the fire is to make me cling to the last vestiges of my faith. How could such circumstance be so fateful? Many a day, when danger seemed nigh, we protected our children. Such evil lulled us into a false sense of security. It was as if the damned French and their savage allies were beckoned by Satan's calling. We have heard much from the Reverend of his insidious work, but I cannot recuse my part.

Her green eyes sparkled with a curiosity that reminded me so much of my own spirit when young. Of all my children, she is most like me. Our bond ... It has just occurred to me that today is the Sabbath, the day we were to see our dear one again, the day I had promised her — promised her — we would meet again. My words leave me. One cannot express that which I feel, and so, my friend, I will not try.

Edward

# 44

〰️

"**S**arah, help me. They shall slay me if you do not. Please, dearest." Lying in a heap at the bottom of the riverbank, arms outstretched, grasping for help, Mrs. Frary's terrified face suddenly changes to that of, "*Mother!*" The forlorn expression of her morphing companion precipitates such a frantic reaction that Sarah feels her body begin to tingle with the debilitating immensity of her own desperation to save her. Try as she might, she cannot cause her legs to move. Even as she looks to see what holds her in place, she wills them to lift from the deep snow, to carry her to her mother, who is crying out, "*Sarah, they are here to slay me. Do not abandon me to this fate!*" The scream she forces as she watches the blade fall makes no sound. Staring into her mother's deep-blue eyes, she begs, "*Dear God, spare Mama. Mama, no!*"

Waking with a start, Sarah sits up, not knowing where she is. Sweating with the effect of her restless night, she cannot shake the truth of the experience. She wipes away the tears that blur her vision. Feeling her cold hands brush against her burning cheeks, she allows the cooling effect to revive her. Searching the scene around her, she is struck by the stark surroundings: a white world with barren trees soaring into a grey sky, a few evergreens in the distance provide the only colour in a dull landscape. Amidst this, a jumbled mass of bodies lie scattered about, giving the impression that no life remains in this world at all. Nearby Mrs. Frary shakes with the convulsions of a fever that took hold the day before. Sarah cannot bear the thought of being alone, even amongst the others. Her tortured dreams, the longing for her family, the dread that consumes her as the final light of day fades, leaving her at the mercy of the sinister creatures that inhabited the darkness — all of this is only made bearable by the presence of Mrs. Frary. The wolves that lulled her into her slumber, their presence once holding a fascination, now become that which she fears as she watches the others cower at their melancholy howls.

"Eat!" One of warriors of their group hands Sarah a piece of cold meat left over from the night before. He does not wait for those lying upon the ground to fully emerge from sleep, before tossing their food at them. Sarah watches in disgust as the others scramble to recover all the meat that is strewn about, they seem as savages not accustomed to propriety in the least. She is ashamed at what they have become. Looking to her own tattered clothing, she instinctively tucks strands of hair falling about her face behind her ear. Trying to convince herself the others are more dishevelled in appearance than she is, she realizes this cannot be true, and blushes. Afraid to look upon the warrior now offering her water, she averts her eyes. The usual practice of their meal being supplied to one amongst them to share with the others makes close contact rare, and usually fatal. When even once unfamiliar routine is abandoned, it gives cause for alarm. Mrs. Frary slowly brings herself to a sitting position, and Sarah worries her difficulty in doing so will be noticed. But as their captor passes her the ladle, she gives a breathless, but confident, "Thank you," as if to reassure him that she is stronger than she appears. He does not remove his gaze for many uncomfortable moments, but to her amazement, Mrs. Frary does not shy from his intensity. Sarah feels ill as she contemplates every eventuality. Seemingly satisfied with some unknown consideration, he moves on, throwing the last few scraps of meat to Ebenezer Nims, who does not acknowledge the presence of the food. Sarah heard him quietly crying in the night, and knows what haunted his dreams. Like all, he is forced to suffer his memories and sorrow alone. Instinctively, Sarah leans into Mrs. Frary seeking her reassuring touch.

"Gather, people of Deerfield, for today is the Sabbath." Reverend Williams' booming voice shocks those who sit quietly awaiting the day's march to begin. They have become accustomed to the silence. But for the sound of those begging for the lives of their kin, no words have been uttered in usual volume in many days. "Come gather to me."

Searching the faces of their captors for any sign of what fate might befall the Reverend, the captives remain deathly still. When the warriors simply retreat to a separate fire, confused expressions pass through the groups.

"Please, gather. It is fine. We are given a day of rest to celebrate the Sabbath. Gather together, good people, and take comfort in the Lord's holy words, and in our communion with one another." The Reverend's tone softens as he looks to his own children. Speaking directly to them, he repeats, "Come to me, and be consoled."

Simon Beamon, a devout man and leader amongst his neighbours, hesitantly rises. Following his example, the captives move one after another to sit in front of the Reverend, who despite his injured foot, stands with the aid of a large branch. Though somewhat unsteady, his demeanour reverts to that in Deerfield as more gather to him. Straightening his posture, he raises his voice, "Yes, come hear the word of our Lord. Gather, gather."

Releasing Sarah, Mrs. Frary struggles to pull herself upright with the flimsy trunk of a nearby sapling. Weakened by the effort, she stands a moment to catch her breath before slowly moving to join the growing crowd. Glancing back, she beckons, "Come, it is the Sabbath." Sarah makes no effort to move.

"Father comes today," she whispers to someone unseen. "He promised. It is the Sabbath. He promised."

"Sarah, dear, come with me. The Lord will provide comfort; He will work in our favour, *if* we remain trusting."

Sarah follows, but looks wildly about as if expecting someone's arrival. Mrs. Frary links her arm in Sarah's to not only ensure her obedience, but to aid her own short walk, made nearly impossible by the seizing in her legs and the faintness caused by a now raging fever. Feeling Sarah start to lag, she looks upon her finding all colour drained from her pale face. Ignoring her own bodily woes, she grabs Sarah's hand, squeezing it gently to remind her she is there.

"Good people, we have suffered much, but it is with the knowing that our Lord sent His only son to suffer that we are saved — no matter the outcome in this life." Overcome, Reverend Williams abandons his usually staunch manner and motions for his children to come to him. He picks up Warham who has run to him, and takes Eunice by the hand. They are quickly followed by Samuel who gathers to his father's side. Hesitating, Esther looks about fearfully as if she will be noticed by the enemy keeping a close eye in the distance.

"Come, gather with your brothers and sister," the Reverend gently encourages. "Come, daughter, come to me." His words breaking her trance, Esther leaps instantly to her feet, running to her father. Collapsing into his open arms, she sobs so distressingly that even the Reverend cannot contain himself. Through choking words, he pulls his children tightly into his frantic embrace. Seeing the many eyes upon him as he communes in grief with his own children, he says in a soft, fatherly tone, "Gather with your families, for we do not know when such blessings will be bestowed upon us once more."

"Mama! Father!" The words wound Sarah as she watches families embrace one another. Anguished with the reminder of what is lost to her, she shuts her eyes tight, unable to endure it further. Putting her hands about her ears to muffle the sounds of reunion, she rocks back and forth, soothing her own broken spirit. With the voices finally dissipating, she tentatively opens her eyes again. As families huddle together, it soon becomes apparent she is not the only one alone.

Setting his children at his feet, Reverend Williams begins to preach in his usual, fiery way. "The Lord is righteous, for I have rebelled against his commandment. Hear, I pray to you, all people, and behold my sorrow. My virgins and my young men have gone into captivity."

What the Reverend says after such cutting words matters not, for Sarah retreats into a sheltered place within. Repeating the words spoken from Lamentations quietly over and over, "I have rebelled against his commandment . . . rebelled . . ." she believes they are meant for her alone. *Father is not coming. They are well rid of me, for who should want a daughter who brought such destruction upon her friends and neighbours.* Even the gentle touch of Mrs. Frary cannot pull her from the depths. Sensing nothing can be done to ease her dear one, she embraces what she knows to be her final Sabbath.

As evening falls, all feel revived by the rest and familiar practices. Emerging from the delusion that redemption was ever possible, Sarah finds the reprieve from the march only heightens her sense of what is happening. Each detail affronts her: the ritual indignities of voiding in open spaces; the smell of unclean bodies huddled as swine; babies dripping with filth. But it is the stench of sin that lingers, the result of her wilful nature, of wanting to see the mountains that once loomed in the distance and now cradle them in their sleep.

The radiant fire appears and disappears for unknown interludes as Sarah succumbs to her exhaustion, with nothing more to hold to, her bitter heart gives up what hope yet flickered within.

# 45

⚛️

Waking into a desolate reality from which no further escape of mind or spirit is possible, Sarah dreads the stillness beside her. With the groups around her beginning to stir in response to the harsh command of their masters to quickly prepare for the march, she turns to look upon the inevitable. "Mrs. Frary?"

Sarah is relieved to find she is not abandoned as her companion opens her eyes. Evidently revived by the day's rest, she hastily sits up, affixing the cape that acted as their blanket through the long, painfully cold night.

Overlooking Mrs. Frary's flushed appearance, Sarah continues tying ragged pieces of fabric around her own ankles. Given scarcely enough time to come to full consciousness, they are roughly handed their morning's meal of corn and a smaller than usual portion of dried deer meat. Though tough, the taste of the rich meat makes her mouth water. Taking what is given, Mrs. Frary only looks at it.

"Eat. You must," Sarah says, concerned by her lack of want of it.

"I cannot."

"But you must. Why, only last evening when I had no desire for it, you told me I must or I shan't survive." Sarah reminds her, hoping it will bring the same result.

"This is different," she answers her voice tinged with sadness.

Before Sarah can make any further protestations, their captor reels back, hearing their private conversation and angrily snips, "Vite! Hurry. We do not linger here."

Alarmed by his tone, Sarah looks to the forest, where he and the other warriors keep a close watch. Even the French, who stay isolated amongst themselves, seem suspicious of something unseen within the thicket. The captives are rushed to their feet, without having finished their meal. Sarah knows Mrs. Frary needs sustenance to have any chance at all. She puts the food to her mouth, and it is met with the hoped for response. Chewing for a painfully long time to digest the tough meat, Mrs. Frary studies Sarah closely, attempting to commit her sweet face to memory, so it may be called upon in the end.

To ease Sarah's mind, Mrs. Frary forces herself to swallow despite an overpowering urge to retch. Observing those in their own small group, she knows Sarah will be left utterly alone by her departure. Thomas French, consumed by his effort to meet the demands of their hard masters, attempts to provide aid to his wife, Mary, who falters in her grief in being separated from her three young daughters claimed by other groups. Their son, Thomas, but a boy at fourteen, can barely eat for his fatigue in helping to carry the youngest, and newest member, of their group, Mary Alexander. She was removed from her mother's care in one of the many cruel trades, which continue to be made between the various tribes. Ebenezer Nims, much diminished since his mother's brutal killing but a day ago, has not uttered a word since. Nonetheless, he continues to care for young William Brooks, six, whose own mother and sister, not a year older than he, sit together under the watchful eye of their own captors.

Noticing Ebenezer's deeply bruised, swollen wrist, Mrs. Frary knows the injury puts him and his young charge at risk. *None will come to Sarah's aid. It is survival each must seek for themselves.* Already feeling death shadowing her, her prayers, once for endurance, now turn to ones to spare her dear one.

"It looks as if the sun comes over the horizon; surely it will keep us warm upon the march," Sarah says with feigned optimism, as she hands Mrs. Frary the wooden ladle of refreshing water drawn from the nearby river. Working hard to overcome her fears, Sarah busies herself with affixing her snowshoes. Excruciating spasms seizing her muscles, Mrs. Frary holds tight, careful not to spill the water. *Yes. I shall be sorry to leave you.*

# 46

❧

The dreaded march underway, the captives emerge from the suffering of the bitterly cold night as the sun rises high above. They quicken their pace to meet that of their captors, which is now noticeably faster. The warriors look suspiciously to the stands of cedar and pine surrounding them. With weapons drawn and at the ready, sentries pull back to watch the trail behind them, as if expecting attack at any moment. At the head of the column, deRouville, in council with a number of his allies, suddenly turns and cries, "Ready your muskets!"

The sound of the rattling weaponry catches the attention of many near the front, who see the alarmed expressions on the soldiers' faces. Beginning as a few hushed conversations, the whisper soon lights like a fuse down the column, until Sarah becomes aware of what is so feared.

"We are hunted," Thomas French whispers breathlessly to his wife, but a few steps behind. Labouring under the heavy packs he is forced to carry, making him useless in her defence, he warns, "Stay close. Keep near to our son, if able."

"But what of the girls?" she inquires anxiously. "You must protect them, Thomas." Her panicked voice is noticed. A nearby warrior charges Thomas, pushing him violently to the ground. He raises his club, and Sarah cringes, expecting the death blow. In disbelief, she watches as their own captor attacks the aggressor with equal violence, sparing Thomas, who prays aloud, begging God for deliverance.

Stunned, the captives stop and all watch in disbelief as the warriors viciously fight. Mary French drops to the ground and tends to her husband's bleeding wound from a ruthless strike to his mouth. Harshly pulled to her feet by the warrior who remains with them, she is held at bay as he demands her husband, "Get up!"

Attempting to escape the brutal fight, the column disbands, with a number of women crying aloud in terror at the sudden turn, causing the children to do the same.

"Silence!"

Running to contain the captives, the French soldiers and their allies surround them, which immediately silences all but Benjamin

Hurst, one of the youngest amongst them. Watching Elizabeth Hurst, a girl who was friends with her own dear Mercy, try and soothe her young brother's cries, Sarah feels a rising dread at his continued outburst. Her family scattered amongst the groups, Elizabeth became the caretaker of her youngest sibling, who has cried for nearly two days.

"Quiet him!" demands the warrior who attacked Thomas French, even as he yet gasps to catch his breath.

"But he is only two years and does not understand. He is unwell. Please help him."

It is obvious to all Benjamin is seriously ill. Pale as the snow, his tiny body hangs limp in his distraught sister's arms. His weakened cries only stop when he retches, which no longer produces any result.

"Please," she begs almost inaudibly, looking to her brother as if her pleas will rally him. "Please." His sunken cheeks, evidence of his inability to digest the food offered, make Sarah nauseous. She has never seen a child so sickly. Even with all the death of the march, the sight of Benjamin Hurst's wasting body is more than she can take. Turning away, she retches, unable to control her reaction to such despair.

Seeking reprieve, she looks to Mrs. Frary, but as she does, she notices one of the warriors nearby nod to another as he casts a curious, sidelong glance to Elizabeth and Benjamin.

"Move!"

Consumed by a sense of foreboding, Sarah struggles to maintain the unnerving pace, which has nearly become a run. An unseen enemy stalking them, many scan the forest as if expecting to be pounced on. Even their captors have not eased their vigilant watch. But it is the secret message passed between the warriors that occupies her mind.

Clasping Mrs. Frary's hand to ensure she does not lag, she watches Elizabeth cradling Benjamin as a baby in her arms. His small bare legs bobbing about up and down with every step, he does not seem to feel the lingering bite of winter.

Near the head of the group, Mr. Hurst had occasionally glanced back over his shoulder to his children, a grim look upon his face. On one such instance, he turned more fully, as if trying to understand what was happening. His concerned expression suddenly changed, and he faced forward, not looking back for now nearly an hour. His curious reaction leaves Sarah confused. *Why should he not look to them again?*

BANG!

The echoing of a musket shot behind them makes the group come to a sudden stop, with many nearly falling over one another. The rush of warriors moving to protect their prizes while the French soldiers muster to the rear sends the captives huddling together upon the ground. It is soon evident what has caused the reaction. In a frenzied, uncoordinated fashion, a flock of geese pass overhead, escaping the sound made by the musket of an overzealous French soldier. Angered, one of the Pocumtuck warriors moves through the group, demanding to speak with deRouville.

Her curiosity about Elizabeth and Benjamin had kept her preoccupied, helping her ignore her own condition, but as she sits upon the ground, the pair now shielded from view, Sarah's full attention turns to the painful spasms racking her body. No sooner does she welcome the relief of resting upon the soft snow, when she is roughly hoisted by the arm by her most feared captor. Once upright, she is immediately released, and she stumbles back, her legs refusing to cooperate as they seize under her weight once more. Indifferent to her plight, he leaves to bring the others in line to continue the march.

Quickly reassuming the unforgiving pace, Sarah approaches Elizabeth, who is struggling to pick Benjamin up from the snowy ground. The meaning of the glance exchanged by the warriors becomes clear. Moving to Elizabeth, one of the warriors gently picks up Benjamin, cradling him as a sleeping child — in the way Elizabeth had cradled him. Calmly, he walks away from the group, disappearing behind a dense stand of cedars nearby. Curious to know Elizabeth's reaction, she looks to where her steady gaze rests. As the lone warrior emerges, Sarah is shocked by the realization.

Expecting an outburst, what she finds is more disconcerting: Elizabeth pulls her cape tightly about her, and faces forward once more, marching as the others. No one seems to notice Benjamin has disappeared from this world.

# 47

The march resumes at an unrelenting speed, and Mrs. Frary begins to lose ground. Pulling desperately, Sarah will not relinquish her hold on her. No longer responding to Sarah's encouragement, her mind wanders to the next realm.

Unable to lift her snowshoe from the deep snow, Mrs. Frary falls to the ground unconscious. Finding herself unable to pull her weakened guardian upright, Sarah searches for any help that might be offered, but the others brush past without pause, though many look upon them with pity. She hates them for their knowing glances. The distance growing, Sarah shakes Mrs. Frary vigorously to rouse her, but finds her seemingly already passing from this world to the next. Her eyes shut, only her laboured breathing provides any evidence of life.

"Please," Sarah begs. "Please do not leave me here alone."

As if drawn back by the fervour of her desperate plea, Mrs. Frary's eyes flutter, sending a wave of relief over Sarah. The snap of a branch shatters the illusion of salvation. Knowing the source of the approaching sound, Sarah turns to see their most feared captor nearly upon them.

"No! No! No!" Sarah screams, forgetting the danger it puts her in. Stunned by a violent blow to her head, she releases her grip and is left with only a vague imprint of the feeling of Mrs. Frary's cold fingers pulling away from her own. Trying to regain her senses, Sarah watches through a confused stupor as Mrs. Frary follows the enemy, giving no resistance as she is led away. Suddenly sinking to her knees, she folds her hands in prayer. Just as the tomahawk is raised, Sarah shields her eyes, as was so often done to protect her from such sights, leaving her to witness Mrs. Frary's end by its ungodly, sickening sound.

# 48

"Lieutenant, our allies request council." Not surprised by the message from his solider, deRouville has sensed the rising tension, for he, too, warily scans the forest, seeking those he feels sure hunt them. "Tell them we meet once their captives have been fed."

Bowing, the soldier leaves to deliver his message to each leader. Surprised that yet so many live, deRouville is pleased his allies' knowledge makes their journey expedient. However, the previous evening, upon seeing the captives gorge themselves on their meagre meals, he grew concerned. Taking his brother, René, now healing from his wounds, into his private confidence, he warns, "It is too many. We have not supplies to sustain all. More will die yet." Though he despises them for the troubles they cause, deRouville is not immune to the effect the death of the very young, and the weakened women, have on him. Reasoning it as necessary does not remove his dislike of it.

"A full day's rest should not have been allowed." The first volley of angered protests begins before the council is formally convened.

"What of their need for rest and the words of their Reverend if we are slaughtered by their people?" demands the infuriated, Huron leader. Newly appointed, he has replaced the great chief who perished from his wounds days earlier.

"We are surely hunted. Having given a day's allowance, the men of Deerfield close in on our position," concurs one of the Mohawk warriors of Sarah's group.

"The price of twenty-four miles is steep," continues the Huron chief. "I wonder if they had known such outcomes would result, if they have forgone the day of rest? Do they wager the lives of their women and children for such foolish want? We will drive them as hard tomorrow, and expect loss. But remember, Lieutenant," he warns, "with each loss, our commitment to this expedition wanes."

A roar of agreement rises up from the warriors. Tempering his growing frustration at having his leadership continually challenged, deRouville reminds himself that without the guidance of his allies, none will see Canada, for what lies ahead will make the previous days' march seem effortless.

"Mes amis, our promise to the church to observe the Lord's day was of the utmost importance. It was not necessitated by the captives' need for rest, or the counsel of their Reverend. We rested because our priests warned that only in our observance of it would we continue walking in the footsteps of righteousness and be protected by God."

With his allies' resentment evident in their angry, fixed stares, he continues, "We are within a day's march of the White River. Let us push hard another day, and make further assessment of our enemy's pursuit at that time. For now, the only course to ensure the safety of your captives is vigilance, and to keep them in good order."

"This 'good order' you speak of is to keep them fed, dry, and warm?" comes a sarcastic response from a Mohawk warrior of another group.

"Yes, all of those things," answers deRouville, suspicious of the question.

"And your own group, how do they fair?" the warrior continues.

"Our own captives do well enough, but as two are coureurs de bois, once of Canada, they are well acquainted with the harsh nature of our march and do much to shore up their women and neighbours."

"Well then, you have the advantage, as our own captives have no such experience to draw upon, and we are forced to tend their every need. They falter with each step and require provisions in such quantity that we are all threatened with starvation if we do not hunt soon." His ominous words are met with solemn agreement. "We must split up now if we are to survive."

"Non! Impossible. We must stay as one, for if we are attacked, we will need our numbers to mount a defence. These captives are imperative to our success. We must bring them to Fort Chambly, as you must bring yours to your villages. I do not presume you come to our aid for having been charged to do so by our king, as we are, but by your own people, who await their children."

DeRouville's words hang in the air amidst a tense silence that is finally broken by the Huron leader, who noticeably calmed as he listened to the heated exchange. Now pensive and composed he offers, "If we do not hunt soon, we will all perish from starvation, Lieutenant."

# 49

❧

"Mama! Mama!"

Shoved harshly, Sarah awakens from her dream unsure of where she is.

"Be quiet, you will get us all killed," hisses a dark figure, shrouded by night. The gruff voice she realizes is that of Thomas French, who was sleeping nearby. A heavy frost settling upon her, she pulls her knees tight to her chest, as much to ward off the cold as her growing despair. A couple of warriors tend the central fire, keeping it well stoked. Her own small group lies like most others seeking its feeble heat, but she notices not all rest nearby. The French, setting themselves apart, have their own fire, giving the impression they are of some elevated rank; even their captives seem to fare better than most. The French claimed their own: Jacques de Noyon and his fellow fur traders, so newly arrived in Deerfield, their names yet unknown to most. Considered traitors by the French, they were a curiosity in Deerfield, but de Noyon, having only two weeks earlier married Abigail Stebbins, became as any other amongst them. Now in the company of their own people, they do not suffer deprivations as the others, for they easily speak the language of the soldiers and seem to enjoy cordial conversations on occasion. With the continued hardships and devastating losses, the resentment toward them grows.

Sarah looks in the direction where she noticed a slight movement, but believes it a trick of the firelight. Just then, the warrior who stole her guardian from her moves to take his place by the fire, keeping a steady gaze upon her.

She shuts her eyes to shield herself from him, but even in absolute darkness, she finds his image remains.

# 50

Speeding their way north, the group follows the Connecticut River, as they have for many days, and while it is easier to walk upon the hard surface of the frozen river, the unyielding pace and the changing weather takes its toll.

With the days becoming noticeably warmer, the chill of night seems that much more excruciating. The river, showing signs of the oncoming spring, begins to open up in sections, revealing the rushing water beneath them. It forces them to march through rough, unbroken forest at the river's edge, as a day ago, or in ankle-deep icy water, as now. Treading carefully, fearing one misstep will swallow them up, the captives consider each movement, but Sarah is so absorbed in her memories of her lost companion that she is oblivious to the dangers lying in her path. Walking on the ice near a patch of open water, Sarah does not notice the others moving away from it.

CRACK! A loud noise erupts below her feet, snapping her to attention. Water rises to the snowy surface, but she does not fear what it signals; instead, she finds hope unexpectedly return — the hope that it will swallow her up and carry her back home. Moving closer to the fragile edge, she is grasped by one of her captors, the one she fears most.

"No! Danger." His concerned tone and expression is altered entirely from when he took Mrs. Frary from her. Despite his lack of ferocity she reels from his touch, pulling hard to release his grasp. Stumbling in her yet cumbersome snowshoes, Sarah tumbles to the ice. Shattering beneath her, the ice gives way. Plunged into the frigid water, the shock causes her to instinctively scream, "Help!"

Dropping to the ice and lying upon his stomach, the warrior extends his hand, grappling for her arm just as she is pulled into the depths of the rushing water. Unable to help herself, as the debilitating cold deadens her limbs, she is acutely aware of the battle being waged to drag her to safety. The river is winning, but the warrior grunts with his effort to pull her toward him. Nearly eye level to the ice, Sarah sinks into the blackness. Feeling his grip loosening, and completely helpless, she gives in to fate. Her loved ones suddenly appear crystal clear before her: her father, sisters, brothers, Mrs. Frary, but amongst them one waits for her with outstretched arms, and Sarah runs joyously, calling out, "Mama!"

Just as she reaches her embrace, she is thrust into light and her mother instantly dissipates.

After several minutes of someone frantically trying to grab what limb and fabric they can, she suddenly finds herself terrifyingly face to face with the enemy. Confused by the shocking cold, and his expression of relief, she mistakes him to be a friend and wills her numbed, free arm to embrace his neck. After sliding her slowly to the edge of the river where the ice is thick once more, the warrior takes Sarah in his arms, carrying her to the top of the embankment, where the rest of the group waits. As Sarah violently convulses, the warrior holds her close, attempting to shield her from the exposure, but she does not feel any of it as she closes her eyes.

"Wake." Shocked by a stinging slap, she hears a heavily accented voice break through the confusion, "Wake. Do not sleep." Feeling a warmth enveloping her, a warmth she has not felt in days, she opens her eyes expecting to be in her bed, finding the nightmare over. Instead, she is greeted by the faces of strangers. The warrior leans over her in such close proximity that river water falls from his own face onto Sarah's. Shaking so intensely he has trouble forming his words, he stammers, "Stay awake. Do . . . do . . . not worry . . . we will carry you."

His concerned, almost pleading tone strangely eases her into believing him. Her mind tells her to fear him, but she can see the truth of his words in his eyes. Fighting against the want of warmth, the ease of her burden in travelling mile after mile in painful snowshoes, she does not resist because she yearns for what is promised. Slowly bringing her hand from beneath the furs laid on her, atop the sled where she now rests, she takes the piece of meat offered from his trembling hand and eats.

Pleased with her reaction, the warrior nods at her, moving away to warm himself with the furs now being offered him by his own people. She is left in the hands of the other warrior of their group. He piles another large, heavy black bear fur upon her, and moves away to pull the sled once more. Mary Alexander, the previous occupant, follows in Ebenezer Nims's arms.

* * *

Not having heard the names of her captors used in any conversations, she settles on referring to them as the "Silent Enemy" and the "Observant Enemy."

The Silent Enemy, who now pulls her along, was easily named as she has never heard his voice at all, a trait which somehow makes her more frightened of him than the one who has perpetrated so much killing. Too quiet, he seems to conceal a ferocity that is ready to be unleashed without warning. The Observant Enemy always seems to keep a watchful eye on her, as at the fire only the night before, and in those fateful moments upon the river. Though Sarah has seen him slay many, she finds strange relief in his predictability. One knows that if you transgress any of his expectations, he will be quick to render his judgement, removing the need to imagine what will come of it.

The names are not innocuous, for Sarah gives them as warning to herself to remember that they hear, and see, everything. Even when one might believe them ignorant of the slightest falter in endurance, or hidden message passed with only a glance exchanged, she knows their brutal response will come with a cruel swiftness, robbing the unfortunate of the slightest hope for redemption.

Sarah's fading consciousness is only combated by the continued prods of the stick given to Thomas French to ensure she does not sleep. Shivering with cold, even beneath the furs, Sarah begins to moan as tormenting spasms overtake her. The intense pain robs her ability to reason and her thoughts become confused.

"Mama?" The sharp sting of her bottom lip in speaking, surprises her more than the series of prods that follow. Sarah licks her lips to ease the pain, but the moistness causes the cold to intensify. Tasting the pungent warm liquid, she removes her hand from beneath the furs and places it to her mouth. Pulling it away again, she sees her hand tinged red. Nightmarish memories replay over and over, and she forgets her bodily discomfort, taking no notice of the passing day.

❧

## 51

A sudden heat upon her face, Sarah stirs awake as the sled comes to a stop by the newly set fire. Watching great billows of white smoke give way to orange flames rising from within, Sarah realizes they are making camp for another desolate night. Easing into the soothing warmth, she rests her head on the packs beneath her. Looking to the sky above, a deepening blue hue at the cusp of turning black, she detects the first faint glint of stars. Soon, hundreds slowly emerge, and she uses the amusement of the flickering lights to remain conscious, struggling to heed the instruction of her captor to "stay awake."

Lifting her heavy head, she strains to watch her captors as they carry on a hushed conversation. The Silent Enemy, who has pulled her throughout the day, retreats to their group to tend them, leaving her alone with the Observant Enemy. As he stokes the fire, sparks shoot high into the air where they mingle with the stars above. As large cedar boughs catch, Sarah recoils from the intense heat. Realizing it may dry her uncomfortable, drenched clothing, she holds her arms out, seeking its effect. Watching the Observant Enemy rise, he moves to her handing her a piece of meat. Giving her a slight nod, as if to say "eat," he immediately returns to sit upon a fur, not a few feet away to partake of his own small portion.

Once finished his meal, he retrieves a pot set in the coals and hands Sarah water warmed in the fire. The liquid heat has an immediate effect on her aching body, and she leans back, taking a deep sigh of relief.

Drifting in and out of sleep, Sarah's head snaps back each time she realizes it falls. Pushing the blankets back, she allows the cold air to revive her. Unsure of when she is allowed to take her rest, she dutifully waits for permission, which is not forthcoming.

The usual hum of the nightly encampment, now quiet as all sleep, Sarah sees the others shiver, even as they rest. They are afforded no more food or warmth than what will keep them alive. She finds the contrasting nature of the Observant Enemy perplexing. The misery they suffer is at the hands of this brutal man, yet only hours before he saved her, showing mercy where none was expected.

Not realizing her curiosity overtakes her sense, she studies his dark eyes, the very colour of the band of black paint covering them. It seems the enemy, too, understands the power of conveying meaning with just the eyes, for Sarah has seen it often enough at home. To bring attention to them in such a way has a terrifying effect, which she assumes is intended. His eyes are as none she has seen amongst her own people. Not unkind, they are as deep pools of black liquid. A flash of memory of such a sight enters her mind, but despite the images swirling about, sending her stomach into painful spasms again, she is inexplicably drawn to her captor's features. The rest of his face is painted red as the coals of the fire he tends, and she can only see a hint of his true self at his exposed neck. Looking to her own hands resting atop the soft, black fur, she lifts one into the air as if against his neck, and finds it much deeper than her own fair skin.

The prominence of his cheekbones and his full, curved lips give him a pleasant appearance. His straight black hair, longer than her own, is neatly tied back. She unconsciously runs her fingers through her own tussled hair to tame the tangled mess made wild with lack of attention. Glancing to him again, she notes his curious expression. Realizing he watches her observation of him, she expects punishment for her impertinence, and retreats back under the furs, as some form of protection. With this, his demeanour markedly changes. Standing up, he looks upon her with disappointment. Even as she hears the terrified voices of those killed — "savages!" — still echoing in her mind, her heart speaks of a different truth. Turning from her, he moves to where the Reverend rests. They are soon engaged in a tense conversation she knows must be about her, for they often glance at her. Left breathless by the terrifying possibilities rushing at her the men begin dissipating into blackness. As her vision narrows, only a glimmer of light from the fire connects her to this place. Appearing in the void, Mrs. Frary stands before her, as though living. Calmed by her presence, Sarah's mind slows, bringing with it clarity of why the men speak. *The Reverend is to provide a final prayer before I am killed. At least I will have that dignity; at least I will not be alone*, she thinks, smiling at her imagined friend.

Sarah watches as the Reverend struggles to his feet. The toll the march has on this once seemingly strong man is marked. Offered aid by the warrior, he waves it off, using his disdain to strengthen his resolve to rise. His noticeably injured leg leaves him lame, but as he hobbles towards her, she can see his usual authoritative manner survives, even as he winces in pain.

*Dear Lord, please forgive my sins, I ask you might yet accept me into the kingdom of heaven, though I do not deserve it. Please. Please forgive me.* Despite her acceptance that the end is near, the knowing of it tortures her.

As the men approach, the warrior picks up a heavy canvas pack, throwing it hard to the ground beside the sled. THUMP! Startled by the sound, Sarah jumps, despite having watched it being moved. She stares wide-eyed as the Reverend sits upon the makeshift seat. He looks at her with such hard eyes, she is unsure whose presence brings more reassurance, his or the warrior's. Where the Reverend is stern, the Observant Enemy appears . . . *concerned?*

"Leave us," the Reverend orders, seeming to forget his altered circumstances. In a strange role-reversal, the warrior does as told, returning to his place by the fire.

"You must pray, Sarah. Do not give in to what they tell you. They are the enemy that has taken you from your family. They will do much to win your trust — feed you, clothe you — this is but bodily relief; it cannot save you in the afterlife." His stark sermon does not ease her increasing distress. She mistrusted his words long before the march, long before she saw his children slaughtered. He had not saved any of his own. Looking past him, to those lying upon the ground, she cannot reconcile his lack of effort in comforting them. *Even now, they suffer within reach of him. His prayers help none, and on occasion seems to threaten many. Why should he be believed?*

Attempting to appear attentive, Sarah keeps her eyes fixed on him, but pays no mind to his continued efforts. Instead, she mulls over the questions that make her head ache in trying to find a logical reason for the day's confusing events. Without thought to propriety in interrupting his sermon, she begs, "Why did he save me when so many have been slain? Why kill me now for merely looking upon him?"

"Pardon?" the Reverend asks, thinking her delirious.

"Why save me from the river, to kill me now?" she whimpers, imagining her horrifying end alone in the dark forest.

"Sarah, he does not intend to kill you this night. He asks me to pray with you so you might be consoled." With renewed vigour, he proceeds, "Do not succumb to their saving of your body, for they mean to damn you to the eternal flames of hell." Astounded by the revelation, Sarah looks to Mrs. Frary, who slips back into the shadows and vanishes.

"Lieutenant deRouville says they take you, and the other children," the Reverend pauses, looking mournfully upon his own, "as replacement for theirs lost to death. They plan on adopting you into their communities, forcing you to become what *they* are." Seeing the effect his hatred has upon one so frail, so young, he softens his tone. "Do not worry, Sarah of Deerfield, we will not let such tragedy come to pass. You will be redeemed. The will of the Lord is mightier than these damned French and their savage allies." Tempering his growing rage, he continues gently, "You will see the face of your father and mother again."

*If only I could remember them,* she thinks, desperately searching the darkness before her for any sign of their appearance. Compelled to confess her sin, she haltingly admits, "I have brought this upon us."

"What do you mean, child?" he asks, the furrow of his brow deepening with his increasing concern for her well-being.

"This. All of this. You said so on the Sabbath. Your words — 'The Lord is righteous for I have rebelled against his commandment' — were for me. I cannot recall Father's face, for I am being punished for my impudence. I always looked to the hills wondering what lay beyond, and here . . . *here* we are in those very hills and mountains, suffering the bitter cold, the agony of injury, and even in our rest, the dark night cruelly gives time to yearn more ardently for home, which seems lost to me, now that I am...alone. Though Mrs. Frary said I was not, I know I am the cause. I am sorry . . ." Sobbing uncontrollably, Sarah draws the attention of the warrior, who rises to more closely observe the situation. The Reverend forcefully slaps his hand about her mouth, stopping any further noise from escaping. Worried she will give cause for his own safety to be called into question, he angrily orders, "Sarah, stop! Stop." Met with bewildered eyes, he releases his hand, whispering a hollow reassurance, "You will be redeemed to your family. But," he gravely warns, "you must pray, for if in your heart you are wanting more, you will not find redemption in the afterlife."

Disheartened by his lack of the fatherly comfort she has prayed for, Sarah looks past him to the enemy now standing by the fire. The images of tomahawks and war clubs being raised, once seared in her mind's eye, are replaced by the sight of dark eyes gazing upon her with the concern, the care, she craves.

# 52

"Call the leaders together," deRouville orders. Around the fire nearest the French encampment, the council gathers for a second night.

"The evidence lacking that we are pursued brings me to the conclusion that we are not to expect the men of Deerfield. As so evidently pointed out last evening, our true enemy is starvation, which now lurks. I seek your counsel to ensure we make Fort Chambly, with as many captives as we may spare."

"We remind the Lieutenant that we will be leaving your company once we have reached our home territory at Cowass," says the Pennacook leader, not so subtly reminding deRouville of the conditions of their aid.

"Oui, I know, and our agreement has not changed, but allow me to remind the honoured leader of the Pennacook that what consideration is given to the captives on this march is expected to continue when you bring them to your people." DeRouville, having seen the harsh treatment of the two men held by the Pennacook, doubts they will last long with such unforgiving masters.

"We do with our slaves as we want. Once in Cowass, we no longer adhere to the rule of les Français; by our ways, and our chief's rule alone, are we guided." DeRouville struggles to keep his anger in check. Knowing any attempt to set conditions on this fierce warrior will be met with brutal violence, he lets the seditious remark pass. Being but two or three days' march from the warrior's village, he will soon be rid of such aggravation. He turns his attention to the larger group.

"Mes amis, many have been lost these first days of our journey north. I do not wish to see you depleted of further prizes for your people. Our own group has only enough to sustain but a day or two, and then we are without provisions. I rely on your wise counsel of how we might resupply for the many miles yet ahead of us." Having rationed his own food supplies to ensure none amongst their own group would starve so early, deRouville finds the lack of daily sustenance draining. The pain of such want now rivals that of his injury, which still grieves him eight days on.

The misery of the march bears down on them. This council, at the junction of the White River, is a turning point. The decisions made around this fire will determine the fate of all.

"We must separate, for if we are to survive, we must hunt," advises the Mohawk warrior who had assumed care of the Reverend at the Lieutenant's request. "Travelling together as we are, we give warning to our prey, and even if we are to go out in hunting parties, it will come to nothing."

"I understand what you say, but would it not be wiser to stay as one and share what supplies we may have need of? The unknown nature of what hardships we may yet face leads me to believe we are best to stay together." Already holding limited control over the factious groups, deRouville should welcome the reprieve of their separating, but for the knowledge that the most gruelling part of the trek, the imposing and perilous Green Mountains, lie ahead. Even with the relative ease of walking upon the frozen river, the deep, soaking snows and increasing speed of the march has exacted a devastating toll on both the captives and his allies.

Succumbing to their injuries, several warriors have been buried along the trail. With the loss of even a single ally, he knows their ability to ensure their captives reach Fort Chambly is jeopardized.

"Non, impossible! We will not continue with such a large group. We make for Lorette on our own. You will have us all starve to retain command. Such arrogance les Français possess that they think they are the masters of nature, the mountains, the animals; you prove the foolishness of your people again and again." The Huron leader, much less interested in negotiation than his predecessor, mocks deRouville. Bolstering the validity of his claim, a number of warriors nod as a few shrill yells pierce the silence of the night. With intensifying severity, he continues, "*You* do not determine our fate by your assertion of authority, Lieutenant. Perhaps you would be best to remember that it is by our medicines that you survived at all. The ache of your wound should serve as a reminder that you live by our hand, and may yet — " Stopping mid-sentence, as if to keep his next thoughts from escaping, the incensed warrior leaves no doubt of his intended meaning.

"I have been charged with the duty to bring the people of Deerfield back to Canada," deRouville says, raising his voice above the murmurs of agreement. Not allowing the momentum the Huron has

sparked to continue, he unleashes the intense anger the warrior elicits. "*All* understood when we set out from Fort Chambly, many days
ago, it was under my leadership that this expedition would take place,
and while we seek to strengthen our alliances with your people, it is
my charge to make decisions based on the rule of les Français, not
the divergent ideas of those who *freely* entered this alliance. Therefore, while I seek your counsel, I do not seek your permission." Glaring at them, he allows his words to settle upon them for a few tense
moments. Suddenly rising, he adds, "I will take your counsel under
consideration." DeRouville leaves their company with his senior
officers, confident he has shown his resolve, and willingness, to die
to retain command.

   He retreats to his encampment to consider the options. Unfurling
the maps, he traces their route with his finger, following the Connecticut River until the junction of the Wells River, which they will follow
northwest until the small black line indicating its flow abruptly ends.
Staring at the void between the end of the Wells and the beginning of
the Winooski River, he remembers the soaring mountains and the dif-
ficulties they pose even when in good constitution and well supplied.

   "Lieutenant? Jean."

   He turns to find the welcome sight of his brother René. "Oui?"

   "Might I help in some way?"

   "Oui. I should like your aid in determining our course."

   "Whatever you may have need of, brother, I shall do."

   Giving him a weak smile, deRouville resumes mapping out their
track, calculating the number of days and amount of supplies needed.
His brother provides no more than company as he works, for his
concentration is absolute. His finger continues west on the Winooski
until it reaches Lake Champlain, where they will move north along its
frozen surface, he prays, for the new season approaches quickly, until
crossing over its vast surface to the Richelieu River and Fort Chambly. Seeing the stark reality before him, of marching these already
weakened people over such merciless terrain, no river existing to ease
their passage in parts, he knows his allies have given the only option:
to survive, they must separate.

# 53

⚮

The warmth of furs and softness of the packs beneath Sarah afford a deep, restful sleep, and where this would have been welcomed in usual times, the rest provides cruel clarity.

Resting comfortably upon the sled, Sarah searches in vain for any amongst those following behind that might make the faintest connection. She finds only vacant eyes that show neither fear, nor spirit. Frightened by the spectres, she looks away. Holding tight to the packs secured beneath her, afraid of being thrown from the sled, pitching and swaying violently over the rugged terrain, she turns her attention to the only ones who show any signs of life: their captors. Finding the one who saved her from a watery grave, she keenly observes his alert eyes, speaking of determination and an awareness of the world they inhabit. He is so in contrast to her own people, she cannot resist yearning to connect with the living, despite him being the enemy. Following the sound of a bird overhead, the warrior watches with much interest. Curious to know what holds his attention, Sarah searches the white, cloud-covered sky, seeking the only sound breaking the oppressive silence. Unable to get a sense from where the shrill call comes, she looks to the Observant Enemy to see where he casts his gaze. Startled to find him studying her, she shies away. Keeping her eyes trained upon the blackness of the furs covering her, as the minutes pass without punishment, her curiosity, revived with her returning strength, compels her to look again. He motions to the sky with a slight gesture of his head. A large bird soars high above, its wide wingspan and distinctive features coming into view. The eagle's call echoes about them, though only the Observant Enemy and Sarah take notice. It turns in the gentle breeze that makes the barren tree tops sway without so much as a flap of its wings. As it soars higher into the sky, it disappears from sight. Craning her neck to follow its now faint call in the distance somewhere behind her, she twists her body, searching for it in vain. The slip of her hand sends her tumbling toward the ground. She desperately grasps the large ropes securing the packs, but her fleeting salvation slips from her fingers. Just as she feels a cold rush as she releases from the furs, Sarah is consumed by dread as the faces of those following behind contort in terror. As a blur, the Observant Enemy's fearsome painted face appears only inches from her own. She is hoisted roughly atop the sled, and they continue moving forward, having not missed a step.

Without a word, he steadies Sarah, pulling the furs to her shoulders, tucking them in forcefully about her as if trapping her within. Offering no resistance, she remains stunned by the mind-numbing immensity of facing certain death, only to find salvation. Existing in neither fear nor gratefulness, she does not avert her eyes from him. Seeing her expressionless face, he falls back, following the sled, paying no further attention to her.

# 54

⁓

Bidding farewell to the Mohawk party carrying the greatest prize of the expedition with it, deRouville worries as he watches them veer from the Connecticut.

They chose a route they know well, but it offers no ease of passage, as they will only follow the White River for a short few miles before heading directly north through the mountains to the headwaters of the Winooski. Assurances that this is their best chance to find food and ensure the safety of the Reverend did not ease his concern. Having to make Fort Chambly at all cost, deRouville knows he wagers the lives of many for the safety of one. He does not doubt the ability of his allies to supply sustenance as they hunt on the long march north, but questions the endurance of the captives, or lack of will to do so in the absence of their spiritual leader. His ongoing preaching has had much effect in driving them steadily onward. By their despondency, he can see many envy the dead. They endure the agony of frozen, wounded feet, continually injured by hidden protruding branches when forced upon the river bank by open water. And when again following the easier route upon the icy surface, the soaking meltwater makes them swell and unable to heal in the least. With the return of the bitter, penetrating cold each night they curl into themselves, protecting what insignificant warmth comes of it. The protests of deprived stomachs rise above their muffled footsteps when moving, and echo distractingly throughout the encampment when at rest. He understands all too well the great effect prayer has in overcoming such suffering, for he holds to his own over the many punishing miles.

Noticing Reverend Williams move away from them, his people wail, watching their final hope take his leave. Their unguarded reaction confirms deRouville is not mistaken to worry.

Hearing their mournful cries, the Reverend turns back, calling out, "Continue to pray, good people of Deerfield, for we will be shown mercy if we hold true to the Lord's teachings." Attempting to take one last look at his children, he catches only a glimpse before they slip from sight, and he descends onto the ice of the White River.

Terrified by the departure from the larger group, each small party sets forth separately. Sarah, taking a last lingering look on her once neighbours, sees Esther crying inconsolably, desperately reaching for her father. Held back by Samuel, she fights to break free, showing more life in this moment than in the many days since her mother's death, reminding Sarah of the dear friend she had once played with in happier days.

With the Reverend's sorrowful words, "Goodbye, my children," carried on the wind, Sarah and the five of Deerfield that remain with her take leave of even the most foreign comfort of captivity amongst many and are swallowed up by the rugged landscape.

# 55

As the denser forest surrounds them threatening to extinguish what light remains, Sarah is uneasy, realizing they are in the midst of the mountains that once loomed before them.

Holding the ropes in a painful grip as the sled continues to heave on the unbroken trail adjacent to a river, Sarah knows mercy shown once is not to be had again if she releases. Watching the others labour to take each step in snow much deeper than before, she is grateful for the ease afforded by the sled. Beads of sweat upon their brows give evidence of the fight they mount against the steadily rising terrain. Following their wanting gaze to the open river, she knows they seek the reprieve of treading upon its frozen surface. A faint sound of rushing water beyond the trees reminds her of the stabbing cold of such waters, bringing a severe reaction, and she begins to convulse. Wincing with the pain, she whimpers in response. With disapproving frowns cast upon her, she retreats under cover to escape their envious stares.

Sarah's vantage point gives her ample opportunity to take account of those who remain. Studying each, she has only now become aware of the others in their group, though they have travelled many miles, many days, in each other's company. Her curiosity proving resilient, Sarah makes a game of determining the thoughts and nature of each man, woman, and child.

*Mr. French struggles the most. I wonder why he should carry more than the boys? And why he does not wear snowshoes?* Remaining focused on each step, Thomas French would seem completely unaware of his surroundings if not for the occasional sidelong glance to his wife and son, following nearby. Sarah watches for any response to his secret attentions, but no discernible acknowledgement from Mary French, nor their son, Thomas, is given. Each is so wholly consumed by their efforts to navigate the rough trail, only newly made by the impression left by the sled, that they seem oblivious to their groans that caught this poor man's attention in the first place. Sarah, feeling the sled rise awkwardly over unseen rocks as it cuts the trail, wants to warn the others as she sees them stumble over the offending objects. But, noticing the intensity with which the Observant Enemy takes interest in each small change in pace or the faintest sound escaping them, she does not want to fall under the same scrutiny, and so remains quiet.

The Silent Enemy grunts with the effort to pull the sled up a steep rise, but gains only a few inches at a time. Sarah looks back down upon the group clawing their way up, grabbing tree branches, protruding rocks, and each other, to aid in their ascent. She feels the sled give slightly. Shaking with the strain to keep it from going any further back down the immense hill, the warrior calls out in distress, "Otentiani!"

Even without understanding the word, his voice makes the danger clear. With Thomas French before her groaning with the effort of merely taking a single step, she knows he cannot avoid the resulting calamity if the warrior loses his grip.

Before she has time to imagine the outcome, the Observant Enemy runs at her and brings the sled to an abrupt stop. Finding herself now facing with him, Sarah is about to avert her eyes from his intense gaze when she realizes it is not upon her, but upon the hill directly behind. She is awash with relief as the sled speeds to the top. Perched high upon the ridge, she watches as the Observant Enemy takes his leave of her and rushes to the others, now completely stalled on the ascent. Plucking Mary Alexander from Ebenezer's arms, who vehemently protests, he pulls hard forcing her release. He bolts up the nearly vertical rise as if it does not impede him in the least. His swiftness leaves only a few seconds to observe young Mary's growing alarm as she tries to leap from his arms. Unceremoniously, he drops her on Sarah's lap with a stern, "Hold her." Pulling the fur back, she puts Mary under cover.

"Quiet now!" she cautions the squirming child, as she would her own precocious brother, Samuel. His sweet, cherubic face flashing before her, she instinctively holds tight, humming a low lonely lullaby to calm her. Rocking Mary gently, Sarah enjoys her fleeting memory of him.

"Up! Up!"

Spellbound, Sarah watches Thomas French, the last of the group to reach the top, lurch forward, his legs shaking, attempting to follow the increasingly angered command of the Observant Enemy. Each looks on with bated breath, silently willing him to take the next step.

Sarah pities him each time he has to begin anew, for it is plain the dire condition he is in. Buckling under the weight of the packs, and nearly consumed by knee-deep snow that has an unrelenting grip on him, he wavers in his final attempt. Sinking down, he hangs his head in defeat. Sarah is captivated by the contrasting sight before her. Below, a solitary, conquered soul awaits death, while before her lies the sweeping view afforded from the top of the ridge: white mountains that carry on as far as the eye can see, soaring into a sky dotted with patches of blue as the clouds part here and there. Sarah, nor any amongst them, has seen such grandeur, but it is this vista, this immensity before them that makes them seem all the more insignificant. Looking back upon Thomas, she knows his fate is one they share, separated perhaps by but a day or two. The affliction of her curiosity will not release her from witnessing what is to come. The Observant Enemy raises his tomahawk as she watches in disbelief.

Felling a sapling with the shiny blade of his weapon, he quickly fashions it into a rod, prodding Thomas harshly with it as he shouts, "Up!"

Offered no aid beyond the rudimentary walking stick, Thomas, emerges from the shock of being spared, and looks to his wife and son gazing down upon him. Using the reviving strength of his deliverance, he hoists himself from the ground. Harshly driven to the top, never alleviated of his heavy packs, he eventually makes the ridge, and its breathtaking view.

"Thanks be to God," he pants. "I am delivered."

Their journey has been hastened since mounting the craggy ridge, which in parts is swept clean of snow by the constant, whipping winds. The sun, having broken free from the bonds of the winter's heavy clouds, revives them with its warmth, and the views hold them in awe of such unknown places. Nestled to her, a now sleeping Mary Alexander gives Sarah a renewed sense of purpose. Leaning in close to her ear, she whispers, "I will watch over you, as I was once watched over." Tenderly cradling her, Sarah feels her bony frame, realizing her clothing conceals how frail she truly is. Casting her eyes to the horizon, Sarah searches for ways to save her tiny companion as a single tear streams down her cheek.

Dropping down the backside of the ridge, they are once again plunged into a shadowy world. Exhausting any possibilities that would change young Mary's fate, Sarah feels her mood darken, as the forest around her. Thomas takes his usual position ahead of his wife and son, and Sarah sees he keeps an eye on them once more. She envies young Thomas the presence of his mother and father. *He does not seem to take much notice of them at all. Surely if my own . . .* The despair of being unable to conjure her own family in any way, leaves Sarah bitter that he is not seeming to rejoice in having them near. *He always was an ungrateful boy,* she thinks jealously.

Feeling Mary stir, she pulls her in close, instinctively stroking her hair as she continues her observations. Searching the sun-dappled faces of each, afforded by the light of the setting sun streaming through barren trees, she suddenly realizes one amongst them is missing. A vague memory brings the name of one who had once been in the care of the forlorn Ebenezer.

"William Brooks," she whispers, as if his name even spoken in hushed tones will provide a marker of his existence, where a memorial does not.

Ebenezer walks in such melancholy that even with the suffering that abounds, he stands apart. His eyes steady upon the ground, he does not seem to notice Mary French falter nearby. Moving around her, his pace does not ease. It is her son Thomas who rushes to her aid, though it would not require much of Ebenezer to do so. His concentration on his own unsteady stride consumes him entirely.

*I do not believe he had snowshoes the day his mother died.* Perplexed, she tries to recall any detail of that day. The awkward way in which he walks in them speaks of inexperience. In comparing his gait to that of young Thomas, who does not continually stumble, the reason dawns on her. Staring at Ebenezer's feet, she realizes she is familiar with the source of this particular pair, for she affixed them to the feet of another not but a few days before.

# 56

❧

The sled striking a hidden rock causes Mary to wake with a start, and she begins to cry, alarming Sarah. Laboured and unnatural, the sound is more akin to moaning than the robust cry one would expect.

"Mary, it is alright. You are alright." Trying to comfort the inconsolable child, Sarah notices her lack of awareness, and tries to revive her. "Mary? Mary?"

Despite, being shaken, Mary simply closes her eyes. Her body goes limp, and Sarah realizes something is terribly wrong. Afraid to draw the attention of the Observant Enemy, who lags behind, she does not know if she should attempt to wake her or leave her to sleep, which she fears signals she is slipping away. Sarah decides to chance any retribution from her captors, for she cannot fathom the alternative. Removing her arm from under the fur, she takes a handful of the cold snow brushing the edges of her legs as the sled sinks deep under its weight. Taking one final glance to the enemy to confirm he keeps a steady watch of the forest, she puts the snow to Mary's face. A passionate cry rings out. Sarah's relief in having her wake, for she is now most aware and upset by the shock, is short lived. Turning to face the consequences, she slowly lifts her head, finding the others staring at them with dread.

Attempting to defend herself from the enemy now fixated on her, she pleads, "She is hungry. I feel her tiny body even now." She embraces the now whimpering Mary. "Her bones protrude, she fades! Please. I only wanted to soothe her. She suffers so." Sobbing, Sarah gives no consideration to her own safety, wanting nothing more than to save the life entrusted to her.

His dark, penetrating eyes do not waver. Sensing he understands, Sarah whispers, "Please."

He calls something out in his own language to the Silent Enemy, who grunts in response, and the sled lurches forward. They continue the march as though nothing has happened, and it is only that he no longer looks to the forest surrounding them, that she believes something has changed.

*Will he help Mary? Kill her? Kill me?* The confusing light of dusk obscuring the features of the others, Sarah can no longer gain any clarity about what each might be thinking. Feeling Mary become increasingly restless, she takes what opportunity she can to tend her. Melting snow in her own hand, she is relieved as the small droplets are eagerly accepted. She continues offering them until her hands become too cold to have any further effect. Holding Mary tight, Sarah sways her, humming a low tune as the little one slips back into sleep.

As the sled finally slows to a stop, Sarah sees exhausted bodies slump to the ground, their silhouettes only scarcely visible in the last vestiges of light. Protected from the chilling winds in a hollow amid a forest of towering pines, she is glad to see the day come to an end. Though it brings a lonely night, it also brings the longed for opportunity to feed Mary, with hopes that she will rally. Lying motionless in Sarah's arms, she sleeps soundly. Her slow, steady breathing assures Sarah she merely rests. As the warriors, Thomas, and the boys gather wood for the nightly fire, Sarah waits for light and warmth to return. Once fearing the dark, of being alone, she remembers Mrs. Frary's care of her, and hopes her friend in heaven is proud she does the same for Mary. Thinking to how the story of her own arrival made their reality disappear, if only for a little while, she decides to tell Mary her most favourite tale. *I shall tell Samuel — Mary,* she corrects, *of Captain Lamberton. Surely she will be amused by it.* Harkening back to a time when Samuel and the others had listened at length to her dramatic rendition of the story of a long-ago grandfather, she smiles.

Flickering to life, the first spark of flame catches on the white bark set atop the sticks piled high. Sarah's mouth waters thinking to the meat that will soon cook over it. Eager for release from her relentless pangs of hunger, she wonders how Mary has fared so long, knowing one so young must feel them all the more. "Poor darling," she whispers as she gently strokes Mary's face.

Sarah is given a small ration of corn, which they have largely subsisted on over the past several days, and she gags at the thought of eating the bland meal again. The tough texture forces her to chew the kernels until her jaw aches in trying to break it down enough to swallow. She hands Mary a piece, but she spits it out with each offering.

"Mary, chew. Chew!" The inconsolable child fights Sarah's effort to put the kernel back in her mouth. "Eat!" Absorbed in the effort, Sarah does not realize she has fallen again under watchful eyes.

"No!" comes Mary's determined reply as she spits the kernel onto the fur. Seeing no other way, Sarah chews it herself and, turning it into mash, spits it into her hand and feeds it to Mary, who seems to accept the food more readily. But, after only a few kernels, she once again refuses to open her mouth. Crying, Mary holds her stomach, moaning in pain. *Perhaps she will fare better with a little meat.* Waiting for her usual portion, Sarah is surprised to find the warriors sit in place, not attending them as usual. Believing she has been so preoccupied she has missed the offering, she looks to the others to beg them to share a morsel to shore up Mary. She notices none eats anything but corn, including their captors, whose own meal consists of but a few measly pieces. In fact, looking at her own small pile, golden against the black fur it sits upon, Sarah realizes she and Mary have more than the others. With Mary's pained cries increasing, Sarah desperately shoves more mash in her mouth, holding it closed, hoping it will force her to swallow.

"Mary, eat one more . . . please." To her great relief, it has the intended effect, and Mary swallows hard. The mash no sooner reaches her stomach than it is violently thrown back up. Beyond herself, Sarah cries desperately, chastising the ill child, "No, Mary. You must eat. No, Mary!" Frightened to find Mary declining rapidly, Sarah is forced to face the unspeakable suffering of what is to come. Attempting to make more mash, she starts the process over again. Suddenly the Observant Enemy stands and walks towards them. Unable to stop her own sobs, Sarah watches his blurred image approach. Streaming down her cheeks, her salty tears cause her mouth to water profusely, making the lack of succulent meat all the more bitter. Sinking into total despair, she is completed defeated by her inability to soothe either Mary or herself.

As the warrior attempts to take Mary, Sarah holds fast, determined not to let her be taken to her doom. Even as Mary wails at being handled so roughly, she does not surrender her. Her fear replaced by the want to safeguard her small companion, she finds strength she did not know she possessed. Finally, losing the brief battle, the Observant Enemy releases his grip on Mary, and she falls roughly back at Sarah's side. Scrambling to her protector, Mary holds tight, shielding her face in the crook of Sarah's neck. Glaring at him, Sarah leaves no doubt of her determination to save the child. Standing firm, the warrior looks to them as if contemplating something. Finally, he bends by their side.

"I will try and feed her."

She does not trust him, for only days before he had taken the last vestige of comfort from her.

"You will kill her," she yells defiantly, not caring to live if he takes Mary from her.

"She starves, young one," he says gently. The words wind her, as if struck by a vicious blow. Paralyzed by the incomprehensible truth, she releases her grip, and Mary is carried off towards the fire.

The warrior lays Mary beside him on his own soft bed of hides. He puts snow into a small pot and heats it on the fire while he sets about grinding corn between two rocks. Soon, noticing white wisps of steam rising from the pot, he pours the flour in, stirring it to create a heavy broth.

Sarah, not having released her gaze from Mary, watches with hopeful anticipation as her enemy brings the ladle to her mouth. Mary immediately accepts it. Awaiting the upheaval she is sure will come, Sarah finally relaxes realizing he was right to take her. No longer grabbing at her pained stomach, as she was only moments before, Mary seems relieved of her terrible suffering, and, furthermore, does not seem afraid to be in his care.

Soon falling asleep, cradled in his arms, Mary seems as a child in the arms of a father. Sarah looks on in disbelief as their enemy soothes Mary with an unknown song. Sarah listens to words sung in low tones, and though she does not understand them, they have a familiar effect. Easing back onto the packs, she pulls the fur to her neck, leaving the fire to warm her face. Gazing into the orange coals glowing within the flames, she watches the pile of branches being slowly consumed. As pieces of soft, grey ash fall from the remnants of blackened wood, Sarah closes her eyes, lulled to sleep by the lilting rhythm of the enemy's haunting song.

# 57

〰

"Might we not make our escape, Thomas?"

Sarah is woken by the piercing sound of Mary French's frantic voice. She panics, seeing them in such close proximity to one another.

"Hush, Mary," comes the stern response.

Scanning the scene, Sarah searches for their ever-present captors, expecting punishment to be swift. Confused by their absence, Sarah looks to young Mary tucked in tightly by her side. Sleeping soundly, she had evidently been placed there as Sarah slept. The thought that she did not wake when the enemy was so close makes her tense.

"But Thomas, they have abandoned us. We must make for Deerfield," Mary French pleads, looking nervously about expecting them to pounce. Thomas's lack of response angers her. With a surge of desperation, she yells, "Why do we not move, Thomas?"

Slapping her harshly across the face, he looks fearfully to the thick forest surrounding them. "Mary, do not speak. They are not far. We are not abandoned. They hunt for food." Seeing her calm, he pulls her instantly into a tender embrace, weeping, "Oh, Mary; my dear."

Stunned to see him break down in the arms of his wife, Sarah picks young Mary up, cradling her with the want of comfort, as Thomas and Mary French have with one another.

"Come to us." Thomas French beckons his son, not a few feet away. "We may have little opportunity for such blessings in the coming days."

Looking nervously about, young Thomas seems unable to move, despite his obvious urge.

"Son, it is safe," his father reassures.

Rushing to them, he is pulled into their embrace. Bowing their heads together, the three remaining members of the family shield themselves from the world around them. Sarah's heart aches as she imagines herself in the scene. She yearns for such comfort. *If only it were me being held close by Mother and Father.* Overcome with grief, she chastises herself. *What would they want of me? I have brought this retribution on us.* With the Reverend's words weighing heavily upon her wounded heart, she whispers, "The Lord is righteous, for I have rebelled against his commandment." The bitter realization that she has brought this upon herself, *and these poor people,* she thinks, putting her arm around the tiny one beside her, makes it impossible to ask the Lord for redemption. Watching this family bask in the relief of being reunited, guilt bears down on her.

"Why do we not escape, dear Husband?" Mary asks again, confused by his lack of will. Sarah listens for his reply, for even as she has not believed it possible, the very word "escape" makes her heart leap. Her hands trembling with anticipation, she watches Thomas look to the dense forest surrounding them, the sheer ridge behind, and upon those in their group, including Sarah, who shies from his gaze.

"Where would we go?"

Sarah feels small and helpless hearing his prophetic words. *It is true. Even if our enemy is gone, we are captives nonetheless,* she reasons, thinking to the endless mountains she witnessed atop the rocky peak a day earlier. She wants her captors to return, for even as she fears them, the thought of suffering with pained stomachs, until they wither away, is so vivid that she would rather meet a swift end by the tomahawk than watch the others — watch young Mary — starve and be consumed by the creatures in this vast, inescapable place. *The wolves will be first.* Thinking to their ominous howls, she allows the gruesome nightmare to play out in her mind. The visions laid bare before her makes the presence of their captors seem comforting.

"Move away. They return." Thomas's alarmed warning stirs Sarah from the sleep she has inadvertently slipped into while waiting the many hours for the enemy's return.

"I will not leave you, Thomas. They may slay me, but I will not be parted again." Mary's resolute defiance brings a harsh response from Thomas, who grabs her by both arms, prying her from his waist, where she holds tight. "No! Do not push me away, dear Husband."

"Mary, please. You must understand, we have hope to be together once our ordeal ends. But we must live to see such a day. Think to the children who will be left orphaned if we do not survive."

She instantly looks to her son, who already rejoins Ebenezer. For what seems an eternity, she stares off into the forest, as Thomas sets her down and leaves her.

"They may yet live?" she asks softly, not turning from where she looks.

"Yes," he whispers.

With tears rolling down her cheeks, Mary's gaze remains fixed, taking no notice as the enemy brushes past, pulling the carcass of a large deer behind them.

The bloodied trail left by the dead animal reminds Sarah of so much killing and loss that she does not realize the salvation its appearance brings. As she stares at the red-soaked snow, her horrifying memories culminate into a deepening hatred for the enemy, who seem pleased with their kill.

Her expression, so full of disdain, surprises the Observant Enemy, for she is much altered since he last saw her. He notices she seems captivated by an unseen vision. Her lips move without sound, and her eyes appear to follows some action, which precipitates in turns sadness, anger, fear. Fear changes her most profoundly. Her eyes widen, but at the precipice of reacting outwardly, her spirit seems extinguished. Her once tense expression and deep furrowed brow give way to a face unmarked by any emotion. Having seen the result of such an effect before, he begins to doubt what once seemed assured. Returning his attention to the bounty lying before him, he leaves her to the shadow world she dwells in.

"You," he says, pointing at young Thomas and Ebenezer. "Come here."

The boys glance at one other with both apprehension and resignation. Doing as they are told, they stand by their captor looking down upon the deer.

"You will help to carve it."

Fear clouding his ability to understand, Ebenezer takes a step back, but as he does, he bumps into the Silent Enemy standing directly behind him, as though anticipating his natural urge to run. Surprised by the impact, Ebenezer reels around. Before he can react, he is pushed forward again to join Thomas, who is standing perfectly still.

The Observant Enemy takes the leg of the animal and begins to butcher it, doing so slowly, to show the boys his technique. Handing the bloodied knife to Ebenezer, he says, "You try."

Petrified, Ebenezer looks down at the blood dripping from his captor's hand. "No!" he says, turning away from the sight. "I will not."

The warrior shoves the knife to Ebenezer's chest. Fully expecting to see himself impaled, he is amazed to find it merely rests against him. Confused, he looks to the warrior only inches from him.

"You *will* learn, Kenaskwa." Unsure of the word's meaning, but understanding what is expected, Ebenezer takes the knife in hand, and this time he does not retreat from his enemy's steady gaze. Suddenly feeling defiant at being called the name of another, he drops to kneel beside the animal, grumbling almost inaudibly, "Ebenezer Nims. My name is Ebenezer Nims."

Warm to the touch, the deer's flesh makes the thought of butchering it much more palatable as Ebenezer's cold fingers tingle with returning feeling. Doing as shown, he slowly cuts the meat from the bone, handing the pieces to the Silent Enemy standing next to Thomas. His silence is disconcerting. Though they have not seen him kill any captives, as the other amongst them, it does not diminish the unnerving effect of his presence, for his disdain of them is clear.

"Give the knife to other boy, *Kenaskwa*," the Observant Enemy orders in a mocking tone, reminding Ebenezer of his place.

His own hands now dripping in blood, Ebenezer hands the knife to Thomas, who seems equally apprehensive to carve the animal. A small nod from Ebenezer, not three years older than he, is enough to reassure him to continue the process as shown. Thomas has a natural talent for the butchering, and the Observant Enemy seems pleased with his skill.

"Good, Shonatakakwani," he praises.

The work and approval, even being given by this captor, buoys Thomas's spirits. Given a hearty pat on the back, he rises, having finished cleaning the bone. Smiling with pride, he suddenly remembers where he is as he glances to the disturbed expressions of his parents, who watch their son be seduced by the praise and encouragement of their enemy. Ashamed, he averts his eyes from their disappointed stares, and looks back upon the carcass before him.

To revive the fire, which was left to smolder during the hunt, Thomas French is sent in search of more branches. With no need to keep watch of him, the warriors pile the meat beside the fire, where they will cook it over the coming days to sustain them on the march.

Wafting about the hollow, the smell of the roasting meat induces all to watch it sizzle above the flames. They are impatient to partake of its goodness as they have had no meal whatsoever since the last few kernels of corn the night before. This has weakened all, including the warriors. Having awoken to the smell, young Mary is left unable to muster anything more than a few breathless whimpers. Sarah sees her strength rapidly deplete with such slight effort. Desperate not to lose her to starvation, and knowing the meat will be too late in coming, she hesitantly asks, "Might she have some corn?"

Her words break the intensity of the group's anticipation. Without response, the Observant Enemy, who had successfully given Mary the reviving broth, opens his bag, showing nothing remains. Unsure of what to do, Sarah begins melting water in her hand, as before, giving the drops to her young charge, hoping a few will make it down her parched throat. Upset by the cold drips falling upon her face, Mary's tries to say "no," but no sound escapes. With every protest, Mary's dry, cracked lips bleed, and Sarah's sense of helplessness increases. Instinctively licking her own lips, she feels the jagged roughness of them, making her shudder at the realization of her own repulsive state. Her noisy, pained stomach and dwindling energy a constant reminder that starvation now stalks them, Sarah joins the others in their vigil as they watch the succulent meat brown. Sputtering flames soar into the sky as each drip of the juices falls from it, intensify the aroma, which torments them unmercifully.

During the long wait, the Observant Enemy carefully keeps an eye on the girls, who are set apart on the sled. His suspicions confirmed, he notices the little one slip in and out of consciousness.

Cutting a small outer piece from the meat upon the fire, he puts it in a clay pot, along with some snow, and sets it back upon the flame to warm. As the boiling vapour hits the frigid night air, the mist swirls about giving Sarah a small diversion to occupy Mary, who continues to moan and threatens to sleep again.

"Look at the dancing smoke," she says, pointing as Mary struggles to follow her instruction. "See how it moves about."

Hearing her words, their captor blows over the pot, sending the steam tumbling over the fire. Mary stops fussing and watches as he continues to do this over and over.

"Is it not curious? Like clouds, but on earth," Sarah says, feeling the delight in it herself. Mary looks to her, giving a small smile, which brings immense relief. "Keep watching," she continues to encourage as Mary's head bobs this way and that with the effort to hold it up.

"Drink slow," the Observant Enemy cautions, handing the bowl to Sarah, a piece of blood-stained cloth wrapped around it to shield her hands from its burning surface. Blackened by the flames, it holds the steaming broth she hopes will provide some energy to the wavering child. "Do not let her eat the meat." With his final warning given, he returns to help continue roasting the large pile of meat.

After blowing on the broth, Sarah brings it to her lips to test the temperature, not wanting to cause injury to Mary, who clamours for the bowl.

"Wait, dear. It is too hot." The taste of the broth lingers on Sarah's lips long after Mary has started eagerly drinking it. "Slowly," she warns gently, knowing the urge its taste elicits, for she continues to lick her own lips though the flavour of the rich liquid has long since disappeared.

With each sip, given at intervals to slow her natural greed of it, Mary's rigid body relaxes as the warm, filling broth eases her hunger pains. Sarah stares at the meat resting at the bottom of the bowl, yearning to eat it. Grabbing the bowl for more, Mary cries as it is harshly taken from her by Sarah, who fears she will attempt to eat the meat.

"No, Mary. It is all gone."

"Me hungry," she protests.

Despite the pitiful sight of Mary's dark, sunken eyes beseeching more, Sarah holds it off to the side, just out of reach of her small hands.

"Mary, no," she scolds. "You will be sick."

As if on cue, Mary begins to retch with the effort to attain more food, causing what little is in her stomach to go to waste.

"No!" Sarah gasps. Rubbing Mary's back, trying to calm the wailing child, Sarah wells up, watching the energy being sapped from her with each upheaval. "Sssh, ssh. Calm now, dearest."

She is devastated as Mary's cries suddenly cease; her head falling back limp shows the protruding bones at her neck. The effort is hopeless. Seeking the guidance of the Observant Enemy, Sarah is sure he will know what to do. Her heart sinks as he looks away from them and stares into the fire, offering no further aid.

# 58

*Will they do nothing to save Mary? Why must I be responsible for her? Our enemy show more mercy than they!*

Confused and angry, Sarah finds it impossible to accept that Thomas and Mary French, the only adults of Deerfield amongst them, will not offer the aid so desperately needed to save Mary.

Slumped into the crook of a large tree, Mary French shelters herself from the cold, eating so voraciously that Sarah is ashamed for her. Wiping the juices from her mouth with her sleeve, ignoring her husband's concerned glances, Mary descends into madness. Her mumbling makes no sense, but the occasional words that rise above the others — "my children . . . gone . . . they are all gone . . . dead, they must be dead" — give evidence to what runs incessantly through her mind. Even if allowed to provide comfort, Thomas knows nothing can be done for his wife. The words she speaks lie upon his own heart. The weight of guilt he carries in not being able to save them proves the cruellest of all the assaults he has faced these many days. Somehow, even exposed to such brutality as they have been, it is knowing they cannot escape, even without threat of violence — that no attempt is to be made to rescue their children — that has pushed Mary beyond her ability to endure. Unable to bear the sight, Thomas returns his focus to the work of packing the meat. Overhearing his son's questions of the enemy who instructs him on their ways, Thomas cannot object, for the miracle of his presence alone is enough to sustain. *When we reach Canada, we shall reclaim you,* he silently promises his boy.

"Here, Sarah, eat." The friendly voice speaking her name is like a ray of blinding sunshine piercing the dark, unsettling places of her mind. Giving a faint smile to Ebenezer, she looks to the meat he hands her. She suddenly feels ill. Despite the stabbing pains reminding her of her need of it, she waves it off.

"No, thank you, Ebenezer."

Unable to hide his deep disappointment in the refusal, he looks behind him before continuing. "But, I cooked it myself, Sarah. It is good. He . . . I mean, um . . ." Hesitant to admit his pride in having the enemy pleased with him, he stammers. "What I mean to say is, it is well cooked."

Warm and soothing in her cold hands, it does not make her mouth water as before; rather, her stomach heaves at the mere thought of eating it.

"I am sorry. It does look delicious, Ebenezer," she whispers, knowing he is afraid of drawing the attention of the Silent Enemy, for he looks over his shoulder with great concern.

"If you refuse, I will be punished." He flushes a deep crimson with the need to admit his own fear to one much younger than himself. She is tempted to refuse once more, simply on the basis of continuing the conversation, but looking into his pleading eyes, she is unable to deny him further.

"Thank you, Ebenezer, I will eat it," Sarah says, releasing him from the fear that grips him.

Replying with only a sigh of relief, he turns to resume his position alongside young Thomas. She envies their camaraderie, even if they may only sit together in silence.

With the relief of their brief conversation restoring her, Sarah finally takes a bite of the meat. Her apprehension and ill feeling soon give way to a ravenous hunger that she fights against, knowing the outcome of devouring the meat too quickly will only further her misery. Recalling Ebenezer's deep, hoarse voice, *from lack of use,* she reasons, she closes her eyes, imagining herself continuing the conversation with this boy with whom she has little acquaintance. Strangely, it does not occur to her to imagine herself anywhere else. Any memories of what was are replaced by a need to survive. Somehow, as once-longed-for faces begin to fade, it is made more bearable. The sound of Ebenezer's voice resonating in her mind, she lingers in her daydream.

# 59

The return of blustery winds brings further agony where none seemed possible. Unable to shield themselves against its force, they shake unyieldingly day and night, despite the demands of the taxing march. Though the days lengthen, there is little evidence of the coming spring in the desolate mountains. Ascending and descending so many times in the past two days that Sarah has no bearings whatsoever, she walks using the snowshoes that prove clumsy and weighty again after so many days of being pulled on the sled. The need to carry the deer meat prepared by their captors, Ebenezer, and Thomas, and her improved condition, means Sarah is again made to endure as the others.

At the head of the group, Thomas French cuts through the deep snow. He plunges his leg in thigh-high, then labours to bring the other to set it but a few inches ahead. The contrast of his treatment is stark, even with the deprivation all suffer. The degradation of Thomas French makes it seem as if he only exists as a slave to cruel masters. He is driven unmercifully with vicious jabs in his back with the end of a sharpened stick, as he struggles under the burden of heavy packs.

Mary French is obviously left to live or die as she wishes, and is given no special attentions. But Ebenezer, Thomas, and Sarah herself are watched carefully and aided when needed — though only when absolutely necessary. The weakened, but living, Mary Alexander is now carried by the Observant Enemy. His voice singing the same melancholy tune of a few nights earlier carries on the wind. Mary does not lift her head, but nuzzles into his neck, and he wraps his arm around her in response. Sarah senses the adults are in much more dire circumstances than the children. Despite them not showing any concern for them, their son included, Sarah needs their presence if only to make that of the enemy somehow more bearable. It is strange to both fear and seek the attentions of these strangers, this enemy, but with each small gesture of food, water, or warmth, Sarah seeks it none the less.

Watching the Observant Enemy cradle Mary — he, too, strains with the effort to carry her, tiny as she is — Sarah is glad for his presence. The truth is, the burden of trying to keep a dying child alive was too much, and when he took Mary from her, she was relieved.

Rarely stopping for a rest, the group moves forward through sheer will, for even with the nourishment of the meat, they falter. Their captors are unrelenting in their push north. More miles are travelled each day now than any previously. There is a palpable urgency in reaching their destination, and when the group slows, their captors become agitated.

"Walk!" cries the Observant Enemy, attempting to spur the exhausted group on. The shock of his raised voice stirs Mary from her rest upon his shoulder, and she begins to whimper, unable to be soothed by his gentle pats upon her back. Sarah glimpses an unspoken but fierce exchange between their captors. Infuriated by it, the one carrying Mary pushes Thomas to the ground. With only his packs visible, he struggles to regain his footing, but only seems to be further consumed. "Thomas! Thomas!" Mary French screams. Attempting to save her husband, she runs in his direction, only to be brutally pushed to the ground herself by their silent, menacing captor. The group comes to a complete stop, and the tension rises as young Thomas takes a step towards his father. Ebenezer grabs him by the arm, as he senses slaughter may be at hand if any further advance is made. To Ebenezer's surprise, a nod of allowance is given by the Observant Enemy, who over time has been revealed as their leader. Releasing himself of Ebenezer's hold, Thomas runs to his father, pulling the packs from his back, giving him a small chance at dislodging himself from the suffocating snow. His wife, held to the ground with a stick as an animal being held at bay, reverts to her usual silent, disconnected state, posing no further trouble to them. Tugging hard on his father's tattered coat, Thomas pulls him upright with one try, his desperation to save him fuelling his unusual strength.

"Thank you," says his father as he gasps to catch his breath.

"Walk!"

With no time to recover from the terrifying incident, Thomas hands his father the heavy pack and helps to position it once again on his back.

Sarah is pulled roughly to the front of the group by the Observant Enemy, who no longer attempts to soothe Mary. Something has changed in his demeanour, and it frightens her. Unsure of what has caused her to be targeted in this way, a surge of sickening dread rises up. Wounded by his sudden scorn, Sarah looks upon his angered face, now very close to her own.

"What did I do to offend?" she asks beseechingly, stifling her tears. His manner instantly changes, becoming calm as if he can read her thoughts. The teardrops fall upon her wind-burned cheeks, stinging as they slowly roll down to her neck. As tiny arms reach for her, Sarah makes no attempt to take the writhing child from the warrior. Turning from her, he wraps his arm around Mary to control her and moves to take his place at the rear of the group once again.

Searching for any kind gesture or evidence of sympathy from her fellow captives, Sarah finds each solely focused on putting one foot in front of the other. Paying no mind to one another, it is as if they are walking alone, not as a group. As they trudge through the forest of soaring pines within the unending mountains that engulf them, Sarah ponders the reasons for the Observant Enemy's abrupt actions and the reversal of his once — almost — gentle way with her and Mary.

As the coming night casts deep shadows around them, Sarah looks into the darkened woods, seeking the source of the muffled sound from a creature that seems to lurk just out of sight. Relieved Mary sleeps, for her silence makes the straining to hear much easier, Sarah tenses as the sound comes closer. The snap of a branch from the tree she brushes against makes her shut her eyes momentarily. Her raw nerves make even the most subtle sound fearful. Tripping as her snowshoe catches the heavy snow, she opens her eyes to stop her descent to the ground. Suddenly appearing before her, the Observant Enemy swiftly passes as he makes his way to his companion, who brings the group to a stop to make camp for the night. Gripped by the jarring absence, Sarah stares at his empty arms.

# 60

❦

The deep snow made soggy by the rising sun, Sarah struggles to maintain her pace. Her body drenched with the effort, she takes no notice of her physical pain, for the renewed and festering hatred of her enemy occupies her mind entirely. A long and lonely night spent cloistered in the solitude of her confusion over the fate of poor, sweet Mary has left Sarah too exhausted to think of the long day's march yet ahead of them. They now walk from dawn until dark. Evoking the tiny image that haunts her, she allows her loathing to fuel her every step.

Throughout the previous fateful evening she studied the Observant Enemy. She wanted to believe it was the silent message of his companion that caused the destruction of such innocent life, but the truth is, she could see no evidence he himself was sorry for it. When he approached with the nightly meal, the only food offered in a day without rest, Sarah rebuffed him, shooting him a distrustful glare. Treated as an animal at the command of its master, she has lost all rights to exert her will, so this small act gave her a rush when it elicited a fleeting response akin to sorrow. Exhilarated by her victory, she felt empowered and sought to inflict further injury if only done through her refusal of his aid. Throughout the long day, she can feel his eyes upon her, but even during their brief rests, she refuses to meet his gaze.

Descending a steep embankment, Sarah stumbles, only briefly leaving the dark, sinister places of her revenge. The sight of the river before her signals a return to the easier passage of its icy surface. The last time they tread on such a surface was many days before, when they had last seen the other captives of Deerfield. As if to further the burden they already carried in being separated from one another, the ease afforded by the frozen rivers was denied them. Languishing in drudgery day after torturous day, they traverse the mountainous terrain that seems to undulate endlessly, never arriving at any particular destination. They see the same sights, suffer the same indignities, and are subjected to the same cruelties. Even now, Sarah takes no pleasure in the sparkling glints of sunlight that burst upon the shimmering pools of open water. *Surely they mean to rid themselves of us all*, she reasons, knowing Mary's life had only been an illusion to give false hope, and a reason to endure.

As the others bend to drink the refreshing, crisp waters flowing in small openings here and there, Sarah denies her enemy the relief of seeing her revive, despite her own desperate thirst. Gesturing how to scoop the water in her hands and drink, the Observant Enemy is met with deadened eyes, devoid of any acknowledgement. Hearing him call to Ebenezer, who quickly comes to his side, Sarah is sorry he has fallen under his spell. She hopes Ebenezer finds release from its powerful grip, as she has. But, thinking to the cruel way in which she was set free of its insidious hold on her, she swallows hard, understanding it is she who will suffer the needed blow to release him. Though she cannot hear the exchange, it soon becomes clear as Ebenezer makes his way to her side.

"Sarah, drink."

"I will not."

"But it refreshes, and we have many a mile before us," he urges in a forced, friendly manner. Despite the effort to seem natural, he cannot hide his concern.

"He has sent you to tell me to drink, and I tell you I will not by *his* command."

Ebenezer glances to the one she speaks of, finding him watching them with great interest. Fearing the result of Sarah's refusal, Ebenezer again pleads, "Do not drink for him, Sarah, but for yourself, for your family."

The sudden reminder of her family, whom she has buried in her memory for many days, weeks perhaps, suddenly stirs in her a longing that consumes her. Feeling as a small, lost child again, she abandons all defences. Sobbing inconsolably, she covers her face, trying desperately to conjure them.

"But what of my family?" she finally ventures in a tentative voice, hoping to hear the impossible — that Ebenezer somehow knows they wait for her arrival.

"If you have any hope to see them again, you must drink and eat when you are able."

Devastated to find her implausible dream shattered, Sarah's defiance rears up again.

"*He*, will probably kill us anyway," she says glaring at the enemy nearby, "What is the purpose of staying strong when I might well find my end by my own efforts?"

"Sarah, I promise you, we are almost to our destination. A few short days and we will have food in abundance once more, I am told. And then there is reason to believe we will be redeemed," he adds in a tone hinting at his own hopes.

"If we are as close as you say, why kill . . ." she stops herself mid-sentence, for as her anger spills over, her voice rises, and she sees Ebenezer's growing alarm as he looks over his shoulder to their captors, now both watching closely. "I am sorry," she whispers, truly contrite for her outburst. She does not want to cause Ebenezer's demise, for somehow his friendly presence in particular comforts her.

"Sarah, we are nearly there," he says, believing what he has been told to be true. Pausing, he adds shyly, "Do it for me?"

After looking into his pleading eyes, Sarah sinks slowly to the ice and kneels by the open water. Removing her deerskin mittens, she plunges her hands into the freezing pool. The sensation makes her instantly crave its refreshing relief. Unable to stop her desperate response, she brings the water to her parched mouth. Sliding down her throat, it soothes the burning pain that has plagued her since being taken from Deerfield.

"Thank you," he whispers.

Now oblivious to his presence, she drinks as fast as her hands can carry the water to her mouth. Relieved to have succeeded, Ebenezer rejoins his new friend, Thomas, who, having had his fill, sits quietly looking at the landscape, now more majestic, more imposing, upon the ice.

"Winooski." Securing the packs that have shifted on the rough trail, the Observant Enemy does not look up, but seems to answer the unspoken question of the boys. He has not provided any bearing of where they are, how many miles they have marched, or how many more are yet before them, but at least they know the name of the river that provides their passage.

The winds that had only hinted at their strength when they were amid the swaying pines within the forest now make themselves plainly felt as they walk along the frozen river. Its cold rush burns Sarah's raw cheeks, tingling with prickled barbs, unseen, but suffered severely. Trying to shield her face, she winces with the misery of the abrasive tattered woollen cape she wears rubbing against her exposed skin. Pressing her hands to her cheeks, she tries to comfort her growing distress caused by the physical agony she endures. The softness of the deerskin gives some relief, but as she releases them from her cheeks, she stares at her mittens, now bearing the evidence of her misery. The reddened stains left upon them leave no doubt of the poor condition she is in. Of the wounds she has acquired upon the march, one seems a mercy: retreating to a place within, Sarah is protected from her inconceivable reality; thinking nothing, feeling nothing, she simply exists.

Despite voracious hunger precipitated by a long day upon the hard surface of the ice, no one sits idly awaiting their ration by the growing flames of the nightly fire. Superseding their desire for the warm, filling meat is the need to tend their wounds. No distinction being made between captive and captor; all suffer in equal measure.

Bloodied by the constant rubbing of the straps from their snowshoes, their feet, soaked in the freezing meltwaters, are made soft, injuring them more deeply than before. Numbed by the endless marching they found some reprieve from the suffering, until they stopped.

Not wanting to touch the horrific injuries, Sarah stares at her feet. Unnaturally pale, they are swollen and wrinkled beyond recognition. Submitting to the despair, she cries looking upon them. The seeping blood slows as they lie exposed to the frost of the night air.

Having quickly tended to his own wounds, the Observant Enemy moves to Sarah's side to clean and wrap her feet. The warmth of his touch upon her numbing foot causes her to retreat. Pulling her knees close, she drags her unresponsive feet in the snow, leaving a trail of blood, evoking memories of such trails by his doing. She stops his attempts with one unwavering look of scorn. She is hardened by his betrayal of an understanding she believed they had, and no attempt at kindness, not even the want for relief, overcomes her mistrust. Angrily throwing the scraps at her, he turns to rejoin the boys, now untying the packs upon the sled.

She stays perfectly still for a few minutes to show her resolve. Finally giving in to the demanding pain, she picks up the fabric strips strewn about her. Meticulously wrapping her seemingly brittle feet, she moves slowly to reduce the agony of the slightest touch. Finding them icy cold, she attempts to rub them warm, which instantly sends a shock of excruciating pain throughout her body. Before she can proceed any further, a sharp cry from the opposite side of the fire rings out, echoing mournfully over the surface of the river they camp by. Watching the commotion, she sees Thomas French, reduced to little more than a pack mule, crying over his own wretched, blackened toes. The Silent Enemy, usually devoid of any care for his captives, moves to aid the poor man, signalling the dire nature he is in. Not understanding why toes would turn such a colour, she notices the concern in their captor's eyes as he examines Thomas's feet. His quick assessment complete, he turns, calling to his companion, who immediately rushes to pull more scraps from their packs.

After gingerly wrapping Thomas's feet, they quickly pull him by the fire, his legs outstretched near the flames.

"No! It hurts too much." As Thomas retracts his legs, the Silent Enemy brings his hands hard upon them, keeping him in place.

"You will lose toes if not warmed." Silenced as much by the ghastly warning as by the one that spoke it, Thomas bites his lips to stifle any further outbursts. Staring at his feet, he sits quietly suffering the feeling returning to his frost-bitten toes.

Having seen the enemy's grave concern, Sarah moves her legs to the fire, soon followed by Mary French and the boys, who have finished taking the meat from the packs. After the rations are passed around, all eat with outstretched legs seeking the heat of the flames. Sarah senses life return to her feet, not by a soothing warmth, but by sharp, painful twinges that grow in number until they give way to a steady throbbing, mimicking that of her heartbeat. Despite the ache that persists, she finds relief in it. Her mind free from such concentration of physical suffering, Sarah resumes her observation of the others, with one in particular holding her attention. The memory of his voice gently asking, "Do it for me?" makes her notice Ebenezer as never before. In Deerfield, she thought no more of him than as a friend of her brother Edward, but as she watches him closely tending the fire, she is astonished by his much altered appearance. The boy she knew in their innocent days has taken on the features of so many a man of their village, though much more dishevelled than one is used to seeing. His wiry beard, patchy and uneven, is much in contrast to Thomas French's full one, which nearly consumes his face in silvery grey and black whiskers. But it is his eyes that captivate her most. As he sweeps his hand across his forehead to control his golden, tussled hair, now long and unruly, his eyes are revealed to be a blue that reminds her of their own windy river in a bright summer day.

Feeling the effects of returning warmth, the abating ache in her feet, and the weight of plentiful food in her belly, Sarah eases into a dreamlike state, comfortable, and safe — for now.

# 61

❧❧

"He promised it would only be a few days more, and a few days I can last," Sarah whispers trying to convince herself as she affixes her snowshoes to her feet for another day. She gasps as the straps pull tight over the open sores on her swollen feet. The extra padding of the wrapping provided the night before proves an insufficient barrier and the wounds quickly reopen and the red stains on her moccasins deepen. As she attempts to bring herself upright, her stiff, weakened muscles resist her efforts, making her unsteady. It is now the painfully familiar way she greets each day. With nothing to look forward to, the effort seems insurmountable, but today is different. Holding to the promise of but "a few days more," made by a most unexpected friend, Sarah looks to the horizon across the frozen river, beginning to show signs of the day's impending arrival. As the others finish their small meal, she stands watching the wispy clouds in the sky become deep reds and pinks, transforming into fiery orange with the growing light. Surprising her as if it was not expected at all, the first spark of day suddenly appears, filling Sarah with a nearly forgotten emotion — happiness. Instantly transported to another time, another place, she is in awe at the speed at which the growing, blazing orb rises from the far shore. Clinging to the land by a small tether of light, it suddenly lets go, floating into the sky. The warmth setting her free from the grip of the piercing cold, Sarah closes her eyes, soaking in the temporary release from purgatory.

Sounds from within the camp soon invade Sarah's reprieve, reminding her of the ordeal ahead. Opening her eyes, she stares so long at the searing, radiant sun, now ascending to take its usual place in the sky, that when she turns to look at the group, only a black spot exists where faces should be. A strange notion washes over her. Looking to the enemy who had once shown false concern, she stares at his featureless face, feeling a sense of retribution in taking his identity from him. *We are nothing to you, and now you are nothing to me,* she thinks vengefully. As her vision returns, she finds herself under his ever-watchful gaze, and is instantly made the captive once more.

The day, having begun with the promise of a reviving sun, soon gives way to changing fortunes. As the clouds grow dark and ominous on the horizon, Sarah notes the increasing speed at which their captors drive them. Even the smooth surface of the frozen river cannot hasten their march. With no impediment on the open space of the river, the gusting winds blow with such force it seems they make no progress at all. Ice rain pelts their already raw faces like shards of glass, but even as it turns to the heavy snow of an oncoming late-winter storm, it provides no relief. The captives are exhausted by the effort of walking through the heavy sludge of the accumulating snow mixed with the meltwaters, but their captors have no mercy.

"Move!" Yells are heard over the winds when the group falters, and the captors poke and prod ruthlessly as the march stalls. Mired by the increasing clumsiness caused by lifting the heavy weight accumulating on her snowshoes, Sarah is cruelly connected to reality by the severe pain of her seizing muscles and the fear of being lost in the tempest they now face. The shoreline having disappeared in a veil of white, she loses all bearings. Desperately relying on maintaining pace with the obscured figures ahead of her, she knows if she lags she will be swallowed up by the storm.

*Is that talking I hear?* Sarah wonders, straining to make sense of faint sounds in the distance. Isolated from the others by several paces, she marches near the end of the group, the Observant Enemy taking up the rear of their dwindling, ragged band as usual. With the voices swirling about, she cannot tell where they come from. Confused by their changing direction, she begins to wonder if her imagination is playing tricks on her or if it is simply the sound of the raging winds. She dares not look about trying to follow the sounds, for she can feel eyes fixed upon her and she can now clearly hear his laboured breath only steps behind. Disturbed by his proximity, Sarah wills herself forward to put some distance between them. Making gains in her stride, despite the sharp pains of her injured feet, she takes satisfaction in her continued defiance, and soon loses focus on the unknown sounds that persist, instead revelling in the imagined distress of her enemy.

Through the blinding white before her, a figure begins to take shape. As the gap between them closes, Sarah recognizes the source of the sound she has heard on the winds. Lamenting her losses, Mary French, weakened and despondent, cries so pitifully Sarah cannot fathom what drives her on. She knows that even as all struggle, it is this heartsick woman who is in the most peril. No help is offered to any. As Sarah slowly passes Mary, she takes a sidelong glance to see if she comprehends her fate. Finding her looking into a void, Sarah takes strange comfort in it.

Unable to resist the urge to look back once last time, Sarah finds the lone figure standing still in the pure-white backdrop of the storm. Suddenly shrouded by the driving snow, Mary French ceases to exist. Only the occasional, fading cry caught on the wind gives any evidence of the forlorn mother yet calling to her lost children.

# 62

Stumbling with every step, the group not having walked a mile since losing one to the ravages of the storm, they can no longer combat the wrath Mother Nature unleashes on them. The snow is becoming too deep, the winds too strong, and what strength they have called upon is now no match for the storm's fury.

Led up the embankment to shelter in the trees that line the river, Sarah finds herself too weak to make this small rise. Standing in place, she is unable to take another step toward the unexpected rest awaiting her. The mercy of such exhaustion is the absence of fear. As with the void that welcomed Mary French, such liberation awaits Sarah that she does not struggle against it. Her body easing, her shoulders drop and her breathing slows as a warmth from deep within washes over her. The tense expression of unrelenting torment relaxes, and any remnants of memories of what had been, of what could be, dissipate into nothingness.

The Observant Enemy, fully expecting her to follow once he overtakes her, turns back briefly to shoot her a look he knows will compel her to move, but the serene, wraithlike beauty who stands motionless stuns him.

"Kaniehtiio!" Shocked by the drastic change, he rushes to her, shaking her violently to bring her back from what he knows will soon be an irreversible journey. Finding his efforts have no effect, he sweeps her into his arms. Despite his own waning strength, he carries her to where the others are now building makeshift shelters from boughs being stripped from the surrounding trees.

Slumping to the ground, he cradles Sarah as he once cradled young Mary.

"Shonatakakwani! Bring furs," he calls to young Thomas, who responds instantly, now recognizing the Mohawk name he has been given. He rushes to secure the immediate aid his captor requires. Turning to Thomas French, he commands harshly, "You build her a shelter!"

* * *

The cocoon where Sarah finds sanctuary remains impermeable. The faint, disconnected sounds beyond neither alarm nor give hope, their hum simply resonating as the winds swirling about.

Sheltering in the tightly woven lean-to, the Observant Enemy, having assumed care of Sarah, watches as the last shafts of light entering through slight cracks are snuffed out. The snow burying them turns day as night. He holds Sarah closely as she lies unconscious with fatigue. Pulling what furs he has negotiated from his companion over her, he tucks them in around her to ward off the chill. The Silent Enemy is unconvinced of her making their homelands and sees no value in her, for she proves to be defiant in nature. The warriors have nearly come to blows over the issue. Singing what he once sang to Sarah's young charge — the song he oft sings to his own children — he cradles her for what seems hours, sensing no change at all. Limp in his arms, she is unresponsive to his voice, his shifting positions, or his unrelenting shivering, for he takes no furs for himself. But as the hours pass and the winds calm, he can hear her slow, steady breathing indicating she rests easy.

Knowing if she wakes it will frighten her to be so close, he gently lifts her, resting her by his side on top of one of the furs he has smoothed out to make a comfortable bed in the deep snow below them. Closing his eyes only briefly, he keeps himself occupied by occasionally adjusting the furs to ensure Sarah's comfort, and imagining the joy his wife will feel when he brings their daughter home. Despite her resistance, and this distressing turn, he senses the curiosity that is so evident in this young one will serve her well, not allowing her to succumb to the fate of the other weak ones once amongst them.

"Sarah. Sarah." Woken by the forgotten sound of her mother's voice, Sarah scrambles to her feet, attempting to follow the voice calling her. Hitting her head hard on the boughs overhead, she is momentarily stunned by the sharp blow. Crawling about in the dark as a trapped, wild creature, she grasps for anything that will help her escape the black world she has awoken to.

"Mama! Mama, I am here," she desperately calls out.

"Kaniehtiio, you are safe. Safe," the warrior says, trying to calm her. She stops at the sound of his deep voice. She remains perfectly still, and only her laboured breathing gives any sign of her yet being within the confines. Regaining some sense of what is happening, she rapidly retreats to the far corner of the tiny shelter, which removes her but a few inches. Unable to see who is next to her, she listens for any noise, but cannot hear anything above her own racing heart. Beating painfully, it deafens her to the unknown danger. Making herself as small as possible, as though she will not be found if she does so, she concentrates on steadying her fast, laboured breathing so she might hear the still being in the darkness with her. The wind having died down, she can barely make out the steady breathing of someone so close she feels the warm breath upon her, causing her to pull back until the sticks of the rough shelter dig deeply into her back. Trying to focus on the black form before her, as her eyes adjust to the dark, Sarah does not scream, for even in the confusion, she remembers no help will come. Despite the painful jabs in her back, she dares not move in the slightest.

"Kaniehtiio." Breaking the tension, the warrior gently repeats his earlier message. "You are safe."

Knowing who now shelters in this cramped space with her does not ease her fear. For a long time she does not move, nor does the Observant Enemy attempt any further conversation. Having pulled her back from the brink of madness, he does not want to chance pushing her further, for the outcome is decisive. His companion made it clear that no aid will be given to a lost cause. If she threatens their own survival, he will take matters into his own hands. With no doubt this is the last chance afforded this girl, and the warrior treads carefully, pulling her back from the edge with patience. In his silence, he allows her to ease into an understanding that he will not harm her. He is not oblivious to the effect the mercy killings have had on this young girl, unaccustomed as she is to their ways. As with les Français, it seems brutal to les Anglais. He had not welcomed the rendering of fate, but would not see the young, the weak, and the old suffer a lingering death. At the very least they deserved a swift end to meet their creator. Knowing the ache of loss, and now sitting so near the hope of a new beginning, he does not want to break her spirit, for it is fragile. He had not known when starting this journey who might be chosen, but he quickly felt a bond to this one who is so much his own lost daughter that, though she was born Anglaise, she is surely Mohawk at heart. He will not let his hopes be dashed by his own impatience, and so he calmly awaits her first move.

Sarah's tattered clothing provides no relief from the penetrating chill, and she tentatively reaches into the darkness to grab the furs that rest on her feet. Realizing there is no option for escape, and wanting for the relief of its warmth, she slowly tugs until the furs cover her to her neck. Not wanting to accidently brush up against her captor, she does not release her knees from their position, even as her legs cramp with the lack of movement. Waiting for some sign that her captor is displeased with her taking the furs, she hears almost no sound at all come from his direction. The shelter, thick with pine needles and buried under the weight of the fallen snow, makes it impossible for her eyes to adjust any further, and so she sits motionless with the darkened silhouette set against the blackness of night.

Above the rich aroma of pine that fills the small space, Sarah smells the familiar pungent scent that makes her mouth water, and her stomach greets its welcome appearance. Feeling the meat being placed atop the fur near her feet, she resists its temptation for a few agonizing minutes. As her stomach growls in protest to her hesitation, she knows the only way to quell its disquieting noise is to partake of the nourishment she desperately needs. Cautiously, she pulls her hand from beneath the cover. Fumbling for the meat, she runs her hand over the coarse surface until she reaches the reward she seeks. Tentatively bringing it to her mouth, she takes the first bite. Pulling the tough meat with her teeth until a small piece releases, her mouth instantly fills with water at its arrival, but she minds to chew it slowly. Hungering for more, she finishes the last morsel of her meagre meal. Her stomach finally ceasing its deafening noises, which she admonished herself for. Sitting quietly for a few minutes she weighs the decision to stretch out her legs, which now cause more grief than is bearable. With her feet numbing from the lack of movement, she warily begins to allow her legs to unfurl from their cramped position. Not knowing exactly where her captor is, or if she will brush against him, she breaks into a sweat with the strain of meticulously moving her legs gradually, inch by inch, until they are, thankfully, extended straight in front of her. The tingling in her feet quickly intensifies as they come back to life, but the throbbing of injuries is not nearly as painful as she expected. Trying to understand why they feel so relieved, she wiggles her toes, and in doing so realizes her feet are bound tightly with what she assumes are new wrapping applied by the unseen enemy. Feeling such hatred, then such . . . gratitude, makes her uneasy. The urge to thank him is only diminished by the damaging images replayed over and over in her memory. The voice of her mother, reminding her of an almost forgotten place, makes the knowledge of now sheltering with the one who ripped her from her life unbearable. Unable to flee, she holds to Ebenezer's promise, "Only a few short days."

# 63

Heaving on the makeshift door of the shelter, the Observant Enemy grunts with the effort to escape from under the weight of the heavy snow. As a few dim shafts of light break through, Sarah gets her first glimpse of just how small the space is, making it more disconcerting than when in total darkness. Rearing back, the warrior throws his body against the door, bringing day flooding in. Momentarily disoriented as her eyes adjust to the early morning light, she realizes she is being buried by a rush of snow filling the space. Panicked, she scrambles toward the light of the open door, where her captor is already fighting to halt the torrent.

"Dig!" he orders. Immediately heeding his command, for she is now trapped to the waist, she digs frantically, trying to break free of the snow's grip. Crawling away from the shelter, now wholly consumed, they struggle to their feet. Sarah is stunned by the desolation of the landscape that greets them. There is no indication that the others are yet amongst them, and her heart sinks, thinking them lost.

Scared to be alone with him, and realizing there is nowhere to run, she is unable to stop the tears, and she cries softly.

"Quiet!" The order is given with such severity that she instantly stops and scans the scene, looking for the reason for the warrior's intense concentration. Cocking his head, he listens to the silence of the forest, seeming to hear something just out of sight.

With visions of being hunted by wolves, Sarah tries to hear any sound at all. As he turns his head suddenly in another direction, she wonders if the faint noise she too hears is the creature approaching. But as the muffled sounds around them grow from beneath several mounds, Sarah sees the camp come to life, as one shelter after the other reveals its once buried occupants. The last to emerge from his snowy cave is the one she longs to see. Brushing off the snow from his clumsy exit, Ebenezer stretches to his full, tall height. Sarah's gaze rests upon him for a moment. When he gives a faint smile acknowledging her notice of him, she blushes and turns her attentions to the others, pretending that is what she was doing in the first place.

Awash with grief, Thomas French and his son seem much altered since Sarah last saw them. Imagining another mound upon the ice of the river, she understands the depth of their despair.

*Four . . . there are only four of us left*, she thinks mournfully. The loss of even one now seems to decimate their group. She does not take their captors into account, for though they march as one — sheltered as one — they are yet the enemy, separating them in the utmost from the experience of those at their mercy. Looking at each forlorn face, she makes a startling realization: *I am the only girl.* Rare was the interaction between she and Mary French, but there was comfort in her presence. Now, standing amongst the men and boys, Sarah feels the full weight of isolation.

Handed a large piece of meat by her captor, Sarah takes it without meeting his gaze. Realizing the others must think her sinful for being alone with the enemy — a transgression of all propriety — she flushes with embarrassment. Though she dreads their disapproval, she can resist no longer to know what judgement exists in their eyes. Not one takes any notice of her.

Eating her meal, she contemplates the judgement that awaits her upon her return to Deerfield, for surely they know not what sacrifices of pride and dignity must be made to survive. Despite her desperate reasoning in imagined conversations, she is unconvinced they will understand.

Her stomach filling after only a few bites, Sarah is unsure of what to do with the large portion remaining. They have not been given so much before, and she wonders what such a change in the usual ways means. Anything out of the strange but customary practices of their march poses questions she fears the answers to. *Are they going to leave me behind with only this meat to sustain me until I freeze or starve? I am of no use. I carry nothing. I do not hunt and learn as the boys do. They are going to leave me here.* Even as the others move to the river, she stands fixed to the ground, overwhelmed by each devastating possibility.

"Come! You. Come now," the Observant Enemy summons as he turns to ensure Sarah moves to take her place ahead of him. Seeing her alarmed expression, he runs back, roughly strapping her snowshoes on. The group stops upon hearing him beckon Sarah. They seem to wait patiently, but he knows well the thought running through his companion's mind. Wincing as the straps pull tightly about her feet,

Sarah does not make a noise, sensing her situation is already precarious. Grabbing the meat from her hand, he pulls a small pouch from around his neck and tucks it inside. Quickly placing it around Sarah's neck, he looks directly at her.

"We do not stop until we make the big water. Eat when you walk," he says in a cautionary tone. He shoves her, as if to show his companion he maintains control of his captive, and Sarah stumbles forward, taking the first of many steps in a long day that will see them fight for every inch gained through the freshly laid snow on their way to the "big water."

# 64

The snowshoes heavy and cumbersome on the powdered surface of the river, often gathering as much snow on top as they have below, but the captives do not seem to mind, for their feet remain relatively dry, allowing them to make good progress. Such small mercies as this newly formed barrier from the soaking water below, gives contentment in disproportionate measure. As if they are not bothered by the hours of marching without rest, they eat while en route, each keeping pace, which eases the tension that existed when those weakened by the march threatened the survival of all.

With a constant eye to her new friend near the front of the group, Sarah wonders if he hopes, as she does, to have occasion to speak again. Thinking to their brief conversation, she ponders just how many days "a few more" really are. Having no sense of how many days now separate her from home, for it seems an eternity, she decides to keep track going forward, if only to keep alive the hope Ebenezer has reignited. *I think we have seen a few days pass since we walked upon the river.* She dreads to think upon the marker events of those days, but they give a measure of time passing, so she uses what she can. *Upon the first day, he spoke to me. The second . . . the second . . .* she pauses. The memory of the disappearing figure standing motionless as it was consumed by a blanket of white makes her heart feel the full weight of sadness so evidently suffered by Thomas French and his son. *We lost Mrs. French.* Perplexed, she searches for days gone missing. *Was it only yesterday she was lost? That does not seem right.* The days mix frustratingly together, some seeming endless and others a shadowy nightmare, the details confused by the horror they brought. Her head aches with the effort to bring clarity. *Today must be the third day. The "big water" must be the end of our journey. That is why we push on.* Momentarily jubilant by the prospect, she feels a surge of energy rush through her, hastening her pace. Searching the river stretched out before them, she notes the warrior guiding them toward a narrow branch of the river shrouded in darkness, as the forest closes in around it. *Surely that is not the way,* Sarah thinks uneasily.

With Ebenezer ahead by several paces, Sarah looks to him for any sign that will give confirmation that he, too, feels apprehension. From the mere gate of his stride, little can be determined. Regardless, for many miles Sarah stares at his back, taking notice of the slightest movement: the swing of his arms as he walks — *Did it slow? Speed up?* — the tension in his shoulders, the turning of his head as he scans the narrowing river before him. Frustratingly, he never turns enough to reveal his expression. The intensity of studying these insignificant gestures does not ease her mind, as she often imagines she sees meaning in the smallest changes.

Unexpectedly, the sun suddenly bursts forth from below a bank of clouds resting on the horizon. Penetrating the forest, flashes of sunlight dance upon them, but Sarah is not captivated, as once she was, but curses its deceiving effect. *Now I shall not be able to see what he thinks at all.* Feeling the comfort of his presence, if only from the back, slip from her, she casts her eyes to the snow at her feet, retreating to her protective, insular world.

Turning into a sharp bend where the river begins to widen, Sarah, having wished for such opportunity during the day's long march, strains to see Ebenezer's face as it comes into profile. Searching the furrow of his brow for any sign of concern, she is taken aback by what she finds. There is a keenness in his eyes, and what she is sure is a growing smile upon his bearded face, and she follows his gaze. Rounding the bend, she sees what holds his attention. Opening up before them, wide and expansive, awash in a pink mist of the setting sun, is the big water.

# 65

No sooner has Sarah laid eyes on the immense frozen lake before them than they stop on its banks to make camp. The men and boys, setting about their usual routine, prepare the fire and unload the furs to set them about for each to take his or her place. As they do so, Sarah notes a relaxing of her captors' usual stern manner, making her believe they are near their destination.

*Perhaps it is hidden in the forest upon the far shore*, Sarah thinks, attempting to quiet her nagging distrust. She tries to see any signs of habitation — a glint of a fire in the distance, an unnatural structure amid the barrier of trees as evidence that others exist — but as darkness consumes them, any hope of making sense of the far shore vanishes with the last hint of day.

By the light of the growing flames, Ebenezer looks to Sarah, ensuring she partakes in the offerings of food and water. Feeling a growing sense of responsibility for her, this young girl amongst men, he looks upon her as a sister. Burdened by the memory of his own lost sisters, he cannot recall their sweet, cherub faces; instead, he is only left with their final moments when in the clutches of terror. Distraught at having witnessed so many of his own family meet a horrific end, he looks to Sarah, vowing to protect that which his friend surely holds dear. *I will protect her in your stead, Edward.*

The full moon illuminating the lake before them quickly ascends in the sky, casting a bright glow upon the vast open space. Night turns to a false day, and the trees on the opposite shore cast long shadows upon the ice and bathe those around the fire in a surreal light that transforms the re-emerging landscape. Captivated, Sarah imagines they have passed into another realm. Gazing upon its pure, unknown beauty, none amongst them but their captors have seen such vastness. The unimpeded views of the big water leaves them momentarily in awe of such natural wonder.

They are silent in their observations. Only the occasional snap of the fire sending burning embers floating into the sky pulls their attention from the unfolding spectacle. Shadows shift upon the patchwork of windblown drifts set about on the clear, icy surface, making the scene change with every inch the moon climbs higher into the night sky. Sitting under this infinite canopy, alive with countless glimmering stars occasionally streaking across the sky, they cannot comprehend the scale of such places. Where once they lived sheltered on the frontier, wilderness surrounding them on all sides, here that world seems to fall away, giving way to a beautiful expanse that is neither tamed by borders nor burdened by man, for it seems wholly untouched. Their own presence seeming insignificant, they sit in the reverence it commands.

Sarah watches once-radiant stars dissolve into the luminous white glow as the light consumes them. Assuming them absorbed by the moon itself, she watches as it steadily glides through the sky consuming others and allowing the once-lost stars to flicker to life once more. The rebirth of each stirs in her a powerful sense of hope, a wanting for them to prevail, though they pale in size to that which threatens their existence. At twelve, Sarah cannot understand that she is much like the stars she gazes upon. A small flickering light against the backdrop of a great struggle for continental supremacy, she, seemingly insignificant — seemingly extinguished — yet exists, yet has hope of emerging from that which consumes her.

"Les Français call this place Lac Champlain after our enemy." Shattering the hold night has on them, the Observant Enemy's voice catches the attention of his captives. Paying no mind to their perplexed expressions, he continues, "We know it as Caniaderi Guarunte. When we journey across the ice tomorrow we will once again be upon the trails laid by our own people." Speaking in a low voice, as though he, too, does not want to disturb the ancient ways of night, he is barely audible above the crackling fire. Thomas French, the usual target of his admonishments, shifts uncomfortably, expecting the opposite to what his almost genial tone implies. Thomas's suddenly rigid posture seems to instill in the others a similar expectation, and Sarah looks about, confused by the rising tension. "We have travelled many days in the lands of the Gannongagehronnon, but this night will be our last." The warrior's voice remains steady as he settles back against a drift, relaxing into it. "Tomorrow we are amongst the Kanien'kéha."

*Ebenezer was right, it was only a few days until we arrived at our destination.* Now understanding it is their captors' lands they march to tomorrow, Sarah is buoyed by the anticipation of it. The unknown of what awaits does not distress her, for the possibility of the arduous march coming to an end provides such relief that she basks in its release. As the flames soar, Sarah looks to her true friend, momentarily lost in her admiration of his striking figure. *He seems more handsome, more a man with his beard. I hope he is not quick to go back to looking the boy.*

Fascinated by the captor's unfamiliar words, spoken in his thick accent, young Thomas seems to forget his father's nervousness and hesitantly ventures, "What is Ga-nien-ge-ha?" He pronounces it nearly as well as the warrior, and his father is taken aback by his son's aptitude in speaking the language of the enemy.

Motioning to himself and his silent companion, he answers, "We are Kanien'kéha." The slip of a smile crossing his lips, his pleasure at his young student's interest and ability is evident. "Our people, the Ka-nien-ké-ha," he reiterates slowly, allowing Thomas to perfect his pronunciation, for he silently mouths it as his teacher speaks, "are the keepers of the eastern door of the Haudenosaunee lands. Our alliances have taken us far from these places," he says, his voice fading as he casts his eye to the shadowy world awaiting on the far shore. The conversation abruptly ends as his lingering gaze rests upon their lands. The small weary group is left with only the distant howl of wolves and the hissing wet branches set atop the fire to fill the chasm which has suddenly opened up, engulfing them. The longing for home is a strange bond they share.

For nearly an hour, no one speaks. Taking comfort in his presence, Sarah watches Ebenezer as he casts his eyes to the sky above. Drifting in and out of sleep, she struggles against it, not wanting to seem a child. She knows she is at a disadvantage. Even as she mourns the loss of so many, there was a peculiar consolation in knowing she was not the weakest, not the focus of her captors' attentions. But now, she stands out amongst the group.

"It is good that we cross the big water now."

Bolting upright, unsure of where she is, Sarah quickly regains her senses as she catches Ebenezer's concerned gaze. Gasping to catch her breath, she quickly calms with his reassuring nod. Blushing at her undignified reaction, she lowers her eyes, wringing her dry, cracked hands nervously, as the warrior continues his story.

"While the waters are still we will not have to fear waking Chaousarou, now sleeping in the depths." The ominous tone of his cryptic words piques the attention of the captives, who rally despite their growing fatigue. Though the late hour and relative comfort afforded by the robust fire conspires against them, they are no match against the curiosity, and fear, his words instill.

"Our people tell of the onyarekowa dwelling in Caniaderi Guraunte." Noticing the confused expressions of his rapt audience, he translates using the words of the English. "A great horned serpent. For many generations he has taken our people to the depths. In the time of snow and ice, we need not fear him, but when the waters flow once more, we watch for signs of his return: a ripple upon the water, a darkening shadow below the surface. As our warriors are masters of silence on land, he is the master of the water. There is no escape if detected."

Despite the fearsome nature of the legend, he seems transformed, becoming animated as he tells of the poisonous breath of the serpent, and how it capsizes canoes, devouring the bravest warriors and smallest children alike. Sparing no effort to ensure his audience is thrilled, appalled, and always eager to know more, he harkens familiar times, memories, of telling the stories of his people around a fire such as this to the ones he longs to see. The nature of this audience fades into the background, as he regales them into the early hours of the morning. As his own exhaustion takes hold, he quiets. Silent for a few moments, his expression changes as if contemplating something of a worrying nature.

"Though he sleeps, he will know of our presence tomorrow."

# 66

The next morning, as the group pulls away from the shore, they are exposed to the elements once more upon the vast expanse of the lake they begin to cross. The winds kicking up remind them that winter still has them in its grip. Affixing her cape tightly around her to protect herself against its bite, Sarah studies the patchwork that revealed itself in the moonlight. Light glints on the barren ice, and she is captivated by the wispy snow shifting weightlessly over the gleaming sheets. As it races across the surface as a rippling thread of white, she watches it gather and disperse as if it has a spirit that revels in the freedom of such unimpeded movement.

"Freedom," she says aloud, unaware she does so.

Having come to know her nature, the Observant Enemy watches Sarah carefully, understanding instinctively that the word revives her. He knows she will never fully assent to his will, accept her fate, but he respects her more for her resistance of it, believing it shows great promise for her new life. A daughter such as this will bring him honour, but until that time, he needs a diversion to change her mind, to steal her from the longing for who she once was.

"Ratirontaks," he says pointing to the towering mountains in the distance. Set against the clear blue morning sky, the mountains across the river, many miles away, rise jagged and foreboding. *Are we meant to cross them?* Sarah wonders with dread. *Why point them out if we are not to make for them?* The possibility of renewing the march through mountainous terrain, even now with the rest of a few days treading level ground, overwhelms her, for she knows she has not the endurance to survive.

The anticipated end of their gruelling march does not alleviate her alarm. Too many times she has witnessed hope snatched from the naive to believe with any conviction that she will be saved. *I am the weakest of the group,* she reminds herself, feeling her own insignificance as she looks to the treacherous mountains far beyond the treeline of the opposite shore. Fuelled by her growing panic, the once entrancing lake now takes on a more ominous quality.

Staring into the darkness beneath her moccasin-shorn feet, for no snowshoes are needed on such a surface, she stands on one of the barren sheets of ice she had only moments before taken delight in. Her imagination running rampant, visions of the giant serpent lingering in the depths besiege her. Feeling exposed upon the open ice, she cannot reason it traps the beast, nor that it is merely a legend of their captor's people. It is as real — the fear as real — as any cutting experience of the journey. Terrified, she searches for escape. Seeing the shore behind her fading as a veil of mist rises on the lake, she looks to the shore ahead of them, to the lands of their enemy. The distance to each is crushing; they are in the middle of the big water.

With no choice but to continue walking, she does so avoiding any glance at the slippery surface. Struggling to recall the name of the creature, she fights the compelling urge to look at the ice; it is as if something is willing her to do so. Convinced the beastly face of the serpent will surely appear, she pants uncontrollably, becoming dizzy. In her confusion, the name suddenly rings out in her mind — *Kanien'kéha.*

Her senses heightened, she is terrified of the slightest nuance. Glints of light catching her eye become the shine of the serpent's wet scales rising from the bitterly cold water; the sound of the snow racing across the ice becomes the sound of it slithering over the smooth surface, but none jar her more than the occasional snap of the ice, which brings hellish visions of Kanien'kéha breaking through. Her only reprieve is to set foot on one of the many drifts. It only slightly alleviates her fear, but even the slightest shield from the clear ice below gives her wits enough to follow the group.

With the promise of salvation now only a few feet away, Sarah forgets herself and sprints the few last terrifying steps. Scrambling up the small embankment, she is relieved in such measure that she lets out an audible sigh, catching the attention of the others. Ashamed to have acted in such a way, she sits down and affixes her snowshoes, hoping if she ignores the Silent Enemy, he will release her from his angry stare. Even the necessity of strapping on these painful contraptions cannot make her sorry for their use. They are shielded by the thicket of the forest, and the mountains that precipitated her panic have disappeared from sight, making her forget the daunting prospect of their crossing. But walking upon the shore, Sarah keeps a wary eye on the lake. Though she calms, the name of the serpent Kanien'kéha continues to echo in her mind.

"Are we upon your land?" asks young Thomas in a voice more assured than his tentative attempt at conversation the night before.

The evening spent enthralled by the stories shared by the warrior has given him a sense of confidence that asking such is acceptable.

"Yes," comes the response from a rarely heard voice. The Silent Enemy does not turn to answer, remaining fixed upon his slave ahead of him. Demoralized, Thomas French is defeated not in his captivity alone, but in the luring of his son into such comfortable conversation. "It is good to be amongst the Kanien'kéha again."

Hearing the word spoken aloud in such context, Sarah realizes she has been mistaken in using it for the beast. After glancing side-long at the lake, she turns her gaze to the Silent Enemy, as much a threat to her as the creature in the depths had been. *Let them have the name of the beast,* she thinks spitefully.

"Where do we journey?" continues young Thomas, seeming eager for the answer.

"My brother has guided us many days, and he will guide us now to our home, Kahnawà:ke," comes the pride-filled reply from behind her.

*Brother?* Shocked, Sarah looks ahead to see if Thomas and Ebenezer are as stunned by the revelation as she is. Simply nodding in understanding of what he says, they give no sign that they think much of it. *Did they not understand?* she wonders, hoping it the reason for their indifference. Shaken by the blow of such news, she has not fully realized until now that she took some small comfort in an assurance that she was protected, that the Observant Enemy would fight his rival to safeguard her. *But he will not fight his brother.* It becomes frighteningly clear that she is much more vulnerable than she had imagined.

# 67

⚛

The mood changes once upon the eastern shore. Casting off a tense vigilance their captives were not aware of until it ceased to exist, the warriors no longer seek the source of every sound echoing about them, nor do they keep a wary eye to the trail behind. The assured manner they now assume has much effect on their captives. Even Sarah's initial shock at the revelation of her captors being brothers eventually wears off as they continue their steady march along the lake's edge. An unnatural calm settles upon them. Her visions of the serpent dissipating, Sarah scans the horizon beyond the far shore, seeing for the first time the vista of imposing mountains that had only days before consumed them. Held in awe, she studies the contrasting effect of each layer, one upon the other, with the peaks slowly disappearing as they become ever more shrouded in the mists. She might have imagined them unending if she did not remember the places beyond — they, too, now shrouded in a confusing haze in her mind. She feels no victory in having survived. Despite her youth, she is burdened with a knowing beyond her years — an insight into darkness not many can claim to so intimately understand. Amongst the group walks a ghost: the Sarah Allen of Deerfield, who knew so little of the world as to yearn to explore beyond the horizon, now lies with those lost in the very mountains she gazes upon.

# 68

The searing rays of the late winter sun quicken the snowmelt, causing the group to wilt with the exertion of marching through water-logged snow in such seemingly sweltering heat. Sweating profusely, they shed the few layers they can. Welcoming the rush of the cooling breeze whipping up off the lake from time to time, its icy surface is now a series of shallow puddles. The constant glare of the sun on the water is blinding. Sarah squints to protect her eyes from the burning pain it causes, making it treacherous to navigate the uneven trail. Where once heavy snows and bitter cold made the march punishing, the changing season is no less demanding. With the sun hovering above the western sky, the group finds a clearing in the forest to make camp for the night.

"We hunt for food," calls out the once Silent Enemy to Ebenezer and young Thomas. He throws the clothing he shed earlier in the day atop the sled, not yet brought to a full stop by Thomas French. Immediately forgetting their exhaustion, the boys eagerly jump at the chance to hunt for the evening's meal. Each is handed a musket they are surprised to see has been hidden amid the supplies. Following the warriors into the forest, they disappear from sight.

Left behind in the stillness of the clearing, Sarah would believe herself alone, had she not seen the dejected Thomas French standing by the sled looking to where his son stood only moments before. Charged with readying the camp, he tends his usual chores, while Sarah goes to gather sticks from the nearby underbrush, as she has seen the boys do. Afraid to venture too far into the dense forest, she tugs on what branches protrude from the ground, piling them in her arms. After placing her unstable bundle in the center of the clearing, she goes back, looking for more to keep the fire burning brightly for a long night of storytelling, which is now expected and looked forward to. Sarah returns with a third bundle just as the sun sets, bringing with it the return of the damp frost. The tentative flickering of a small flame from the interior of the fire suddenly blazes to life, illuminating the camp in a brilliant glow.

"Ow!" She cries, reeling from the stinging pain. The intense heat feels as if it scorches her face, now red and peeling from the burning sun.

"Sarah, you must wrap some cloth about your face, for it bleeds," comes an unexpected response from the far corner where Thomas is pulling the furs from the sled. Reminded of her appalling condition, she thinks not to the injury, but to what Ebenezer must think of her. Pulling her hand from her mitten, she runs it over her raw cheeks, which are in much worse shape than the last time she checked her appearance. Grabbing a handful of snow to relieve the burning, Thomas suddenly appears at her side.

"Let me see," he says in a low, raspy voice that compels her to obey by the surprise of it. Turning to see his heavily bearded face and catching sight of his dark, sunken eyes, seeming to retreat into the caverns of their sockets, she only now notices his emaciated state. Bringing a clean remnant of cloth to her face, he dabs it gently. Flinching occasionally, she does not stop him from cleaning her wounds, nor can she stop staring at his abhorrent features.

"The snow will dry it further, Sarah; best to do as I am each night, and during the day. I know it is warm, but cover your cheeks so they do not suffer further damage." His gentle voice falters in speaking the final word, the result of his weakened state, making her sorry he suffers so. Having thought him indifferent, she sees his true nature emerge. Alone and free to do as he will, he takes no time for himself, but gives her comfort. Unable to suppress the rush of emotion overtaking her, she begins to cry, her tears burning as they roll down her raw, wounded cheeks. As she averts her eyes, he continues to dab her face. Swallowing hard to tame the sobs, she looks up to thank him, and finds him gazing upon her in way she has nearly forgotten. His lip quivers as if his mind speaks words his voice cannot convey. His eyes, welling with tears, show such pain that Sarah wants nothing more than to look away, to escape the reminder, but in her heart, she knows in maintaining his gaze, she offers him comfort — a connection he has not felt in many weeks, the same connection she once knew so well. She yearns for him to embrace her, to tell her everything will be as it was, that she will be saved — redeemed. Though the face she looks upon is unfamiliar, her heart dreams it is her father. Hearing the drone of voices coming from the forest, they look in the direction from where they come, and Thomas walks away to resume his work.

As they eat the rabbit, proudly supplied through Ebenezer's hunting ability, the nightly tale begins.

## 69

"**M**any centuries ago, there was much war in our lands," the Observant Enemy says, looking about the darkness around him. A cloudless night, the moon reflects only dim light upon them, as it is now nearly cut perfectly in half from its former glory of their first night upon the shores of the great lake. The stars dancing above no longer hold the attention of the captives as the night's story does.

"Tekana:wita, the Peacemaker brought harmony to our peoples." As has become usual, the warrior pauses, listening carefully to young Thomas attempting to pronounce the word, correcting as needed. His grasp of the language is extraordinary, bringing much pride to his captor, knowing Thomas's place amongst their people will be welcomed.

"Dega...na...wida," he repeats. The special attention young Thomas receives leaves no doubt in his father's mind that his son has been claimed by his enemy. He had often heard news in the meeting-house of boys being assimilated into the villages of those who had stolen them, but at the time he did not believe it could be true. *They are a cunning enemy*, he concedes, observing those captivated, even enjoying, the story. *They tempt our children with such small mercies that they do not recognize they are ensnared in a trap.* Having seen his son, Ebenezer, and now Sarah, once the most resistant by her ways and lack of attempt to conceal her unmistakable thoughts, succumb to the false humanity, he doubts it no more.

"Tekana:wita was sent by the Creator to bring peace, for we had lost our way. No longer did the voices of our elders ring in our ears, no longer did we listen to our wise women; only the war cries rang in our ears and in our hearts. The Onkwe honwe became enemies."

"Oh-gwey-ho-wey," Thomas repeats, with Ebenezer now joining the attempt, the fire capturing the pleasure in his eyes. *They seem to sparkle*, Sarah admires, unknowingly mimicking his broad smile. Settling against a large soft drift covered with one of the furs, Sarah eases into the warmth of the bright fire, watching Ebenezer closely, secretly hoping for a glance in her direction.

Though he does his best to speak the language of his captives, the warrior often reverts to French, and as the story intensifies, he speaks his own language, often forgetting to translate his words..

"Kaheto ktha became upset that her daughter could not explain the changes in her body as Tekana:wita grew within her. Believing it to be the work of a . . . sorcière," he stumbles, trying to find the right word, looking to his student for aid.

"Sorcery?" Thomas offers.

"Non, the person who does sorcery," the warrior repeats, using his word.

"Witch," Ebenezer offers in a grave, hesitant tone. The word hangs heavy over them.

"Oui, witch," he repeats, nodding at Ebenezer in thanks, oblivious to the effect the word has on his captives. With troubles at Salem not twelve years before, the cautionary tale often cited from the pulpit, the mood suddenly changes. Continuing with his story, he does not note the shift, but his brother, ever-observant of his captive's ways, watches their brows furrow as they draw back slightly from their once-eager anticipation of the unfolding tale.

His experience in war and knowledge of the way of the English being greater than his brother's, he is wary of their seeming submission, knowing it is often insincere, a ploy to deceive their true intentions of escape. Only one has not wavered, but he is subdued by the labour he supplies. Holding no value after their return, his slave will be bargained away, but this seemingly indistinguishable sign around the fire speaks of the trouble the others may yet pose to those awaiting them in their village. The influence of the Reverend is far-reaching, for even now he holds the young ones in his grip.

The Observant Enemy, using his natural ability as a storyteller, brings his words to life and has a profound effect upon his rapt audience.

"Kahetehsuk gave birth to Tekana:wita, but her mother would not accept him. Intent on killing the child she believed to be the result of evil deeds, she took him for a walk as her daughter slept. Cutting away the ice, she dropped Tekana:wita in to be swept away."

Sarah shivers, remembering herself slipping under the ice. The memory is so vivid she can almost feel the strong pull of the frigid water dragging her under, the ache to be carried home, and its promise stolen from her.

"When the grandmother returned to her daughter, she heard a baby crying, and there in the arms of his mother was Tekana:wita. Wanting to rid them of this evil, she stole the baby away again, digging a hole in the snow and burying him."

Sarah becomes increasingly agitated as his story evokes ghastly images — memories of such things much like what he now speaks of — and she ceases listening, instead becoming preoccupied with a pressing matter. *We have been five . . . six . . . days in their lands?* Struggling to make sense of each sunrise and sunset since crossing the lake, Sarah is furious at herself for forgetting to keep track. *On the first day . . . or was that the second? When did we cross the lake, day two?*

SNAP! Burning embers fly in all directions, and those gathered around the fire flick the hot, glowing pieces from their clothing, except Sarah, who glares at her enemy, finding herself released from the spell he has cast.

Turning her attention to Ebenezer, who is again absorbed in the tale of their enemy, a dire question rings out in her mind. *Has he been a willing participant in the deception?*

⚜

## 70

Embracing the agony of her pained body, Sarah realizes it keeps her connected to the hate and anger she will not relinquish again. Unable, unwilling, to control a rage that has simmered too long, she unleashes her disgust at such injustice, sparing none from her internal tirade. Holding no further illusions and her admiration now replaced by fury, Sarah turns her attention to her once-trusted friend ahead of her on the trail, the one who had promised their march would soon end. *He lied to keep my obedience.*

*Does he not seethe with anger?* She scowls, watching Ebenezer carry on an easy conversation with young Thomas. *They took his brothers peacefully working in the fields, not this past harvest season. His mother died in plain view. He saw her take the fatal blow.* Cringing at the memory of the ghastly sound, she shakes her head as if to deny any further affliction from it. *A beloved sister disappeared into the forest, led away by her captors, and who knows the loss he suffered when they attacked . . .* Vivid flashes now relentlessly attacking her senses, it is as if she relives the carnage left behind in Deerfield. Imagining the very enemy, now walking relaxed in their stride, to have perpetrated it all, she cannot fathom how Ebenezer so easily forgets. *Surely he must, for I see him lean forward captivated by each word of the nightly tales, as once I was with the ones of Grandfather Lamberton.* The very thought of it stirs feelings once buried in the ruins. She knows the memory of listening to her mother tell of the adventures of her ancestors must be denied. Where once it might have brought comfort, it now only brings her damaging loss to bear. Wiggling her feet, knowing it will cut and injure, she watches the bright red stains grow on her already stained moccasins. Relaxing as the physical pain consumes her, she is released from that which pains her more.

Turning from Ebenezer, whose betrayal threatens her ability to control her consuming outrage, she takes aim at young Thomas. *Such a foolish boy! Did he not see his own mother consumed by the storm, calling to his brothers and sisters? I did not see him shed a tear. I am haunted by the image of her standing there still, calling out, and yet he sits nightly, enamoured with the stories they tell, trying to speak their words and seeming to shun our ways to become more like our enemy,* she angrily thinks, observing him walking in unison with the Silent Enemy. *Look, even now he has not a care but to look around like a naive child.*

Ahead of them, Thomas French languishes under his usual heavy load, forced to now not only carry all the supplies, but to pull the sled so the boys may walk with the enemy and learn their ways. He sinks hopelessly in the wet snow, occasionally becoming mired with no aid offered but instead a threat to urge him on. She believes she has seen him glance to her a few times, but it is so fleeting she is unsure if it is just wishful thinking. She can find no fault with him, for she has seen, and felt, his pain.

Thomas French prays his own son might be saved, released from the enemy's grip, as Sarah most surely is. He saw her change the night before as she pulled away from the others, her hate evident once more. At every opportunity, he looks upon her to ensure she remains resolute in her return to being *one of us.* He is relieved to see she is.

For Sarah, the broken trust of a once-cherished friend carries with it a punishing consequence: not only the loss of faith in the false bearer of it, but in herself. Her final and most brutal judgement is rendered. *You precipitated this with your sinful want, Sarah. You brought this upon yourself — and the others. Had you not wanted for more, daydreamed of the places beyond, you would still be with . . .* she dares not think the word, for she wants no more the pain of their loss. *No one will redeem a girl such as you. No one.* Feeling the last connection to that life sever, she accepts her fate for such sin. *Deemed by God, the punishment is just.*

Leaving the vast lake behind them, the group covers many miles upon the narrow river they now follow. Speeding north, nearly sprinting as is possible through the quagmire of the spring melt, they are occasionally forced into the deep snow upon the shore.

The view of the soaring mountains from where they have travelled now gives way to small, seemingly disconnected hills in the distance, which protrude from the generally flat landscape. Once, it would have reminded Sarah of the hills at home, but now she makes no such connection. In accepting blame for all that has happened, she is finally free of the cruelty of want — of hope. Anticipating nothing, wanting for nothing, she does not count the days, nor wonder at the miles that separate her from home. The barren landscape of her mind, now unencumbered, allows her to sleep more deeply as disturbing fragments of dreams cease, strangely bolstering her stamina. Sarah keeps pace, for she has not lost her sense of survival; that innate instinct supersedes even her vehemence. In finally surrendering herself to an unknown fate, Sarah has freed herself.

The source of the growing noise ahead on the trail, at first unrecognizable, now comes into view as they move onto the riverbank. Before her, the open water cascades down the slight incline of the river.

Marching closer to the roaring, frothy tempest, Sarah is enthralled by the river's violence. Forced to move deeper into the forest to avoid the water that consumes the shoreline, she stares at the strange spectacle of trees immersed in the turbulent river, standing perfectly still against its force. Great plumes of water spray into the air as the rushing water moves by each. Small shrubs with ice-covered branches, consumed by the ferocious torrent, suddenly escape its grip. They bob and weave as if to avoid being taken below the surface, but with a great surge of its watery hand, the river pulls them under once more, if only briefly. Keeping a wary eye on the water lapping against the edge of her snowshoe, Sarah carefully chooses each step. Grabbing tree branches to anchor her to the shore, she knows there is no escape if she is swept up in its relentless surge. Even in her fascination of it, the power of the river frightens her.

Her attention diverted, she has not noticed the reason for their sudden departure from the river's edge. Blinded by the full sun beating down upon them as they emerged into a clearing, Sarah shades her eyes with her hand to her forehead, attempting to make sense of the dark mass before them. As her eyes adjust, an eerily familiar sight appears: palisades.

# 73

"Mes amis, you have made it!" Rushing to greet them as they enter the gate of Fort Chambly, deRouville's sincerely joyous, almost surprised tone gives the impression their arrival was all but unexpected. Having left their company now weeks before at the fork of the White River, he finds the sight of more of his allies arriving with their prizes intact a sign of God's pleasure in the righteousness of their cause, though he had not doubted it. The numbers arriving are smaller than when he left them, but he always knew the groups, isolated and at the mercy of the harsh conditions they faced, would be reduced. It is a truth that is not to be fretted about, for he knows even a few captives are of great value to their cause. His allies proved almost too successful. With more captives taken than planned, even in the earliest days, he could estimate the losses, and further, determine which individuals he would see arrive.

Brushing past deRouville with an almost imperceptible nod, the warriors take leave of their captives and walk directly to an elongated, wooden building sitting solitarily in the center of the compound. For the weary group, it is a strange feeling to be left amongst the soldiers. Even the familiar face of deRouville does not ease their apprehension, for it is obvious by his suddenly stern demeanour that he is affronted by the snub of his allies. He harshly orders something in French, and the dishevelled group instinctively huddles together, looking nervously about to understand any response in movement or gesture. Now that they have been abandoned by their masters, the sense of peculiar protection they have been afforded suddenly disappears, making their response as primal as the early days. Standing nearly shoulder to shoulder, quivering with dreaded anticipation, they are reduced to acting as the creatures they once commanded. Though they bear the shame of it, for they can see the evident disgust in the eyes of the soldiers staring curiously at them, they cannot help but cling to that which will provide any relief from the terrible burden of the unknown. Scowling at them with an arrogance that shows his evident distaste at their reaction, deRouville spins around and suddenly departs, walking quickly in the direction of the far end of the building where his allies have gone. Left alone with the soldiers, the captives are quickly surrounded and pushed roughly toward the nearest door. As they enter, they are plunged into darkness.

Standing perfectly still, not knowing what lies before her, Sarah hears shuffling about and muffled conversation coming from the far reaches of the building. Struggling to adjust to the dim light, she can do no more than remain close to Ebenezer, who she knows has been shoved in directly after her. Feeling him close, she forgets that only before entering the palisades she despised him for his deceit. Now she wants for his presence, or that of any of Deerfield. Those who take custody of them may only differ in language and custom, but in not sharing the kinship of experience, the presence of the warriors was preferred, for these men know nothing of the places from where they have come, the immensity of their suffering, nor their profound grief. Exposed and at the mercy of a new enemy, Sarah finds solace in knowing the swiftness of the tomahawk.

Ominous and unusual in shape, the darkened figure before her slowly comes into focus.

"Bonjour, mes enfants. We are glad to welcome you to Fort Chambly." The friendly voice should not instill fear, but a shiver rises up Sarah's back upon hearing it, paining her as the cold of all the days and nights upon the march bear down on her at once. Faltering, she feels a hand steady her, and then instantly remove itself. Shocked, she stands still, though her legs yet threaten to cast her to the ground. Strangely focused on the once-familiar surface at her feet, she wiggles her toes, feeling the floor beneath her. Pushing hard against it until it hurts, as if to assure herself it is real, she plants her feet steadily upon its immovable, solid surface, revelling in the familiarity of it. As if this solitary sensation has unlocked all those that have been muted by the absence of them, the sweet smell of baking bread wafting through the building mixes with the pungent odour of the men surrounding them. The combination creates a nearly overwhelming sensation that tugs at her stomach, making it churn in response. The heat of the room is stifling. The air is thick and stale, and she cannot catch her breath; she feels as if she is drowning. As her vision begins to fade, the door behind them suddenly opens, bringing with it the welcome relief of a cold blast of fresh air.

Revived, Sarah looks to the man before them. Expecting to see a soldier, she is taken aback to find a short, stout, aged man in a long black robe. Though he wears a large cross hung from a plain rope around his waist, she cannot make sense of it, for he looks nothing like Reverend Williams.

"Je suis . . ." He pauses, nodding deferentially to them. "Excuse me," he continues in an accent so thick it is almost indiscernible as English. "I am Père Barthélemy. We rejoice at your arrival. That you may now be saved must bring joy to you as well." Anticipating the response, he ignores Thomas French, who straightens his stance, meeting the priest with a very direct stare. Moving from the table he stands before, the priest motions with his extended arm as if to highlight the abundance of the offering. "You must be hungry, please sit and enjoy."

Before them are loaves of bread. Illuminated by the candles at either end of the table, the steam rises from them, making their mouths water. Once a mundane staple of their diet, it has never before created such desire in Sarah. She yearns to rush to the steaming loaves and devour them entirely, but does not move. Her stomach growls loudly at the denial. Embarrassed, she crosses her arms over to muffle the sound of her want.

"Please." The priest laughs. "Do not torment yourself further. It is for you. Eat of it as you will, and there is more should you want for it. You will find fresh water and ale to wash it down."

By the sounds that rise from the captives' stomachs, it is obvious they all yearn to partake, but will not be the first to give in to their enemy. Finally, exasperated by their refusal, a soldier roughly pushes young Thomas forward, grabbing his shoulder in a harsh grip to force him to sit upon the bench. Pulling a loaf in front of him, he orders, "Mange!"

Though he does not understand the word, the lure of the warm bread proves more than he can resist. Grabbing it, he tears it apart, shoving a large piece in his mouth. Chewing faster than Sarah has ever witnessed him eat, he nearly chokes on every piece. Tentatively moving forward, Thomas French slowly sits beside his son, and as if the feeling of having him near is more tempting than the bread, he remains still for a moment, simply enjoying their proximity to one another again. Handing a piece to his father, young Thomas gives a shy smile, acknowledging the distance that has grown between them. Feeling a gentle push from behind, Sarah moves forward, followed to the opposite side of the table by Ebenezer. After quickly pulling a steaming loaf toward them, he breaks it in two, putting half on her plate. Tearing it apart, she cannot stop, even as the heat burns her hands. Putting the bread into her mouth, she is surprised by the deafening crunch of the crusty outer layer, but she only gives it brief notice, as the warm, soft center fills her mouth with an explosion of familiar taste. Not caring that they are a spectacle, they eat and drink with abandon.

Père Barthélemy is no longer appalled by the reaction, for he has seen such uncivilized behaviour in the groups that have already passed through in similar conditions, and some worse. While it may have disheartened some to see people in such a state, the priest is well pleased. *Mon Dieu, Your will be done,* he silently prays, looking upon the proof of the Lord's will to bring these heathens to salvation. Believing their suffering as penance, he will not delay having them converted to the true religion. *Surely those who suffer as they have, stripped of all dignities, pained and tortured with every step, have seen the truth of what they have suffered — the retribution for their sins against the Lord. Yes, I have no doubt they will quickly embrace the one true way.* In his victory, his once-friendly demeanour gives way to smug righteousness. Sensing he is being observed, Père Barthélemy looks up to find Thomas French staring at him suspiciously. Smiling broadly to ease his look of concern, the priest knows even in their decimated state, some will not be so easily convinced. Using this knowledge, he realizes the influence of this man over his son will need to be removed to ensure those who are prime for conversion will have no impediment to their salvation. The adults have proven difficult to convince, no matter their suffering, and serve no purpose but as slaves to their masters. The priest determines to advise Lieutenant deRouville that this man will prove a problem if left with the younger ones, and should be relegated to the Lieutenant's purposes, for this is the true reason for his being amongst them. As with all who pass through Fort Chambly, he is to assess their role as either a pawn in negotiations with les Anglais or as a converted member of their society, whether amongst the French themselves or their Catholic allies.

Holding a small morsel of bread in her hand, Sarah stares down, not understanding how she can feel so full after so few bites of the delicious fare before her. One would expect that with the ravenous way in which they began their meal, more bread, which is at the ready on a nearby side table, would be called for. But after only a few bites, the group suddenly slows, feeling the effects of the heavy weight in their empty stomachs. Even with the nourishment of meat, it had never been in sufficient quantity, and in the last few days of the march, less so. Tattered clothing hangs off their nearly skeletal bodies, and despite the want to eat of all that is offered, they cannot, for the dire effects of their captivity will not allow it.

"You will have what bread you have need of. It is usual that you fill so easily in these early days, but as with the others, you will find your appetites and strength restored," says Père Barthélemy at the abrupt conclusion of their meal.

The uttering of "the others" stuns them. Peering at him in disbelief, they had not considered others may yet exist. Their dark, sunken eyes, having been dull and lifeless only moments before, now glint with the possibility that others have survived. None speak, but it is clear to the priest and the soldiers that they are encouraged by this news as they glance at one another as if to confirm what they have heard. Using their tempered, but unmistakably affected, reaction to his advantage, he offers, "We have welcomed a number of Deerfield here at Fort Chambly. All have now found comfortable accommodations in our communities and amongst our allies. Tonight you shall sleep in the fort, then tomorrow you journey on to your destination, where you will find abundant food, comfortable beds to sleep upon, and clean clothing, restoring the dignity you once had." In reminding them of all they have lost, he knows they will want dearly for it again. Through his experience, Père Barthélemy understands that in cases such as these, the promise of restitution wields a mightier victory than the threat of having it taken away. They have already survived losing everything but their lives, which mattered little to them as they neared the end of the march, but with the return of even such common, basic dignities, ones nearly entirely forgotten, he knows they will not so easily part with them again, making the captives perfectly situated to their influence.

Turning to make arrangements for their nightly accommodation, Père Barthélemy stoops as he approaches a low doorway into an adjoining room. Stopping before making the threshold, he turns back, sensing a lingering question resting on the lips of the captives. With a final tactical move, he says in a cheerful manner, "And you may expect to find those of whom I spoke waiting for you." His darkened silhouette instantly disappears into the next room, leaving the weight of such news, of such hope, to rest upon them.

Sarah, alone in a small, confining room with a fire flickering in the heavy stone fireplace, remains awake despite overwhelming fatigue. Even as her body finds, for the first time in days, a warm softness beneath her, she is unable to ease her mind. She has been given one of the officers' rooms; she heard the priest arguing for it earlier, insisting that it was not proper for a young girl to be left amongst the men. At one time, she, too, would have found it entirely inappropriate, but such proprieties as once existed no longer seem to be of any consequence. With the absence of fear, whether of death or damage of reputation, she is not bothered to sleep alongside the others. In truth, it is the cause of her current unrest. Separated from them, she feels isolated in the tiny, sparsely appointed room, which only magnifies her loneliness. Every unfamiliar sound within the fort — the echo of distant voices yelling commands, the thunder of heavy boots upon the wooden floors, the small creak of a floorboard outside her door — reminds her she is yet under guard and leaves her increasingly anxious. Without the reaction of others to observe and take her cue from, she is left with only her vivid imagination as her guide, and finds herself unable to determine whether trouble is at hand, or if it is merely the usual sounds of such a place. Ripping the blankets from her, she gasps to catch her breath. Pulling at the neck of the clean nightshirt she has been provided, she feels as if she is suffocating. As the walls and ceiling of the room slowly close in on her, she shuts her eyes, trying desperately to imagine the stars that glimmered above in the wide-open spaces upon the march. She yearns for the cold rush of the open air, for her chest and throat hurt as she inhales each breath of the stagnant, acrid smoke in the cell she is confined to. Struggling to control what she knows will rob her of her senses, Sarah stumbles to the corner of the room where a basin of water has been set on a small table for her. Plunging her cupped hands into the warm water, she splashes it on her face, hoping for its refreshing relief, but finds none. Sitting back upon the bed, her face and hair dripping, she realizes her only escape is to pretend she is not here at all.

"Come now, Sarah, it was only last night. Think. Think hard about the cold snow beneath you, the stinging wind upon your face, your bones rattling with the shiver that has been your constant companion. Breathe it in, Sarah, breathe . . ." In a low voice, she speaks as if to another. She continues her encouragement until her own whispered pleas lull her into an uneasy sleep.

For all that has been restored, much has been taken.

# 74

"**M**ademoiselle, êtes-vous prêts? Pardonnez-moi — are you ready?" Père Barthélemy corrects, as he speaks through the door of the stuffy interior room where Sarah is finishing washing and dressing as earlier instructed. Groggy with the exhaustion of having been jolted from her sleep throughout the long, lonely night, Sarah dutifully answers, "Yes, I am nearly ready."

"Very good. I shall wait for you and then take you to breakfast." She can hear the priest's feet shuffle back from the door, and though he cannot see within, she is glad to have the distance and privacy of his departure, even if he is but a few feet away.

*Ready for what?* Sarah wonders warily as she finishes preparing herself. She has been thrown into the unknown time and again, and to some it may seem she is a strong girl. The priest believes this, for he reported such to deRouville himself the evening before when giving account of the captives' status. The truth is, she has not been made stronger or resilient in any way. Each twist and turn imposed on her leaves her heart so burdened with their injury that she simply acquiesces to the will of others, having lost her own will many terrifying days before.

With the fire dimmed to only a few smoldering coals, Sarah strains to see herself in the old, blackened mirror provided to her. The deep shadows cast by her much-altered appearance make her feel as if a stranger peers back. It is nearly inconceivable that it is she herself. Studying the drawn features of the girl in the mirror, she looks at the cheekbones protruding where once there were rounded, rosy cheeks. The soft golden curls she used to curse as they sprang from beneath her cap now burst forth in all directions, dry and brittle. Trying to smooth her hair with water from the basin, she finds it is not to be controlled, no matter the effort. Frustrated, she pulls the kerchief over her head and ties it tight, pushing all the wiry strands beneath it to hide them from sight. Tucking in a final curl, she stands back to inspect herself, not out of pride, but to ensure she is presentable to meet her master's command. The sunken eyes staring back at her disturb her so much she turns away from their deep, troubled stare. No matter the truth, she does not recognize the girl in the mirror, nor does she want to know her.

Rushing to the bed, leaving the stranger's company, Sarah sits down to affix the new pair of moccasins she has been provided. These are devoid of the darkened stains of her former pair that had seen her walk many miles. For a moment the pain of each step is seemingly erased, but when she pulls tight, she feels the reminder acutely. Looking down to the new clothing she wears, Sarah still vividly sees tattered rags. Lost in the swirling memories caving in on her, she is startled from her dark places by the creak of the floorboard, and she rises, putting the heavy woollen cloak on, tying it with a wide sash. Pulling the hood over her head until it nearly hides her face entirely, she is glad for the small sense of protection it gives as she opens the door, revealing the priest.

"Good, good," he says excitedly in his heavy accent. He tempers his impatience, though does so poorly, for Sarah can clearly see he is agitated and wanting to leave immediately. As he quickly turns, Sarah simply follows. His black cloak billows with the speed at which he is leading her, she presumes, to meet with the others.

Entering the room where the day before she ate her first familiar meal in many weeks, Sarah waits for the others to arrive. A burly man sets several newly baked loaves of bread upon the table before her, and her mouth waters, remembering the chewy texture. Staring at it, she hopes the others will not be long in coming, for she craves it as much now as when she first arrived.

"Eat quickly. You leave in only a few minutes. I am afraid there is no time to enjoy the food to any great degree."

Confused as to why she should not wait, she does as instructed. Tearing off a piece, releasing a great cloud of steam, she smells its rich, tangy scent. Bringing it to her mouth, she savours the first burst of flavour.

"Mademoiselle, do you not pray before eating the bounty of God?" the priest severely admonishes.

Feeling the bread begin to fill her mouth as it absorbs the water, which continues to freely flow with the want of more, she does not chew or swallow. Staring down at the wooden slates beneath her feet, she dares not look to him as she awaits her punishment.

"Excuse me, I did not mean to frighten you," he continues in a gentle voice. "It is only that *we* believe in giving thanks before eating."

Offended by his insinuation that they, the French, are somehow superior to her, she flushes with anger. But, as much as she wants to defend herself, she cannot, for she has long ago fallen out of God's favour.

"I will pray for you, until you learn the Catholic prayers yourself." As the priest's voice fills the room with his lilting prayer, Sarah does not pay attention, for it is all she can do not to choke on the bread still sitting idly in her mouth. Upon hearing "Amen," she glances to him, seeking permission to continue eating.

"Eat; eat!" he commands, gesturing to the bread with the flick of his finger. His impatience having returned, he looks about anxiously in the direction of noises coming from both the adjacent room and outside in the courtyard.

The rush of boots from all directions suddenly closes in on the room. Setting the bread down, Sarah waits for the impending attack, for she cannot imagine what else would cause such a charge. Bursting open with a loud bang, the door hits the wall, making the cup on the table rattle with the force. Light streams in from behind the figure standing in the doorway, and Sarah does not need to see his features to know who it is. The Observant Enemy and priest immediately engage in an angered exchange.

"Père Barthélemy, it has been settled; the girl leaves immediately," comes the stern voice of deRouville, entering from an adjacent room, with a small group of soldiers from within the fort.

"Very well then, Lieutenant, as you wish, but it has been agreed upon that her conversion should not be delayed," the priest continues, an air of concern in his voice evident, despite his agreement.

"Yes, as discussed, she will be brought to the church to begin her education; it shall not be delayed."

Sarah listens as they speak in turns English and French, she assumes, as it does not sound like her captor's now familiar language. The Observant Enemy seems impatient with the banter, for his stance becomes more menacing, and he puts his hand upon his blade.

"Take your leave, *mon ami*," deRouville says, exaggerating his words, leaving no doubt of his contempt.

"You, come," the warrior abruptly orders Sarah, his infuriation now directed at her. Not understanding what is happening, but knowing enough to obey, she immediately rises and follows him.

Greeted by a dull, warm day, they quickly exit the palisade walls, leaving Fort Chambly behind. Sinking nearly ankle-deep in the cold mud beneath her feet, Sarah pulls her clean skirt up to avoid soaking

it in the muck. As she does so, she is sorry to see her new moccasins ruined so quickly. Caught up in the haste of their departure, and
believing they will soon meet with the others, it is only when she and
the warrior are alone on the trail for a number of miles that she realizes what the priest's protestations were about.

Easily assuming the familiar rhythm of the march, Sarah follows
her captor throughout the long day. His mood has darkened since
last she saw him. Thinking to the loud, raucous banging and yelling
coming from the far end of the fort where she had seen him and his
brother disappear into, she now realizes that the friendly welcome
of the French Lieutenant had masked their true relationship, which
is not at all friendly. *I wonder if his brother and the others have gone
ahead. The priest did seem impatient. Perhaps they did not want to
delay on my behalf*, she reasons, grasping at the faint hope that this
is the case. Scanning the land around them, she cannot see any tracks
in the snow. As much as she hates her captors, she knows to look for
such signs, having listened in to their instructions to the boys on such
things. With the sound of the unbridled river behind them, they head
inland. Sorry to have been so unforgiving of her companions, she
now finds herself wishing them here — not praying for it, for this she
knows is lost to her.

〜❦〜

## 75

"Kahnawà:ke," the warrior announces as they suddenly break free from the confines of the heavily wooded forest. Sarah is stunned by the view before her. She cannot make sense of the structures in the peculiar village. Their vantage point from the opposite shore of the partially frozen river gives her a sweeping view of rounded houses, neatly arranged in rows. Her reason for assuming them houses is not only the familiar smoke rising from the top of each, though they lack chimneys, but the people, many of them children, entering and exiting them carrying pots, logs, and going about what seems a daily routine. Some, she can see, cordially greet neighbours and stop to talk. At the far edge of the village stands a building whose dimensions are more familiar. The building, boasting a large cross rising from a tall spire, is much grander than their meetinghouse, and is undoubtedly the location of the "conversion" the priest spoke of. Looking to her captor, expecting his order to continue forward, she notices he seems as captivated by the sight as she is. Seeing his once-brooding demeanour change to one that gives a hint of a smile, she glances back to the village, seeing a small gathering begin to take shape. As the group stares at them, a small child's hand suddenly waves in the air. Curious to know her captor's response, she watches his smile broaden and his hand rise in kind.

"Kahnawà:ke. Home," he says, stepping from the edge of the land onto the small slip of ice connecting the two shores. It is their long-awaited destination.

The cries and yelps growing in volume as more and more people gather together at the edge of the river frighten Sarah. She has only known these sounds in such magnitude once. The memories of acrid, ungodly smells, chaotic, desperate screams, mixing with the ones she now hears as clearly as the ones ringing in her mind proves bewildering. Standing on the thin ice near the midpoint of their crossing, she looks at the water slipping beneath the edge, but a few feet from where she treads. Every raw memory, once buried in the far reaches of her mind, unleashes in a torrent of unrelenting cruel images, laying waste to what remains of the defences she has unknowingly created to protect herself. Each face lost to her — those of Deerfield, those on the march — and every intense, overwhelming feeling of revulsion, disbelief, desperation, and yearning threatens to consume her in a final violent act. But the same cold hand that had stolen this release from her too many times before takes her arm in a tight grip, as if understanding her desire. Pulled across the icy surface, she sets foot in Kahnawà:ke, the home of her enemy.

Jostled about by the rush of humanity that engulfs them, Sarah finds herself quickly being ushered into one of the strange structures she saw from across the river. With nowhere to retreat from the curious stares and shrill sounds of celebration, she feels violated by the intensity of their attentions to her.

"Shé:kon," the adults and children greet her as she passes by, though the wary stares of a few do not go unnoticed. Sensing the deep distrust they have of her draws her strangely to them, for their sentiment is akin to her own. The joyous welcome and their continued attempts to greet her with a mix of "Bonjour" and "Shé:kon" do not bring any response from Sarah. In the rush of what is happening, it is impossible to make sense of her situation.

After being thrust instantly into the dim interior, Sarah stands inside one of the large structures. The intense smells rouse her from the confusion: cedar, smoke, and unfamiliar sweet aromas. Shadowy silhouettes stand silent, their presence, quiet and unobtrusive, does not alarm her, for she is relieved to leave behind the boisterous mob. The expansive open space is as nothing as she has ever seen. A high, rounded ceiling allows shafts of light to stream in from openings above. As the smoke of three fires set in the middle escapes, the effect is captivating. Diffused into a hazy glow, it brightens the space, bringing it into sharper focus. Directly before her, a clay cooking pot is set upon the small fire. As she passes by, the smell reminds her of how famished she truly is. Their abrupt departure from the fort left her with no more than a morsel of bread.

The women and children of all ages coming toward her stare at her curiously. Many of the children have shy smiles on their faces, but the women are not so quick to rejoice in her presence; most look her over carefully as if considering her nature. Each new, mystifying situation brings with it questions that have yet to be answered, the most troublesome echoes in her mind as she walks by the silent, sharp-eyed spectators. *What purpose do I serve?*

A commotion at the far end of the dwelling captures her attention. Surrounded by those few allowed to enter, she has not noticed the absence of her captor at her side until she sees him illuminated by a shaft of light at the far end. She is astounded. Taking a woman into his arms, he holds her close, whispering something which brings her to tears. Children rush to his legs, and he places his arms around them, patting them on the heads as . . . *a father?* So changed is her captor that Sarah finds him nearly unrecognizable. His demeanour already much relaxed upon entering the village, he now takes on an expression of what can only be described as relief. His tender embrace of his wife and children makes her feel abandonment to such a degree that she could have ill-conceived feeling worse than she has the many days since Deerfield, but cast out and discarded, she does. Once she was his captive, and though it was unwanted, it was at the very least defined. Now, his broad smile transforms him into someone else. Sarah can no longer rely on her familiar hatred of him. Entirely without connection, she stands amongst them, the only one of her own kind.

## 76

Some great excitement outside the longhouse sends the occupants pouring out to see what it is, and Sarah is left alone for the first time in an unknown number of days since she has arrived in the village. The time has passed in a blur of activity. Still adapting to having so many near, she is alarmed by the deafening noise of even murmured voices. The indelible mark of fearing being hunted, that any slight noise should draw the attention of an unseen enemy, puts her on edge. Though she no longer marches, the fear that bore down so heavily upon her has not left. Assaulted by the constant barrage of movement, noise, and a disconcerting feeling of being in the presence of so many of the enemy, she desperately yearns to retreat to her quiet place, and not think of what is happening. With such close contact and with her every move being observed, she finds it impossible.

She is forced to sleep in a cramped, walled-off area with the family of the Observant Enemy, and while such close proximity is uncomfortable, she is relieved to have quiet return. Not able to see the stars above, she pretends she is alone, until sounds from the other families remind her it is only an illusion. Even these once-intrusive noises do not cause alarm for over the nights since her arrival, she has come to understand they are just the usual ways of the longhouse, and pose no threat. Sleep was elusive in the beginning when she attempted to reason her situation, and think of how she might escape with so many near. Eventually, she found herself waking in the morning, not remembering when she had lost her grip on remaining alert. Falling into the oblivion of sleep has not been wholly unwelcome, for in pondering her flight from the village, she has realized there is nowhere to go.

Though the dress, customs, and language of the Mohawk people differ from what she knew, the rhythm of daily life is the same in many ways. Sarah is charged with preparing meals, completing chores, such as weaving, mending and cleaning, and entertaining the children, of which there are always many running about. Had not these tasks been somewhat familiar, Sarah would be entirely unable to follow the command of her master, who is now the wife of the Observant Enemy. She is known as Ihsta'a to the children, but he calls her Skawennahawi.

Not able to speak any English, as her husband, she relies on using gestures to try and bring about what is needed of Sarah. She is not unkind. In fact, Sarah feels she earnestly tries to help her understand, often smiling at her to put her at ease. Her eyes, deep wells of sadness, make it difficult for Sarah to look upon her for any length as they reflect back that which she feels in her own broken heart. Fearing if she remains transfixed, the grief will consume her, she averts her eyes. But on occasion, when Sarah's curiosity takes hold, she sees the hurt she inflicts, and while she revels to bring such injury to her enemy, to this gentle woman, she cannot deny, she is sorry to do so.

Since her enemy's family is a young one, the children she tends are few: the youngest, Katsitsanéron, about two or three years old, is a precocious, petite girl, who very often runs off, causing the others to chase after her before she can exit at the far end of the longhouse. Giving chase, Kahntineta, about five, is swift, and often is the one to seize the little one, as Sarah always delays, awaiting her instructions for every small task. The oldest, Taronhiorens, whom Sarah surmised to be about eight by his size and responsibility, is quiet. Observing her cautiously, which she appreciates, he seems to most understand her own apprehension. At night she practices the names of the family over and over, for she likes the rhythmic sounds of them; but she will not repeat the name of her enemy. Like the day she blotted out his face with the sunspot, she will not name him, taking from him what she can — his identity. He is now held fully to account for all that has befallen her. Unsure of where the others of her once group are, she judges him to be the reason for it. What progress she makes in the presence of his family is quickly undone when he appears as her seething anger gives her strength to deny his instructions, and his attempts to converse with her — even using English on occasion to try and illicit some response. She can see he is not as wounded as his wife, whom she figures does not understand what atrocities her husband is capable of, for she, and the children, seem to love him. To assume them unaware of his true nature, absolving them of his guilt, is the only way she quiets the constant panic that threatens to plunge her into madness.

Stirring the pot over the small fire near the family's space in the longhouse, Sarah mindlessly tends a porridge of corn and water. Lulled into a trance by the repetitive motion, she does not notice the flames begin to die down.

"Kaniehtiio," comes a soft voice from within the recesses of the room directly in front of her. Searching the darkness, Sarah sees the form of an elderly woman begin to appear as she slowly pulls herself into the dim light at the edge of the platform. Dressed as the others, she hunches over, trying to catch her breath with the strain of her moving. Small in stature, the old woman stares at her. Uncomfortable with her steady gaze, Sarah looks back to the pot. *Has she been watching me since my arrival?* she wonders, worried she has been observed much more closely than she assumed. The thought of this woman sitting in the dark watching her every move makes her question each action she has made. The silence the woman maintains quiets Sarah's apprehension and she looks up. Captivated by her dark eyes and long, silvery hair worn in a simple braid, Sarah studies the woman's features. As if understanding her natural curiosity, the woman remains still, allowing her time to take in each detail.

Sarah does not feel threatened by her presence, which furthers her confusion. Forced as she is to live so intimately amidst her enemy, what once seemed clear about her role in this foreign place now leaves her more unsettled with every gesture of kindness.

Remembering the pot on the fire, Sarah stirs it noting the bubbles of a rapid boil have retreated into only a few now barely breaking the surface. Searching about to find more logs to stoke the fire and finish cooking the meal, she finds none. Unsure of the movement she is allowed, she sits staring anxiously at the thickening contents of the pot. The family, having scurried out in a great rush not several minutes ago, left her with the singular instruction: to stir. Not wanting to leave her post, she looks for even one stick that will help the situation. Only the ones set by the other fires are evident, but she knows enough of the rules not to touch them. Sarah looks to the old woman, hoping to be offered wood, but she finds her working on applying colourful beads to a new pair of moccasins. *They will be angry*, she worries, her heart beating faster. After gathering a few measly pieces of bark, which have fallen from one of the logs in the pile, she puts them on the fire, hoping they will restore some heat, but they do not. Creating a heavy white smoke, the dirt that accompanies them further smothers the fire she is hoping to spare. Thinking to every possibility of what punishment to expect, Sarah begins to tremble.

"Kaniehtiio, óyente," a calm, steady voice says, interrupting her terrible daydream.

Sarah looks up to find the woman has laid her beading down momentarily upon her lap and is again watching her.

"Kaniehtiio," she says, extending a bony, crooked finger at her. Finally understanding, Sarah points to herself. The woman nods, "Kaniehtiio." Sarah smiles in kind, but quickly catches herself, resuming her usual serious demeanour. "Kaniehtiio, ó-yen-te," the women repeats slowly. When Sarah shakes her head to show she does not understand, the woman again extends her finger, but this time to the firepit. "Óyente."

"Wood?"

With a broadening smile and a nod, the woman repeats, "wood."

Entering the village, Jean Quenet and his companion Pierre Lamoureux are eager to make the deal they seek and leave as soon as possible. While his business relies on his relations with their allies, he has enough experience to distrust them. The men of Kahnawà:ke assemble upon seeing them, followed closely by the many women and children who are curious about their visitors; Jean turns to his friend.

"Let us make quick work of this and be gone before dark."

Staring warily at the throngs awaiting them, Pierre nods his agreement.

"Bonjour!" With a hearty greeting and forced smile, Jean enters the village, extending a genial greeting to the chief, who is first of his people to meet the men.

"Shé:kon" comes the stern reply. Even with alliances proven with the recent raid into the English territory, there still exists a tense relationship that speaks of a time, not long past, when Jean and Pierre would not find themselves so welcome, nor likely find themselves leaving. With their approach to the negotiations being of the utmost importance, Jean tenses as he enters the longhouse.

"We come here seeking to broker a deal for les Anglais, whom you now have amongst you. Monsieur Lamoureux has drafted our offer, for Père Millet of your parish has sent word to Père deBreslay that there may be interest in the sale of one or more of these unfortunates."

After removing the agreement from his pack, Pierre hands it to a warrior seated beside the chief, who reads through it before advising the leader of its terms. Speaking at length in their native tongue to exclude the men from their discussions, they glance at various members of the group, and always when looking upon their visitors, they eye them with suspicion the men well understand. Unsure of what the discussion is, Jean worries they have offended with the offer made. Their information was that a young girl of twelve has not been easy to integrate into the community and therefore does not serve the purpose for which she was taken. The mourning wars were something Jean, Pierre, and their compatriots can little understand; the idea of replacing children with ones stolen is abhorrent to them. That Kahnawà:ke is a devout Catholic community matters not. Most amongst the French believe children of European descent should be raised by others who share such origins, no matter that they are English. Jean and Pierre have not merely come seeking a domestic for Jean's household, but feel it their duty to save all they can from the clutches of the savages. It is not their place to question the king's wisdom, for they realize the victory depends on their alliance, but in equal measure, Jean and many in their society work to negotiate the release through sale, trade, or any means that will save these poor souls from what the French deem a fate worse than death.

As another warrior is called forth, the discussion continues, at times becoming heated. With a final word from the chief, the discussion ends abruptly and the warrior that was called is handed the agreement prepared by Pierre. As he looks it over, the chief finally speaks directly to the men.

"We have one and no more."

"Forgive me, but it was our understanding that there are others that may be considered. We will give fair payment for their — " Catching himself before he says "release," Pierre continues minding his words. "For them. My client is eager to secure the services of these captives for his growing household and farm."

With no discernible change in demeanour, the chief looks directly at the men. "One, or none," he says, his tone emphasizing the definitive nature of his answer.

Sensing their questioning escalates the already tense exchange, they acquiesce. "We understand."

Reading each word of the agreement, the warrior with whom they are evidently negotiating finally looks to the chief and gives a slight nod.

"The offer is acceptable. You will take l'Anglaise with you now?"

"Yes, we depart immediately, if that is agreeable."

"It is." Standing to end the negotiation, the chief and the warrior who struck the deal exit the longhouse, leaving Jean, Pierre, and the others gathered in council to await the arrival of their purchase.

Outside her longhouse, Sarah grabs a final log from the pile that only the day before she helped to create; she is startled by a rough hand upon her arm. Assuming she is caught by her master for doing wrong, for she knows him by the harshness of his grip, she turns to face him.

"I am sorry, there was no more wood for cooking. I did not know what to do. Your wife asked me to cook, and I was trying."

Surprised by the speed of her pleas, he releases his hand, looking at her in disbelief that she yet fears him in such measure. If it had not been obvious before, this makes it plain: the girl will never accept the life he offers. She will never be the daughter they wanted for . . . again. His disappointment, disguised by his hard demeanour, does not betray his true feelings on the deal newly inked.

Dropping the bundle she has steadied in her hands, Sarah is pulled roughly towards two men standing stone-faced outside a longhouse nearby. Shoved toward the strangers before her, she stumbles as her foot catches in the deep mud. Grasping her before she falls to the ground, Jean steadies her, using his aid to deliver a guarded message he whispers in her ear.

"It is all right. We have freed you from their clutches."

Her heart leaping at the possibility of redemption that her nightmare is over, Sarah's emotions swell, but she does not allow them to burst forth. Now wise in the art of survival, she has been disappointed too many times to believe what her heart so fervently wants.

## 77

"**I** am afraid we must walk through the mud, for the river runs too quickly this time of year and our horses will go no faster with our weight upon their backs; we would surely find them sinking knee-deep. But no mind, we shall clean up, and you will be given new clothing when we arrive at my home," Jean says in a cheerful manner. His thick accent makes him difficult to understand, but he does not lack in the proper use of English, as with the few who had made attempts to speak with her in the village they hastily left but an hour before. For the duration of their early journey, the three travellers walk in silence, the gait and speed of their step signalling the urgency of their departure.

Sarah does not respond to any of their attempts at conversation, but simply follows. Neither man has ever seen such a person, let alone a child. It is not well-mannered obedience that makes her so quick to do as directed, but the absence of will to do anything other than what she is told. Jean was warned by his parish priest, Père deBreslay, of such things — that only education in the Catholic faith and steady work will renew such a fragile being. He is glad for his priest's guidance and experience in such things, for upon seeing her, he shuddered looking at her thin, frail body and despairing eyes. Subdued by his realization that this child is much more affected that he has imagined, he attempts once more to appeal to her and ease some of her suffering.

"Now, ma petite," he says gently, using the term he calls his own daughter, for he cannot help but feel she needs protection, "you will not have to linger under the cruelty of the savages. We pray more of your people will find a similar fate, for though we may be allied with them, it is no place for people of our own kind." Hoping to see her rally with such news, he studies her sullen face and rigid posture for some evidence of release from her stunned state, but he finds nothing. The blank stare she maintained the few miles they have already walked remains. Looking to Pierre, he shrugs, confounded by what to do. Shaking his head as if to silently signal to his companion that nothing can be done, Pierre strikes up a conversation about other business dealings they have to attend to upon their arrival back in Beaurepaire.

With an estimated two days' journey ahead of them, Jean and Pierre keep each other company, rarely interacting with their charge, for it seems their efforts to reassure her are wasted.

Roaring just in sight of the well-worn, muddy trail, the river, now alive with the spring melt, rushes in a torrent to unknown places. Sarah knows the river will lead them to wherever they are headed, for she understands the way of her enemy in using the land as a guide. She assumes these men are no different, for despite the fact that they are French, and the path veers inland after leaving the village, the river is never completely out of sight. Reassured by this now familiar practice, Sarah turns her attention to try and make sense of what is happening.

*You will not have to linger under the cruelty of the savages.* Sarah wonders what cruelty she has escaped. *Perhaps they found out I was to be punished,* she shudders, imagining the result. It was clear her captor was becoming increasingly frustrated with her, but her disobedience was not rooted in spite, for that sentiment had proven to hold no power in altering her circumstances. It was her inability to escape her own guilt, which was as a yoke weighing her down. Even in accepting her fate — to live amongst the enemy — she found painful memories occupying her mind, leaving her unable to fully comprehend what was expected. Devoid of her physical suffering, her mind was left fully, and agonizingly, engaged.

Her short time in the village did not inflict further suffering as expected. Her body was warm for the first time in countless days; the scars upon her feet, which once bled from the straps that cut deeply into them, began to heal; she was fed adequately, though her appetite waned as her fate became clear; she even slept soundly on occasion, but always woke with a start, expecting to be somewhere she was not. Had not the sight of the Observant Enemy been a constant reminder of having fallen out of the Lord's favour—he, having shown her the desolation one would suffer for such disobedience — she wonders if she would not have found her stay bearable. Thinking of her encounter with the old woman in the village, she begins to question whether the extension of kindness was real or had a more sinister purpose. *Was it all to fool me? To put me at ease before he . . .* As she stops her next memory from coming into full view, her stomach heaves, remembering well the way of her enemy: *Give hope where none exists.*

Confused by her unexpected removal from Kahnawà:ke, she stares at the men ahead on the trail. Their manner of dress, more formal, even ornate, than the men of Deerfield, along with the self-assured way in which they carried themselves, gives them a sense of authority. The few words by the shorter man, the one seemingly in charge by his confident, slightly bold manner, did not strike her as threatening in any way. The other more refined man appears to enjoy the spirited conversation they hold, unconcerned by her presence. Yet, not knowing more of their intentions makes her uneasy. As she attempts to understand their motivations for taking her from the village, an impossible notion comes through with such clarity that all other reasons dissipate: *Have they been sent to save me?*

Entering a small stand of trees budding with new leaves, they are shaded from the blazing, midday sun. Although it is unusually warm for this time of year, Sarah shivers with the changing temperature, for amid the trees, the memory of winter lingers. As they move closer to the shore, the sound of the river becomes less a beacon of its familiar presence and more menacing. As the roar of its turbulent waters increase, so, too, does her unease.

Free from its icy grip, the water speeds along, carrying sheets of ice upon it, which tumble about, often disappearing under the roiling waters for a time only to reappear down river. Unnaturally captivated, she watches the white fragments rush by.

Sarah turns her attention to the men, who are raising their voices to be heard over the raging river. She listens to them speak in animated tones, and actions, for they use both their fanciful, rolling words and excessive hand gestures in conversation, as if to highlight the importance of what they are saying. Unexpectedly, a voice from the past seems to whisper in her ear, "the damned French." Whether Reverend Williams has survived, Sarah is unsure, but his voice is as alive as when he spoke the words so often on the pulpit. After scanning the empty trail behind her to be sure he is not there, Sarah pulls back slightly from the men, the distance providing some relief from the source of the shame the voice instills. *How could you so freely follow these French?* it echoes in her mind.

Throughout his conversation with Jean, Pierre has been quietly studying the girl. Even though they walk ahead of her, with each turn to speak to his companion, he takes a sidelong glance to see if he can determine anything at all about her disposition. The last few fleeting looks have revealed a growing anxiety upon her face. Assuming it the unbridled river, which drowns the shoreline and comes very near the trail, he calls over his shoulder, "We are on good footing here. The Fleuve Saint-Laurent will not swallow us up today, Mademoiselle."

Surprised by the intrusion into her punishing thoughts, Sarah looks at him for moment, contemplating his words. Despite her own apprehension and the convictions of Reverend Williams, she moves closer, as before. It had not been the river itself, but the memories it stirred, that upset her, but the very notion of its dangers, now planted, makes her seek the safety of proximity to the men.

Jean, engrossed in the discussion about his recent legal woes, pays no attention to Pierre's exchange, or the reason for it. Only glancing at Sarah as she rushes up behind them, he continues uninterrupted.

Having only left the confines of the longhouse to fetch wood, Sarah had not put on the deerskin cloak that would have now helped shield her from the bite of the returning cold quickly descending upon them with the setting sun. Her instincts for survival taking hold, she notes how few supplies the men carry. She wonders how they are to shelter, stay warm, and eat. Hunger crept up on her slowly throughout the day, but with the effort of slogging through deep mud, it now turns into a painful reminder of such want as was on her march to this place. She has grown weak from a day without food, and the image of the porridge bubbling in the pot she left behind is summoned in such vivid detail she can almost taste it.

Sure these fine men lack the knowledge to survive such conditions, she wonders why they are not more concerned. Realizing she will be left with no aid, she looks about, taking account of what might be scavenged to eat, and searches for pine trees, whose boughs may be used to give warmth through a long, miserable night. As a chill runs down her back with the memory of such pain, a once familiar sight comes into view as they crest a small rise.

Gleaming white in the murky light of dusk, a house of substantial size, set back from the river, seems an apparition. With the welcoming glow of candlelight escaping through its windows, and wispy grey smoke rising into the night sky, the house seems the trick of a desperate heart. As she turns away to subdue her painful yearning for it to be true, a jubilant voice shatters the silence.

"Ah, bien! We have made our destination," Jean says in a tone that reveals his own relief at their long day's journey coming to an end. "Tonight we are the guests of Monsieur Caillier and his family."

## 78

Moving from one side of the open barn door to the other, a boy, shrouded in darkness, carries a pile of hay on his pitchfork. Judging from the sounds within, the cows are being fed and bedded down for the night, a custom Sarah knows well. Coming upon the homestead transports her to such familiar places that reality and memory clash. Believing the boy to be Edward, her heart overrides the logic of it. She smiles broadly, picking up her pace, as if she is about to rush to greet him. Turning toward the barn, pulled by an invisible force, her advance is only but a few steps.

"Where are you going?" Perplexed by her sudden departure from behind them, Jean catches her by the arm, just before she walks out of reach.

Sarah wilts, realizing her mistake. "I am sorry," she says meekly, unable to offer an explanation that will make any sense. Believing these instances of confused reality to be part of the burden she is to bear as the result of her sin, she now rebounds from them quickly, making them less noticeable to others — though not always.

"Sorry? Why, you were expecting to sleep in the barn, were you not?"

Unsure of what to answer, she remains silent. His brief grip of her arm has only been to stop her, and it does not leave a memory of its touch by any harshness.

"You will sleep upon a proper bed tonight. It has all been arranged." He motions for her to take the lead, and she notices the boy standing still in the doorway of the barn, observing the exchange. Sarah is glad to escape his curious stares, for in not being Edward, she does not want his attentions, and hurries to slip past the house to be shielded by it.

"Bonjour!" The door swings open just as she approaches. Startled, Sarah jumps back. With wide eyes fixed on him, Monsieur Caillier can see the alarm he affects with his abrupt greeting.

"Oh, no, please. Come in. We have been waiting for you." The burly middle-aged man before her seems overly welcoming with his exaggerated movements and apologetic voice, the result being that

Sarah feels more exposed than ever by the knowing of her by all these strangers. As he moves off to the side, waving her in, a gentle nudge from behind pushes her through the door and into the warm, well-appointed interior.

It is as nothing she has ever seen. In such contrast to homes in her own village, which were plain and unadorned, this place, with its ornate, rich excess, makes it difficult for her to take in all there is to look at. The candles lighting the rooms are not set in simple stands, but shimmering ones that twist and turn in such intricate designs that she wonders they use such finery for such a mundane purpose. The fabrics upon the furniture and pulled back from the windows are in shades of rich burgundy, blue, and gold. All of it, from the various objects set about for no other purpose than to look at, she assumes, to the everyday implements turned into objects of beauty, removes any semblance of familiarity that she felt before entering this sumptuous place.

From the corner of the room they are now ushered into, a woman, whom Sarah assumes is the man's daughter, approaches them with a demure greeting.

"Bonjour," she says dipping into a slight curtsey.

The men bow in kind. "We thank you for your hospitality, Madame Caillier. We pray our company does not interrupt your home too much while we are here," Jean says apologetically.

*She is his wife.* Sarah is surprised that such a young woman should marry a man his age.

"You are most welcome to. . . ." Madame Caillier blushes, attempting to find the right words in English. ". . . to . . . to stay as long as you . . . wish." She smiles at Sarah, who cannot help giving one in return, sensing the effort is made for her benefit. She hardly understands the words, as Madame Caillier's English is rudimentary and her accent much thicker than that of the men, but she feels a kinship, despite their differing circumstances.

Madame Caillier is a beautiful woman with a refined demeanour. Her clothing, as lavish as their surroundings, are made of fine, delicate fabrics, layered upon her in such abundance Sarah wonders how she is not wilting under the weight of it, for the house is stifling. The well-stoked fire in the ornate hearth directly before her emits more heat than is comfortable. It seems to bother no one but her, for she soon feels beads of sweat rolling down from her brow, but notes no such discomfort in the others. Hunger and the effects of such suffocating heat collude against her, and her knees weaken. Noticing her eyes flutter, Madame Caillier can see Sarah struggles to maintain herself. Not wanting to alarm her, as she has been told of the girl's delicate state, she calls out into the adjoining room, "Lizette."

"Oui, Madame," replies a servant who quickly appears.

"Please show our guest to her room."

"Oui, Madame."

Brushing past Sarah, Lizette stops, realizing she is not following. Not understanding why the girl does not move, Madame Caillier looks to the men to see if they might give insight.

"It is okay. You may go," Jean says, knowing Sarah believes him her master, and the only one who may give such permission.

Glancing to Madame Caillier before leaving the room, Sarah notices her mournful expression. Even through the fog that envelops her, Sarah can see she pities her.

"She does not understand but to do as she is told," Jean adds, reverting back to French once Sarah leaves the room. "We received word only a few days after her arrival that she was already deemed unmanageable by the Indians, which to her advantage was so, for we have heard a number of the children have been adopted into the communities, and we see no way to negotiate their release."

"Isabelle, if you will excuse us, we will retire to my study." Believing the nature of the discussion is more than his wife should hear, Henri Caillier moves to leave the room. Jean and Pierre give genial bows to her and they follow.

"Did you see others at Kahnawà:ke?" inquires Henri, before he is fully seated in the large armchair by the fire, only newly lit by the boy from the barn who watches it closely, ensuring the kindling takes.

"Yes, we saw others." Guarding his answer, Jean eyes the boy, not wanting to reveal too much while he is in the room.

"C'est tout. Leave us, Jacques," Henri snaps, impatient to know the news Jean has to share.

"Oui, Monsieur." Quickly retreating from the room, the fire is left to sputter to life on its own.

"As you know, Henri, the great tragedy of such wars is that we must rely on those who we not so long ago called enemy. It is inconceivable that they should then be allowed to adopt children who share nothing in common with them."

"This is true, Jean, but we must be thankful that they are followers of the Catholic faith and will impart the church's teaching on these poor unfortunates, for there is hope in this, is there not?"

"No! There is no hope in that argument," rebuts Jean heatedly. "Their ways differ too much from our own. It is not right that a girl such as the one I now have in my possession be subjected to living amongst them. Do not forget, I have seen the result of their savagery."

Henri and Pierre look to one another, knowing Jean will unleash his usual tirade against the alliance, which he deems gives too many concessions to the Mohawk. His sentiments are precisely the reason Pierre accompanied him to the village. To ensure negotiations went smoothly, he had to use his influence over Jean, whose temper often got the best of him. The occupants of the study, however, will not be spared.

"You may well forget, but I lived many years amongst the Mohawk before the peace accord of three years ago, and I do not so easily forget the screams in the fields as my tenant, neighbour, and *friend*," he emphasizes for effect, "Jean deLalonde was cut down along with eight others of our parish while they tended to their farms. What threat did they pose, I ask you? You do not have the memory of Jean's widow crying at her loss and the destitution as babes clung to her skirt, but I do. I do!" Jean is almost yelling now, and Henri knows he can do nothing to stop his friend, but not wanting to alarm Isabelle and the others, he pleads, "Jean, please. Lower your voice."

"Oh, excuse, I forget we are not alone," he offers sincerely, glancing to the room where they left Madame Caillier's company. Where one might have expected the reminder to restrain his emphatic telling of his story, Jean is undeterred.

"You may well say, 'but it has been seventeen years, Jean; time has moved on,' but I tell you, friends, such things do not so easily escape your memory, and I am equally a victim of such terror. I am as injured by the remembrance of it as I sit here now as on that day. Yes, a peace has been signed, and they may follow the Catholic faith, but only last year we had to abandon our beloved Saint-Louis parish because of the ongoing threat from our *allies*."

"You are right," Pierre concedes. "It is a great loss to see Saint-Louis close. And we do not know what memories you carry of that day many years ago."

They sit in silence for a few moments, allowing Jean to regain his composure, for he pants with the effort of making his point clear.

Rising from his chair, Henri moves to a side table where a bottle of cognac and glasses are neatly set. Pouring an unusually generous amount of the amber liquid into each glass, he nimbly picks them up and distributes them to his companions. Sipping the warming aperitif, he finally offers. "We must rely on the assurances we have been given that our alliance is strong. Surely we shall not see conflict as we once did. With the guidance of Père Millet in their village, they will not transgress our newly forged peace accord. To renew such sentiments would be an act of war."

"Do not be so sure, mon ami. Do not be so sure," Jean says, swirling the liquid around in his glass, as though he sees in it what he recounts to them.

❧

## 79

"Jean, you must be joking. No man has ever attempted such an ambitious expedition."

"I tell you, Pierre, with Henri's backing — which I do count on, mon ami," he says, smiling cunningly at their host, "we shall mount the expedition and be richly rewarded for it."

Laughing heartily, Henri adds, "You may count upon the investment, Jean, but I count upon its return."

With the wine flowing throughout the meal, the men have become more jovial, and boisterous, as a result. They speak of business matters, a topic that does not interest Madame Caillier, nor her young guest, she assumes. She rises from her place at the end of the table, opposite her husband. Giving him a knowing look, she proceeds to take Sarah from their company.

"Come," she whispers softly in her ear, gently grabbing her hand. Sarah is sorry to leave the table, which holds her rapt in the sheer abundance before her. Having had her fill, she has spent the last several minutes simply taking in the sight so sorely missed. The meal itself seems an impossible vision: succulent beef with juices flowing over her plate, boiled potatoes, and bread with freshly churned butter, a fact which Monsieur Caillier did not overlook, for he regaled his guests at length at how fortunate they are to have the best cattle from which they are able to enjoy such luxuries. Though he reveals himself boastful, he is not unfriendly. Sarah studies his wife carefully, trying to determine her situation.

Calm and refined, she seems the opposite of her husband's gregarious nature. Sarah wonders if it is lack of experience due to age, for Sarah guesses she can be no older than seventeen, or perhaps the fact that she is only newly his wife, for Sarah heard the men make their apologies at not having attended their recent wedding as they were in Ville Marie finalizing the purchase of new lands. Their customs, manner of elaborate dress, language, and overt, sometimes arrogant, behaviour are the opposite of the life Sarah knew.

Madame Caillier wears an extravagant green dress with an exposing neckline that made Sarah blush when she first saw her appear for the evening meal. A string of pearls at her neck further highlights her bare white flesh. Sarah watches her carefully, imagining each shy aversion to her husband's lingering gaze a sign that she, too, finds the situation bewildering. Such kinship, however slight, stirs within her something that reminds her that she is alive — a yearning to connect, to be seen.

Without releasing her grip, Madame Caillier holds to Sarah the entire length of the narrow hall to the bedroom she was taken to earlier to wash in preparation of the evening meal. She leads Sarah to the chair at the fanciful table with deeply carved flowers across the front, holding a wash basin and small mirror. Madame Caillier does not speak, but squeezes Sarah's hand tight, smiling sweetly at her before turning to her servant, who is already preparing the bed for the night.

"Lizette . . . water . . . please," she says in halting English. Having less grasp on the language than Madame Caillier, Lizette looks at her in confusion. "L'eau, de l'eau," she repeats, with only the slightest impatience. Rushing toward Sarah, Lizette grabs the jug and leaves the room.

Alone, Sarah and Madame Caillier remain in uncomfortable silence, knowing they cannot hold a conversation with so few words understood between them. Seeking to break the impasse, Madame Caillier picks up the ivory brush from the table. Shifting Sarah by the shoulders to straighten her in the chair, she begins brushing the tangled mess. With the first few strokes, Sarah tenses, uneasy with such attention, but as each pass becomes smoother, she relaxes into the sense of relief engulfing her. Marked by such damaging experiences, she does not entirely forget her place as captive, but allows herself a brief reprieve, trusting that what her heart tells her of the kindness of this woman is true.

Captivated by Madame Caillier, Sarah uses the mirror to more closely study the details of her elegant appearance. Stealing a few fleeting glances of her throughout the meal, Sarah feared being caught, for she could sense them closely watching her, as if she were a curiosity to them. Madame Caillier had on occasion done the same, but Sarah did not feel scrutinized by her as with the men.

Set high atop her head, Madame Caillier's raven hair, twisted about itself, is affixed with a green ribbon, the perfect match to her dress. Tucked in around it, cascading down one side, are delicate orange and red flowers, which Sarah can see are not real, for in the candlelight they shimmer much as the sheen on her dress. A few curls allowed to escape encircle her face as if to highlight her great beauty, for she is undoubtedly the most beautiful girl Sarah has ever seen. Even in her admiration, Sarah is not sorry to be so plain, for she clings to the familiar comfort of it. But looking at them together in the mirror, she is struck by just how different they are.

The sound of quick footsteps in the hallway startles Sarah. Looking to the mirror to see the cause of her sudden tensing, Madame Caillier feels her own heart leap at the girl's terrified expression. She spins around to see Lizette come into view, and sets her hand upon Sarah's shoulder, which draws her back. Giving her a weak, reassuring smile, she finishes brushing the final twisted curl, and neatly sets it back in place. All the while, she works to maintain her own composure so the frightened child before her will not sense her own shock in seeing such immense fear rise up and consume Sarah so wholly.

Setting the basin in front of them, Lizette puts the jug down warning, "C'est chaud, Mademoiselle."

Seeking direction of what is expected, Sarah turns to Madame Caillier.

"It is hot. Be careful," she warns.

Leaving the room to afford privacy, Madame Caillier waits in the darkened hallway, saying a silent prayer, caressing the child only yet known to her.

Left to wash, Sarah is sorry to sully the crisp white linen she has been left. It is embroidered with fine blue thread, and she traces the swirling pattern over and over, nearly forgetting what she has been asked to do. Hearing a soft knock at the closed door, she quickly dries her face.

"You are not ready?" Madame Caillier says, confused to find Sarah yet fully dressed.

"I am sorry," Sarah says, looking at the floor in shame. Moving past her, Madame Caillier picks up the nightgown she had Lizette lay out on the bed for her.

"You put this on, et . . ." Searching to find the words, she tries again. "We will . . . pris?" Repeating it again, "Pris," she hopes it will strike Sarah as familiar, for she knows the word she seeks is very near to this one.

"Pray?" Sarah ventures, thinking to her once customary routine.

"Oui, pray!" Madame Caillier repeats enthusiastically, pleased they have found the word between them. "Here," she says, handing the garment to Sarah. Staring at the beautifully made white nightgown with lace detailing at the neck, Sarah does not move to put it on. It should have seemed obvious that it is meant for her, but having lived with such depravation of pride and kindness, she is unable to accept it.

"I can sleep in these," she says, peering down at what she wears.

"Mais, non!" Madame Caillier replies, shocked at the notion.

Embarrassed, Sarah averts her eyes to avoid the incredulous stare. With only the ongoing, loud conversation of the men in the study penetrating the absolute silence of the room, Madame Caillier walks to the table where the basin now sits full of water, waiting to be emptied.

"You dress," she says decidedly, hoping this will work, for she senses she will not convince the girl of her worthiness to have use of such a thing. She had been sorry her husband would not tell her more of the girl's story — of where she came from, how long she travelled — "For her own sake," he had reasoned, but is now glad for his wisdom. *Such sadness.* She does not want to know what makes a child have such evident torment that it was profoundly felt upon meeting her. Pretending to busy herself, she watches Sarah in the mirror's reflection. As she slips the nightgown over her head, Madame Caillier swallows hard, trying not to gasp at seeing her frail, wasted body. She feels the tears well. Wanting to do anything that might ease Sarah's suffering, she says, "The gown is yours."

Thinking no one watching, Sarah runs her hands over the lace neckline, giving just a hint of a smile. "Thank you . . . Madame," she whispers, shyly attempting to address her as Lizette.

Nearly letting out an audible sigh of relief, Madame Caillier turns to her and says, "We will pray."

Sarah looks at her with fretful eyes. Knowing she will never understand what has such a hold on her, Madame Caillier seeks the solace of prayer, making this girl her particular intention this night. After kneeling at the side of the bed, she folds her hands and closes her eyes. When Sarah does not join her, she remembers what her husband told her: "She is a heathen, my dear, and will only be saved with the guidance of the church." She pats the floor beside her, and Sarah dutifully slips off the bed and onto her knees, doing as Madame Caillier. Listening to her recite her prayers, though she does not understand them, Sarah finds herself relaxed by the cadence of her voice. She likes the sound of the language when spoken quietly as now, as Madame speaks.

"Amen." Rising from the cold floor, Madame Caillier pulls back the blanket for Sarah to slip under. Sinking into the soft mattress, Sarah feels sleep quickly take hold.

"Bonne nuit. Good night."

Wanting to thank her for all she has done, so much that cannot be expressed, Sarah looks to Madame Caillier hovering over her and haltingly attempts, "Bonne . . . nuit? Madame."

Leaning down to blow out the candle on the bedside table, Madame Caillier takes one last look at Sarah, who dreamily stares back at her.

# 80

Sarah clutches a small bag that holds her only possession beyond the clothes she wears: her delicate, lace-detailed nightgown. Finding herself revived, she walks once again upon the muddy trail to their next unknown destination.

Never straying far from the icy shore, Sarah notes the changing temperament of the river. She watches as the once-raging tempest calms, and in these reprieves, when the river slows, it reminds her of another she knows well.

"Adieu, Pierre." Jean waves to his friend, who returns the gesture. Remaining on the trail nearest the river, he is unconcerned by the departure. Occasionally Sarah turns back to see the distance growing between them and Pierre Lamoureux until he finally disappears into the forest.

The silence of the walk, devoid of the continual hum of conversation, seems to suit Jean, for he looks this way and that, following the sound of the birds in the distance and turning to see great sheets of ice break up when they hit the islands dotting the river.

"My friend goes to Ville Marie to attend to his work," Jean says as if to himself, for he never turns to address Sarah directly. She ardently wishes he will speak more, for it fills the space where darkness occupies her mind, pulling her to places she wants to forget, but he does not. For a few miles, he contentedly observes the river, unaware that she fights to subdue her unrelenting, vicious memories.

"We will soon cross the river and arrive at my home, Mademoiselle." His tone suddenly changes, becomes much more authoritative. Straightening his posture, he turns to her and says, "Until your baptism, you will be known in our home simply as Mademoiselle."

"But I have a name."

"You are best to forget that name," he says without asking what it is. "Embrace what is being offered. It is more than you would find in the village we only a day ago released you from. Let me be clear: little opportunities exist for you beyond this."

Only now, in realizing he does not intend to see her redeemed, does she realize how ardently she had held to such an impossible hope. Sensing he has inflicted unnecessary fear into his new servant, for he cannot help but feel sorry for her, he softens his tone as he continues. "Do you have any questions?"

She has many, but one has tormented her for many days. "How . . . how many days did we journey?"

"Five weeks. Five," he repeats, seeming to say it as if not believing it himself. "The final group arrived at Fort Chambly only four days ago."

"And how many were there?"

"Just four of you, from what I understand."

"Excuse me, no, what I mean . . . what I mean to say is, how many of us were taken?"

"One hundred and twelve, we have estimated," comes the flat response, with no way to shield the magnitude of it.

"And how many are here now?"

"Mademoiselle, it is best we speak no more of this. It serves no purpose to know such things."

She can tell he is uncomfortable with the questions. "Please, it will not upset me to know. I have," she pauses, stopping the tears welling. "I know, not all made it . . . I know . . ." Her voice fades.

"Very well then, if you promise to ask no more of it, I will tell you."

"I promise."

"Eighty-nine." As if knowing the question to follow, he finishes, "And no more expected."

# 81

Cupping his hands around his mouth, Monsieur Quenet yells "Bonjour!" Waving vigorously to capture the attention of two men working near the opposite shore, he hollers again, "Bonjour!" This time his greeting is met with a return wave and a quickening of their pace as they jump into a large canoe and begin paddling ferociously against the strong current of a smaller, seemingly more powerful river, which flows into the now expansive river they have followed since leaving Kahnawà:ke. Sarah watches the men dipping their paddles deeply into the water, their grunts echoing as they pull with all their might to carry themselves forward. Drifting toward the open water of the slow, lumbering river, the men seem to wage a losing battle against the tempest of white water. They are frantically paddling, seeking an escape from its unyielding grip, and fear rises up in Sarah as she watches the unfolding scene. It is not only the knowledge that she will soon be ensnared in the river's grip that frightens her, but also the almost imperceptible hazy peaks in the distance, as if a fate once denied stalks her, reminding her it has not forgotten.

Only as they approach the shore downstream does the river release them from its grip, and, using the calmer water at the shoreline, they paddle their way back to where she and her master stand.

Panting with the exhaustion of their struggle, the men pull the canoe up on dry land. Quickly approaching Monsieur Quenet, they point further up river, speaking as quickly as the water flows. After listening attentively, he glances at Sarah doubtfully. When he finally nods in agreement, the men nimbly pick up the canoe, hoisting it over their heads, and carry it a short distance.

"We will have to walk along the shore, for with the added load we will surely be swept into the Saint-Laurent," he says, turning to Sarah, who is already quickening her pace. "Mademoiselle, there is no reason to worry yourself. Lucien and Jean-Baptiste are strong and quite used to traversing the river in such a temperament." His tone does not instill confidence, but instead reveals his own apprehension at the crossing. The dead brush at their feet catches them about the ankles, but the men seem well aware of each step. Paying more attention to the rapid waters and the feeling of the ominous mountains at her back, Sarah stumbles in her distraction.

"Come now, keep up," orders Monsieur Quenet impatiently.

Holding the canoe tight to the shore, the men first settle Monsieur Quenet near the back. Then Lucien extends his hand. "Mademoiselle."

Feeling the steady ground give way to a wobbly footing, she nearly tumbles over the side, only saved from a watery grave by Lucien, who lunges to grasp her waist and roughly set her in place ahead of Monsieur Quenet, who exhales audibly in relief. Without warning, the two men jump in, and they are instantly thrust into the untamed river. The canoe bobs wildly about, and it seems the men have no control whatever. Cringing with every jolt and violent sway, she grips the sides of the unstable vessel. Her knuckles white and fingers paining with the cold water washing over them, Sarah shuts her eyes to blot out the vision of the maelstrom.

Miraculously, the canoe soon slows and the water beneath her calms. Opening her eyes again, she sees Lucien grab the dried, winter-worn reeds at the river's edge, holding tightly until Jean-Baptiste, who has guided them from the rear, can bring them fully alongside the shore. Both grasp any manner of shrubs or grasses to stop them drifting towards the larger river, until a boy, who has been waiting for them, can steady them enough for Lucien to jump out and help Sarah and Monsieur Quenet disembark. Awkwardly scrambling up the slick, muddy embankment, Sarah uses her only free hand, for she will not loosen her grip on the bag she carries. Covered in filth by the time she makes the top, her only concern is that her one precious possession has remained pristine. Relieved, she can see the pure white lace collar, jostled slightly from its encasement by the rough ascent, is unsoiled.

"Ah, bravo! Bravo!" Monsieur Quenet congratulates the men with a hearty handshake, seeming as if he is surprised they have made it at all. "François," he calls out to the boy dragging the canoe up the embankment.

"Oui, Monsieur?" After giving the vessel a good tug to secure it, François rushes to Monsieur Quenet. Receiving his orders, he runs off in the direction of the house in the distance. With all the commotion, and so many readily available to be at the master's calling, Sarah knows their return has been expected, and she believes François is off to announce their arrival to those who live in the house set on a high point overlooking both rivers.

"La Maison Quenet, Mademoiselle," Monsieur Quenet announces proudly. The stone home, not as grand as the Cailliers', is no less substantial with its large, roughhewn stones and sharply sloped roof. The sun of the late afternoon shines brightly upon it, and the door opens, revealing two small children, fidgeting impatiently as a servant urges them back into the shadows. Quickening his pace, he walks up the narrow path, followed by Sarah, leaving Lucien and Jean-Baptiste to attend the work that was interrupted by their arrival.

"Papa, Papa!" Before he can take a further step into his home, the children, jubilant at his return, grasp his legs. They are exposed upon the rise of land, and a chilled breeze nips at them. Monsieur Quenet fumbles under their enthusiasm, trying to move from the door to allow the servant to shut it.

"Mes enfants, attendez! Wait," he says in English for Sarah's benefit.

Noticing her, the children stare at her with gaping mouths, making her feel uncomfortable at the curious attention.

"Papa, c'est la fille?" a young girl asks shyly.

He hushes them, putting his finger to his mouth in a gesture for the benefit of the small boy urging him to do the same.

Just as the children dislodge from him, a woman, heavy with child, enters from an adjoining room. "Jean!" she cries with a hint of relief in her voice. He greets her with a kiss on each cheek, and the family moves to a sitting room, leaving Sarah in the darkened entryway with a woman who is evidently a servant, judging by her plain manner of dress and lack of attention from Monsieur Quenet.

"Madesmoiselle, viens avec moi," she orders harshly. Snatching the bag from Sarah's hand, she ascends a steep, narrow staircase at the back of the house. She does not understand what is asked of her, but as she watches her bag leave her, it precipitates the desired effect and she follows.

The servant leads her to a poorly lit room. The low, slanted ceiling makes it difficult to navigate the cramped space. Hurrying to her bag, which has been thrown as if discarded, onto a bed along the far wall, Sarah clutches her treasure. Turning, she finds the girl frowning at her. She points to the bed Sarah stands beside, then directly at her, as if to indicate the already obvious point that it is to be hers.

"Julienne? Julienne?" The soft voice of a woman calls out. Sarah assumes it to be Monsieur Quenet's wife, for she is the only other adult she has seen thus far in the house. Exaggeratedly rolling her eyes, the servant answers, "Oui, Madame." Before exiting the room, she scowls at Sarah with contempt. Her heavy footsteps descending the stairs seem to mimic her discontent of her changed situation.

Tucking her head as she sits on the edge of the bed, Sarah hears the crunch of the hard straw mattress beneath her. Lacking the abundant character and comfort of the bed she enjoyed at the Cailliers', this is much more in keeping with the simplicity of the life she had known. But this bleak room stands in contrast to even that plain existence, for it has no evidence that anyone dwells in the eaves at all; save the two beds and primitive, wooden chests at the end of each, it looks abandoned.

A small window at one end, furthest from her, allows a solitary shaft of light to enter the dismal, unadorned space. Even as the dust floats about, catching sparks of light in them, it does not ease her growing panic at being in such an enclosed space. Days before she had only the stars above her, but since her arrival she has been forced into the confines of suffocating rooms, this being the smallest yet.

Listening to the bustling household — orders being called to Julienne in quick succession — Sarah remembers her parting from Madame Caillier, who shed a tear at her departure. Believing at the time she was simply sorry to see her leave, Sarah now focuses on one significant, but overlooked detail — the pity in her eyes. Suddenly, she understands the reason for it. The notion that the men have saved her vanishes, and is replaced by a stark reality: from the lack of acknowledgement by Madame Quenet and the curious stares of the children, to the inhospitable manner of Julienne's welcome, Sarah does not require further explanation of her role. She is as Lizette, as Julienne: a servant.

## 82

Tying up her long, white apron, the final piece to her servant's attire, Sarah joins Julienne in the kitchen to prepare the evening meal. Peeling the potatoes, she watches Julienne feed the children with no sign that she loves them whatsoever, though they seem to beg her attention. With every misstep, they are scolded, making them cry inconsolably, which does nothing to slow her rapid feeding of them, even as they choke. Once finished, they are whisked from their chairs and taken away to be put to bed. Charlotte, small for seven years, is taken roughly by the hand, while Pierre, four, trails close behind; both seem to understand the consequence of any lagging.

Taking her meal in the kitchen after Monsieur and Madame Quenet have finished theirs, Sarah picks at her food, much to Julienne's consternation, who mumbles under her breath. Over the clanging of the dishes, Sarah hears Monsieur Quenet's voice with the occasional soft responses from his wife. Sarah is unsure of her duties, beyond peeling the potatoes, which gives her time to ponder the disposition of the woman she has yet to meet.

Upon returning with more dishes in hand from the adjoining room, Julienne points to the door, flicking her finger at Sarah. "Allez! Le Monsieur veut parler avec toi!" she barks. Opening the door, she dares not disobey, for she will suffer further from Julienne's wrath. Standing in the empty room, only a few dishes left as any evidence of her master having eaten in there, she waits for any sign of what she is to do next.

"Julienne!" Monsieur Quenet calls from a room just out of sight. Hastening to his command, Julienne almost knocks Sarah over. Upon seeing the girl standing stationary in the empty room, she knows what he is calling for. Harshly grabbing Sarah's arm, she pulls her to a more formal sitting room where Monsieur Quenet sits in a large armchair, directly across from his wife, who is occupied with her embroidery.

Positioning Sarah in the center of the room, Julienne retreats to attend to her work.

"Mademoiselle, please meet my wife, Madame Quenet."

Raising her eyes, the lady of the house takes her first notice of their new servant.

"We have brought you to our home out of a duty to provide you the opportunity to be saved into the one true faith — and to release you from the hands of our allies." Monsieur Quenet says in a tone which causes his wife to put down her work to see the reason of his sudden change.

Easing her concern with a shake of his head and tender smile, he continues. "We have a growing family and Julienne has much to do, leaving many chores unattended. My dear wife suffers from it and as such, I seek to remedy the situation, which now may be accomplished through aiding an unfortunate, such as yourself." The reference stings. *An unfortunate?* Sarah's cheeks flush with the shame of it.

"While you will not earn a wage, as Julienne does, for the payment for your release was dear, you may be assured that you will be housed, fed adequately, and provided education in the Catholic faith. This, I believe, will bring you much happiness."

Staring at the floor, embarrassed to be such a burden, Sarah does not answer.

"As a father would punish his children to provide proper guidance, so too may you expect punishment to be adjudicated when necessary," he adds, reinforcing his role in her life. Offended at the lack of appreciation for his great sacrifice, he glances to his wife who seems equally insulted.

"Your duty will be to tend the children. Julienne will teach you. Once on your own, you may expect no further assistance from her, so learn well," he sternly warns. "You will find that none amongst my family or servants speaks your language, and though I use it now, and in matters of business on occasion, you are not to speak it in my house. Pay close attention and you will come to understand Français quickly." Realizing no response will be forthcoming, he abruptly ends the conversation. "You are dismissed."

Just as she reaches the threshold of the room, he adds in a sympathetic tone, "My duty, Mademoiselle, is to ensure you are ensconced in the ways of our society so that when you are of age, you will marry and be a faithful servant of God, our king, and your husband. This is as much as any woman of New France can pray for."

# 83

❧

"**P**ut on your cloak, Mademoiselle, for we go to meet Père deBreslay at Sainte-Anne-de-Bellevue to begin your education."

At the front of the church, near what Sarah believes is the pulpit, a man in a black robe, the same as the one at Fort Chambly, waits.

"Bonjour, Père deBreslay," Monsieur Quenet calls out, his voice echoing in the grand space. Given a slight nod by the priest, her master instantly excuses himself, leaving Sarah alone with him.

Appraising her as he slowly makes his way down the central aisle, his solemn demeanour gives no indication of the powerful tirade he will soon unleash in order to begin the process of her education. Older than many of the children he has previously converted, he expects resistance. Though she looks weak, a trait all captive children possess to some degree after their trials, he knows the Puritan teachings use fear as control, particularly over children, and the undoing will be difficult.

Now a guest, albeit a captive one, of deRouville's father, Joseph François Hertel, at his home near Fort Chambly, Reverend Williams was amongst the final captives to arrive. He is highly prized for the value he offers the Marquis de Vaudreuil in his negotiations with the enemy, and his comfort is an efficient method by which to gain his trust, or at the very least, information that will be of value. Missives in these early days already confirm he is a fiery preacher, using the touchstones of fear of the Catholic faith, and the French themselves, upon the pulpit. To fracture any remaining ties to these heathen beliefs, and the life this girl has known, the priest will have to use equally jarring tactics.

"Monsieur Quenet has explained your place here in his household and in our community?" he asks in a serious tone.

"Yes," Sarah answers meekly.

"And you understand why you come to see me today?"

"Yes."

"And you know that you are to learn to speak French quickly?"

"Yes."

"Very well, come with me," he beckons, already moving up the nave. Turning his head slightly so that Sarah can hear him, he warns, "This day will be the only I shall speak to you solely in the language of les Anglais. By our next meeting, you shall be expected to speak our language."

Sitting her upon an uncomfortable stool in a cloistered room, Père deBreslay rails for hours of damnation, eternal hell fires, and lost souls, conversion being the only deliverance from this fate. Believing he has to convince her of the sin she carries, he sweats profusely with the fervour of his convictions. He does not realize the lack of necessity for it. As Sarah is already condemned a sinner in her own mind, this conversion is not met with the resistance he imagines. The broken child before him, burdened by sin, by knowing intimately the desolation of hell, craves the promise of salvation being offered. Believing she deserves it is the final impediment to accepting it.

"No light, no sound, no love shall exist while you languish in eternal misery." Incessant in his methods, he stands over her, watching for any sign that the critical moment is at hand.

As the occasional nervous wringing of her hands turns to trembling, he can see the final stronghold give. Sensing he must strike now, he loudly commands, "Confess, my child, that which lies upon your heart."

"I believe I brought this upon us."

"Of what do you speak?" he inquires, not understanding the response. He expects her to voice her resistance to her conversion.

"All of it," she answers, quietly sobbing, her head bowed in shame.

"Go on," he urges, patting her hand gently, his vehemence calmed.

"I wanted for more, thinking my life . . ." She is distraught, contemplating the devastation her sin wrought, and her voice fails her.

"Thinking your life what?"

"Plain," she whispers, struggling to hold back the torrent, which will not be denied further. Streaming down her face, the tears flow unimpeded. Wiping them from her cheeks to thwart the stinging pain she knows they will cause, she is surprised to find her face . . . *soft*. She touches her cheeks lightly again to confirm what she can scarcely believe, for in finding her once-raw, wounded face healed, she realizes her heart has not.

"No," Père deBreslay replies almost breathlessly, shocked at the immensity of guilt she carries. "No, it is not your doing. It was your heathen ways, and those of your people. Your miseducation led you to believe you were saved, but eternal hell fires always awaited. Purgatory has been shown to you on earth. If you now embrace and follow our Catholic teachings *faithfully*," he emphasizes, "you will find salvation." Lifting her face by her chin, he repeats, "Salvation." Recognizing a willing student, he changes tactics: kindness and love will be the tools of conversion.

## 84

Drawing a shawl tightly about her to ward off the chill, Sarah prepares to exit the house into the early morning fog signalling the advent of another season. Bundling the children, who are at her heels, as always, she ties Charlotte's shawl tightly about her and makes sure Pierre's buttons are properly affixed. Having recently found the practice of undoing them fascinating, he lacks the skill to find their match when attempting to do them up again, making him look dishevelled, much to the dismay of Madame Quenet. Sarah does not welcome her mistress's upset, but gives Pierre a smile each time, for he is pure joy to her. She cannot resist his large, brown eyes so full of a sense of accomplishment, even when the task is incorrectly done. Taking their small hands in her own, she sets out for the long walk to church, Monsieur and Madame Quenet following in the carriage.

Passing by the farmyard, Sarah sees Jean-Baptiste, Lucien, and Jacques quickly feeding the animals so they, too, might attend mass. When able, she watches them from a window as the children play, or as she feeds them their meals. She envies their camaraderie, for even as she has the children for companionship, her life remains one of solitude in many ways.

Madame Quenet sometimes gives a small compliment on how the children progress under her care, which has slowly led to short conversations, always on the subject of the children. Jealous, Julienne makes her sentiments known. Though they share a room, she does not extend the hand of friendship no matter the offer of help, or gratitude shown for her guidance. Sarah soon accepts that her efforts to become companions in their work will not change Julienne's opinion. Now, having to stay behind to care for Marie Josephe, born only two months previously, does not ingratiate her further. Her education being at a critical stage, Sarah is given privileges that sour their relationship all the more. Julienne, thinking herself superior to the orphan Anglaise, as she refers to her under her breath, glares at Sarah in their parting, huffing in disgust so that she might hear as she closes the door behind them. Even her ire cannot dissuade Sarah from welcoming the day.

The sun, only newly risen, sets the leaves ablaze with gold, red, and orange hues that stun with their beauty. Set against the gently flowing river, the Quenet home affords a breathtaking vista. Often in the summer months, she took Charlotte and Pierre near the shore to walk along its banks, where they delighted in the small fish who nibble the stones. Where once only a few ducks and summer birds frolicked, now great flocks of geese gather upon the water as the chill, not felt in many months, returns. Their presence brings a strange realization: time has passed. Dew covered, the empty fields glisten. The harvest is in. As she studies the contrast of the expansive field bordered by the brilliance of the autumn leaves in the thick forest surrounding them, something begins to take shape in the mists of a shadowy distant corner of the field. Squinting to make sense of it, Sarah stops. As she studies its familiar form, her heart pains with the injury of what is becoming clear. Robbed of her breath, she mouths a word as if calling out, but just as she expects a response, the sun rises above the trees, banishing him with the light.

"Mademoiselle?"

Seeing Charlotte's confused expression, Sarah smiles reassuringly at her before moving forward into the forest along the well-worn path to church.

In the months since her arrival at the Quenet's, she has become adept at ignoring such episodes, which are mercifully rare as so little of this new life seems familiar to her. But even as she refuses to dwell on these false visions, the deceit of them injures her heart. Overwhelmed by the lingering effects, she seeks that which offers reprieve from these cruel memories. Searching the horizon, she is released from its grip as when the white cross high upon the steeple of Sainte-Anne comes into view.

Sarah's strongest attachment within this new society is to the church, and Père deBreslay, for it, and he, offers that which she could not have expected — deliverance. It did not come easy, but once accepted, she leapt at it, grasping to it steadfastly.

Her early days amongst the French saw the restoration of dignity afforded by cleanliness, adequate food, and privacy, but these revived confusing fantasies about redemption. For weeks, she dreamt of her father having come for her and believed this true until she woke and the anguish of reality slay such hope. They would not seek to reclaim such a sinner.

Père deBreslay, impassioned by his belief that this girl has been rescued by God himself, could see the struggle she waged in accepting wholeheartedly her absolution from blame.

"Heathen beliefs can only lead to desolation," he imparted. "A child, such as yourself, cannot be held to account. To be unfairly influenced by the adults is to condemn you."

Even with the insinuation that the adults in her life had wrought the outcome, he was careful not to alienate her affections by accusing those by name he knew she may well yet come to the defence of. Instead, he targeted a common foe, he suspected, as an early mention of his name elicited a marked response: all colour drained from her usually rosy complexion, her posture became rigid, and a deep furrow appeared upon her brow, as if besieged by dread.

"Reverend Williams, my dear, does the devil's work." But it was in posing one final question that he found the key to unlocking that which held her back. "Have you not suffered enough to trust my words, Mademoiselle?" There was no necessity of an answer, for it was plain enough to see. "You imagine what may be? Perhaps you find yourself thinking to, or dreaming of, the faces you have known?"

Surprised that he should know her innermost thoughts, she recoiled, averting her eyes to the floor as she often did when trying to protect herself.

"Yearning for such things is human, but your salvation is divine. It is God's will that you are here, that you should be saved. Salvation," he explained, noting the almost imperceptible reaction to the word, "lies in the life you are offered. What has befallen you once could happen again; God is not so easily dissuaded. To lose it all — to lose *them* all," he emphasized, using what he knew would be most affecting, "I should think was most difficult, Mademoiselle. To lose them twice," he paused, "well, to lose them twice . . . it would be beyond measure. Do not want such things, dear girl."

The vicious memories of all that had transpired, and the suggestion it could happen again, found her beseeching his protection. "I cannot," she whispered gravely.

Placing his large palm upon her forehead, he bowed his head and closed his eyes, "You are chosen to come to the loving arms of the Father and take your rightful place amongst us."

Meeting with Père deBreslay regularly, Sarah, now an eager student and quick study, looks forward to their time together, for he soon became a trusted guide in navigating the myriad of customs, language, and most importantly, teachings of the Catholic faith. Always greeting her with a genuine smile and gentle voice, he never again employed fear as his method — beyond the reasonable measure of imparting the teachings of the church, which was considerably less than she had been raised with.

With the children in tow, she enters her refuge. The distress of the earlier episode in the field washes away and she relaxes, comforted by her faith.

Taking in a deep breath the distinct sweet, pungent fragrance of incense hanging in the air, Sarah sits the children on a pew beside the confessional, warning them to behave before slipping into the darkness behind a deep burgundy velvet curtain. Kneeling, she clasps her hands and closes her eyes, awaiting the screen to be pulled back. Her faults and secret desires laid bare in confession each Sunday frees her from the weight of sin. Sarah always makes it — and its promise of forgiveness — her first priority each time she enters Sainte-Anne.

After completing her prescribed penance, two Our Fathers and six Hail Marys, Sarah and the children take their usual seats at the back of the church with the other servants of the community. A number of families have already settled into their places ahead of her and are kneeling in quiet prayer, their hands clasped and their heads bowed, awaiting the mass to begin. The pews at the front of the church, where the Quenets sit, remain empty. Though they arrive by carriage, they are very often the last to enter the church, as if to make a grand entrance so that all might observe the arrival. Their dress is markedly finer than most habitants, Monsieur Quenet's status as one of the wealthiest landowners affording him such luxury.

Sarah has been given an appropriate set of clothing for Sunday mass, but her dress is not fine in any manner, but it is no less than the majority that make up the church, and therefore has the effect of giving her a sense of pride to be accepted amongst them. All that Père deBreslay promised would come to pass has been proven true.

Waiting for mass to begin, Sarah enjoys looking around the beautifully adorned church. There are numerous statues of various saints, with a particularly touching one of the Virgin Mary holding her infant son being her favourite. A large golden cross above the alter seems to emit its own light even on dreary days, and paintings on the wall depict the twelve stations of the cross, which Sarah enjoys doing on her weekly visits with Père deBreslay. But on a sunny morning such as this, it is the light streaming in through the stained-glass windows that captivates her. Drenched in a multitude of colours, the people sitting in the pews seem unaware of the beauty surrounding them. The sight so overtakes Sarah's emotions that it seems a message from God, and she gives silent thanks for His gift. The life offered her since accepting the Catholic faith has filled her with such abundance, that even in her position as servant, she is thankful.

"God has truly saved me," she whispers under her breath.

Everyone stands with a suddenness that shocks her to attention, and Sarah looks about, finding the Quenets seated at the head of the church, along with all other usual parishioners. Realizing she has been lost in her observations, she sings along with the choir as Père deBreslay, preceded by altar boys and deacons carrying crosses and holy objects, slowly makes his way past her up the nave to take his place upon the alter. After a few moments spent in silent prayer, he slowly, reverently, turns to face the congregation.

"In nómine Pátris et Fílii et Spíritus Sáncti. Amen."

Making the sign of the cross, she falls into the comforting rhythm of the highly ritualized mass. Although the mass, said in Latin, remains elusive in understanding, she gives the appropriate responses as expected, making her feel part of the larger community that gathers. Their voices mix together, *as though harkening the angels to bring their prayers to God's ear*, Sarah thinks, swallowing hard to subdue the emotions moving her to tears. Filled with such joy, such peace, she embraces it wholly.

With the encouragement of Père deBreslay and the routine of daily life, Sarah begins to rebuild herself into a girl of New France.

# 85

❧

"You have learned well since your arrival only last year, Mademoiselle," Monsieur Quenet congratulates Sarah upon hearing her give final instructions to Julienne regarding the children before her departure.

"Merci," she replies, dipping into a clumsy curtsy, a little distracted by the excitement of the day.

With an impressive ability to learn the language, Sarah quickly became fluent in French. Now able to ascertain what visitors speak about, it gives her insight into news of the community. None of it is of any consequence, but it provides distraction from her usual concerns of rearing the children. Pierre Lamoureux, their most frequent visitor, has proven himself kind, often asking of her instruction with Père deBreslay, a subject she gladly engages in. She sometimes finds herself offering more than he may have expected, but he never cuts her off or makes her feel as if she has transgressed his good nature. However, she does pray to learn to control her enthusiasm for that which makes her most happy: her faith and the children.

"Mademoiselle!" Hearing her named called impatiently by Monsieur Quenet, Sarah rushes from the house and takes her place beside Madame Quenet in the carriage. The vantage point gives her an opportunity to take a lingering look at the changing landscape.

Released from a long, hard winter, the late spring brings the welcome return of sun and life to the Quenet farm. She does not complain as some do about the hardships of cold, dark months, yet Sarah rejoices in seeing a landscape of abundance — fragrant flowers budding amid newly sprouting green grasses, leaves only now able to give shade, rustling in the light breeze, and the river beginning to return to its gentle nature — for she will soon enjoy bringing the children to search for the creatures within, as last summer. The season matches the joy in her heart.

Monsieur Quenet, often away on business, usually pays no mind to her at all, leaving this usual duty to his wife. He has, however, come back especially for this day. Driving his horse at a good clip, he sits proudly as they make their way to Sainte-Anne, for today Sarah is to be baptized into the faith she has come to love and faithfully embrace.

Reflecting on the day, Père deBreslay is filled with pride in his accomplishment. Usually only those much younger are so easily converted. Where he has witnessed — experienced — resistance to conversion by many who were brought under similar circumstances, some from the very group she was once a part of, Marie Magdeleine Hélène is a testament to his instruction, for she has fully embraced Catholicism and is now living as though naturally born amongst them. Taking credit for his expert handling of this child of God, he smiles as he reads the parish registry:

Marie Magdeleine Hélène, Anglaise

The thirty first day of May, seventeen hundred and five, the baptism ceremony was given to Marie Magdeleine Hélène, Anglaise, living at the home of Sieur Quenet of this parish, age thirteen, who previously lived in her own country. The Godfather, Pierre Lamoureux, Sieur de St-Germain, who aided in procuring the girl of Sr. Quenet. The wife, Etiennette Hurtubise, of said Jean Quenet, who did not know how to sign this document, the said Jean Quenet signed.

Jean Quenet
R.C. de Breslay

## 86

"Marie Josephe, I am given a name today," Sarah whispers to the little one cradled in her arms, as she rocks her tenderly in the glow of the soft moonlight coming through the window of the children's room.

As the baby fusses, she rises from the chair to close the window where the curtains flutter in the warm evening breeze. Glinting high above, the night sky calls forth parts of herself left dormant. Swaying to and fro, she allows herself to drift to the past — to places where the same stars shine upon those now living in the shadows.

"I heard my name today, not the name of this place, but the name I once had." Speaking as if to the night itself, rather than to the baby now lulled to sleep by the gentle motion and soothing sound of her soft voice, she speaks her name aloud for the first time, "Marie Magdeleine . . . Hélène." Almost breathlessly, she repeats in her own language ". . . Allen." Recognizing it at once at her baptism, she felt as if an unseen presence made itself known to her, the same presence she now speaks to.

She does not know her once-familiar name is a gift from Madame Quenet, now her Godmother, as a way to show her gratitude for the aid with, and the love of, her own children, who thrive in her care. Only weeks before her baptism, she had made a special request of her husband that Marie Magdeleine should have a small reminder of her lost family. Not a sentimental man, he believed the move ill-advised, but quickly acquiesced, finding the persuasion of his wife in such cases touching. She asked for little, but when moved, was compelling.

The quiet of the night removing all distractions, consciously and unconsciously sought, she is faced with matters left unfinished, with goodbyes never uttered. Seeking the solace of prayer to subdue that which if allowed to manifest will prove unbearable, she places Marie Josephe gently in her cradle to return to her own small room on the other side of the wall.

"Your Maman is my Godmother, I am tied to this place," she says, looking lovingly down upon the sweet, rounded face of the baby she has come to see as a sibling. They have all become as those she once knew — as those once lost to her. Even if customs and language differ, some things about the normalcy of a family home remain the same: joy, laughter, affection — these things have revived her, saved her.

The heart that wanted for more has been quenched by a terrible torrent of misery, and now beating within her, though much diminished, it is grateful.

Kneeling upon the hard floor at her bedside, Marie Magdeleine folds her hands and bows her head in prayer. With her new rosary, a baptism gift from Père deBreslay, in hand, she gives thanks for the abundant blessing in her life: for salvation in the Catholic faith, for the guidance of Père deBreslay, for the name that renews her sense of being, for her beloved brothers and sisters, whom she cares for, for her Godmother, Madame Quenet, and Monsieur Quenet for providing the means of her deliverance from her ordeal, and for her Godfather, Monsieur Lamoureux. But on this night, when the names she once knew resonate in her heart, she takes her time finishing what must be done to move on. Praying for them, wishing them love and happiness, she allows her own family to recede into her past and the darkness of disjointed dreams.

# 87

## 1 May 1709

"Oh, it is beautiful, Charlotte," Marie Magdeleine says as she runs her hand gently over the delicate needlework, studying the embroidered scene. The view from the Quenet farm has always enchanted her. The children, having spent their days frolicking with such a background, seem to pay no attention to it, but with this precious gift, she realizes her own days contemplating the joy of such a place has been noticed, and she is grateful for the memento of it. Captured at its most beautiful, the small image set in a plain wooden frame shows the narrow Rivière des Outaouais in the foreground flowing to join the mighty Fleuve Saint-Laurent. The darkened silhouettes of the distant mountains on the horizon are set against a clear blue sky, and all the glory of a midsummer's day lies in between with the colour of such richness. It seems a perfect study of the memories she has of it. Rubbing the small flecks of yellow, white, and purple flowers they often pick to adorn a summer table, Marie Magdeleine closes her eyes, breathing in slowly and deeply as if their scent fills the air.

"I made it special for your birthday." Charlotte hesitates, finding the pensive silent examination of her gift disconcerting.

Opening her eyes, Marie Magdeleine smiles broadly. "It is as I remember, and we only have a month or two until your work comes to life." Putting her hands on Charlotte's plump, rosy cheeks, she pulls her close, placing a soft kiss on her forehead, whispering, "Thank you, dearest. It is the loveliest of all that I have." Releasing her, she can see the pride upon her sister's face.

"Maman had the thread ordered from Ville Marie and Papa brought it to me months ago," she shares excitedly, relishing in the delight that her gift has been such a welcomed surprise. "Of course, I did not construct the frame, but I asked Lucien to make it, for he is a master craftsman, Papa says. He did not charge me whatsoever for it, and though Papa tried to pay him for his services, he said to tell you 'bonne fête' from him and that he wishes you well."

The reminder of small kindnesses in her early years floods back with a name she has not heard in some time. Only a few months after her arrival, Lucien had married and started his own farm, but while in the Quenet's employ he had proven sympathetic, showing her the work of caring for the chickens and collecting eggs with a helpful heart, not ridiculing her for the errors she often made. Having little occasion, or cause, to speak with him since his departure, she now only sees him and his growing family when attending church. She cannot find reason for such generosity to someone of no consequence to him, but is thankful as much for the sentiment as for the joy it brings Charlotte in placing her beautiful work in it.

Listening to Charlotte detail her clandestine work, Marie Magdeleine soon hears the familiar ruckus of the children coming to find her, as it is breakfast time. "Let us go eat, and you may tell me and the others more of your ruse," she says, knowing Charlotte will enjoy recounting her story for the others.

Finding the children, now numbering six, seated around the table, she joins Suzanne in finishing the preparation of their porridge. Suzanne Duquet, a shy girl from a neighbouring farm, was hired only a month earlier, at Madame Quenet's request. Marie Magdeleine is to train her to help with the children. She is somewhat surprised, for she has no need of an assistant, the youngest, Louis, already being two years of age, and Charlotte often helping, but she does as asked without question.

While the addition of one more bed in the already cramped room upstairs further aggravates Julienne, now considered too old to marry, *and too sour*, in Marie Magdeleine's opinion, she makes sure Suzanne has an ally, despite the uneasy feeling she has about the change.

The day passes with little fanfare. Marie Magdeleine attends to the children and household duties as any other day, though the elevated spirits of the young ones do on occasion require tempering. Distracted by an inexplicable feeling of the day being somehow different, she ignores it, believing it the result of the children's influence.

As dinner draws to an end, the children gather their plates from the table to hand them "politely," they are reminded, to Julienne, anxious for their removal from the room. Unexpectedly, Monsieur Quenet appears at the door.

"I wish to speak with you after the children have been put to bed. Please find me in my study," he says, looking directly at Marie Magdeleine.

"Oui, Monsieur," she answers simply, feeling a sense of apprehension rise within her.

"Please sit." Monsieur Quenet motions to the large armchair set by the hearth laying dormant as the evening is warm yet. Doing as told, she sits, wondering what news warrants such an unusual request.

"This is a significant day, Marie Magdeleine. Many years ago, when you first came to us, I should think . . ." Pausing as if calculating something in his mind, he offers, "Five?" He looks to her, awaiting confirmation. "Yes," she answers hesitantly, unsure of why he asks.

"Very well, five years ago when you first came to us, I explained to you that you would be given a home and treated as any in our community. I hope you have found my word was kept?" he says in a tone of expectant gratitude.

"Yes, I thank you for all you have given me."

"At that time, I also said our duty was to give you opportunity until such time as you would marry."

Shyly, she averts her eyes, looking to the ground, a habit she has never broken, despite his efforts.

"Marie Magdeleine," he says harshly, attempting to assure her full attention to the important matter at hand. "You are eighteen years of age today, a grown woman, much older than many who are already married. If we delay further, you risk becoming as Julienne." The very mention of becoming as Julienne makes her shudder. *Such a miserable* — before finishing her thought, she suddenly feels remorse for such unkind judgement. The conversation makes previously unknown truths come to bear, and she feels sorry for her, now understanding the true source of the poor girl's unhappy state.

"You might well have wondered why we have hired Mademoiselle Duquet?" he continues, oblivious to her inner turmoil. "It is best we begin now, so that the transition will not be so affecting on my dear wife."

Utterly confused, she tries to understand what he means by "transition."

"Monsieur Lalonde has taken note of you at Sainte-Anne these many years, and judges you have grown into an appropriate match for that which he seeks. I have arranged for him to come to call on Sunday afternoon after mass. You will help Julienne prepare for our special visitor."

"Oui, Monsieur," she answers instinctively, unable to reason, or think, at all. Her impulse to run from the room, which seems to close in on her is only thwarted by the sternness of Monsieur Quenet's steady stare.

"You may be excused," he says dryly.

Rising from the chair, she makes her way to the door, only to be stopped steps from being released from the upsetting change in her circumstance.

"Will you not thank me for such an advantageous match?"

"Oui, Monsieur," she answers, oblivious to her inappropriate response. She does not turn back, embarrassed to look upon him, for her heart now confirms that which her mind will not accept.

# 88

⚜

Père deBreslay's sermon, usually so carefully listened to by his most devoted parishioner, fades into the background as Marie Magdeleine mulls over questions she has about Guillaume Lalonde, sitting only a few pews ahead of her. Of course she has seen him each Sunday, but only a child when she first arrived, she has not taken notice of him in any way that mattered. Now, faced with their futures being intertwined, she sees him differently.

Having watched him enter the church with his brother, Jean-Baptiste, and his family, she believes he had cast a fleeting glance in her direction, but she cannot be sure. The scene plays over and over in her mind as she tries to ascertain the truth.

She performs the rituals of the mass — kneeling, responding, singing — as expected, and none might have noticed her level of distraction, except that the final benediction given does not send Marie Magdeleine pouring out into the day as the others. She jumps, startled, at the gentle tap on her arm.

"Mademoiselle, mass has ended," Suzanne whispers quietly, trying to spare her companion any embarrassment. It is too late, for she looks to those impatiently waiting for her to allow them to exit the pew and feels the warmth of a deep crimson blush appear upon her face. She quickly moves, offering a contrite, "Oh, I am so sorry. Excuse me."

Pretending to have forgotten her missile in the pew, she delays her own departure, hoping the evidence of her embarrassment will subside in case she runs into Guillaume. Already her nerves threaten to betray her as childish and inexperienced. Not wanting to compound what is already difficult to conceal, she takes a few deep breaths, feeling her face return to normal, though she still feels slightly nauseous, a symptom which has not subsided since her talk with Monsieur Quenet a few nights before.

Entering the bright sun, she finds it difficult to ascertain where Guillaume and his family might be. As her eyes adjust, she notices Suzanne waiting with the Quenet children on the trail leading home. Louis waves for her to join them. Searching the crowd of parishioners carrying on friendly conversations and sharing news of the community, she does not see the one she seeks. Just as she waves, answering the calls of the children, she hears a voice from behind.

"Mademoiselle."

Turning, she finds Guillaume unexpectedly standing only a few feet from her. Dipping into a deep curtsy, she addresses him in the even tone she has practiced over the days since learning of his intentions.

"Bonjour, Monsieur Lalonde." Trying not to let her pride show, she silently congratulates herself on the perfect execution of her greeting.

"Monsieur Quenet has arranged for me to visit with you this afternoon." He pauses, seeming to choose his next words carefully. "I pray you find this arrangement agreeable?"

Lost in his captivatingly blue eyes, she admonishes herself for being so concerned with his evident good looks. Wanting to end the conversation before she inevitably betrays herself, she matter-of-factly says, "Yes, I look forward to it. I must go now." With a quick curtsy, she immediately leaves his company to find Suzanne and the children, which provides a welcome excuse to escape the discomfort of their initial meeting.

Once out of sight, Suzanne clings tightly to Marie Magdeleine's arm as the children rush excitedly ahead, asking her to detail every word spoken by the handsome gentlemen coming to call.

Strolling along the trail at the river's edge after a light repast with the Quenet family, Guillaume and Marie Magdeleine have not looked upon one another for some time, avoiding the resulting shyness it induces. Each silently contemplates what to speak of, as they know so little of one another. Without the ready conversation offered by Monsieur Quenet, Guillaume seems quite at a loss about what to say, and equally, Marie Magdeleine had been content to listen to the answers he gave, not knowing what she should say, or do, once left alone in his company. Her mind, dizzy with the effort to surmise such things on her own, furthers her distress. The fresh air has done nothing to clear her mind.

Walking with this man gives her such a queer sensation. Instead of their meeting subduing her nervousness, as she expected, it only intensifies it. Her heart feels as if it beats forth from her chest, and she imagines it so violent that it will give her away. She prays he will ask her a question, or even offer an observation of the season — anything to break the awful standoff they have unwittingly entered. Finally, much to her relief, he does.

"I am twenty-six now, and have been living with my brother for a number of years . . . My mother remarried when I was young," he shares hesitantly, looking over the landscape to avoid her gaze. Drifting off in private thought, Marie Magdeleine notes his demeanour change as a concerned expression overtakes his once-pleasant appearance. "My family has been here since the founding of Saint-Louis. It is gone now, replaced by Sainte-Anne," he says with a tinge of anger evident in voice. "I am glad you were brought here. Monsieur Quenet was right to fear for your well-being. Few know what he . . . or I know of our allies." The ring of disdain in his voice sounds like that in her master's, and she finds the comparison disconcerting.

He offers no more for many tense minutes, as they walk slowly back towards the Quenet home. As the mystery of this man deepens, Marie Magdeleine questions the wisdom of Monsieur Quenet in making such a match. Having been polite, even charming, throughout the meal, he now seems moody and distant. For one who craves companionship, who has known the void of loss, these traits are worrying, and she feels anticipation turn to apprehension.

Upon reaching the door, he turns to her and with the return to his former charm inquires, "Might I call on you again next Sunday afternoon?"

"I shall ask Monsieur Quenet," she answers, not knowing the custom.

A broad, amiable smile crosses his lips, showing the kindness in his eyes. Carefully wording his next statement to avoid making her feel the embarrassment of her inexperience, he says, "He has given his permission to call on you if I wish. The decision to do so rests with you, Mademoiselle."

Overwhelmed by the effect his words, she feels a rush of joy consume her. Meeting his direct, beseeching gaze, she gives her answer: "You may."

❧

## 89

One afternoon, as the harvest approaches, Monsieur Quenet prepares to go to Sainte-Anne to meet with Père deBreslay, Guillaume, and his friend Pierre Lamoureux. Having come to understand the usual ways of such matters, Marie Magdeleine has prayed for this day, the day her union to Guillaume will be confirmed. Once she came to know him, she wanted for the life he offers — an offer he cannot know means so much to her. Even Julienne's attempt to dampen her excitement by saying, "It is not unheard of for such contracts to be broken" did nothing to diminish her belief in Guillaume's sincere intentions. What has evidently been Julienne's undoing, she is truly sorry for. The sting of Julienne being near such future hope has a terrible effect on their already strained relationship, but Marie Magdeleine will not be infected with her bitterness. Over the summer, Guillaume has proven himself forthright and honourable, traits of the utmost importance to her. Though she does not share her innermost desires or secrets, he has become a trusted friend, and this, she believes, is the basis of her love for him.

Her guardian, Monsieur Quenet will do the negotiating on her behalf, but he has deferred the telling of the details to Guillaume when they are to have their usual Sunday afternoon visit, which is an agonizing two days away.

"I have secured the date of our marriage with Père deBreslay," Guillaume says, smiling broadly in delivering the news he has been eager to share.

"When shall it be?" she asks calmly, not wanting to seem too excited, though beneath her apron she wrings her hands with the anticipation.

"Next spring, on the 27th of April."

*Next Spring?* Her heart sinks. While she does not share her disappointment in the delay, she cannot respond, winded by the shock of such an unexpected answer.

Misconstruing her silence, he offers in a low, almost mournful tone, "A contract may be broken by either party."

Worried he may be reconsidering her as his choice, as suggested by Julienne's prophetic warning, she looks away to the distant mountains, overwhelmed by a terrible, familiar sense of loss. She is unable to control her reaction to it, and tears stream down her cheeks. Protecting what dignity she still has, she does not wipe them away so as not to draw attention to her disappointment.

Her lack of response creating a strange, uncomfortable distance between them, Guillaume looks to her, expecting that she is contemplating the offer, but what he finds surprises him. "Marie Magdeleine, why do you cry?" he asks, sincerely confused by her reaction.

"Do you wish to break the contract?" she asks, embarrassed at having made such a poor impression on him that he should want to nullify it so soon.

"Me? No! What I meant — what I intended," he corrects, realizing her misunderstanding, "was, you do not have to be bound to me."

Unabated, she cries with relief, unconcerned with the spectacle she makes of herself. She feels safe with Guillaume and does not subdue that which is in her nature. To express herself in both fear and joy releases her captive heart. Unknowingly, she has languished in a muted life, protecting herself from feeling too much, and it is only in being released from such bondage that she recognizes the one who has truly saved her. His blue eyes glinting in the sun look upon her with such love that it is as if light burst forth from her, shattering oppressive palisades keeping her spirit at bay. In his love, she is transformed.

Sitting upon a fallen log under the large maple tree near the river, a favourite place because of its expansive views of the Fleuve Saint-Laurent, and because of its privacy, Guillaume explains that with the harvest so near his attentions will be called away from building their home, which he works on every spare moment he has, the result of which is that it will not be ready before winter.

"I am sorry for the delay, for I know it will seem an eternity," he says, smiling sweetly at her.

Hearing him speak of his commitment to their future together, and sharing his disappointment in not beginning it sooner, Marie Magdeleine wants to remove any doubt of her growing love for him, and her desire to be his. Unreservedly, she exposes her true feelings, saying, "I shall be proud to be your wife."

She basks in the pure joy of being in his company as they sit quietly together, her soul at peace.

⊰❧⊱

## 90

The heavy snows and relentless frigid winds of so many days over the long, harsh winter months often make travel impossible, even to attend mass. Enduring the seemingly unending hours until they may meet again, Marie Magdeleine busies herself with her usual duties, and a special task she has undertaken to occupy her mind and pacify her yearning heart.

Using the small wage she began to receive three years after her arrival, she purchased fabric to make her wedding dress, which Monsieur Lamoureux delivered to her on his last visit from Ville Marie. He, as with most visitors, and one in particular, will not call again until the thaw begins. Lonely Sunday afternoons are passed in the making of her dress and daydreaming of the spring day when she will finally be able to wear it. The fabric is plain, but remnants given to her by Madame Quenet from one of her worn dresses adorn the sleeves and bodice, making it finer than anything she should have hoped for. When she has a few quiet moments to herself, Suzanne asks to help in the hemming of the skirt. Listening to Marie Magdeleine share her dreams for the future fills her with excitement at what she may one day know. Having become so much a sister, Suzanne's companionship is always welcomed, for it settles an unshakable sense of longing, as if something, or someone, is missing. Assuming it her extended separation from Guillaume, she will not entertain any other reason for it, though it persists.

After three agonizing weeks during which attending mass was not possible, the drifts having risen to the height of the window sills, the winds calm, and Amable and Rhéal — two recently hired farm hands — and Monsieur Quenet are finally able to extract them from their snowbound imprisonment. Entering Sainte-Anne, Marie Magdeleine sees Guillaume sitting amongst his family, and as if sensing her arrival, he inconspicuously turns his head only far enough to confirm it with a sidelong glance. Seeing the slight curve of his lip, she bends her head to conceal her own smile in response. Through the unhappy hours, she has fought against worrisome thoughts that his affection might diminish with their prolonged separation, but his sincere joy in seeing her makes it now seem as if no time has passed at all, their connection as strong as when they last laid eyes on one another.

Kneeling before God, she clasps her hands and gives thanks for the gift of such an unimaginable miracle.

# 91

❧

## 27 April 1710

Spring, only newly born, brings the world back to life. Marie Magdeleine is renewed by sunny days and the blossoming landscape, but it is the return to her afternoon visits with Guillaume that has truly revived her. Now, the day that once seemed so distant is finally upon her.

The Quenet household is abuzz with activity. Chasing after the children, trying to dress them in their finest outfits for the part they will play in the wedding, Suzanne finds it no easy task as they scatter about the house singing, laughing, and of course, trying to steal a glimpse at Marie Magdeleine preparing in her room. Julienne, at first unhappy with being tasked with aiding her, now surrenders to the excitement of the day, humming a cheerful tune under her breath as she meticulously affixes each of the buttons at the back of Marie Magdeleine's dress. Finishing the final one, she stands back, offering a genuine compliment.

"You have done wonderfully in the making of it. You look . . ." she pauses, a mournful expression overtaking her, "lovely."

"Thank you," Marie Magdeleine says turning to the pitiful woman. "Is there no way you might join us?" she asks generously, hoping this will change her disposition.

"No. There is too much that must be attended to with all the extra work *this* has caused." Almost glad for the barb, Marie Magdeleine is released from the sorrow of Julienne's disappointment. With their relationship back as it should be, she is able to bask in the joy of the moment. As she looks into a mirror borrowed from Madame Quenet, it is difficult to reconcile that the woman she gazes upon is herself. Without noticing Julienne's departure, she stands mesmerized by the beauty of her gown as the light streaming in the small window illuminates the full, cream-coloured skirt as if it is sunlight itself. She swishes it back and forth like a bell, watching the ample material fold and then right itself. Running her hands over the decadent bodice, accented with light pink silk from Madame Quenet's old dress, she studies the detailed workmanship. Beneath a long veil, an unexpected gift from the Quenets, her golden curls, tamed by Julienne's efforts, are neatly affixed with early-season flowers, the delicate purple violets being her favourite. Pleased with the reflection in the mirror, her silent prayer is that Guillaume will be proud to claim her.

Arriving at Sainte-Anne, Marie Magdeleine is surprised by the welcome of the excited crowd. She is seated high atop the carriage, which has not come to a complete stop when a rush of guests come at her. Already overwhelmed by her own excitement and emotions, she pulls back as if shielding herself from them.

"They are excited to see the bride," says Madame Quenet, her hand placed on Marie Magdeleine's arm to steady her nerves. Their relationship never having transgressed the boundaries of master and servant, Marie Magdeleine has found her recent generosity comforting. Beyond the offering of her old dress for the making of the wedding gown, Madame Quenet enjoyed helping Marie Magdeleine navigate the plethora of considerations in the planning of her special day. But it has not come without some trepidation on her part, for though she has adequate servants, Marie Magdeleine has held a special place amongst them since arriving a shell of a girl only six years before. Filled with a sense of accomplishment at having provided the means for that girl to become the woman that sits beside her in the carriage, she imparts one final kindness. "Calm will return once you are inside, you will see," she assures, remembering well the nervous anticipation just prior to entering the church.

Listening to the hum of hushed conversations within the church, Marie Magdeleine shuffles nervously in the small vestibule, hidden from sight by closed doors to the main sanctuary. Père deBreslay is preoccupied with instructing the altar boys about the order they should assume for the procession, and she is left to contemplate what lies ahead, which only adds to the anxiety of the wait. Bowing his head, listening for the first notes from the choir, he suddenly reaches out, taking her hand, whispering, "He has chosen well." Before she can respond, the door suddenly opens and he slips through into the sanctuary. Only able to catch a glimpse of the church filled to capacity before the doors close again, she prays for the calm Madame Quenet promised.

The door opens for a final time as joyful voices fill the air, and she looks upon Guillaume, immersed in fractured, coloured light.

Marie Madeleine, on the arm of her master, Monsieur Quenet, slowly, reverently — and calmly — walks towards her future.

# 92

⚭

The raucous festivities at Guillaume's brother's home left behind, Marie Magdeleine can still hear sounds of the violins, singing, and laughter ringing in her ears. Even as the hour approaches midnight, they have left their many guests behind, yet dancing, drinking the finest ales and cognacs, and eating of the enormous feast provided by Monsieur Quenet. For a mile or more the resonating sounds carry over the darkened landscape, but as they draw nearer to their own home and the faint glint of candles in the windows becomes visible through the mists, the sounds fade and the usual drone of the frogs fills the night air.

After a day of endless merriment, the slow, steady ride home is the first occasion Marie Magdeleine and Guillaume have spent alone as man and wife. Instead of reminiscing excitedly of all that has entertained them, they ride in silence, contemplating what mysteries lie ahead.

After slowing to a stop, Guillaume jumps from the carriage, extending a hand to his wife to aid her dismount, so she might gather her ample skirt, sparing her dress, which he knows she has worked painstakingly on to impress him. She wraps her hand around his arm and he holds tight as they walk up the short path to their newly completed home. Freshly whitewashed, it stands out even in the darkness of the moonless night.

Opening the door, they are greeted by a welcoming sight: a number of candles are placed not only in the windows, the beacons that guided them home, but also upon the mantle, illuminating the comfortable room with a soft, warm glow. A bottle of fine cognac and two glasses are set on a small table near the fireplace, where flames sputter and dance within. Reading the small note set with the bottle, he shares, "It is a gift from the Quenets." She smiles, thankful for all they have done to make the day special. The children cried mournfully upon realizing she would not be returning to them, but she promised she would visit from time and time, and they would see her at mass every Sunday, which seemed to ease their distress. She shares their apprehension for such change. Even as the wait has seemed unbearably long, once upon them, the day passed too quickly to fully comprehend.

It seems strange to be alone with Guillaume, without the ever-watchful Monsieur Quenet lurking about in the background. She often caught a glimpse of him in some inconspicuous position to observe their Sunday visits, and now she cannot help but look to the dark corners of the room, expecting to find him there. Suddenly, as if her suspicions are confirmed, she hears soft footsteps in the adjoining room, where a shadow can be seen moving about on a far wall. Just as she moves to be nearer Guillaume, fearful of the unknown presence, Claudette, his brother's servant, swiftly enters the room announcing, "All is prepared." Avoiding eye contact, she curtsies and leaves the house. Confused by her presence, thinking her yet to be amongst the revellers, she turns to Guillaume.

"But where does she go?" she asks, concerned how she will find her way back to Jean-Baptiste's house in the dark night.

"Etienne followed not far behind to fetch her. She is perfectly safe, ma belle."

*Ma belle.* The tender sound of his voice in expressing this special name brings her such joy. Taking the glass he offers, she sits across from him on a comfortable chair set before the fire. Nervously swirling the amber liquid about, she studies the pattern in the etching, realizing amid the fanciful filigree is an L in the center.

"Marie Magdeleine . . . Hélène . . . Lalonde," she whispers haltingly.

"Pardon?"

Realizing she has been lost in thought, she looks to Guillaume, who nervously smiles at her. "I was just saying my new name.

"And what do you think of it?"

"I am proud to be known by it," she says demurely, shying away from his steady gaze.

They fall into a prolonged silence, and Marie Magdeleine stares into the fire, reflecting on the eventful day. Despite her best efforts to savour each glorious detail, she finds it all blends together, the only clear part being the memory of seeing Guillaume smile at her as she walked up the aisle. His loving gaze had proven intoxicating, and though the church had been full, it was if everyone else had faded away, leaving only she and him in that moment.

"Morning comes, perhaps." Guillaume pauses, unsure of how to proceed. "Well, that is, perhaps we should get some . . . sleep." Instead of his nervous stammer making her uncomfortable with the delicate nature of the insinuation, she is glad to know he feels as she does, for even as she appears composed and at ease sitting by the fire, her heart beats forcefully as a confusing multitude of thoughts and feelings churn about: from apprehension to excitement, even embarrassment. Her stomach flutters as she waits for the inevitable, but not unwelcome, next step. With Guillaume's own unsure nature revealed, she suddenly relaxes, feeling a kinship in being of one mind as they navigate their first few intimate times together.

"Yes, you are right, morning comes quickly. I will go and prepare the room — our room," she says, giving Guillaume a shy smile as she takes her leave.

Her effects having been delivered earlier in the day by Amable, Marie Magdeleine opens the wooden chest, which once sat at the end of her bed at the Quenets, to unpack the few items she has brought with her. Finding it empty, she opens a nearby cupboard to find her dresses neatly hanging within, Claudette's work now revealed. She looks for the one item she cherishes most.

Her precious nightgown having become threadbare many years before, she turns to find the one replacing it laid out upon the bed, a gift that arrived a couple of weeks earlier from one who knew how much such a thing meant to her. Enclosed, a simple note read, "Many congratulations to you on your wedding. Madame Caillier."

Soft, hesitant footsteps stop just outside the threshold of the room, and Marie Magdeleine assures, "I am dressed."

Entering the soft glow of the candlelit room, Guillaume looks upon his wife, stunned to find her more beautiful now than in any other moment he has known her. Moving only slightly closer to her, he says, "I have news I hope you will find makes you happy. I wanted to wait until . . . tonight to share it with you," he says, nervously striking up a conversation, tempering his eagerness to sweep her up into his arms.

Drawn to him by an unknown, compelling force, without response she takes a small step forward, precipitating a sympathetic motion. As he wraps his arms around her waist, she places her hands upon his chest, easing into the first embrace she has known in seven long years.

"You are to be made a French citizen in only a couple of weeks. Your place amongst us is assured."

*Oh, to be held in love again, I had not realized the true ache of its absence until now.*

She is hardly able to suppress the rising want to weep with relief. *He does not — cannot — understand what gift he has given me.*

Moving her hand to take his that now bears the band of gold signifying their unity, she brings their hands between them, twirling the ring around his finger, struck by what it symbolizes. Holding to him, Marie Magdeleine looks up to find him gazing upon her with such love and she is instantly released.

"Guillaume, your gift of such a home is lovely and your news most welcome, but it is not these, which you have imparted, that I now thank you for. You have restored something to me, something I believed lost, that has already assured my place here, and for this I thank you." She feels the tears brim, but does not stop them.

As he pulls her hard to his chest, Guillaume's heart beats in time with hers. "And what is that, ma belle? What have I restored?"

"A family of my own."

# 93

❧

## 1712

"I love you mon bébé, mon Edouard," Marie Magdeleine whispers, setting her baby into his cradle made by his father's hand. Her nights spent by his side, attending to his small, whimpering cries, are a most precious gift. Often she passes the time gazing upon him, marvelling at such a miracle. But his birth has strangely signalled a death — a death of her childish notions.

These two years with Guillaume have brought such joy, such renewal, that she believed no further sadness existed within. Even dreams, which at times leave confusion, were not so well formed that they impacted her days. Truly, a heart filled with love aches as sadness in many ways. So fulfilled was she, she misjudged its source. Such strange notions have only occurred to her since his birth. His name, once chosen as Adelard, seemed impossible once he was laid in her arms. As she looked upon him, new to the world, *Edouard* rang out in her mind and seemed so well suited that it was incomprehensible he should be anyone else. Guillaume did not question her choice of his name, for she believes he knows of her past.

But in these quiet hours, such dreadful truths shatter her childish wishes.

Soon after her arrival at the Quenets, she overheard whispered conversations about some of Deerfield who had been redeemed. Part of her always expected to see her father. For days after hearing such news, she took note of movements upon the horizon, but never did she see him. Then, she believed it was her sin preventing it.

Now, with the clarity of maturity, she supposes they met their fate the morning she was taken, unprotected as they were outside the palisades — though these provided no protection. It seems an insurmountable task to accept such realities as these, and why it should never have occurred to her before looking upon her own child she does not know — but such violence as ripped her from the embrace of her home must surely have rendered a brutal fate upon her beloved family.

"Father, Mother, Edward, Mercy, Martha, Jemima, Hannah, Samuel. Oh, to whisper these names!" The memory of them strikes at her heart. *How I wish to see them once more, even if only conjured in my mind.*

A scream rises in her, a desperation not so keenly felt in years. She clings to that which provides comfort — her sleeping baby, moving his mouth as if yet suckling, and Guillaume peacefully asleep in their bed — and her wounded heart calms by their very presence. Looking to the stars of her childhood, she remembers the lovely things of each of them, and to days once thought mundane, now fondly recounted.

Père deBreslay once told her they were lost to God, but her heart tells her they are not.

*I will hereafter pray for them at night, in a prayer that rings familiar to their ears,* she promises silently.

Knowing she must take her rest, for morning comes too soon, she leans over her baby, watching his small chest rise and fall with life. After kissing him a final time on his delicate, warm cheek, she whispers softly in his ear, "Sleep well Edouard — Edward — for you are looked upon by angels."

# 94

⚜

## 1740

"**M**a belle, please come with me a moment."

Marie Magdeleine quickly agrees, for Guillaume seems distracted by a serious matter. He hands her a letter, and she sees a name not known in many years.

"I will have Geneviève take the children outside so that you may have a few moments to read it."

Life has passed in a steady, full manner with her thirteenth child soon due, but today Marie Magdeleine suddenly feels as if she is twelve once more. Though she is apprehensive to open old wounds, her curiosity rears up with a strength she cannot deny. Her hands shake as she breaks the seal.

14 May 1740

Dear Madame Lalonde,

Please find a letter, written in my father's hand some years ago, which as part of his will I am to deliver to you at a specified time. The reason for this will become clear with the reading of his letter.

John Sheldon, Jr.

Within this short letter, written nearly nine weeks ago, she finds another, yellowed with age, the seal almost completely released from the paper it affixes. Simply written upon it, in an unsteady hand, is "Madame Lalonde. Baie D'Urfé."

23 June 1733 at Hartford

Dear Madame Lalonde,

Many years ago, a man I called neighbour and friend suffered a most grievous loss, the depth of which cannot be expressed in mere words, but I believe you shall come to understand more fully by the end of my letter.

A burden which has laid heavy upon my heart these many years is now relieved in the writing of this account in my last few days upon this earth. Many years ago, I entered into a covenant to keep a secret that I now reveal. As life has brought me many blessings, and the end provides clarity, it is my truest belief that it is right that you should know your father did not forsake you.

Dear lady, I am sorry to share this news when it is too late to reunite with your own father and mother again, the receipt of this letter confirming their passing, but in honouring a choice made long ago, it must be so.

Herein, I shall tell you the events of the day when last your father set eyes upon his daughter so long ago taken.

In an attempt to regain that which had been so brutally ripped from him, your father and I, along with others of our community, ventured many days and nights seeking that which was lost. Our first attempts thwarted with the renewal of conflict, we finally made our way to Ville Marie. The year was 1709. We made inquiries about where you might be found, for we had heard you had survived the long march, our own Reverend Williams having been redeemed three years earlier. Our guide found you living as a servant in a home along the St. Lawrence River, and we set out immediately to negotiate your release. But the blessing of finding you was soon replaced by the reality of so many years passed.

When we arrived at the Quenet farm, the gentleman spirited us away to a seldom-used barn, knowing the confusion you would feel at finding us there. We learned from him that you were betrothed. I will say, Monsieur Quenet was understanding of the situation, and told your father he was sorry for his trials. What only then became apparent was that the woman we saw down by the river with a young man at her side, much as any in Canada, was you. He had not recognized his own daughter, for you were much grown — a woman. I shall never forget his face awash with such grief it haunts me still. He asked Monsieur Quenet if there might not be a place where he could quietly observe you, for he had much to consider. He brought us to a rise in the land where a stand of trees would shield us from sight. I could see he struggled to hold himself back from rushing to you. After a few tense moments, he turned to us, then walked back along the trail from whence we had come. We did not follow too closely, for it was evident he was overcome by what I knew to be a bitter defeat. Thanking Monsieur Quenet, we followed, leaving you to the life you had come to know.

In his great love for you, dear lady, once Sarah of Deerfield, your father decided not to burden you with which life to choose. Seeing your evident happiness with your soon-to-be husband, he relinquished all claims on your heart. Our journey home was spent in quiet contemplation, but as the days passed, his disappointed resignation turned to a peacefulness that was evident to all his companions. Two days away from our return to Deerfield, after many weeks of journeying, he finally revealed the deception that had been the reason for this change. We all swore to abide by his decision.

Upon our return, knowing that no comfort would come to a mother yearning for a child already lost to the realm of adulthood, and to a new life much opposed to our own humble lives, he told your dear mother you had been lost on the trail many years before. Devastated by such news, she was much affected for many months. Mercifully, she found joy in the growing families of your brothers and sisters, though they were ever marked by your loss, for it was plain enough in their diminished manner. Years on, when we had occasion to visit our once home, my own dear wife remarked that one could yet see the depth of their loss in their eyes.

That you were ever-mourned by your family, and the knowledge that only the deepest and truest love of a father could make such choices as he did, I pray brings you some measure of comfort.

Your servant,

John Sheldon

Folding the letter back to a position that very nearly makes the seal appear as if it has never been broken, Marie Magdeleine lays it before her. Running her hand over it, time and again, as though a loved one, she does not know what to feel. Searching for direction, she looks out the window to the golden fields ablaze in the midday sun.

After struggling to remember his face for so many years, he stands before her now amidst the field of wheat swaying in the light breeze. Its rhythmic motion and her father's familiar features do not stir her feelings, but instill such peace that she allows herself to drift to places in her past.

As he turns his gaze to her, she looks into the gentle blue eyes that so oft looked upon her in childhood. A knowing crossing between them, he smiles. Raising his hand, he waves at her, as a day long ago.

As his faint image dissipates into the sunlight, she whispers, "Goodbye."

# 95

⤜⤐

Marie Magdeleine's journal arrived with Guillaume's return from Ville Marie, where he journeyed to pick up supplies, but she had found the anticipation of setting the first few words upon the page daunting. So much she has to record that it seems impossible to begin.

Alone in the silence of the late night, her family at their rest, she sits staring at the open, blank page lying upon the small table set near the window by Guillaume for her special purpose. He knows how she looks to the stars, finding comfort in them. Tonight their brilliance shines down upon her, and so with a whispered prayer lifted to the heavens, she dips her quill into the ink well.

4 August 1740

Mes enfants, where once I had no story to tell, I find my memories renewed and now share on these pages the story of the journey that brought me to you.

Do not be sorry for the trials I have endured, for they are small payment for the life I have shared with you and your Papa. Had not your arrivals and the love of my dearest Guillaume brought me such renewed spirit, I fear I should have wilted with the weight of sorrow I carried, but love shows mercy in its ability to heal — and endure.

I am of two worlds, forged in the flames of war. The place where my life began lies many miles, many memories, away from here. Though I am equally your Maman, Marie Magdeleine Hélène Lalonde, always I remember Deerfield, and the girl I once was. Recalling little of the language of les Anglais, I now reclaim this part of myself and declare: Je suis Sarah Allen, and I am the daughter of conflict.

# Epilogue

"They are back!" Samuel calls out excitedly.

Running from the house, Mercy, sure her daughter has returned, she looks beyond the men in the group, seeking the familiar form of Sarah amongst them.

Taking his leave of them, Edward walks upon the trail leading home. Suddenly Mercy stops, meeting his gaze, which is awash with the look of defeat. The blow of devastation brings her to her knees. She gasps for the breath that will not come until the throngs of consuming grief finally allow the horrified scream of a mother to ring out, "Sarah!"

Her cry echoing in air, the group of men stop, but do not look back. Looking over his distraught wife, Edward is unable to offer comfort. Consumed by his own grief, it is the shame of not being able to return a child to her mother that renders him incapable of doing so. The mortification that he is the cause of such sorrow leaves him speechless, and he merely looks to the sun setting through the trees with the memory of his last moments with his unsure, sorrowful Sarah playing repetitively in his mind as it had upon much of the trek back to Deerfield. "We shall see you upon the Sabbath, but six days from now." Bitter at having uttered such hollow words, he chastises himself. *Fool.* Fighting the tears welling in his eyes, the image of his once precocious Sarah playing within the forest before him proves too much. Moving past his crumpled, sobbing wife who lies inconsolable upon the ground, he takes refuge at his desk.

17 September 1709

Sarah is lost to us.

# About the Author

With deep ancestral roots in New France/Quebec, Upper Canada/ Ontario, and colonial America, Jennifer is interested in exploring the human story within this rich history. Combining her passion and experience in writing, education, history, and genealogy, she writes fact-based, historical fiction that engages readers in "discovering the humanity in the history." A dynamic and knowledgeable speaker, Jennifer is a sought-after presenter at historical, literary and community events. *Daughter of Conflict* is her third novel.

Other works by author and ordering information:

*www.jenniferdebruin.com*